A CHATTO & W

THE SWEET CHEAT GONE

Marcel Proust's continuous novel *À la Recherche du Temps Perdu* (REMEMBRANCE OF THINGS PAST) was originally published in eight parts, the titles and dates of which were: I. *Du Coté de Chez Swann* (1913); II. *À l'Ombre des Jeunes Filles en Fleurs* (1918), awarded the Prix Goncourt in 1919; III. *Le Coté de Guermantes I* (1920); IV. *Le Coté de Guermantes II, Sodome et Gomorrhe I* (1921); V. *Sodome et Gomorrhe II* (1922); VI. *La Prisonnière* (1923); VII. *Albertine Disparue* (1925); VIII. *Le Temps Retrouvé* (1927).

Du Coté de Chez Swann has been published in English as SWANN'S WAY: *À l'Ombre des Jeunes Filles en Fleurs* as WITHIN A BUDDING GROVE: *Le Coté de Guermantes* as THE GUERMANTES WAY: *Sodome et Gomorrhe* as CITIES OF THE PLAIN: *La Prisonnière* as THE CAPTIVE: *Albertine Disparue* as THE SWEET CHEAT GONE: and *Le Temps Retrouvé* as TIME REGAINED. The first seven parts were translated by C. K. Scott Moncrieff; the eighth by Stephen Hudson.

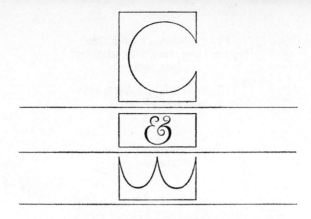

THE
SWEET CHEAT
GONE

MARCEL PROUST

Translated by
C. K. Scott Moncrieff

CHATTO & WINDUS
LONDON

First published in English 1930
Reprinted 1941, 1944, 1949, 1952, 1957,
1962, 1968

This edition first published in 1969
by Chatto & Windus
London

*

Clarke, Irwin & Co. Ltd.
Toronto

SBN 7011 1069 4

© Chatto & Windus Ltd. 1930

Printed in Great Britain by
R. & R. Clark, Ltd., Edinburgh

CONTENTS

✽

Chapter I   *page* 1
Grief and oblivion

Chapter II   195
Mademoiselle de Forcheville

Chapter III   287
Venice

Chapter IV   327
A fresh light upon Robert de Saint-Loup

TRANSLATOR'S NOTE

[*We regret that Mr. Scott Moncrieff was not
able to write this note before his death.*

THE PUBLISHERS]

THE SWEET CHEAT GONE

CHAPTER I

GRIEF AND OBLIVION

"MADEMOISELLE ALBERTINE has gone !"
How much farther does anguish penetrate in
psychology than psychology itself ! A moment ago, as I
lay analysing my feelings, I had supposed that this separation without a final meeting was precisely what I wished,
and, as I compared the mediocrity of the pleasures that
Albertine afforded me with the richness of the desire
which she prevented me from realising, had felt that I was
being subtle, had concluded that I did not wish to see her
again, that I no longer loved her. But now these words :
" Mademoiselle Albertine has gone ! " had expressed themselves in my heart in the form of an anguish so keen that I
would not be able to endure it for any length of time. And
so what I had supposed to mean nothing to me was the only
thing in my whole life. How ignorant we are of ourselves. The first thing to be done was to make my
anguish cease at once. Tender towards myself as my
mother had been towards my dying grandmother, I said to
myself with that anxiety which we feel to prevent a person
whom we love from suffering : " Be patient for just a
moment, we shall find something to take the pain away,
don't fret, we are not going to allow you to suffer like this."
It was among ideas of this sort that my instinct of self-

preservation sought for the first sedatives to lay upon my open wound : " All this is not of the slightest importance, for I am going to make her return here at once. I must think first how I am to do it, but in any case she will be here this evening. Therefore, it is useless to worry myself." " All this is not of the slightest importance," I had not been content with giving myself this assurance, I had tried to convey the same impression to Françoise by not allowing her to see what I was suffering, because, even at the moment when I was feeling so keen an anguish, my love did not forget how important it was that it should appear a happy love, a mutual love, especially in the eyes of Françoise, who, as she disliked Albertine, had always doubted her sincerity. Yes, a moment ago, before Françoise came into the room, I had supposed that I was no longer in love with Albertine, I had supposed that I was leaving nothing out of account ; a careful analyst, I had supposed that I knew the state of my own heart. But our intelligence, however great it may be, cannot perceive the elements that compose it and remain unsuspected so long as, from the volatile state in which they generally exist, a phenomenon capable of isolating them has not subjected them to the first stages of solidification. I had been mistaken in thinking that I could see clearly into my own heart. But this knowledge which had not been given me by the finest mental perceptions had now been brought to me, hard, glittering, strange, like a crystallised salt, by the abrupt reaction of grief. I was so much in the habit of seeing Albertine in the room, and I saw, all of a sudden, a fresh aspect of Habit. Hitherto I had regarded it chiefly as an annihilating force which suppresses the originality and even our consciousness of our perceptions ; now I beheld it as a dread deity, so riveted to ourself, its meaningless aspect so incrusted in our heart, that if it detaches itself, if it turns away from us, this deity which we can barely distinguish inflicts upon us sufferings more terrible than any other and is then as cruel as death itself.

The first thing to be done was to read Albertine's letter, since I was anxious to think of some way of making her return. I felt that this lay in my power, because, as the future is what exists only in our mind, it seems to us to be still alterable by the intervention, *in extremis*, of our will. But, at the same time, I remembered that I had seen act upon it forces other than my own, against which, however long an interval had been allowed me, I could never have prevailed. Of what use is it that the hour has not yet struck if we can do nothing to influence what is bound to happen. When Albertine was living in the house I had been quite determined to retain the initiative in our parting. And now she had gone. I opened her letter. It ran as follows :

" MY DEAR FRIEND,

" Forgive me for not having dared to say to you in so many words what I am now writing, but I am such a coward, I have always been so afraid in your presence that I have never been able to force myself to speak. This is what I should have said to you. Our life together has become impossible ; you must, for that matter, have seen, when you turned upon me the other evening, that there had been a change in our relations. What we were able to straighten out that night would become irreparable in a

3

few days' time. It is better for us, therefore, since we have had the good fortune to be reconciled, to part as friends. That is why, my darling, I am sending you this line, and beg you to be so kind as to forgive me if I am causing you a little grief when you think of the immensity of mine. My dear old boy, I do not wish to become your enemy, it will be bad enough to become by degrees, and very soon, a stranger to you ; and so, as I have absolutely made up my mind, before sending you this letter by Françoise, I shall have asked her to let me have my boxes. Good-bye : I leave with you the best part of myself.

" ALBERTINE "

"All this means nothing," I told myself, " it is even better than I thought, for as she doesn't mean a word of what she says she has obviously written her letter only to give me a severe shock, so that I shall take fright, and not be horrid to her again. I must make some arrangement at once : Albertine must be brought back this evening. It is sad to think that the Bontemps are no better than black-mailers who make use of their niece to extort money from me. But what does that matter ? Even if, to bring Albertine back here this evening, I have to give half my fortune to Mme Bontemps, we shall still have enough left, Albertine and I, to live in comfort." And, at the same time, I calculated whether I had time to go out that morning and order the yacht and the Rolls-Royce which she coveted, quite forgetting, now that all my hesitation had vanished, that I had decided that it would be unwise to give her them. " Even if Mme Bontemps' support is not sufficient, if Albertine refuses to obey her aunt and

4

makes it a condition of her returning to me that she shall enjoy complete independence, well, however much it may distress me, I shall leave her to herself; she shall go out by herself, whenever she chooses. One must be prepared to make sacrifices, however painful they may be, for the thing to which one attaches most importance, which is, in spite of everything that I decided this morning, on the strength of my scrupulous and absurd arguments, that Albertine shall continue to live here." Can I say for that matter, that to leave her free to go where she chose would have been altogether painful to me? I should be lying. Often already I had felt that the anguish of leaving her free to behave improperly out of my sight was perhaps even less than that sort of misery which I used to feel when I guessed that she was bored in my company, under my roof. No doubt at the actual moment of her asking me to let her go somewhere, the act of allowing her to go, with the idea of an organised orgy, would have been an appalling torment. But to say to her : " Take our yacht, or the train, go away for a month, to some place which I have never seen, where I shall know nothing of what you are doing,"—this had often appealed to me, owing to the thought that, by force of contrast, when she was away from me, she would prefer my society, and would be glad to return. " This return is certainly what she herself desires; she does not in the least insist upon that freedom upon which, moreover, by offering her every day some fresh pleasure, I should easily succeed in imposing, day by day, a further restriction. No, what Albertine has wanted is that I shall no longer make myself unpleasant to her, and most of all—like Odette with Swann—that I shall make up my mind to marry her. Once she is married, her independence will cease to matter ; we shall stay here together, in perfect happiness." No doubt this meant giving up any thought of Venice. But the places for which we have most longed, such as Venice (still more, the most agreeable hostesses, such as the Duchesse de Guermantes, amusements such as the theatre), how pale, insignificant, dead they become when we are tied to the heart of another person by a bond so painful that it prevents us from tearing ourself away. "Albertine is perfectly right, for that matter, about our marriage. Mamma herself was saying that all these postponements were ridiculous. Marrying her is what I ought to have done long ago, it is what I shall have to do, it is what has made her write her letter without meaning a word of it ; it is only to bring about our marriage that she has postponed for a few hours what she must desire as keenly as I desire it : her return to this house. Yes, that is what she meant, that is the purpose of her action," my compassionate judgment assured me ; but I felt that, in telling me this, my judgment was still maintaining the same hypothesis which it had adopted from the start. Whereas I felt that it was the other hypothesis which had invariably proved correct. No doubt this second hypothesis would never have been so bold as to formulate in so many words that Albertine could have had intimate relations with Mlle Vinteuil and her friend. And yet, when I was overwhelmed by the invasion of those terrible tidings, as the train slowed down before stopping at Parville station, it was the second hypothesis that had already been proved correct. This hypothesis had never, in the interval, conceived the idea that Albertine

6

might leave me of her own accord, in this fashion, and without warning me and giving me time to prevent her departure. But all the same if, after the immense leap forwards which life had just made me take, the reality that confronted me was as novel as that which is presented by the discovery of a scientist, the inquiries of an examining magistrate or the researches of a historian into the mystery of a crime or a revolution, this reality while exceeding the meagre previsions of my second hypothesis nevertheless fulfilled them. This second hypothesis was not an intellectual feat, and the panic fear that I had felt on the evening when Albertine had refused to kiss me, the night when I had heard the sound of her window being opened, that fear was not based upon reason. But—and the sequel will shew this more clearly, as several episodes must have indicated it already—the fact that our intellect is not the most subtle, the most powerful, the most appropriate instrument for grasping the truth, is only a reason the more for beginning with the intellect, and not with a subconscious intuition, a ready-made faith in presentiments. It is life that, little by little, case by case, enables us to observe that what is most important to our heart, or to our minds is learned not by reasoning but by other powers. And then it is the intellect itself which, taking note of their superiority, abdicates its sway to them upon reasoned grounds and consents to become their collaborator and their servant. It is faith confirmed by experiment. The unforeseen calamity with which I found myself engaged, it seemed to me that I had already known it also (as I had known of Albertine's friendship with a pair of Lesbians), from having read it in so many signs in which (notwithstanding the contrary affirmations of my reason, based upon Albertine's own statements) I had discerned the weariness, the horror that she felt at having to live in that state of slavery, signs traced as though in invisible ink behind her sad, submissive eyes, upon her cheeks suddenly inflamed with an unaccountable blush, in the sound of the window that had suddenly been flung open. No doubt I had not ventured to interpret them in their full significance or to form a definite idea of her immediate departure. I had thought, with a mind kept in equilibrium by Albertine's presence, only of a departure arranged by myself at an undetermined date, that is to say a date situated in a non-existent time ; consequently I had had merely the illusion of thinking of a departure, just as people imagine that they are not afraid of death when they think of it while they are in good health and actually do no more than introduce a purely negative idea into a healthy state which the approach of death would automatically destroy. Besides, the idea of Albertine's departure on her own initiative might have occurred to my mind a thousand times over, in the clearest, the most sharply defined form, and I should no more have suspected what, in relation to myself, that is to say in reality, that departure would be, what an unprecedented, appalling, unknown thing, how entirely novel a calamity. Of her departure, had I foreseen it, I might have gone on thinking incessantly for years on end, and yet all my thoughts of it, placed end to end, would not have been comparable for an instant, not merely in intensity but in kind, with the unimaginable hell the curtain of which Françoise had raised for me when she said : " Mademoiselle Albertine has gone." In order to form an idea of an

unknown situation our imagination borrows elements
that are already familiar and for that reason does not form
any idea of it. But our sensibility, even in its most
physical form, receives, as it were the brand of the lightning,
the original and for long indelible imprint of the novel
event. And I scarcely ventured to say to myself that, if
I had foreseen this departure, I would perhaps have been
incapable of picturing it to myself in all its horror, or
indeed, with Albertine informing me of it, and myself
threatening, imploring her, of preventing it! How far
was any longing for Venice removed from me now! As
far as, in the old days at Combray, was the longing to know
Mme de Guermantes when the time came at which I
longed for one thing only, to have Mamma in my room.
And it was, indeed, all these anxieties that I had felt ever
since my childhood, which, at the bidding of this new
anguish, had come hastening to reinforce it, to amalgamate
themselves with it in a homogeneous mass that was stifling
me. To be sure, the physical blow which such a parting
strikes at the heart, and which, because of that terrible
capacity for registering things with which the body is
endowed, makes our suffering somehow contemporaneous
with all the epochs in our life in which we have suffered; to
be sure, this blow at the heart upon which the woman specu-
lates a little perhaps—so little compunction do we show for
the sufferings of other people—who is anxious to give the
maximum intensity to regret, whether it be that, merely
hinting at an imaginary departure, she is seeking only to
demand better terms, or that, leaving us for ever—for
ever!—she desires to wound us, or, in order to avenge herself, or to continue to be loved, or to enhance the memory

that she will leave behind her, to rend asunder the net of weariness, of indifference, which she has felt being woven about her—to be sure, this blow at our heart, we had vowed that we would avoid it, had assured ourself that we would make a good finish. But it is rarely indeed that we do finish well, for, if all was well, we would never finish! And besides, the woman to whom we show the utmost indifference feels nevertheless in an obscure fashion that while we have been growing tired of her, by virtue of an identical force of habit, we have grown more and more attached to her, and she reflects that one of the essential elements in a good finish is to warn the other person before one goes. But she is afraid, if she warns us, of preventing her own departure. Every woman feels that, if her power over a man is great, the only way to leave him is sudden flight. A fugitive because a queen, precisely. To be sure, there is an unspeakable interval between the boredom which she inspired a moment ago and, because she has gone, this furious desire to have her back again. But for this, apart from those which have been furnished in the course of this work and others which will be furnished later on, there are reasons. For one thing, her departure occurs as often as not at the moment when our indifference—real or imagined—is greatest, at the extreme point of the oscillation of the pendulum. The woman says to herself: " No, this sort of thing cannot go on any longer," simply because the man speaks of nothing but leaving her, or thinks of nothing else; and it is she who leaves him. Then, the pendulum swinging back to its other extreme, the interval is all the greater. In an instant it returns to this point; once more, apart from all the reasons that have been given, it is so natural. Our heart still beats; and besides, the woman who has gone is no longer the same as the woman who was with us. Her life under our roof, all too well known, is suddenly enlarged by the addition of the lives with which she is inevitably to be associated, and it is perhaps to associate herself with them that she has left us. So that this novel richness of the life of the woman who has gone reacts upon the woman who was with us and was perhaps planning her departure. To the series of psychological facts which we are able to deduce and which form part of her life with us, our too evident boredom in her company, our jealousy also (the effect of which is that the men who have been left by a number of women have been left almost always in the same manner because of their character and of certain always identical reactions which can be calculated: each man has his own way of being betrayed, as he has his own way of catching cold), to this series not too mysterious for us, there corresponds doubtless a series of facts of which we were unaware. She must for some time past have been keeping up relations, written, or verbal or through messengers, with some man, or some woman, have been awaiting some signal which we may perhaps have given her ourself, unconsciously, when we said: " X. called yesterday to see me," if she had arranged with X. that on the eve of the day when she was to join him he was to call upon me. How many possible hypotheses! Possible only. I constructed the truth so well, but in the realm of possibility only, that, having one day opened, and then by mistake, a letter addressed to my mistress, from this letter which was written in a code, and said: " Go on waiting for a signal to go to the Marquis de Saint-

Loup; let me know to-morrow by telephone," I reconstructed a sort of projected flight; the name of the Marquis de Saint-Loup was there only as a substitute for some other name, for my mistress did not know Saint-Loup well enough, but had heard me speak of him, and moreover the signature was some sort of nickname, without any intelligible form. As it happened, the letter was addressed not to my mistress but to another person in the building who bore a different name which had been misread. The letter was written not in a code, but in bad French, because it was written by an American woman, who was indeed a friend of Saint-Loup as he himself told me. And the odd way in which this American woman wrote certain letters had given the appearance of a nickname to a name which was quite genuine, only foreign. And so I had on that occasion been entirely at fault in my suspicions. But the intellectual structure which had in my mind combined these facts, all of them false, was itself the so accurate, so inflexible form of the truth that when three months later my mistress, who had at that time been meaning to spend the rest of her life with me, left me, it was in a fashion absolutely identical with that which I had imagined on the former occasion. A letter arrived, containing the same peculiarities which I had wrongly attributed to the former letter, but this time it was indeed meant as a signal.

This calamity was the greatest that I had experienced in my life. And, when all was said, the suffering that it caused me was perhaps even exceeded by my curiosity to learn the causes of this calamity which Albertine had deliberately brought about. But the sources of great events are like those of rivers, in vain do we explore the earth's surface, we can never find them. So Albertine had for a long time past been planning her flight; I have said (and at the time it had seemed to me simply a sign of affectation and ill-humour, what Françoise called " lifting her head ") that, from the day upon which she had ceased to kiss me, she had gone about as though tormented by a devil, stiffly erect, unbending, saying the simplest things in a sorrowful tone, slow in her movements, never once smiling. I cannot say that there was any concrete proof of conspiracy with the outer world. Françoise told me long afterwards that, having gone into Albertine's room two days before her departure, she had found it empty, the curtains drawn, but had detected from the atmosphere of the room and the sounds that came in that the window was open. And indeed she had found Albertine on the balcony. But it is hard to say with whom she could have been communicating from there, and moreover the drawn curtains screening the open window could doubtless be explained by her knowing that I was afraid of draughts, and by the fact that, even if the curtains afforded me little protection, they would prevent Françoise from seeing from the passage that the shutters had been opened so early. No, I can see nothing save one trifling incident which proves merely that on the day before her departure she knew that she was going. For during the day she took from my room without my noticing it a large quantity of wrapping paper and cloth which I kept there, and in which she spent the whole night packing her innumerable wrappers and dressing-gowns so that she might leave the house in the morning; this was the only incident, it was more than enough. I cannot attach any importance to her having almost forced upon me that evening a thousand francs which she owed me, there is nothing peculiar in that, for she was extremely scrupulous about money. Yes, she took the wrapping paper overnight, but it was not only then that she knew that she was going to leave me! For it was not resentment that made her leave me, but her determination, already formed, to leave me, to abandon the life of which she had dreamed, that gave her that air of resentment. A resentful air, almost solemnly cold towards myself, except on the last evening when, after staying in my room longer than she had intended, she said—a remark which surprised me, coming from her who had always sought to postpone the moment of parting—she said to me from the door: " Good-bye, my dear; good-bye, my dear." But I did not take any notice of this, at the moment. Françoise told me that next morning when Albertine informed her that she was going (but this, for that matter, may be explained also by exhaustion for she had spent the whole night in packing all her clothes, except the things she had to ask Françoise for, as they were not in her bedroom or her dressing-room), she was still so sad, so much more erect, so much stiffer than during the previous days that Françoise, when Albertine said to her: " Good-bye, Françoise," almost expected to see her fall to the ground. When we are told anything like this, we realise that the woman who appealed to us so much less than any of the women whom we meet so easily in the course of the briefest outing, the woman who makes us resent our having to sacrifice them to herself, is on the contrary she whom now we would a thousand times rather possess. For the choice lies no longer between a certain pleasure—which has become by force of habit, and perhaps by the insignificance of its object, almost nothing—and other pleasures, which tempt and thrill us, but between these latter pleasures and something that is far stronger than they, compassion for suffering.

When I vowed to myself that Albertine would be back in the house before night, I had proceeded in hot haste to cover with a fresh belief the open wound from which I had torn the belief that had been my mainstay until then. But however rapidly my instinct of self-preservation might have acted, I had, when Françoise spoke to me, been left for an instant without relief, and it was useless my knowing now that Albertine would return that same evening, the pain that I had felt in the instant in which I had not yet assured myself of her return (the instant that had followed the words: " Mademoiselle Albertine has asked for her boxes; Mademoiselle Albertine has gone ") this revived in me of its own accord as keen as it had been before, that is to say as if I had still been unaware of Albertine's immediate return. However, it was essential that she should return, but of her own accord. Upon every hypothesis, to appear to be taking the first step, to be begging her to return would be to defeat my own object. To be sure, I had not the strength to give her up as I had given up Gilberte. Even more than to see Albertine again, what I wished was to put an end to the physical anguish which my heart, less stout than of old, could endure no longer. Then, by dint of accustoming myself to not wishing anything, whether it was a question of work or of anything else, I had become more cowardly. But above all, this anguish was incomparably keener for several reasons, the most important of which was perhaps not that I had never tasted any sensual pleasure with Mme de Guermantes or with Gilberte, but that, not seeing them every day, and at every hour of the day, having no opportunity and consequently no need to see them, there had been less prominent, in my love for them, the immense force of Habit. Perhaps, now that my heart, incapable of wishing and of enduring of its own free will what I was suffering, found only one possible solution, that Albertine should return at all costs, perhaps the opposite solution (a deliberate renunciation, gradual resignation) would have seemed to me a novelist's solution, improbable in real life, had I not myself decided upon it in the past when Gilberte was concerned. I knew therefore that this other solution might be accepted also and by the same man, for I had remained more or less the same. Only time had played its part, time which had made me older, time which moreover had kept Albertine perpetually in my company while we were living together. But I must add that, without my giving up the idea of that life, there survived in me of all that I had felt about Gilberte the pride which made me refuse to be to Albertine a repellent plaything by insisting upon her return; I wished her to come back without my appearing to attach any importance to her return. I got out of bed, so as to lose no more time, but was arrested by my anguish; this was the first time that I had got out of bed since Albertine had left me. Yet I must dress myself at once in order to go and make inquiries of her porter.

Suffering the prolongation of a spiritual shock that has come from without, keeps on endeavouring to change its form; we hope to be able to dispel it by making plans, by seeking information; we wish it to pass through its countless metamorphoses, this requires less courage than retain-

16

ing our suffering intact; the bed appears so narrow, hard
and cold on which we lie down with our grief.   I put my
feet to the ground; I stepped across the room with endless
precaution, took up a position from which I could not see
Albertine's chair, the pianola upon the pedals of which she
used to press her golden slippers, nor a single one of the
things which she had used and all of which, in the secret
language that my memory had imparted to them, seemed to
be seeking to give me a fresh translation, a different version,
to announce to me for the second time the news of her
departure.   But even without looking at them I could see
them, my strength left me, I sank down upon one of those
blue satin armchairs, the glossy surface of which an hour
earlier, in the dimness of my bedroom anaesthetised by a ray
of morning light, had made me dream dreams which then I
had passionately caressed, which were so far from me now.
Alas, I had never sat down upon any of them until this
minute save when Albertine was still with me.   And so I
could not remain sitting there, I rose; and thus, at every
moment there was one more of those innumerable and
humble " selves " that compose our personality which was
still unaware of Albertine's departure and must be informed
of it; I was obliged—and this was more cruel than if they
had been strangers and had not borrowed my sensibility to
pain—to describe to all these " selves " who did not yet
know of it, the calamity that had just occurred, it was
necessary that each of them in turn should hear for the first
time the words: " Albertine has asked for her boxes "—
those coffin-shaped boxes which I had seen put on the train
at Balbec with my mother's—" Albertine has gone."   To
each of them I had to relate my grief, the grief which is in

17

no way a pessimistic conclusion freely drawn from a number of lamentable circumstances, but is the intermittent and involuntary revival of a specific impression, come to us from without and not chosen by us. There were some of these "selves" which I had not encountered for a long time past. For instance (I had not remembered that it was the day on which the barber called) the "self" that I was when I was having my hair cut. I had forgotten this "self," the barber's arrival made me burst into tears, as, at a funeral, does the appearance of an old pensioned servant who has not forgotten the deceased. Then all of a sudden I recalled that, during the last week, I had from time to time been seized by panic fears which I had not confessed to myself. At such moments, however, I had debated the question, saying to myself: "Useless, of course, to consider the hypothesis of her suddenly leaving me. It is absurd. If I were to confess it to a sober, intelligent man" (and I should have done so to secure peace of mind, had not jealousy prevented me from making confidences) "he would be sure to say to me: 'Why, you are mad. It is impossible.' And, as a matter of fact, during these last days we have not quarrelled once. People separate for a reason. They tell you their reasons. They give you a chance to reply. They do not run away like that. No, it is perfectly childish. It is the only hypothesis that is absurd." And yet, every day, when I found that she was still there in the morning when I rang my bell, I had heaved a vast sigh of relief. And when Françoise handed me Albertine's letter, I had at once been certain that it referred to the one thing that could not happen, to this departure which I had in a sense perceived many days in advance, in spite of the logical reasons for my feeling reassured. I had said this to myself almost with satisfaction at my own perspicacity in my despair, like a murderer who knows that his guilt cannot be detected, but is nevertheless afraid and all of a sudden sees his victim's name written at the head of a document on the table of the police official who has sent for him. My only hope was that Albertine had gone to Touraine, to her aunt's house, where after all, she would be fairly well guarded and could not do anything very serious in the interval before I brought her back. My worst fear was that she might be remaining in Paris, or have gone to Amsterdam or to Montjouvain, in other words that she had escaped in order to involve herself in some intrigue the preliminaries of which I had failed to observe. But in reality, when I said to myself Paris, Amsterdam, Montjouvain, that is to say various names of places, I was thinking of places which were merely potential. And so, when Albertine's hall porter informed me that she had gone to Touraine, this place of residence which I supposed myself to desire seemed to me the most terrible of them all, because it was real, and because, tormented for the first time by the certainty of the present and the uncertainty of the future, I pictured to myself Albertine starting upon a life which she had deliberately chosen to lead apart from myself, perhaps for a long time, perhaps for ever, and in which she would realise that unknown element which in the past had so often distressed me when, nevertheless, I had enjoyed the happiness of possessing, of caressing what was its outer shell, that charming face impenetrable and captive. It was this unknown element that formed the core of my love. Outside the door of Albertine's house I found a poor little girl who gazed at me open-eyed and looked so honest that I asked her whether she would care to come home with me, as I might have taken home a dog with faithful eyes. She seemed pleased by my suggestion. When I got home, I held her for some time on my knee, but very soon her presence, by making me feel too keenly Albertine's absence, became intolerable. And I asked her to go away, giving her first a five-hundred franc note. And yet, a moment later, the thought of having some other little girl in the house with me, of never being alone, without the comfort of an innocent presence, was the only thing that enabled me to endure the idea that Albertine might perhaps remain away for some time before returning. As for Albertine herself, she barely existed in me save under the form of her name, which, but for certain rare moments of respite when I awoke, came and engraved itself upon my brain and continued incessantly to do so. If I had thought aloud, I should have kept on repeating it, and my speech would have been as monotonous, as limited as if I had been transformed into a bird, a bird like that in the fable whose song repeated incessantly the name of her whom, when a man, it had loved. We say the name to ourselves, and as we remain silent it seems as though we inscribed it on ourself, as though it left its trace on our brain which must end by being, like a wall upon which somebody has amused himself by scribbling, entirely covered with the name, written a thousand times over, of her whom we love. We repeat it all the time in our mind, even when we are happy, all the more when we are unhappy. And to repeat this name, which gives us nothing in addition to what we already know, we feel an incessantly renewed desire, but, in course of time, it wearies us. To carnal pleasure I did not even give a thought at this moment; I did not even see, with my mind's eye, the image of that Albertine, albeit she had been the cause of such an upheaval of my existence, I did not perceive her body and if I had wished to isolate the idea that was bound up—for there is always some idea bound up—with my suffering, it would have been alternately, on the one hand my doubt as to the intention with which she had left me, with or without any thought of returning, and on the other hand the means of bringing her back. Perhaps there is something symbolical and true in the minute place occupied in our anxiety by the person who is its cause. The fact is that the person counts for little or nothing; what is almost everything is the series of emotions, of agonies which similar mishaps have made us feel in the past in connection with her and which habit has attached to her. What proves this clearly is, even more than the boredom which we feel in moments of happiness, that the fact of seeing or not seeing the person in question, of being or not being admired by her, of having or not having her at our disposal will seem to us utterly trivial when we shall no longer have to set ourselves the problem (so superfluous that we shall no longer take the trouble to consider it) save in relation to the person herself—the series of emotions and agonies being forgotten, at least in so far as she is concerned, for it may have developed afresh but in connection with another person. Before this, when it was still attached to her, we supposed that our happiness was dependent upon her presence; it depended merely upon the cessation of our anxiety. Our subconscious was therefore more clairvoyant than ourself at that moment, when it made the form of the beloved woman so minute, a form which we had indeed perhaps forgotten, which we might have failed to remember clearly and thought unattractive, in the terrible drama in which finding her again in order to cease from expecting her becomes an absolutely vital matter. Minute proportions of the woman's form, a logical and necessary effect of the fashion in which love develops, a clear allegory of the subjective nature of that love.

The spirit in which Albertine had left me was similar no doubt to that of the nations who pave the way by a demonstration of their armed force for the exercise of their diplomacy. She could not have left me save in the hope of obtaining from me better terms, greater freedom, more comfort. In that case the one of us who would have conquered would have been myself, had I had the strength to await the moment when, seeing that she could gain nothing, she would return of her own accord. But if at cards, or in war, where victory alone matters, we can hold out against bluff, the conditions are not the same that are created by love and jealousy, not to mention suffering. If, in order to wait, to " hold out," I allowed Albertine to remain away from me for several days, for several weeks perhaps, I was ruining what had been my sole purpose for more than a year, never to leave her by herself for a single hour. All my precautions were rendered fruitless, if I allowed her the time, the opportunity to betray me as often as she might choose, and if in the end she did return to me, I should never again be able to forget the time when she had been alone, and even if I won in the end, nevertheless in the past, that is to say irreparably, I should be the vanquished party.

As for the means of bringing Albertine back, they had all

the more chance of success the more plausible the hypothesis appeared that she had left me only in the hope of
being summoned back upon more favourable terms. And
no doubt to the people who did not believe in Albertine's
sincerity, certainly to Françoise for instance, this was the
more plausible hypothesis. But my reason, to which the
only explanation of certain bouts of ill-humour, of certain
attitudes had appeared, before I knew anything, to be that
she had planned a final departure, found it difficult to
believe that, now that her departure had occurred, it was a
mere feint. I say my reason, not myself. The hypothesis of a feint became all the more necessary to me the
more improbable it was, and gained in strength what it lost
in probability. When we find ourself on the brink of the
abyss, and it seemed as though God has forsaken us, we no
longer hesitate to expect a miracle of Him.

I realise that in all this I was the most apathetic, albeit
the most anxious of detectives. But Albertine's flight had
not restored to myself the faculties of which the habit of
having her watched by other people had deprived me. I
could think of one thing only: how to employ someone else
upon the search for her. This other person was Saint-
Loup, who agreed. The transference of the anxiety of so
many days to another person filled me with joy and I
quivered with the certainty of success, my hands becoming
suddenly dry again as in the past, and no longer moist with
that sweat in which Françoise had bathed me when she
said: " Mademoiselle Albertine has gone."

The reader may remember that when I decided to live
with Albertine, and even to marry her, it was in order to
guard her, to know what she was doing, to prevent her

from returning to her old habits with Mlle Vinteuil. It had been in the appalling anguish caused by her revelation at Balbec when she had told me, as a thing that was quite natural, and I succeeded, albeit it was the greatest grief that I had ever yet felt in my life, in seeming to find quite natural, the thing which in my worst suppositions I had never had the audacity to imagine. (It is astonishing what a want of imagination jealousy, which spends its time in weaving little suppositions of what is untrue, shews when it is a question of discovering the truth.) Now this love, born first and foremost of a need to prevent Albertine from doing wrong, this love had preserved in the sequel the marks of its origin. Being with her mattered little to me so long as I could prevent her from " being on the run," from going to this place or to that. In order to prevent her, I had had recourse to the vigilance, to the company of the people who went about with her, and they had only to give me at the end of the day a report that was fairly reassuring for my anxieties to vanish in good humour.

Having given myself the assurance that, whatever steps I might have to take, Albertine would be back in the house that same evening, I had granted a respite to the grief which Françoise had caused me when she told me that Albertine had gone (because at that moment my mind taken by surprise had believed for an instant that her departure was final). But after an interruption, when with an impulse of its own independent life the initial suffering revived spontaneously in me, it was just as keen as before, because it was anterior to the consoling promise that I had given myself to bring Albertine back that evening. This utterance, which would have calmed it, my suffering had not heard. To set in motion the means of bringing about her return, once again, not that such an attitude on my part would ever have proved very successful, but because I had always adopted it since I had been in love with Albertine, I was condemned to behave as though I did not love her, was not pained by her departure, I was condemned to continue to lie to her. I might be all the more energetic in my efforts to bring her back in that personally I should appear to have given her up for good. I decided to write Albertine a farewell letter in which I would regard her departure as final, while I would send Saint-Loup down to put upon Mme Bontemps, as though without my knowledge, the most brutal pressure to make Albertine return as soon as possible. No doubt I had had experience with Gilberte of the danger of letters expressing an indifference which, feigned at first, ends by becoming genuine. And this experience ought to have restrained me from writing to Albertine letters of the same sort as those that I had written to Gilberte. But what we call experience is merely the revelation to our own eyes of a trait in our character which naturally reappears, and re-appears all the more markedly because we have already brought it into prominence once of our own accord, so that the spontaneous impulse which guided us on the first occasion finds itself reinforced by all the suggestions of memory. The human plagiarism which is most difficult to avoid, for individuals (and even for nations which persevere in their faults and continue to aggravate them) is the plagiarism of ourself.

Knowing that Saint-Loup was in Paris I had sent for him immediately; he came in haste to my rescue, swift and efficient as he had been long ago at Doncières, and agreed to set off at once for Touraine. I suggested to him the following arrangement. He was to take the train to Chatellerault, find out where Mme Bontemps lived, and wait until Albertine should have left the house, since there was a risk of her recognising him. " But does the girl you are speaking of know me, then? " he asked. I told him that I did not think so. This plan of action filled me with indescribable joy. It was nevertheless diametrically opposed to my original intention: to arrange things so that I should not appear to be seeking Albertine's return; whereas by so acting I must inevitably appear to be seeking it, but this plan had the inestimable advantage over " the proper thing to do " that it enabled me to say to myself that some-one sent by me was going to see Albertine, and would doubtless bring her back with him. And if I had been able to read my own heart clearly at the start, I might have fore-seen that it was this solution, hidden in the darkness, which I felt to be deplorable, that would ultimately prevail over the alternative course of patience which I had decided to choose, from want of will-power. As Saint-Loup already appeared slightly surprised to learn that a girl had been living with me through the whole winter without my having said a word to him about her, as moreover he had often spoken to me of the girl who had been at Balbec and I had never said in reply: " But she is living here," he might be annoyed by my want of confidence. There was always the risk of Mme Bontemps's mentioning Balbec to him. But I was too impatient for his departure, for his arrival at the other end, to wish, to be able to think of the possible consequences of his journey. As for the risk of his recognising Albertine (at whom he had resolutely refrained from looking when he had met her at Doncières), she had, as everyone admitted, so altered and had grown so much stouter that it was hardly likely. He asked me whether I had not a picture of Albertine. I replied at first that I had not, so that he might not have a chance, from her photograph, taken about the time of our stay at Balbec, of recognising Albertine, though he had no more than a glimpse of her in the railway carriage. But then I remembered that in the photograph she would be already as different from the Albertine of Balbec as the living Albertine now was, and that he would recognise her no better from her photograph than in the flesh. While I was looking for it, he laid his hand gently upon my brow, by way of consoling me. I was touched by the distress which the grief that he guessed me to be feeling was causing him. For one thing, however final his rupture with Rachel, what he had felt at that time was not yet so remote that he had not a special sympathy, a special pity for this sort of suffering, as we feel ourself more closely akin to a person who is afflicted with the same malady as ourself. Besides, he had so strong an affection for myself that the thought of my suffering was intolerable to him. And so he conceived, towards her who was the cause of my suffering, a rancour mingled with admiration. He regarded me as so superior a being that he supposed that if I were to subject myself to another person she must be indeed extraordinary. I quite expected that he would think Albertine, in her photograph, pretty, but as at the same time I did not imagine that it would produce upon him the impression that Helen made upon the Trojan elders, as I continued to look for it, I said modestly : " Oh! you know, you mustn't imagine things, for one thing it is a bad photograph, and besides there's nothing startling about her, she is not a beauty, she is merely very nice." "Oh, yes, she must be wonderful," he said with a simple, sincere enthusiasm as he sought to form a mental picture of the person who was capable of plunging me in such despair and agitation. " I am angry with her because she has hurt you, but at the same time one can't help seeing that a man who is an artist to his finger-tips like you, that you, who love beauty in everything and with so passionate a love, were predestined to suffer more than the ordinary person when you found it in a woman." At last I managed to find her photograph. "She is bound to be wonderful," still came from Robert, who had not seen that I was holding out the photograph to him. All at once he caught sight of it, he held it for a moment between his hands. His face expressed a stupefaction which amounted to stupidity. "Is this the girl you are in love with?" he said at length in a tone from which astonishment was banished by his fear of making me angry. He made no remark upon it, he had assumed the reasonable, prudent, inevitably somewhat disdainful air which we assume before a sick person—even if he has been in the past a man of outstanding gifts, and our friend—who is now nothing of the sort, for, raving mad, he speaks to us of a celestial being who has appeared to him, and continues to behold this being where we, the sane man, can see nothing but a quilt on the bed. I at once understood Robert's astonishment and that it was the same in which the sight of his mistress had plunged me, with this difference only that I had recognised in her a woman whom I already knew, whereas he supposed that he had never seen Albertine.

But no doubt the difference between our respective impressions of the same person was equally great. The time was past when I had timidly begun at Balbec by adding to my visual sensations when I gazed at Albertine sensations of taste, of smell, of touch. Since then, other more profound, more pleasant, more indefinable sensations had been added to them, and afterwards painful sensations. In short, Albertine was merely, like a stone round which snow has gathered, the generating centre of an immense structure which rose above the plane of my heart. Robert, to whom all this stratification of sensations was invisible, grasped only a residue of it which it prevented me, on the contrary, from perceiving. What had disconcerted Robert when his eyes fell upon Albertine's photograph was not the consternation of the Trojan elders when they saw Helen go by and said: " All our misfortunes are not worth a single glance from her eyes," but the exactly opposite impression which may be expressed by: " What, it is for this that he has worked himself into such a state, has grieved himself so, has done so many idiotic things! " It must indeed be admitted that this sort of reaction at the sight of the person who has caused the suffering, upset the life, sometimes brought about the death of someone whom we love, is infinitely more frequent than that felt by the Trojan elders, and is in short habitual. This is not merely because love is individual, nor because, when we do not feel it, finding it avoidable and philosophising upon the folly of other people come naturally to us. No, it is because, when it has reached the stage at which it causes such misery, the structure composed of the sensations interposed between the face of the woman and the eyes of her lover—the huge egg of pain which encases it and conceals it as a mantle of snow conceals a fountain—is already raised so high that the point at which the lover's gaze comes to rest, the point at which he finds his pleasure and his sufferings' is as far from the point which other people see as is the real sun from the place in which its condensed light enables us to see it in the sky. And what is more, during this time, beneath the chrysalis of griefs and affections which render invisible to the lover the worst metamorphoses of the beloved object, her face has had time to grow old and to change. With the result that if the face which the lover saw on the first occasion is very far removed from that which he has seen since he has been in love and has been made to suffer, it is, in the opposite direction, equally far from the face which may now be seen by the indifferent onlooker. (What would have happened if, instead of the photograph of one who was still a girl, Robert had seen the photograph of an elderly mistress?) And indeed we have no need to see for the first time the woman who has caused such an upheaval, in order to feel this astonishment. Often we know her already, as my great-uncle knew Odette. Then the optical difference extends not merely to the bodily aspect, but to the character, to the individual importance. It is more likely than not that the woman who is causing the man who is in love with her to suffer has always behaved perfectly towards someone who was not interested in her, just as Odette who was so cruel to Swann had been the sedulous " lady in pink " to my great-uncle, or indeed that the person whose every decision is calculated in advance with as much dread as that of a deity by the man who is in love with her, appears as a person of no importance, only too glad to do anything that he may require of her, in the eyes of the man who is not in love with her, as Saint-Loup's mistress appeared to me who saw in her nothing more than that " Rachel, when from the Lord " who had so repeatedly been offered me. I recalled my own stupefaction, that first time that I met her with Saint-Loup, at the thought that anybody could be tormented by not knowing what such a woman had been doing, by the itch to know what she might have said in a whisper to some other man, why she had desired a rupture. And I felt that all this past existence—but, in this case, Albertine's—towards which every fibre of my heart, of my life was directed with a throbbing clumsy pain, must appear just as insignificant to Saint-Loup as it would one day, perhaps, appear to myself. I felt that I would pass perhaps gradually, so far as the insignificance or gravity of Albertine's past was concerned, from the state of mind in which I was at the moment to that of Saint-Loup, for I was under no illusion as to what Saint-Loup might be thinking, as to what anyone else than the lover himself might think. And I was not unduly distressed. Let us leave pretty women to men devoid of imagination. I recalled that tragic explanation of so many of us which is furnished by an inspired but not lifelike portrait such as Elstir's portrait of Odette, which is a portrait not so much of a mistress as of our degrading love for her. There was lacking only what we find in so many portraits—that the painter should have been at once a great artist and a lover (and even then it was said that Elstir had been in love with Odette). This disparity, the whole life of a lover—of a lover whose acts of folly nobody understands—the whole life of a Swann goes to prove. But let the lover be embodied in a painter like Elstir and then we have the clue to the enigma, we have at length before our eyes those lips which the common herd have never perceived, that nose which nobody has ever seen, that unsuspected carriage. The portrait says: "What I have loved, what has made me suffer, what I have never ceased to behold, is this." By an inverse gymnastic, I who had made a mental effort to add to Rachel all that Saint-Loup had added to her of himself, I attempted to subtract the support of my heart and mind from the composition of Albertine and to picture her to myself as she must appear to Saint-Loup, as Rachel had appeared to me. Those differences, even though we were to observe them ourself, what importance would we attach to them? When, in the summer at Balbec, Albertine used to wait for me beneath the arcades of Incarville and spring into my carriage, not only had she not yet put on weight, she had, as a result of too much exercise, begun to waste; thin, made plainer by an ugly hat which left visible only the tip of an ugly nose, and at a side-view, pale cheeks like white slugs, I recognised very little of her, enough however to know, when she sprang into the carriage, that it was she, that she had been punctual in keeping our appointment and had not gone somewhere else; and this was enough; what we love is too much in the past, consists too much in the time that we have spent together for us to require the whole woman; we wish only to be sure that it is she, not to be mistaken as to her identity, a thing far more important than beauty to those who are in love; her cheeks may grow hollow, her body thin, even to those who were originally most proud, in the eyes of the world, of their domination over beauty, that little tip of a nose, that sign in which is summed up the permanent personality of a woman, that algebraical formula, that constant, is sufficient to prevent a man who is courted in the highest society and is in love with her from being free upon a single evening because he is spending his evenings in brushing and entangling, until it is time to go to bed, the hair of the woman whom he loves, or simply in staying by her side, so that he may be with her or she with him, or merely that she may not be with other people.

" You are sure," Robert asked me, " that I can begin straight away by offering this woman thirty thousand francs for her husband's constituency? She is as dishonest as all that? You're sure you aren't exaggerating and that three thousand francs wouldn't be enough? " " No, I beg of you, don't try to be economical about a thing that matters so much to me. This is what you are to say to her (and it is to some extent true): ' My friend borrowed these thirty thousand francs from a relative for the election expenses of the uncle of the girl he was engaged to marry. It was because of this engagement that the money was given him. And he asked me to bring it to you so that Albertine should know nothing about it. And now Albertine goes and leaves him. He doesn't know what to do. He is obliged to pay back the thirty thousand francs if he does not marry Albertine. And if he is going to marry her, then if only to keep up appearances she ought to return immediately, because it will look so bad if she stays away for long.' You think I've made all this up? " " Not at all," Saint-Loup assured me out of consideration for myself, out of discretion, and also because he knew that truth is often stranger than fiction. After all, it was by no

means impossible that in this tale of the thirty thousand
francs there might be, as I assured him, a large element of
truth. It was possible, but it was not true and this element
of truth was in fact a lie. But we lied to each other,
Robert and I, as in every conversation when one friend is
genuinely anxious to help another who is desperately in
love. The friend who is being counsellor, prop, comforter,
may pity the other's distress but cannot share it, and the
kinder he is to him the more he has to lie. And the other
confesses to him as much as is necessary in order to secure
his help, but, simply perhaps in order to secure that help,
conceals many things from him. And the happy one of
the two is, when all is said, he who takes trouble, goes on
a journey, executes a mission, but feels no anguish in his
heart. I was at this moment the person that Robert had
been at Doncières when he thought that Rachel had
abandoned him. "Very well, just as you like; if I get
my head bitten off, I accept the snub in advance for your
sake. And even if it does seem a bit queer to make such
an open bargain, I know that in our own set there are
plenty of duchesses, even the most stuffy of them, who if
you offered them thirty thousand francs would do things
far more difficult than telling their nieces not to stay in
Touraine. Anyhow, I am doubly glad to be doing you a
service, since that is the only reason that will make you
consent to see me. If I marry," he went on, " don't you
think we might see more of one another, won't you look
upon my house as your own. . . ." He stopped short,
the thought having suddenly occurred to him (as I supposed at the time) that, if I too were to marry, his wife
would not be able to make an intimate friend of Albertine.

And I remembered what the Cambremers had said to me as the probability of his marrying a niece of the Prince de Guermantes. He consulted the time-table, and found that he could not leave Paris until the evening. Françoise inquired: " Am I to take Mlle Albertine's bed out of the study ?" " Not at all," I said, " you must leave everything ready for her." I hoped that she would return any day and did not wish Françoise to suppose that there could be any doubt of her return. Albertine's departure must appear to have been arranged between ourselves, and not in any way to imply that she loved me less than before. But Françoise looked at me with an air, if not of incredulity, at any rate, of doubt. She too had her alternative hypotheses. Her nostrils expanded, she could scent the quarrel, she must have felt it in the air for a long time past. And if she was not absolutely sure of it, this was perhaps because, like myself, she would hesitate to believe unconditionally what would have given her too much pleasure. Now the burden of the affair rested no longer upon my overwrought mind but upon Saint-Loup. I became quite light-hearted because I had made a decision, because I could say to myself: " I haven't lost any time, I have acted." Saint-Loup can barely have been in the train when in the hall I ran into Bloch, whose ring I had not heard, and so was obliged to let him stay with me for a minute. He had met me recently with Albertine (whom he had known at Balbec) on a day when she was in a bad humour. " I met M. Bontemps at dinner," he told me, " and as I have a certain influence over him, I told him that I was grieved that his niece was not nicer to you, that he must make entreaties to her in that connection." I boiled with rage; these entreaties, this compassion destroyed the whole effect of Saint-Loup's intervention and brought me into direct contact with Albertine herself whom I now seemed to be imploring to return. To make matters worse, Françoise, who was lingering in the hall, could hear every word. I heaped every imaginable reproach upon Bloch, telling him that I had never authorised him to do anything of the sort and that, besides, the whole thing was nonsense. Bloch, from that moment, continued to smile less, I imagine, from joy than from self-consciousness at having made me angry. He laughingly expressed his surprise at having provoked such anger. Perhaps he said this hoping to minimise in my mind the importance of his indiscreet intervention, perhaps it was because he was of a cowardly nature, and lived gaily and idly in an atmosphere of falsehood, as jelly-fish float upon the surface of the sea, perhaps because, even if he had not been of a different race, as other people can never place themselves at our point of view, they do not realise the magnitude of the injury that words uttered at random can do us. I had barely shewn him out, unable to think of any remedy for the mischief that he had done, when the bell rang again and Françoise brought me a summons from the head of the Sûreté. The parents of the little girl whom I had brought into the house for an hour had decided to lodge a complaint against me for corruption of a child under the age of consent. There are moments in life when a sort of beauty is created by the multiplicity of the troubles that assail us, intertwined like Wagnerian *leitmotiv*, from the idea also, which then emerges, that events are not situated in the content of the reflections portrayed in the wretched little mirror which the mind holds in front of it and which is called the future, that they are somewhere outside, and spring up as suddenly as a person who comes to accuse us of a crime. Even when left to itself, an event becomes modified, whether frustration amplifies it for us or satisfaction reduces it. But it is rarely unaccompanied. The feelings aroused by each event contradict one another, and there comes to a certain extent, as I felt when on my way to the head of the Sûreté, an at least momentary revulsion which is as provocative of sentimental misery as fear. I found at the Sûreté the girl's parents who insulted me by saying: "We don't eat this sort of bread," and handed me back the five hundred francs which I declined to take, and the head of the Sûreté who, setting himself the inimitable example of the judicial facility in repartee, took hold of a word from each sentence that I uttered, a word which enabled him to make a witty and crushing retort. My innocence of the alleged crime was never taken into consideration, for that was the sole hypothesis which nobody was willing to accept for an instant. Nevertheless the difficulty of a conviction enabled me to escape with an extremely violent reprimand, while the parents were in the room. But as soon as they had gone, the head of the Sûreté, who had a weakness for little girls, changed his tone and admonished me as one man to another: "Next time, you must be more careful. Gad, you can't pick them up as easily as that, or you'll get into trouble. Anyhow, you can find dozens of girls better than that one, and far cheaper. It was a perfectly ridiculous amount to pay." I felt him to be so incapable of understanding me if I attempted to tell him the truth that without saying a word I took advantage of his permission to withdraw. Every passer-by, until I was safely at home, seemed to me an inspector appointed to spy upon my behaviour. But this *leitmotiv*, like that of my anger with Bloch, died away, leaving the field clear for that of Albertine's departure. And this took its place once more, but in an almost joyous tone now that Saint-Loup had started. Now that he had undertaken to go and see Mme Bontemps, my sufferings had been dispelled. I believed that this was because I had taken action, I believed it sincerely, for we never know what we conceal in our heart of hearts. What really made me happy was not, as I supposed, that I had transferred my load of indecisions to Saint-Loup. I was not, for that matter, entirely wrong; the specific remedy for an unfortunate event (and three events out of four are unfortunate) is a decision; for its effect is that, by a sudden reversal of our thoughts, it interrupts the flow of those that come from the past event and prolong its vibration, and breaks that flow with a contrary flow of contrary thoughts, come from without, from the future. But these new thoughts are most of all beneficial to us when (and this was the case with the thoughts that assailed me at this moment), from the heart of that future, it is a hope that they bring us. What really made me so happy was the secret certainty that Saint-Loup's mission could not fail, Albertine was bound to return. I realised this; for not having received, on the following day, any answer from Saint-Loup, I began to suffer afresh. My decision, my transference to him of full power of action, were not, therefore, the cause of my joy, which, in that case, would have persisted; but rather the " Success is certain " which had been in my mind when I said: "Come what may." And the thought aroused by his delay, that, after all, his mission might not prove successful, was so hateful to me that I had lost my gaiety. It is in reality our anticipation, our hope of happy events that fills us with a joy which we ascribe to other causes and which ceases, letting us relapse into misery, if we are no longer so assured that what we desire will come to pass. It is always this invisible belief that sustains the edifice of our world of sensation, deprived of which it rocks from its foundations. We have seen that it created for us the merit or unimportance of other people, our excitement or boredom at seeing them. It creates similarly the possibility of enduring a grief which seems to us trivial, simply because we are convinced that it will presently be brought to an end, or its sudden enlargement until the presence of a certain person matters as much as, possibly more than our life itself One thing, however, succeeded in making my heartache as keen as it had been at the first moment and (I am bound to admit) no longer was. This was when I read over again a passage in Albertine's letter. It is all very well our loving people, the pain of losing them, when in our isolation we are confronted with it alone, to which our mind gives, to a certain extent, whatever form it chooses, this pain is endurable and different from that other pain less human, less our own, as unforeseen and unusual as an accident in the moral world and in the region of our heart, which is caused not so much by the people themselves as by the manner in which we have learned that we are not to see them again. Albertine, I might think of her with gentle tears, accepting the fact that I should not be able to see her again this evening as I had seen her last night,

39

but when I read over again: " my decision is irrevocable," that was another matter, it was like taking a dangerous drug which might give me a heart attack which I could not survive. There is in inanimate objects, in events, in farewell letters a special danger which amplifies and even alters the nature of the grief that people are capable of causing us. But this pain did not last long. I was, when all was said, so sure of Saint-Loup's skill, of his eventual success, Albertine's return seemed to me so certain that I asked myself whether I had had any reason to hope for it. Nevertheless, I rejoiced at the thought. Unfortunately for myself, who supposed the business with the Sûreté to be over and done with, Françoise came in to tell me that an inspector had called to inquire whether I was in the habit of having girls in the house, that the porter, supposing him to refer to Albertine, had replied in the affirmative, and that from that moment it had seemed that the house was being watched. In future it would be impossible for me ever to bring a little girl into the house to console me in my grief, without the risk of being put to shame in her eyes by the sudden intrusion of an inspector, and of her regarding me as a criminal. And at the same instant I realised how far more we live for certain ideas than we suppose, for this impossibility of my ever taking a little girl on my knee again seemed to me to destroy all the value of my life, but what was more, I understood how comprehensible it is that people will readily refuse wealth and risk their lives, whereas we imagine that pecuniary interest and the fear of death rule the world. For if I had thought that even a little girl who was a complete stranger might, by the arrival of a policeman, be given a bad impression of myself, how much more readily would I have committed suicide. And yet there was no possible comparison between the two degrees of suffering. Now in everyday life we never bear in mind that the people to whom we offer money, whom we threaten to kill, may have mistresses or merely friends, to whose esteem they attach importance, not to mention their own self-respect. But, all of a sudden, by a confusion of which I was not aware (I did not in fact remember that Albertine, being of full age, was free to live under my roof and even to be my mistress), it seemed to me that the charge of corrupting minors might include Albertine also. Thereupon my life appeared to me to be hedged in on every side. And when I thought that I had not lived chastely with her, I found in the punishment that had been inflicted upon me for having forced an unknown little girl to accept money, that relation which almost always exists in human sanctions, the effect of which is that there is hardly ever either a fair sentence or a judicial error, but a sort of compromise between the false idea that the judge forms of an innocent action and the culpable deeds of which he is unaware. But then when I thought that Albertine's return might involve me in the scandal of a sentence which would degrade me in her eyes and would perhaps do her, too, an injury which she would not forgive me, I ceased to look forward to her return, it terrified me. I would have liked to telegraph to her not to come back. And immediately, drowning everything else, the passionate desire for her return overwhelmed me. The fact was, that having for an instant considered the possibility of telling her not to return and of living without her, all of a sudden I felt myself on the contrary ready to abandon all travel, all pleasure, all work, if only Albertine might return! Ah, how my love for Albertine, the course of which I had supposed that I could foretell, on the analogy of my previous love for Gilberte, had developed in an entirely opposite direction! How impossible it was for me to live without seeing her! And with each of my actions, even the most trivial, since they had all been steeped before in the blissful atmosphere which was Albertine's presence, I was obliged in turn, with a fresh expenditure of energy, with the same grief, to begin again the apprenticeship of separation. Then the competition of other forms of life thrust this latest grief into the background, and, during those days which were the first days of spring, I even found, as I waited until Saint-Loup should have seen Mme Bontemps, in imagining Venice and beautiful, unknown women, a few moments of pleasing calm. As soon as I was conscious of this, I felt in myself a panic terror. This calm which I had just enjoyed was the first apparition of that great occasional force which was to wage war in me against grief, against love, and would in the end prove victorious. This state of which I had just had a foretaste and had received the warning, was, for the moment only, what would in time to come be my permanent state, a life in which I should no longer be able to suffer on account of Albertine, in which I should no longer be in love with her. And my love, which had just seen and recognised the one enemy by whom it could be conquered, forgetfulness, began to tremble, like a lion which in the cage in which it has been confined has suddenly caught sight of the python that is about to devour it.

I thought of Albertine all the time and never was

Françoise, when she came into my room, quick enough in saying: " There are no letters," to curtail my anguish. From time to time I succeeded, by letting some current or other of ideas flow through my grief, in refreshing, in aerating to some slight extent the vitiated atmosphere of my heart; but at night, if I succeeded in going to sleep, then it was as though the memory of Albertine had been the drug that had procured my sleep, whereas the cessation of its influence would awaken me. I thought all the time of Albertine while I was asleep. It was a special sleep of her own that she gave me, and one in which, moreover, I should no longer have been at liberty, as when awake, to think of other things. Sleep and the memory of her were the two substances which I must mix together and take at one draught in order to put myself to sleep. When I was awake, moreover, my suffering went on increasing day by day instead of diminishing, not that oblivion was not performing its task, but because by the very fact of its doing so it favoured the idealisation of the regretted image and thereby the assimilation of my initial suffering to other analogous sufferings which intensified it. Still this image was endurable. But if all of a sudden I thought of her room, of her room in which the bed stood empty, of her piano, her motor-car, I lost all my strength, I shut my eyes, let my head droop upon my shoulder like a person who is about to faint. The sound of doors being opened hurt me almost as much because it was not she that was opening them.

When it was possible that a telegram might have come from Saint-Loup, I dared not ask: " Is there a telegram? " At length one did come but brought with it only a postponement of any result, with the message: " The ladies have gone away for three days." No doubt, if I had endured the four days that had already elapsed since her departure, it was because I said to myself: " It is only a matter of time, by the end of the week she will be here." But this argument did not alter the fact that for my heart, for my body, the action to be performed was the same: living without her, returning home and not finding her in the house, passing the door of her room—as for opening it, I had not yet the courage to do that—knowing that she was not inside, going to bed without having said good-night to her, such were the tasks that my heart had been obliged to accomplish in their terrible entirety, and for all the world as though I had not been going to see Albertine. But the fact that my heart had already performed this daily task four times proved that it was now capable of continuing to perform it. And soon, perhaps, the consideration which helped me to go on living in this fashion—the prospect of Albertine's return—I should cease to feel any need of it (I should be able to say to myself: " She is never coming back," and remain alive all the same as I had already been living for the last four days), like a cripple who has recovered the use of his feet and can dispense with his crutches. No doubt when I came home at night I still found, taking my breath away, stifling me in the vacuum of solitude, the memories placed end to end in an interminable series of all the evenings upon which Albertine had been waiting for me; but already I found in this series my memory of last night, of the night before and of the two previous evenings, that is to say, the memory of the four nights that had passed since Albertine's departure, during which I had remained without her, alone, through which, nevertheless, I had lived, four nights already, forming a string of memories that was very slender compared with the other, but to which every new day would perhaps add substance. I shall say nothing of the letter conveying a declaration of affection which I received at this time from a niece of Mme de Guermantes, considered the prettiest girl in Paris, nor of the overtures made to me by the Duc de Guermantes on behalf of her parents resigned, in their anxiety to secure their daughter's happiness, to the inequality of the match, to an apparent misalliance. Such incidents which might prove gratifying to our self-esteem are too painful when we are in love. We feel a desire, but shrink from the indelicacy of communicating them to her who has a less flattering opinion of us, nor would that opinion be altered by the knowledge that we are able to inspire one that is very different. What the Duke's niece wrote to me could only have made Albertine angry. From the moment of waking, when I picked my grief up again at the point which I had reached when I fell asleep, like a book which had been shut for a while but which I would keep before my eyes until night, it could be only with some thought relating to Albertine that all my sensation would be brought into harmony, whether it came to me from without or from within. The bell rang: it is a letter from her, it is she herself perhaps! If I felt myself in better health, not too miserable, I was no longer jealous, I no longer had any grievance against her, I would have liked to see her at once to kiss her, to live happily with her ever after. The act of telegraphing to her: " Come at once " seemed to me to have become a perfectly simple thing, as though my fresh mood had changed not merely my inclinations but things external to myself, had made them more easy.   If I was in a sombre mood, all my anger with her revived, I no longer felt any desire to kiss her, I felt how impossible it was that she could ever make me happy, I sought only to do her harm and to prevent her from belonging to other people.   But these two opposite moods had an identical result: it was essential that she should return as soon as possible.   And yet, however keen my joy at the moment of her return, I felt that very soon the same difficulties would crop up again and that to seek happiness in the satisfaction of a moral desire was as fatuous as to attempt to reach the horizon by walking straight ahead. The farther the desire advances, the farther does true possession withdraw.   So that if happiness or at least freedom from suffering can be found, it is not the satisfac- tion, but the gradual reduction, the eventual extinction of our desire that we must seek.   We attempt to see the person whom we love, we ought to attempt not to see her, oblivion alone brings about an ultimate extinction of desire.   And I imagine that if an author were to publish truths of this sort he would dedicate the book that contained them to a woman to whom he would thus take pleasure in returning, saying to her: "This book is yours."   And thus, while telling the truth in his book, he would be lying in his dedication, for he will attach to the book's being hers, only the importance that he attaches to the stone that came to him from her which will remain precious to him only so long as he is in love with her.   The bonds that unite another person to ourself exist only in our mind. Memory as it grows fainter relaxes them, and notwithstanding the illusion by which we would fain be cheated and with which, out of love, friendship, politeness, deference, duty, we cheat other people, we exist alone. Man is the creature that cannot emerge from himself, that knows his fellows only in himself; when he asserts the contrary, he is lying. And I should have been in such terror (had there been anyone capable of taking it) of somebody's robbing me of this need of her, this love for her, that I convinced myself that it had a value in my life. To be able to hear uttered, without being either fascinated or pained by them, the names of the stations through which the train passed on its way to Touraine, would have seemed to me a diminution of myself (for no other reason really than that it would have proved that Albertine was ceasing to interest me); it was just as well, I told myself, that by incessantly asking myself what she could be doing, thinking, longing, at every moment, whether she intended, whether she was going to return, I should be keeping open that communicating door which love had installed in me, and feeling another person's mind flood through open sluices the reservoir which must not again become stagnant. Presently, as Saint-Loup remained silent, a subordinate anxiety—my expectation of a further telegram, of a telephone call from him—masked the other, my uncertainty as to the result, whether Albertine was going to return. Listening for every sound in expectation of the telegram became so intolerable that I felt that, whatever might be its contents, the arrival of the telegram, which was the only thing of which I could think at the moment, would put an end to my sufferings. But when at length I had received a telegram from Robert in which he informed me that he had seen Mme Bontemps, but that, notwithstanding all his precautions, Albertine had seen him, and that this had upset everything, I burst out in a torrent of fury and despair, for this was what I would have done anything in the world to prevent. Once it came to Albertine's knowledge, Saint-Loup's mission gave me an appearance of being dependent upon her which could only dissuade her from returning, my horror of which was, as it happened, all that I had retained of the pride that my love had boasted in Gilberte's day and had since lost. I cursed Robert. Then I told myself that, if this attempt had failed, I would try another. Since man is able to influence the outer world, how, if I brought into play cunning, intelligence, pecuniary advantage, affection, should I fail to succeed in destroying this appalling fact: Albertine's absence. We believe that according to our desire we are able to change the things round about us, we believe this because otherwise we can see no favourable solution. We forget the solution that generally comes to pass and is also favourable: we do not succeed in changing things according to our desire, but gradually our desire changes. The situation that we hoped to change because it was intolerable becomes unimportant. We have not managed to surmount the obstacle, as we were absolutely determined to do, but life has taken us round it, led us past it, and then if we turn round to gaze at the remote past, we can barely catch sight of it, so imperceptible has it become. In the flat above ours, one of the neighbours was strumming songs. I applied their words, which I knew, to Albertine and myself, and was stirred by so profound a sentiment that I began to cry. The words were:

" Hélas, l'oiseau qui fuit ce qu'il croit l'esclavage,
d'un vol désespéré revient battre au vitrage "

and the death of Manon:

" Manon, réponds-moi donc,
Seul amour de mon âme, je n'ai su qu'aujourd'hui
la bonté de ton cœur."

Since Manon returned to Des Grieux, it seemed to me that
I was to Albertine the one and only love of her life. Alas,
it is probable that, if she had been listening at that moment
to the same air, it would not have been myself that she
would have cherished under the name of Des Grieux, and,
even if the idea had occurred to her, the memory of myself
would have checked her emotion on hearing this music,
albeit it was, although better and more distinguished, just
the sort of music that she admired. As for myself, I had
not the courage to abandon myself to so pleasant a train of
thought, to imagine Albertine calling me her " heart's only
love " and realising that she had been mistaken over what
she " had thought to be bondage." I knew that we can
never read a novel without giving its heroine the form and
features of the woman with whom we are in love. But be
the ending as happy as it may, our love has not advanced an
inch and, when we have shut the book, she whom we love
and who has come to us at last in its pages, loves us no
better in real life. In a fit of fury, I telegraphed to Saint-
Loup to return as quickly as possible to Paris, so as to avoid
at least the appearance of an aggravating insistence upon a
mission which I had been so anxious to keep secret. But
even before he had returned in obedience to my instructions
it was from Albertine herself that I received the following
letter:

49

" My dear, you have sent your friend Saint-Loup to my aunt, which was foolish. My dear boy, if you needed me why did you not write to me myself, I should have been only too delighted to come back, do not let us have any more of these absurd complications." " I should have been only too delighted to come back!" If she said this, it must mean that she regretted her departure, and was only seeking an excuse to return. So that I had merely to do what she said, to write to her that I needed her, and she would return.

I was going, then, to see her again, her, the Albertine of Balbec (for since her departure this was what she had once more become to me; like a sea-shell to which we cease to pay any attention while we have it on the chest of drawers in our room, once we have parted with it, either by giving it away or by losing it, and begin to think about it, a thing which we had ceased to do, she recalled to me all the joyous beauty of the blue mountains of the sea). And it was not only she that had become a creature of the imagination that is to say desirable, life with her had become an imaginary life, that is to say a life set free from all difficulties, so that I said to myself: " How happy we are going to be!" But, now that I was assured of her return, I must not appear to be seeking to hasten it, but must on the contrary efface the bad impression left by Saint-Loup's intervention, which I could always disavow later on by saying that he had acted upon his own initiative, because he had always been in favour of our marriage. Meanwhile, I read her letter again, and was nevertheless disappointed when I saw how little there is of a person in a letter. Doubtless the characters traced on the paper express our thoughts, as do also our features: it is still a thought of some kind that we see before us. But all the same, in the person, the thought is not apparent to us until it has been diffused through the expanded water-lily of her face. This modifies it considerably. And it is perhaps one of the causes of our perpetual disappointments in love, this perpetual deviation which brings it about that, in response to our expectation of the ideal person with whom we are in love, each meeting provides us with a person in flesh and blood in whom there is already so little trace of our dream. And then when we demand something of this person, we receive from her a letter in which even of the person very little remains, as in the letters of an algebraical formula there no longer remains the precise value of the arithmetical ciphers, which themselves do not contain the qualities of the fruit or flowers that they enumerate. And yet love, the beloved object, her letters, are perhaps, nevertheless, translations (unsatisfying as it may be to pass from one to the other) of the same reality, since the letter seems to us inadequate only while we are reading it, but we have been sweating blood until its arrival, and it is sufficient to calm our anguish, if not to appease, with its tiny black symbols, our desire which knows that it contains, after all, only the equivalent of a word, a smile, a kiss, not the things themselves.

I wrote to Albertine:

" My dear, I was just about to write to you, and I thank you for telling me that if I had been in need of you you would have come at once; it is like you to have so exalted a sense of devotion to an old friend, which can only increase my regard for you. But no, I did not ask and I shall not ask you to return; our meeting—for a long time to come—

might not be painful, perhaps, to you, a heartless girl. To me whom at times you have thought so cold, it would be most painful. Life has driven us apart. You have made a decision which I consider very wise, and which you have made at the right moment, with a marvellous presentiment, for you left me on the day on which I had just received my mother's consent to my asking you to marry me. I would have told you this when I awoke, when I received her letter (at the same moment as yours). Perhaps you would have been afraid of distressing me by leaving immediately after that. And we should perhaps have united our lives in what would have been for us (who knows?) misery. If this is what was in store for us, then I bless you for your wisdom. We should lose all the fruit of it were we to meet again. This is not to say that I should not find it a temptation. But I claim no great credit for resisting it. You know what an inconstant person I am and how quickly I forget. You have told me often, I am first and foremost a man of habit. The habits which I am beginning to form in your absence are not as yet very strong. Naturally, at this moment, the habits that I had when you were with me, habits which your departure has upset, are still the stronger. They will not remain so for very long. For that reason, indeed, I had thought of taking advantage of these last few days in which our meeting would not yet be for me what it will be in a fortnight's time, perhaps even sooner (forgive my frankness): a disturbance,—I had thought of taking advantage of them, before the final oblivion, in order to settle certain little material questions with you, in which you might, as a good and charming friend, have rendered a service to him who for five minutes imagined himself your

future husband. As I never expected that my mother
would approve, as on the other hand, I desired that we
should each of us enjoy all that liberty of which you had too
generously and abundantly made a sacrifice, which might
be admissible had we been living together for a few weeks,
but would have become as hateful to you as to myself now
that we were to spend the rest of our lives together (it
almost hurts me to think as I write to you that this nearly
happened, that the news came only a moment too late), I
had thought of organising our existence in the most
independent manner possible, and, to begin with, I wished
you to have that yacht in which you could go cruising while
I, not being well enough to accompany you, would wait
for you at the port (I had written to Elstir to ask for his
advice, since you admire his taste), and on land I wished
you to have a motor-car to yourself, for your very own, in
which you could go out, could travel wherever you chose.
The yacht was almost ready; it is named, after a wish that
you expressed at Balbec, *le Cygne*. And remembering that
your favourite make of car was the Rolls, I had ordered one.
But now that we are never to meet again, as I have no
hope of persuading you to accept either the vessel or the
car (to me they would be quite useless), I had thought—
as I had ordered them through an agent, but in your name
—that you might perhaps by countermanding them, yourself, save me the expense of the yacht and the car which are
no longer required. But this, and many other matters,
would need to be discussed. Well, I find that so long as
I am capable of falling in love with you again, which will
not be for long, it would be madness, for the sake of a
sailing-vessel and a Rolls-Royce, to meet again and to risk

the happiness of your life since you have decided that it
lies in your living apart from myself. No, I prefer to
keep the Rolls and even the yacht. And as I shall make
no use of them and they are likely to remain for ever, one
in its dock, dismantled, the other in its garage, I shall
have engraved upon the yacht (Heavens, I am afraid of
misquoting the title and committing a heresy which would
shock you) those lines of Mallarmé which you used to like:

> Un cygne d'autrefois se souvient que c'est lui
> Magnifique mais qui sans espoir se délivre
> Pour n'avoir pas chanté la région où vivre
> Quand du stérile hiver a resplendi l'ennui.

You remember—it is the poem that begins:

> Le vierge, le vivace et le bel aujourd'hui. . . .

Alas, to-day is no longer either virginal or fair. But the
men who know, as I know, that they will very soon make
of it an endurable " to-morrow " are seldom *endurable*
themselves. As for the Rolls, it would deserve rather
those other lines of the same poet which you said you could
not understand:

> Dis si je ne suis pas joyeux
> Tonnerre et rubis aux moyeux
> De voir en l'air que ce feu troue
>
> Avec des royaumes épars
> Comme mourir pourpre la roue
> Du seul vespéral de mes chars.

Farewell for ever, my little Albertine, and thanks once
again for the charming drive which we took on the eve
of our parting. I retain a very pleasant memory of it.

P.S. I make no reference to what you tell me of the
alleged suggestions which Saint-Loup (whom I do not for

a moment believe to be in Touraine) may have made to
your aunt. It is just like a Sherlock Holmes story.
For what do you take me? "

No doubt, just as I had said in the past to Albertine:
" I am not in love with you," in order that she might love
me; " I forget people when I do not see them," in order
that she might come often to see me; " I have decided to
leave you," in order to forestall any idea of a parting, now
it was because I was absolutely determined that she must
return within a week that I said to her: " Farewell for
ever "; it was because I wished to see her again that I said
to her: " I think it would be dangerous to see you " ; it
was because living apart from her seemed to me worse than
death that I wrote to her: " You were right, we should be
wretched together." Alas, this false letter, when I wrote
it in order to appear not to be dependent upon her, and also
to enjoy the pleasure of saying certain things which could
arouse emotion only in myself and not in her, I ought to
have foreseen from the start that it was possible that it
would result in a negative response, that is to say, one which
confirmed what I had said; that this was indeed probable,
for even had Albertine been less intelligent than she was,
she would never have doubted for an instant that what I
said to her was untrue. Indeed, without pausing to consider the intentions that I expressed in this letter, the mere
fact of my writing it, even if it had not been preceded by
Saint-Loup's intervention, was enough to prove to her
that I desired her return and to prompt her to let me
become more and more inextricably ensnared. Then
having foreseen the possibility of a reply in the negative,
I ought also to have foreseen that this reply would at once

revive in its fullest intensity my love for Albertine. And I ought, still before posting my letter, to have asked myself whether, in the event of Albertine's replying in the same tone and refusing to return, I should have sufficient control over my grief to force myself to remain silent, not to telegraph to her: " Come back," not to send her some other messenger, which, after I had written to her that we would not meet again, would make it perfectly obvious that I could not get on without her, and would lead to her refusing more emphatically than ever, whereupon I, unable to endure my anguish for another moment, would go down to visit her and might, for all I knew, be refused admission. And, no doubt, this would have been, after three enormous blunders, the worst of all, after which there would be nothing left but to take my life in front of her house. But the disastrous manner in which the psychopathic universe is constructed has decreed that the clumsy action, the action which we ought most carefully to have avoided, should be precisely the action that will calm us, the action that, opening before us, until we learn its result, fresh avenues of hope, relieves us for the moment of the intolerable pain which a refusal has aroused in us. With the result that, when the pain is too keen, we dash headlong into the blunder that consists in writing, sending somebody to intercede, going in person, proving that we cannot get on without the woman we love. But I foresaw nothing of all this. The probable result of my letter seemed to me on the contrary to be that of making Albertine return to me at once. And so, as I thought of this result, I greatly enjoyed writing the letter. But at the same time I had not ceased, while writing it, from shedding tears; partly, at first, in the same way as upon the day when I had acted a pretence of separation, because, as the words represented for me the idea which they expressed to me, albeit they were aimed in the opposite direction (uttered mendaciously because my pride forbade me to admit that I was in love), they carried their own load of sorrow. But also because I felt that the idea contained a grain of truth.

As this letter seemed to me to be certain of its effect, I began to regret that I had sent it. For as I pictured to myself the return (so natural, after all), of Albertine, immediately all the reasons which made our marriage a thing disastrous to myself returned in their fullest force. I hoped that she would refuse to come back. I was engaged in calculating that my liberty, my whole future depended upon her refusal, that I had been mad to write to her, that I ought to have retrieved my letter which, alas, had gone, when Françoise, with the newspaper which she had just brought upstairs, handed it back to me. She was not certain how many stamps it required. But immediately I changed my mind; I hoped that Albertine would not return, but I wished the decision to come from her, so as to put an end to my anxiety, and I handed the letter back to Françoise. I opened the newspaper; it announced a performance by Berma. Then I remembered the two different attitudes in which I had listened to *Phèdre*, and it was now in a third attitude that I thought of the declaration scene. It seemed to me that what I had so often repeated to myself, and had heard recited in the theatre, was the statement of the laws of which I must make experience in my life. There are in our soul things

57

to which we do not realise how strongly we are attached.
Or else, if we live without them, it is because we put off
from day to day, from fear of failure, or of being made to
suffer, entering into possession of them. This was what
had happened to me in the case of Gilberte when I thought
that I had given her up. If before the moment in which
we are entirely detached from these things—a moment
long subsequent to that in which we suppose ourself to
have been detached from them—the girl with whom we
are in love becomes, for instance, engaged to someone
else, we are mad, we can no longer endure the life which
appeared to us to be so sorrowfully calm. Or else, if we
are in control of the situation, we feel that she is a burden,
we would gladly be rid of her. Which was what had
happened to me in the case of Albertine. But let a sudden
departure remove the unloved creature from us, we are
unable to survive. But did not the plot of *Phèdre*, combine these two cases? Hippolyte is about to leave. Phèdre,
who until then has taken care to court his hostility, from a
scruple of conscience, she says, or rather the poet makes
her say, because she is unable to foresee the consequences
and feels that she is not loved, Phèdre can endure the
situation no longer. She comes to him to confess her love,
and this was the scene which I had so often repeated to
myself:

On dit qu'un prompt départ vous éloigne de nous. . . .

Doubtless this reason for the departure of Hippolyte is
less decisive, we may suppose, than the death of Thésée.
And similarly when, a few lines farther on, Phèdre pre-
tends for a moment that she has been misunderstood:

Aurais-je perdu tout le soin de ma gloire?

we may suppose that it is because Hippolyte has repulsed her declaration.

> Madame, oubliez-vous
> Que Thésée est mon père, et qu'il est votre époux?

But there would not have been this indignation unless, in the moment of a consummated bliss, Phèdre could have had the same feeling that it amounted to little or nothing. Whereas, as soon as she sees that it is not to be consummated, that Hippolyte thinks that he has misunderstood her and makes apologies, then, like myself when I decided to give my letter back to Françoise, she decides that the refusal must come from him, decides to stake everything upon his answer:

> Ah! cruel, tu m'as trop entendue.

And there is nothing, not even the harshness with which, as I had been told, Swann had treated Odette, or I myself had treated Albertine, a harshness which substituted for the original love a new love composed of pity, emotion, of the need of effusion, which is only a variant of the former love, that is not to be found also in this scene:

> Tu me haïssais plus, je ne t'aimais pas moins.
> Tes malheurs te prêtaient encor de nouveaux charmes.

What proves that it is not to the " thought of her own fame " that Phèdre attaches most importance is that she would forgive Hippolyte and turn a deaf ear to the advice of Oenone had she not learned at the same instant that Hippolyte was in love with Aricie. So it is that jealousy, which in love is equivalent to the loss of all happiness, outweighs any loss of reputation. It is then that she allows Oenone (which is merely a name for the baser part of herself) to slander Hippolyte without taking upon herself the " burden of his defence " and thus sends the man who will have none of her to a fate the calamities of which are no consolation, however, to herself, since her own suicide follows immediately upon the death of Hippolyte. Thus at least it was, with a diminution of the part played by all the " Jansenist scruples," as Bergotte would have said, which Racine ascribed to Phèdre to make her less guilty, that this scene appeared to me, a sort of prophecy of the amorous episodes in my own life. These reflections had, however, altered nothing of my determination, and I handed my letter to Françoise so that she might post it after all, in order to carry into effect that appeal to Albertine which seemed to me to be indispensable, now that I had learned that my former attempt had failed. And no doubt we are wrong when we suppose that the accomplishment of our desire is a small matter, since as soon as we believe that it cannot be realised we become intent upon it once again, and decide that it was not worth our while to pursue it only when we are quite certain that our attempt will not fail. And yet we are right also. For if this accomplishment, if our happiness appear of small account only in the light of certainty, nevertheless, they are an unstable element from which only trouble can arise. And our trouble will be all the greater the more completely our desire will have been accomplished, all the more impossible to endure when our happiness has been, in defiance of the law of nature, prolonged for a certain period, when it has received the consecration of habit. In another sense as well, these two tendencies, by which I mean that which made me anxious that my letter should be posted, and, when I thought that it had gone, my regret that I had written it, have each of them a certain element of truth. In the case of the first, it is easily comprehensible that we should go in pursuit of our happiness —or misery—and that at the same time we should hope to keep before us, by this latest action which is about to involve us in its consequences, a state of expectancy which does not leave us in absolute despair, in a word that we should seek to convert into other forms, which, we imagine, must be less painful to us, the malady from which we are suffering. But the other tendency is no less important, for, born of our belief in the success of our enterprise, it is simply an anticipation of the disappointment which we should very soon feel in the presence of a satisfied desire, our regret at having fixed for ourself, at the expense of other forms which are necessarily excluded, this form of happiness. I had given my letter to Françoise and had asked her to go out at once and post it. As soon as the letter had gone, I began once more to think of Albertine's return as imminent. It did not fail to introduce into my mind certain pleasing images which neutralised somewhat by their attractions the dangers that I foresaw in her return. The pleasure, so long lost, of having her with me was intoxicating.

Time passes, and gradually everything that we have said in falsehood becomes true; I had learned this only too well with Gilberte; the indifference that I had feigned when I could never restrain my tears had ended by becoming real; gradually life, as I told Gilberte in a lying formula which retrospectively had become true, life had driven us apart. I recalled this, I said to myself: " If

Albertine allows an interval to elapse, my lies will become the truth. And now that the worst moments are over, ought I not to hope that she will allow this month to pass without returning? If she returns, I shall have to renounce the true life which certainly I am not in a fit state to enjoy as yet, but which as time goes on may begin to offer me attractions while my memory of Albertine grows fainter."

I have said that oblivion was beginning to perform its task. But one of the effects of oblivion was precisely— since it meant that many of Albertine's less pleasing aspects, of the boring hours that I had spent with her, no longer figured in my memory, ceased, therefore, to be reasons for my desiring that she should not be with me as I used to wish when she was still in the house—that it gave me a curtailed impression of her, enhanced by all the love that I had ever felt for other women. In this novel aspect of her, oblivion which, nevertheless, was engaged upon making me accustomed to our separation, made me, by shewing me a more attractive Albertine, long all the more for her return.

Since her departure, very often, when I was confident that I shewed no trace of tears, I would ring for Françoise and say to her: " We must make sure that Mademoiselle Albertine hasn't left anything behind her. Don't forget to do her room, it must be ready for her when she comes." Or merely: " Only the other day Mademoiselle Albertine said to me, let me think now, it was the day before she left. . . ." I was anxious to diminish Françoise's abominable pleasure at Albertine's departure by letting her see that it was not to be prolonged. I was anxious also to let Françoise see that I was not afraid to speak of this departure, to proclaim it—like certain generals who describe a forced retreat as a strategic withdrawal in conformity with a prearranged plan—as intended by myself, as constituting an episode the true meaning of which I concealed for the moment, but in no way implying the end of my friendship with Albertine. By repeating her name incessantly I sought, in short, to introduce, like a breath of air, something of herself into that room in which her departure had left a vacuum, in which I could no longer breathe. Then, moreover, we seek to reduce the dimensions of our grief by making it enter into our everyday speech between ordering a suit of clothes and ordering dinner.

While she was doing Albertine's room, Françoise, out of curiosity, opened the drawer of a little rosewood table in which my mistress used to put away the ornaments which she discarded when she went to bed. "Oh! Monsieur, Mademoiselle Albertine has forgotten to take her rings, she has left them in the drawer." My first impulse was to say: "We must send them after her." But this would make me appear uncertain of her return. "Very well," I replied after a moment of silence, "it is hardly worth while sending them to her as she is coming back so soon. Give them to me, I shall think about it." Françoise handed me the rings with a distinct misgiving. She loathed Albertine, but, regarding me in her own image, supposed that one could not give me a letter in the handwriting of my mistress without the risk of my opening it. I took the rings. "Monsieur must take care not to lose them," said Françoise, "such beauties as they

are! I don't know who gave them to her, if it was
Monsieur or someone else, but I can see that it was someone rich, who had good taste!" "It was not I," I
assured her, "besides, they don't both come from the
same person, one was given her by her aunt and the other
she bought for herself." "Not from the same person!"
Françoise exclaimed, "Monsieur must be joking, they
are just alike, except that one of them has had a ruby added
to it, there's the same eagle on both, the same initials
inside. . . ." I do not know whether Françoise was
conscious of the pain that she was causing me, but she
began at this point to curve her lips in a smile which never
left them. "What, the same eagle? You are talking
nonsense. It is true that the one without the ruby has an
eagle upon it, but on the other it is a sort of man's head."
"A man's head, where did Monsieur discover that? I
had only to put on my spectacles to see at once that it was
one of the eagle's wings; if Monsieur will take his magnifying glass, he will see the other wing on the other side,
the head and the beak in the middle. You can count the
feathers. Oh, it's a fine piece of work." My intense
anxiety to know whether Albertine had lied to me made
me forget that I ought to maintain a certain dignity in
Françoise's presence and deny her the wicked pleasure
that she felt, if not in torturing me, at least in disparaging
my mistress. I remained breathless while Françoise went
to fetch my magnifying glass, I took it from her, asked her
to shew me the eagle upon the ring with the ruby, she had
no difficulty in making me see the wings, conventionalised
in the same way as upon the other ring, the feathers, cut
separately in relief, the head. She pointed out to me also

the similar inscriptions, to which, it is true, others were added upon the ring with the ruby. And on the inside of both was Albertine's monogram. "But I'm surprised that it should need all this to make Monsieur see that the rings are the same," said Françoise. "Even without examining them, you can see that it is the same style, the same way of turning the gold, the same form. As soon as I looked at them I could have sworn that they came from the same place. You can tell it as you can tell the dishes of a good cook." And indeed, to the curiosity of a servant, whetted by hatred and trained to observe details with a startling precision, there had been added, to assist her in this expert criticism, the taste that she had, that same taste, in fact, which she shewed in her cookery and which was intensified perhaps, as I had noticed when we left Paris for Balbec, in her attire, by the coquetry of a woman who was once good-looking, who has studied the jewels and dresses of other women. I might have taken the wrong box of medicine and, instead of swallowing a few capsules of veronal on a day when I felt that I had drunk too many cups of tea, might have swallowed as many capsules of cafeine; my heart would not have throbbed more violently. I asked Françoise to leave the room. I would have liked to see Albertine immediately. To my horror at her falsehood, to my jealousy of the unknown donor, was added grief that she should have allowed herself to accept such presents. I made her even more presents, it is true, but a woman whom we are keeping does not seem to us to be a kept woman so long as we do not know that she is being kept by other men. And yet since I had continued to spend so much money upon her,

I had taken her notwithstanding this moral baseness; this baseness I had maintained in her, I had perhaps increased, perhaps created it. Then, just as we have the faculty of inventing fairy tales to soothe our grief, just as we manage, when we are dying of hunger, to persuade ourself that a stranger is going to leave us a fortune of a hundred millions, I imagined Albertine in my arms, explaining to me in a few words that it was because of the similarity of its workmanship that she had bought the second ring, that it was she who had had her initials engraved on it. But this explanation was still feeble, it had not yet had time to thrust into my mind its beneficent roots, and my grief could not be so quickly soothed. And I reflected that many men who tell their friends that their mistresses are very kind to them must suffer similar torments. Thus it is that they lie to others and to themselves. They do not altogether lie; they do spend in the woman's company hours that are really pleasant; but think of all that the kindness which their mistresses shew them before their friends and which enables them to boast, and of all that the kindness which their mistresses shew when they are alone with them, and which enables their lovers to bless them, conceal of unrecorded hours in which the lover has suffered, doubted, sought everywhere in vain to discover the truth! It is to such sufferings that we attach the pleasure of loving, of delighting in the most insignificant remarks of a woman, which we know to be insignificant, but which we perfume with her scent. At this moment I could no longer find any delight in inhaling by an act of memory, the scent of Albertine. Thunderstruck, holding the two rings in my hand, I stared at that pitiless eagle whose beak was rending my heart, whose wings, chiselled in high relief, had borne away the confidence that I retained in my mistress, in whose claws my tortured mind was unable to escape for an instant from the incessantly recurring questions as to the stranger whose name the eagle doubtless symbolised, without however allowing me to decipher it, whom she had doubtless loved in the past, and whom she had doubtless seen again not so long ago, since it was upon that day so pleasant, so intimate, of our drive together through the Bois that I had seen, for the first time, the second ring, that upon which the eagle appeared to be dipping his beak in the bright blood of the ruby.

If, however, morning, noon and night, I never ceased to grieve over Albertine's departure, this did not mean that I was thinking only of her. For one thing, her charm having acquired a gradual ascendancy over things which, in course of time, were entirely detached from her, but were, nevertheless, electrified by the same emotion that she used to give me, if something made me think of Incarville or of the Verdurins, or of some new part that Léa was playing, a flood of suffering would overwhelm me. For another thing, what I myself called thinking of Albertine, was thinking of how I might bring her back, of how I might join her, might know what she was doing, With the result that if, during those hours of incessant martyrdom, there had been an illustrator present to represent the images which accompanied my sufferings, you would have seen pictures of the Gare d'Orsay, of the bank notes offered to Mme Bontemps, of Saint-Loup stooping over the sloping desk of a telegraph office at which

67

he was writing out a telegram for myself, never the picture of Albertine. Just as, throughout the whole course of our life, our egoism sees before it all the time the objects that are of interest to ourself, but never takes in that Ego itself which is incessantly observing them, so the desire which directs our actions descends towards them, but does not reascend to itself, whether because, being unduly utilitarian, it plunges into the action and disdains all knowledge of it, or because we have been looking to the future to compensate for the disappointments of the past, or because the inertia of our mind urges it down the easy slope of imagination, rather than make it reascend the steep slope of introspection. As a matter of fact, in those hours of crisis in which we would stake our whole life, in proportion as the person upon whom it depends reveals more clearly the immensity of the place that she occupies in our life, leaving nothing in the world which is not overthrown by her, so the image of that person diminishes until it is no longer perceptible. In everything we find the effect of her presence in the emotion that we feel; herself, the cause, we do not find anywhere. I was during these days so incapable of forming any picture of Albertine that I could almost have believed that I was not in love with her, just as my mother, in the moments of desperation in which she was incapable of ever forming any picture of my grandmother (save once in the chance encounter of a dream the importance of which she felt so intensely that she employed all the strength that remained to her in her sleep to make it last), might have accused and did in fact accuse herself of not regretting her mother, whose death had been a mortal blow to her but whose features escaped her memory.

Why should I have supposed that Albertine did not care for women? Because she had said, especially of late, that she did not care for them: but did not our life rest upon a perpetual lie? Never once had she said to me: "Why is it that I cannot go out when and where I choose, why do you always ask other people what I have been doing?" And yet, after all, the conditions of her life were so unusual that she must have asked me this had she not herself guessed the reason. And to my silence as to the causes of her claustration, was it not comprehensible that she should correspond with a similar and constant silence as to her perpetual desires, her innumerable memories and hopes? Françoise looked as though she knew that I was lying when I made an allusion to the imminence of Albertine's return. And her belief seemed to be founded upon something more than that truth which generally guided our old housekeeper, that masters do not like to be humiliated in front of their servants, and allow them to know only so much of the truth as does not depart too far from a flattering fiction, calculated to maintain respect for themselves. This time, Françoise's belief seemed to be founded upon something else, as though she had herself aroused, kept alive the distrust in Albertine's mind, stimulated her anger, driven her in short, to the point at which she could predict her departure as inevitable. If this was true, my version of a temporary absence, of which I had known and approved, could be received with nothing but incredulity by Françoise. But the idea that she had formed of Albertine's venal nature, the exasperation with which, in her hatred, she multiplied the "profit" that Albertine was supposed to be making out of myself, might to some extent, give a check to that certainty. And so when in her hearing I made an allusion, as if to something that was altogether natural, to Albertine's immediate return, Fran-çoise would look me in the face, to see whether I was not inventing, in the same way in which, when the butler, to make her angry, read out to her, changing the words, some political news which she hesitated to believe, as for instance the report of the closing of the churches and expulsion of the clergy, even from the other end of the kitchen, and without being able to read it, she would fix her gaze instinctively and greedily upon the paper, as though she had been able to see whether the report was really there.

When Françoise saw that after writing a long letter I put on the envelope the address of Mme Bontemps, this alarm, hitherto quite vague, that Albertine might return, increased in her. It grew to a regular consternation when one morning she had to bring me with the rest of my mail, a letter upon the envelope of which she had recognised Albertine's handwriting. She asked herself whether Albertine's departure had not been a mere make-believe, a supposition which distressed her twice over as making definitely certain for the future Albertine's presence in the house, and as bringing upon myself, and thereby, in so far as I was Françoise's master, upon herself, the humiliation of having been tricked by Albertine. However great my impatience to read her letter, I could not refrain from studying for a moment Françoise's eyes from which all hope had fled, inducing from this presage the imminence of Albertine's return, as a lover of winter sports concludes with joy that the cold weather is at hand

when he sees the swallows fly south. At length Françoise left me, and when I had made sure that she had shut
the door behind her, I opened, noiselessly so as not to
appear anxious, the letter which ran as follows:

" My dear, thank you for all the nice things that you
say to me, I am at your orders to countermand the Rolls,
if you think that I can help in any way, as I am sure I can.
You have only to let me know the name of your agent.
You would let yourself be taken in by these people whose
only thought is of selling things, and what would you do
with a motor-car, you who never stir out of the house?
I am deeply touched that you have kept a happy memory
of our last drive together. You may be sure that for my
part I shall never forget that drive in a twofold twilight
(since night was falling and we were about to part) and
that it will be effaced from my memory only when the
darkness is complete."

I felt that this final phrase was merely a phrase and that
Albertine could not possibly retain until her death any
such pleasant memory of this drive from which she had
certainly derived no pleasure since she had been impatient
to leave me. But I was impressed also, when I thought
of the bicyclist, the golfer of Balbec, who had read nothing
but *Esther* before she made my acquaintance, to find how
richly endowed she was and how right I had been in
thinking that she had in my house enriched herself with
fresh qualities which made her different and more complete. And thus, the words that I had said to her at
Balbec: " I feel that my friendship would be of value to
you, that I am just the person who could give you what
you lack "—I had written this upon a photograph which

I gave her—" with the certainty that I was being provi-
dential "—these words, which I uttered without believing
them and simply that she might find some advantage in my
society which would outweigh any possible boredom,
these words turned out to have been true as well. Similarly, for that matter, when I said to her that I did not
wish to see her for fear of falling in love with her, I had
said this because on the contrary I knew that in frequent
intercourse my love grew cold and that separation kindled
it, but in reality our frequent intercourse had given rise to
a need of her that was infinitely stronger than my love in
the first weeks at Balbec.

Albertine's letter did not help matters in any way. She
spoke to me only of writing to my agent. It was necessary to escape from this situation, to cut matters short, and
I had the following idea. I sent a letter at once to Andrée
in which I told her that Albertine was at her aunt's, that I
felt very lonely, that she would be giving me an immense
pleasure if she came and stayed with me for a few days and
that, as I did not wish to make any mystery, I begged her
to inform Albertine of this. And at the same time I
wrote to Albertine as though I had not yet received her
letter: " My dear, forgive me for doing something which
you will understand so well, I have such a hatred of secrecy
that I have chosen that you should be informed by her and
by myself. I have acquired, from having you staying so
charmingly in the house with me, the bad habit of not being
able to live alone. Since we have decided that you are
not to come back, it has occurred to me that the person
who would best fill your place, because she would make
least change in my life, would remind me most strongly of

yourself, is Andrée, and I have invited her here. So that all this may not appear too sudden, I have spoken to her only of a short visit, but between ourselves I am pretty certain that this time it will be permanent. Don't you agree that I am right? You know that your little group of girls at Balbec has always been the social unit that has exerted the greatest influence upon me, in which I have been most happy to be eventually included. No doubt it is this influence which still makes itself felt. Since the fatal incompatibility of our natures and the mischances of life have decreed that my little Albertine can never be my wife, I believe that I shall, nevertheless, find a wife—less charming than herself, but one whom greater conformities of nature will enable perhaps to be happier with me—in Andrée." But after I had sent this letter to the post, the suspicion occurred to me suddenly that, when Albertine wrote to me: " I should have been only too delighted to come back if you had written to me myself," she had said this only because I had not written to her, and that, had I done so, it would not have made any difference; that she would be glad to know that Andrée was staying with me, to think of her as my wife, provided that she herself remained free, because she could now, as for a week past, stultifying the hourly precautions which I had adopted during more than six months in Paris, abandon herself to her vices and do what, minute by minute, I had prevented her from doing. I told myself that probably she was making an improper use, down there, of her freedom, and no doubt this idea which I formed seemed to me sad but remained general, shewing me no special details, and, by the indefinite number of possible mistresses which it

73   D 2

allowed me to imagine, prevented me from stopping to consider any one of them, drew my mind on in a sort of perpetual motion not free from pain but tinged with a pain which the absence of any concrete image rendered endurable. It ceased, however, to be endurable and became atrocious when Saint-Loup arrived. Before I explain why the information that he gave me made me so unhappy, I ought to relate an incident which I place immediately before his visit and the memory of which so distressed me afterwards that it weakened, if not the painful impression that was made on me by my conversation with Saint-Loup, at any rate the practical effect of this conversation. This incident was as follows. Burning with impatience to see Saint-Loup, I was waiting for him upon the staircase (a thing which I could not have done had my mother been at home, for it was what she most abominated, next to " talking from the window ") when I heard the following speech: " Do you mean to say you don't know how to get a fellow sacked whom you don't like? It's not difficult. You need only hide the things that he has to take in. Then, when they're in a hurry and ring for him, he can't find anything, he loses his head. My aunt will be furious with him, and will say to you: ' Why, what is the man doing? ' When he does shew his face, everybody will be raging, and he won't have what is wanted. After this has happened four or five times, you may be sure that they'll sack him, especially if you take care to dirty the things that he has to bring in clean, and all that sort of thing." I remained speechless with astonishment, for these cruel, machiavellian words were uttered by the voice of Saint-Loup. Now I had always regarded him as

so good, so tender-hearted a person that this speech had the
same effect upon me as if he had been acting the part of
Satan in a play: it could not be in his own name that he
was speaking. " But, after all, a man has got to earn his
living," said the other person, of whom I then caught
sight and who was one of the Duchesse de Guermantes's
footmen. " What the hell does that matter to you so
long as you're all right? " Saint-Loup replied callously.
" It will be all the more fun for you, having a scape-goat.
You can easily spill ink over his livery just when he has to
go and wait at a big dinner-party, and never leave him in
peace for a moment until he's only too glad to give notice.
Anyhow, I can put a spoke in his wheel, I shall tell my
aunt that I admire your patience in working with a great
lout like that, and so dirty too." I shewed myself, Saint-
Loup came to greet me, but my confidence in him was
shaken since I had heard him speak, in a manner so different
from anything that I knew. And I asked myself whether
a person who was capable of acting so cruelly towards a
poor and defenceless man had not played the part of a
traitor towards myself, on his mission to Mme Bontemps.
This reflection was of most service in helping me not to
regard his failure as a proof that I myself might not
succeed, after he had left me. But so long as he was with
me, it was, nevertheless, of the Saint-Loup of long ago
and especially of the friend who had just come from
Mme Bontemps that I thought. He began by saying:
" You feel that I ought to have telephoned to you more
often, but I was always told that you were engaged."
But the point at which my pain became unendurable was
when he said: " To begin where my last telegram left you,

after passing by a sort of shed, I entered the house and at the end of a long passage was shewn into a drawing-room." At these words, shed, passage, drawing-room, and before he had even finished uttering them, my heart was shattered more swiftly than by an electric current, for the force which girdles the earth many times in a second, is not electricity, but pain. How I repeated them to myself, renewing the shock as I chose, these words, shed, passage, drawing-room, after Saint-Loup had left me! In a shed one girl can lie down with another. And in that drawing-room who could tell what Albertine used to do when her aunt was not there? What was this? Had I then imagined the house in which she was living as incapable of possessing either a shed or a drawing-room? No, I had not imagined it at all, except as a vague place. I had suffered originally at the geographical identification of the place in which Albertine was. When I had learned that, instead of being in two or three possible places, she was in Touraine, those words uttered by her porter had marked in my heart as upon a map the place in which I must at length suffer. But once I had grown accustomed to the idea that she was in a house in Touraine, I had not seen the house. Never had there occurred to my imagination this appalling idea of a drawing-room, a shed, a passage, which seemed to be facing me in the retina of Saint-Loup's eyes, who had seen them, these rooms in which Albertine came and went, was living her life, these rooms in particular and not an infinity of possible rooms which had cancelled one another. With the words shed, passage, drawing-room, I became aware of my folly in having left Albertine for a week in this cursed place, the existence (instead of the

mere possibility) of which had just been revealed to me.
Alas! when Saint-Loup told me also that in this drawing-
room he had heard someone singing at the top of her
voice in an adjoining room and that it was Albertine who
was singing, I realised with despair that, rid of me at last,
she was happy! She had regained her freedom. And I
who had been thinking that she would come to take the
place of Andrée! My grief turned to anger with Saint-
Loup. "That is the one thing in the world that I asked
you to avoid, that she should know of your coming."
"If you imagine it was easy! They had assured me that
she was not in the house. Oh, I know very well that you
aren't pleased with me, I could tell that from your telegrams. But you are not being fair to me, I did all that I
could." Set free once more, having left the cage from
which, here at home, I used to remain for days on end
without making her come to my room, Albertine had
regained all her value in my eyes, she had become once
more the person whom everyone pursued, the marvellous
bird of the earliest days. "However, let us get back to
business. As for the question of the money, I don't know
what to say to you, I found myself addressing a woman
who seemed to me to be so scrupulous that I was afraid of
shocking her. However, she didn't say no when I mentioned the money to her. In fact, a little later she told
me that she was touched to find that we understood one
another so well. And yet everything that she said after
that was so delicate, so refined, that it seemed to me
impossible that she could have been referring to my offer
of money when she said: 'We understand one another so
well,' for after all I was behaving like a cad." "But

perhaps she did not realise what you meant, she cannot have heard you, you ought to have repeated the offer, for then you would certainly have won the battle." " But what do you mean by saying that she cannot have heard me, I spoke to her as I am speaking to you, she is neither deaf nor mad." "And she made no comment? " "None." " You ought to have repeated the offer." " How do you mean, repeat it? As soon as we met I saw what sort of person she was, I said to myself that you had made a mistake, that you were letting me in for the most awful blunder, and that it would be terribly difficult to offer her the money like that. I did it, however, to oblige you, feeling certain that she would turn me out of the house." " But she did not. Therefore, either she had not heard you and you should have started afresh, or you could have developed the topic." " You say: ' She had not heard,' because you were here in Paris, but, I repeat, if you had been present at our conversation, there was not a sound to interrupt us, I said it quite bluntly, it is not possible that she failed to understand." " But anyhow is she quite convinced that I have always wished to marry her niece? " " No, as to that, if you want my opinion, she did not believe that you had any intention of marrying the girl. She told me that you yourself had informed her niece that you wished to leave her. I don't really know whether now she is convinced that you wish to marry." This reassured me slightly by shewing me that I was less humiliated, and therefore more capable of being still loved, more free to take some decisive action. Nevertheless I was in torments. " I am sorry, because I can see that you are not pleased." " Yes, I am touched by your kindness,

I am grateful to you, but it seems to me that you might
. . . ." " I did my best. No one else could have done
more or even as much. Try sending someone else."
" No, as a matter of fact, if I had known, I should not
have sent you, but the failure of your attempt prevents
me from making another." I heaped reproaches upon
him: he had tried to do me a service and had not succeeded.
Saint-Loup as he left the house had met some girls coming
in. I had already and often supposed that Albertine knew
other girls in the country; but this was the first time that
I felt the torture of that supposition. We are really led
to believe that nature has allowed our mind to secrete a
natural antidote which destroys the suppositions that we
form, at once without intermission and without danger.
But there was nothing to render me immune from these
girls whom Saint-Loup had met. All these details, were
they not precisely what I had sought to learn from everyone,
with regard to Albertine, was it not I who, in order to
learn them more fully, had begged Saint-Loup, summoned back to Paris by his colonel, to come and see me at
all costs, was it not, therefore, I who had desired them, or
rather my famished grief, longing to feed and to wax fat
upon them? Finally Saint-Loup told me that he had had
the pleasant surprise of meeting, quite near the house, the
only familiar face that had reminded him of the past, a
former friend of Rachel, a pretty actress who was taking a
holiday in the neighbourhood. And the name of this
actress was enough to make me say to myself: " Perhaps
it is with her;" was enough to make me behold, in the
arms even of a woman whom I did not know, Albertine
smiling and flushed with pleasure. And, after all, why

should not this have been true? had I found fault with myself for thinking of other women since I had known Albertine? On the evening of my first visit to the Princesse de Guermantes, when I returned home, had I not been thinking far less of her than of the girl of whom Saint-Loup had told me who frequented disorderly houses and of Mme Putbus's maid? Was it not in the hope of meeting the latter of these that I had returned to Balbec, and, more recently, had been planning to go to Venice? Why should not Albertine have been planning to go to Touraine? Only, when it came to the point, as I now realised, I would not have left her, I would not have gone to Venice. Even in my own heart of hearts, when I said to myself: " I shall leave her presently," I knew that I would never leave her, just as I knew that I would never settle down again to work, or make myself live upon hygienic principles or do any of the things which, day by day, I vowed that I would do upon the morrow. Only, whatever I might feel in my heart, I had thought it more adroit to let her live under the perpetual menace of a separation. And no doubt, thanks to my detestable adroitness, I had convinced her only too well. In any case, now, things could not go on like this. I could not leave her in Touraine with those girls, with that actress, I could not endure the thought of that life which was escaping my control. I would await her reply to my letter: if she was doing wrong alas! a day more or less made no difference (and perhaps I said this to myself because, being no longer in the habit of taking note of every minute of her life, whereas a single minute in which she was unobserved would formerly have driven me out of my mind, my jealousy no longer observed the same division of time). But as soon as I should have received her answer, if she was not coming back, I would go to fetch her; willy-nilly, I would tear her away from her women friends. Besides, was it not better for me to go down in person, now that I had discovered the duplicity, hitherto unsuspected by me, of Saint-Loup; he might, for all I knew, have organised a plot to separate me from Albertine.

And at the same time, how I should have been lying now had I written to her, as I used to say to her in Paris, that I hoped that no accident might befall her. Ah! if some accident had occurred, my life, instead of being poisoned for ever by this incessant jealousy, would at once regain, if not happiness, at least a state of calm through the suppression of suffering.

The suppression of suffering? Can I really have believed it, have believed that death merely eliminates what exists, and leaves everything else in its place, that it removes the grief from the heart of him for whom the other person's existence has ceased to be anything but a source of grief, that it removes the grief and substitutes nothing in its place. The suppression of grief! As I glanced at the paragraphs in the newspapers, I regretted that I had not had the courage to form the same wish as Swann. If Albertine could have been the victim of an accident, were she alive I should have had a pretext for hastening to her bedside, were she dead I should have recovered, as Swann said, my freedom to live as I chose. Did I believe this? He had believed it, that subtlest of men who thought that he knew himself well. How little do we know what we have in our heart. How clearly, a little later, had he been still alive, I could have proved to him that his wish was not only criminal but absurd, that the death of her whom he loved would have set him free from nothing.

I forsook all pride with regard to Albertine, I sent her a despairing telegram begging her to return upon any conditions, telling her that she might do anything she liked, that I asked only to be allowed to take her in my arms for a minute three times a week, before she went to bed. And had she confined me to once a week, I would have accepted the restriction. She did not, ever, return. My telegram had just gone to her when I myself received one. It was from Mme Bontemps. The world is not created once and for all time for each of us individually. There are added to it in the course of our life things of which we have never had any suspicion. Alas! it was not a suppression of suffering that was wrought in me by the first two lines of the telegram: " My poor friend, our little Albertine is no more; forgive me for breaking this terrible news to you who were so fond of her. She was thrown by her horse against a tree while she was out riding. All our efforts to restore her to life were unavailing. If only I were dead in her place! " No, not the suppression of suffering, but a suffering until then unimagined, that of learning that she would not come back. And yet, had I not told myself, many times, that quite possibly, she would not come back? I had indeed told myself so, but now I saw that never for a moment had I believed it. As I needed her presence, her kisses, to enable me to endure the pain that my suspicions wrought in me, I had formed, since our Balbec days, the habit of being always with her. Even when she had gone

out, when I was left alone, I was kissing her still. I had
continued to do so since her departure for Touraine. I
had less need of her fidelity than of her return. And if my
reason might with impunity cast a doubt upon her now and
again, my imagination never ceased for an instant to bring
her before me. Instinctively I passed my hand over my
throat, over my lips which felt themselves kissed by her lips
still after she had gone away, and would never be kissed by
them again; I passed my hands over them, as Mamma had
caressed me at the time of my grandmother's death, when
she said: "My poor boy, your grandmother, who was so
fond of you, will never kiss you again." All my life to
come seemed to have been wrenched from my heart. My
life to come? I had not then thought at times of living it
without Albertine? Why, no! All this time had I, then,
been vowing to her service every minute of my life until
my death? Why, of course! This future indissolubly
blended with hers I had never had the vision to perceive,
but now that it had just been shattered, I could feel the
place that it occupied in my gaping heart. Françoise,
who still knew nothing, came into my room; in a sudden
fury I shouted at her: "What do you want?" Then
(there are sometimes words which set a different reality
in the same place as that which confronts us; they stun us
as does a sudden fit of giddiness) she said to me: "Monsieur has no need to look cross. I've got something here
that will make him very happy. Here are two letters
from Mademoiselle Albertine." I felt, afterwards, that I
must have stared at her with the eyes of a man whose mind
has become unbalanced. I was not even glad, nor was I
incredulous. I was like a person who sees the same place

in his room occupied by a sofa and by a grotto: nothing seeming to him more real, he collapses on the floor. Albertine's two letters must have been written at an interval of a few hours, possibly at the same moment, and, anyhow only a short while before the fatal ride. The first said: " My dear, I must thank you for the proof of your confidence which you give me when you tell me of your plan to get Andrée to stay with you. I am sure that she will be delighted to accept, and I think that it will be a very good thing for her. With her talents, she will know how to make the most of the companionship of a man like yourself, and of the admirable influence which you manage to secure over other people. I feel that you have had an idea from which as much good may spring for her as for yourself. And so, if she should make the least shadow of difficulty (which I don't suppose), telegraph to me, I undertake to bring pressure to bear upon her." The second was dated on the following day. (As a matter of fact, she must have written her two letters at an interval of a few minutes, possibly without any interval, and must have antedated the first. For, all the time, I had been forming an absurd idea of her intentions, which had been only this: to return to me, and which anyone with no direct interest in the matter, a man lacking in imagination, the plenipotentiary in a peace treaty, the merchant who has to examine a deal, would have judged more accurately than myself.) It contained only these words: " Is it too late for me to return to you? If you have not yet written to Andrée, would you be prepared to take me back? I shall abide by your decision but I beg you not to be long in letting me know it, you can imagine how impatiently I shall be waiting. If it is telling me to return, I shall take the train at once. With my whole heart, yours, Albertine."

For the death of Albertine to be able to suppress my suffering, the shock of the fall would have had to kill her not only in Touraine but in myself. There, never had she been more alive. In order to enter into us, another person must first have assumed the form, have entered into the surroundings of the moment; appearing to us only in a succession of momentary flashes, he has never been able to furnish us with more than one aspect of himself at a time, to present us with more than a single photograph of himself. A great weakness, no doubt, for a person to consist merely in a collection of moments; a great strength also: it is dependent upon memory, and our memory of a moment is not informed of everything that has happened since; this moment which it has registered endures still, lives still, and with it the person whose form is outlined in it. And moreover, this disintegration does not only make the dead man live, it multiplies him. To find consolation, it was not one, it was innumerable Albertines that I must first forget. When I had reached the stage of enduring the grief of losing this Albertine, I must begin afresh with another, with a hundred others.

So, then, my life was entirely altered. What had made it—and not owing to Albertine, concurrently with her, when I was alone—attractive, was precisely the perpetual resurgence, at the bidding of identical moments, of moments from the past. From the sound of the rain I re-captured the scent of the lilacs at Combray, from the shifting of the sun's rays on the balcony the pigeons in the Champs-Elysées, from the muffling of all noise in the heat of the morning hours, the cool taste of cherries, the longing for Brittany or Venice from the sound of the wind and the return of Easter. Summer was at hand, the days were long, the weather warm. It was the season when, early in the morning, pupils and teachers resort to the public gardens to prepare for the final examinations under the trees, seeking to extract the sole drop of coolness that is let fall by a sky less ardent than in the mid-day heat but already as sterilely pure. From my darkened room, with a power of evocation equal to that of former days but capable now of evoking only pain, I felt that outside, in the heaviness of the atmosphere, the setting sun was plastering the vertical fronts of houses and churches with a tawny distemper. And if Françoise, when she came in, parted by accident the inner curtains, I stifled a cry of pain at the gash that was cut in my heart by that ray of long-ago sunlight which had made beautiful in my eyes the modern front of Marcouville l'Orgueilleuse, when Albertine said to me: " It is restored." Not knowing how to account to Françoise for my groan, I said to her: " Oh, I am so thirsty." She left the room, returned, but I turned sharply away, smarting under the painful discharge of one of the thousand invisible memories which at every moment burst into view in the surrounding darkness: I had noticed that she had brought in a jug of cider and a dish of cherries, things which a farm-lad had brought out to us in the carriage, at Balbec, " kinds " in which I should have made the most perfect communion, in those days, with the prismatic gleam in shuttered dining-rooms on days of scorching heat. Then I thought for the first time of the farm called Les Ecorres, and said to myself that on certain days when

Albertine had told me, at Balbec, that she would not be free, that she was obliged to go somewhere with her aunt, she had perhaps been with one or another of her girl friends at some farm to which she knew that I was not in the habit of going, and, while I waited desperately for her at Marie-Antoinette, where they told me: " No, we have not seen her to-day," had been using to her friend, the same words that she used to say to myself when we went out together: " He will never think of looking for us here, so that there's no fear of our being disturbed." I told Françoise to draw the curtains together, so that I should not see that ray of sunlight. But it continued to filter through, just as corrosive, into my memory. " It doesn't appeal to me, it has been restored, but we shall go to-morrow to Saint-Mars le Vêtu, and the day after to. . . ." To-morrow, the day after, it was a prospect of life shared in common, perhaps for all time, that was opening; my heart leaped towards it, but it was no longer there, Albertine was dead.

I asked Françoise the time. Six o'clock. At last, thank God, that oppressive heat would be lifted of which in the past I used to complain to Albertine, and which we so enjoyed. The day was drawing to its close. But what did that profit me? The cool evening air came in; it was the sun setting in my memory, at the end of a road which we had taken, she and I, on our way home, that I saw now, more remote than the farthest village, like some distant town, not to be reached that evening, which we would spend at Balbec, still together. Together then; now I must stop short on the brink of that same abyss; she was dead. It was not enough now to draw the curtains, I tried to stop the eyes and ears of my memory so as not to see that band of orange in the western sky, so as not to hear those invisible birds responding from one tree to the next on either side of me who was then so tenderly embraced by her that now was dead. I tried to avoid those sensations that are given us by the dampness of leaves in the evening air, the steep rise and fall of mule-tracks. But already those sensations had gripped me afresh, carried far enough back from the present moment so that it should have gathered all the recoil, all the resilience necessary to strike me afresh, this idea that Albertine was dead. Ah! never again would I enter a forest, I would stroll no more beneath the spreading trees. But would the broad plains be less cruel to me? How many times had I crossed, going in search of Albertine, how many times had I entered, on my return with her, the great plain of Cricqueville, now in foggy weather when the flooding mist gave us the illusion of being surrounded by a vast lake, now on limpid evenings when the moonlight, dematerialising the earth, making it appear, a yard away, celestial as it is, in the daytime, on far horizons only, enshrined the fields, the woods, with the firmament to which it had assimilated them, in the moss-agate of a universal blue.

Françoise was bound to rejoice at Albertine's death, and it should, in justice to her, be said that by a sort of tactful convention she made no pretence of sorrow. But the unwritten laws of her immemorial code and the tradition of the mediæval peasant woman who weeps as in the romances of chivalry were older than her hatred of Albertine and even of Eulalie. And so, on one of these late afternoons, as I was not quick enough in concealing my distress, she caught sight of my tears, served by the instinct of a little old peasant woman which at one time had led her to catch and torture animals, to feel only amusement in wringing the necks of chickens and in boiling lobsters alive, and, when I was ill, in observing, as it might be the wounds that she had inflicted upon an owl, my suffering expression which she afterwards proclaimed in a sepulchral tone and as a presage of coming disaster. But her Combray " Customary " did not permit her to treat lightly tears, grief, things which in her judgment were as fatal as shedding one's flannels in spring or eating when one had no " stomach ". " Oh, no, Monsieur, it doesn't do to cry like that, it isn't good for you." And in her attempt to stem my tears she shewed as much uneasiness as though they had been torrents of blood. Unfortunately I adopted a chilly air that cut short the effusions in which she was hoping to indulge and which might quite well, for that matter, have been sincere. Her attitude towards Albertine had been, perhaps akin to her attitude towards Eulalie, and, now that my mistress could no longer derive any profit from me, Françoise had ceased to hate her. She felt bound, however, to let me see that she was perfectly well aware that I was crying, and that, following the deplorable example set by my family, I did not wish to " let it be seen". " You mustn't cry, Monsieur," she adjured me, in a calmer tone, this time, and intending to prove her own perspicacity rather than to shew me any compassion. She went on: " It was bound to happen; she was too happy, poor creature, she never knew how happy she was."

How slow the day is in dying on these interminable summer evenings. A pallid ghost of the house opposite continued indefinitely to sketch upon the sky its persistent whiteness. At last it was dark indoors; I stumbled against the furniture in the hall, but in the door that opened upon the staircase, in the midst of the darkness which I had supposed to be complete, the glazed panel was translucent and blue, with the blue of a flower, the blue of an insect's wing, a blue that would have seemed to me beautiful if I had not felt it to be a last reflection, trenchant as a blade of steel, a supreme blow which in its indefatigable cruelty the day was still dealing me. In the end, however, the darkness became complete, but then a glimpse of a star behind one of the trees in the courtyard was enough to remind me of how we used to set out in a carriage, after dinner, for the woods of Chantepie, carpeted with moonlight. And even in the streets it would so happen that I could isolate upon the back of a seat, could gather there the natural purity of a moonbeam in the midst of the artificial lights of Paris, of that Paris over which it enthroned, by making the town return for a moment, in my imagination, to a state of nature, with the infinite silence of the suggested fields, the heart-rending memory of the walks that I had taken in them with Albertine. Ah! when would the night end? But at the first cool breath of dawn I shuddered, for it had revived in me the delight of that summer when, from Balbec to Incarville, from Incarville to Balbec, we had so many times escorted each other home until the break of day. I had now only one hope left for the future—a hope far more heartrending than any dread—which was that I might forget Albertine. I knew that I should one day forget her; I had quite forgotten Gilberte, Mme de Guermantes; I had quite forgotten my grandmother. And it is our most fitting and most cruel punishment, for that so complete oblivion, as tranquil as the oblivion of the graveyard, by which we have detached ourself from those whom we no longer love, that we can see this same oblivion to be inevitable in the case of those whom we love still. To tell the truth, we know it to be a state not painful, a state of indifference. But not being able to think at the same time of what I was and of what I should one day be, I thought with despair of all that covering mantle of caresses, of kisses, of friendly slumber, of which I must presently let myself be divested for all time. The rush of these tender memories sweeping on to break against the knowledge that Albertine was dead oppressed me by the incessant conflict of their baffled waves so that I could not keep still; I rose, but all of a sudden I stopped in consternation; the same faint day-break that I used to see at the moment when I had just left Albertine, still radiant and warm with her kisses, had come into the room and bared, above the curtains, its blade now a sinister portent, whose whiteness, cold, implacable and compact, entered the room like a dagger thrust into my heart.

Presently the sounds from the streets would begin, enabling me to tell from the qualitative scale of their resonance the degree of the steadily increasing heat in which they were sounding. But in this heat which, a few hours later, would have saturated itself in the fragrance of cherries, what I found (as in a medicine which the substitution of one ingredient for another is sufficient to transform from the stimulant and tonic that it was into a debilitating drug) was no longer the desire for women but the anguish of Albertine's departure. Besides, the memory of all my desires was as much impregnated with her, and with suffering, as the memory of my pleasures. That Venice where

I had thought that her company would be a nuisance (doubtless because I had felt in a confused way that it would be necessary to me), now that Albertine was no more, I preferred not to go there. Albertine had seemed to me to be an obstacle interposed between me and everything else, because she was for me what contained everything, and it was from her as from an urn that I might receive things. Now that this urn was shattered, I no longer felt that I had the courage to grasp things; there was nothing now from which I did not turn away, spiritless, preferring not to taste it. So that my separation from her did not in the least throw open to me the field of possible pleasures which I had imagined to be closed to me by her presence. Besides, the obstacle which her presence had perhaps indeed been in the way of my travelling, of my enjoying life, had only (as always happens) been a mask for other obstacles which reappeared intact now that this first obstacle had been removed. It had been in the same way that, in the past, when some friend had called to see me and had prevented me from working, if on the following day I was left undisturbed, I did not work any better. Let an illness, a duel, a runaway horse make us see death face to face, how richly we should have enjoyed the life of pleasure, the travels in unknown lands which are about to be snatched from us. And no sooner is the danger past than what we find once again before us is the same dull life in which none of those delights had any existence for us.

No doubt these nights that are so short continue for but a brief season. Winter would at length return, when I should no longer have to dread the memory of drives with her, protracted until the too early dawn. But would not the first frosts bring back to me, preserved in their cold storage the germ of my first desires, when at midnight I used to send for her, when the time seemed so long until I heard her ring the bell: a sound for which I might now wait everlastingly in vain? Would they not bring back to me the germ of my first uneasiness, when, upon two occasions, I thought that she was not coming? At that time I saw her but rarely, but even those intervals that there were between her visits which made her emerge, after many weeks, from the heart of an unknown life which I made no effort to possess, ensured my peace of mind by preventing the first inklings, constantly interrupted, of my jealousy from coagulating, from forming a solid mass in my heart. So far as they had contrived to be soothing, at that earlier time, so far, in retrospect, were they stamped with the mark of suffering, since all the unaccountable things that she might, while those intervals lasted, have been doing had ceased to be immaterial to me, and especially now that no visit from her would ever fall to my lot again; so that those January evenings on which she used to come, and which, for that reason, had been so dear to me, would blow into me now with their biting winds an uneasiness which then I did not know, and would bring back to me (but now grown pernicious) the first germ of my love. And when I considered that I would see again presently that cold season which, since the time of Gilberte and my playhours in the Champs Elysées, had always seemed to me so depressing; when I thought that there would be returning again evenings like that evening of snow when I had vainly, far into the night, waited for Albertine to come; then as a consumptive chooses the best place, from the physical point of view, for his lungs, but in my case making a moral choice, what at such moments I still dreaded most for my grief, for my heart, was the return of the intense cold, and I said to myself that what it would be hardest to live through was perhaps the winter.   Bound up as it was with each of the seasons, in order for me to discard the memory of Albertine I should have had first to forget them all, prepared to begin again to learn to know them, as an old man after a stroke of paralysis learns again to read; I should have had first to forgo the entire universe.   Nothing, I told myself, but an actual extinction of myself would be capable (but that was impossible) of consoling me for hers.   I did not realise that the death of oneself is neither impossible nor extraordinary; it is effected without our knowledge, it may be against our will, every day of our life, and I should have to suffer from the recurrence of all sorts of days which not only nature but adventitious circumstances, a purely conventional order introduce into a season. Presently would return the day on which I had gone to Balbec in that earlier summer when my love, which was not yet inseparable from jealousy and did not perplex itself with the problem of what Albertine would be doing all day, had still to pass through so many evolutions before becoming that so specialised love of the latest period, that this final year, in which Albertine's destiny had begun to change and had received its quietus, appeared to me full, multiform, vast, like a whole century.   Then it would be the memory of days more slow in reviving but dating from still earlier years; on the rainy Sundays on which nevertheless everyone else had gone out, in the void of the afternoon, when the sound of wind and rain would in the past have bidden me stay at home, to "philosophise in my garret," with what anxiety would I see the hour approach at which Albertine, so little expected, had come to visit me, had fondled me for the first time, breaking off because Françoise had brought in the lamp, in that time now doubly dead when it had been Albertine who was interested in me, when my affection for her might legitimately nourish so strong a hope. Even later in the season, those glorious evenings when the windows of kitchens, of girls' schools, standing open to the view like wayside shrines, allow the street to crown itself with a diadem of those demi-goddesses who, conversing, ever so close to us, with their peers, fill us with a feverish longing to penetrate into their mythological existence, recalled to me nothing now but the affection of Albertine whose company was an obstacle in the way of my approaching them.

Moreover, to the memory even of hours that were purely natural would inevitably be added the moral background that makes each of them a thing apart. When, later on, I should hear the goatherd's horn, on a first fine, almost Italian morning, the day that followed would blend successively with its sunshine the anxiety of knowing that Albertine was at the Trocadéro, possibly with Léa and the two girls, then her kindly domestic gentleness, almost that of a wife who seemed to me then an embarrassment and whom Françoise was bringing home to me. That telephone message from Françoise which had conveyed to me the dutiful homage of an Albertine who was returning with her, I had thought at the time that it made me swell with pride. I was mistaken. If it had exhilarated me, that was because it had made me feel that she whom I loved was really mine, lived only for me, and even at a distance, without my needing to occupy my mind with her, regarded me as her lord and master, returning home upon a sign from myself. And so that telephone message had been a particle of sweetness, coming to me from afar, sent out from that region of the Trocadéro where there were proved to be for me sources of happiness directing towards me molecules of comfort, healing balms, restoring to me at length so precious a liberty of spirit that I need do no more, surrendering myself without the restriction of a single care to Wagner's music, than await the certain arrival of Albertine, without fever, with an entire absence of impatience in which I had not had the perspicacity to recognise true happiness. And this happiness that she should return, that she should obey me and be mine, the cause of it lay in love and not in pride. It would have been quite immaterial to me now to have at my behest fifty women returning, at a sign from myself, not from the Trocadéro but from the Indies. But that day, conscious of Albertine who, while I sat alone in my room playing music, was coming dutifully to join me, I had breathed in, where it lay scattered like motes in a sunbeam, one of those substances which, just as others are salutary to the body, do good to the soul. Then there had been, half an hour later, Albertine's return, then the drive with Albertine returned, a drive which I had thought tedious because it was accompanied for me by certainty, but which, on account of that very certainty, had, from the moment of Françoise's telephoning to me that she was bringing Albertine home, let flow a golden calm over the hours that followed, had made of them as it were a second day, wholly unlike the first, because it had a completely different moral basis, a moral basis which made it an original day, which came and added itself to the variety of the days that I had previously known, a day which I should never have been able to imagine—any more than we could imagine the delicious idleness of a day in summer if such days did not exist in the calendar of those through which we had lived— a day of which I could not say absolutely that I recalled it, for to this calm I added now an anguish which I had not felt at the time. But at a much later date, when I went over gradually, in a reversed order, the times through which I had passed before I was so much in love with Albertine, when my scarred heart could detach itself without suffering from Albertine dead, then I was able to recall at length without suffering that day on which Albertine had gone shopping with Françoise instead of remaining at the Troca-déro; I recalled it with pleasure, as belonging to a moral season which I had not known until then; I recalled it at length exactly, without adding to it now any suffering, rather, on the contrary, as we recall certain days in summer which we found too hot while they lasted, and from which only after they have passed do we extract their unalloyed standard of fine gold and imperishable azure.

With the result that these several years imposed upon my memory of Albertine, which made them so painful, the successive colouring, the different modulations not only of their seasons or of their hours, from late afternoons in June to winter evenings, from seas by moonlight to dawn that broke as I was on my way home, from snow in Paris to fallen leaves at Saint-Cloud, but also of each of the particu-lar ideas of Albertine that I successively formed, of the physical aspect in which I pictured her at each of those moments, the degree of frequency with which I had seen her during that season, which itself appeared consequently more or less dispersed or compact, the anxieties which she might have caused me by keeping me waiting, the desire which I had felt at a given moment for her, the hopes formed and then blasted; all of these modified the character of my retrospective sorrow fully as much as the impressions of light or of scents which were associated with it, and completed each of the solar years through which I had lived—years which, simply with their springs, their trees, their breezes, were already so sad because of the indissoci-able memory of her—complementing each of them with a sort of sentimental year in which the hours were defined not by the sun's position, but by the strain of waiting for a tryst, in which the length of the days, in which the changes of temperature were determined not by the seasons but by the soaring flight of my hopes, the progress of our intimacy, the gradual transformation of her face, the expeditions on which she had gone, the frequency and style of the letters that she had written me during her absence, her more or less eager anxiety to see me on her return.   And lastly if these changes of season, if these different days furnished me each with a fresh Albertine, it was not only by recalling to me similar moments.   The reader will remember that always, even before I began to be in love, each day had made me a different person, swayed by other desires because he had other perceptions, a person who, whereas he had dreamed only of cliffs and tempests overnight, if the indis-creet spring dawn had distilled a scent of roses through the gaping portals of his house of sleep, would awake alert to set off for Italy.   Even in my love, had not the changing state of my moral atmosphere, the varying pressure of my beliefs, had they not one day diminished the visibility of the love that I was feeling, had they not another day extended it beyond all bounds, one day softened it to a smile, another day condensed it to a storm? We exist only by virtue of what we possess, we possess only what is really present to us, and so many of our memories, our humours, our ideas set out to voyage far away from us, until they are lost to sight! Then we can no longer make them enter into our reckoning of the total which is our personality. But they know of secret paths by which to return to us. And on certain nights, having gone to sleep almost without regretting Albertine any more—we can regret only what we remember—on awakening I found a whole fleet of memories which had come to cruise upon the surface of my clearest consciousness, and seemed marvellously distinct. Then I wept over what I could see so plainly, what overnight had been to me non-existent. In an instant, Albertine's name, her death, had changed their meaning; her betrayals had suddenly resumed their old importance.

How could she have seemed dead to me when now, in order to think of her, I had at my disposal only those same images one or other of which I used to recall when she was alive, each one being associated with a particular moment? Rapid and bowed above the mystic wheel of her bicycle, tightly-strapped upon rainy days in the amazonian corslet of her waterproof which made her breasts protrude, while serpents writhed in her turbaned hair, she scattered terror in the streets of Balbec; on the evenings on which we had taken champagne with us to the woods of Chantepie, her voice provoking, altered, she shewed on her face that pallid

99

warmth colouring only over her cheekbones so that, barely able to make her out in the darkness of the carriage, I drew her face into the moonlight in order to see her better, and which I tried now in vain to recapture, to see again in a darkness that would never end. A little statuette as we drove to the island, a large, calm, coarsely-grained face above the pianola, she was thus by turns rain-soaked and swift, provoking and diaphanous, motionless and smiling, an angel of music. So that what would have to be obliterated in me was not one only, but countless Albertines. Each of these was thus attached to a moment, to the date of which I found myself carried back when I saw again that particular Albertine. And the moments of the past do not remain still; they retain in our memory the motion which drew them towards the future, towards a future which has itself become the past, and draw us on in their train. Never had I caressed the waterproofed Albertine of the rainy days, I wanted to ask her to divest herself of that armour, that would be to know with her the love of the tented field, the brotherhood of travel. But this was no longer possible, she was dead. Never either, for fear of corrupting her, had I shewn any sign of comprehension on the evenings when she seemed to be offering me pleasures which, but for my self-restraint, she would not perhaps have sought from others, and which aroused in me now a frantic desire. I should not have found them the same in any other woman, but her who would fain have offered me them I might scour the whole world now without encountering, for Albertine was dead. It seemed that I had to choose between two sets of facts, to decide which was the truth, so far was the fact of Albertine's death—arising for me from a reality which I had not known; her life in Touraine—a contradiction of all my thoughts of her, my desires, my regrets, my tenderness, my rage, my jealousy. So great a wealth of memories, borrowed from the treasury of her life, such a profusion of sentiments evoking, implicating her life, seemed to make it incredible that Albertine should be dead. Such a profusion of sentiments, for my memory, while preserving my affection, left to it all its variety. It was not Albertine alone that was simply a series of moments, it was also myself. My love for her had not been simple: to a curious interest in the unknown had been added a sensual desire and to a sentiment of an almost conjugal mildness, at one moment indifference, at another a jealous fury. I was not one man only, but the steady advance hour after hour of an army in close formation, in which there appeared, according to the moment, impassioned men, indifferent men, jealous men—jealous men no two of whom were jealous of the same woman. And no doubt it would be from this that one day would come the healing which I should not expect. In a composite mass, these elements may, one by one, without our noticing it, be replaced by others, which others again eliminate or reinforce, until in the end a change has been brought about which it would be impossible to conceive if we were a single person. The complexity of my love, of my person, multiplied, diversified my sufferings. And yet they could always be ranged in the two categories, the option between which had made up the whole life of my love for Albertine, swayed alternately by trust and by a jealous suspicion.

If I had found it difficult to imagine that Albertine, so vitally alive in me (wearing as I did the double harness of the present and the past), was dead, perhaps it was equally paradoxical in me that Albertine, whom I knew to be dead could still excite my jealousy, and that this suspicion of the misdeeds of which Albertine, stripped now of the flesh that had rejoiced in them, of the heart that had been able to desire them, was no longer capable, nor responsible for them, should excite in me so keen a suffering that I should only have blessed them could I have seen in those misdeeds the pledge of the moral reality of a person materially non-existent, in place of the reflection, destined itself too to fade, of impressions that she had made on me in the past. A woman who could no longer taste any pleasure with other people ought not any longer to have excited my jealousy, if only my affection had been able to come to the surface. But this was just what was impossible, since it could not find its object, Albertine, save among memories in which she was still alive. Since, merely by thinking of her, I brought her back to life, her infidelities could never be those of a dead woman; the moments at which she had been guilty of them became the present moment, not only for Albertine, but for that one of my various selves who was thinking of her. So that no anachronism could ever separate the indissoluble couple, in which, to each fresh culprit, was immediately mated a jealous lover, pitiable and always contemporaneous. I had, during the last months, kept her shut up in my own house. But in my imagination now, Albertine was free, she was abusing her freedom, was prostituting herself to this friend or to that. Formerly, I used constantly to dream of the uncertain future that was unfolding itself before us, I endeavoured to read its message. And now, what lay before me, like a counterpart of the future—as absorbing as the future because it was equally uncertain, as difficult to decipher, as mysterious, more cruel still because I had not, as with the future, the possibility or the illusion of influencing it, and also because it unrolled itself to the full extent of my own life without my companion's being present to soothe the anguish that it caused me —was no longer Albertine's Future, it was her Past.   Her Past!   That is the wrong word, since for jealousy there can be neither past nor future, and what it imagines is invariably the present.

Atmospheric changes, provoking other changes in the inner man, awaken forgotten variants of himself, upset the somnolent course of habit, restore their old force to certain memories, to certain sufferings.   How much the more so with me if this change of weather recalled to me the weather in which Albertine, at Balbec, under the threat of rain, it might be, used to set out, heaven knows why, upon long rides, in the clinging mail-armour of her waterproof. If she had lived, no doubt to-day, in this so similar weather, she would be setting out, in Touraine, upon a corresponding expedition.   Since she could do so no longer, I ought not to have been pained by the thought; but, as with amputated cripples, the slightest change in the weather revived my pains in the member that had ceased, now, to belong to me.

All of a sudden it was an impression which I had not felt for a long time—for it had remained dissolved in the fluid and invisible expanse of my memory—that became crystallised.   Many years ago, when somebody mentioned her bath-wrap, Albertine had blushed.   At that time I was not jealous of her.   But since then I had intended to ask her if she could remember that conversation, and why she had blushed. This had worried me all the more because I had been told that the two girls, Léa's friends, frequented the bathing establishment of the hotel, and, it was said, not merely for the purpose of taking baths. But, for fear of annoying Albertine, or else deciding to await some more opportune moment, I had always refrained from mentioning it to her and in time had ceased to think about it. And all of a sudden, some time after Albertine's death, I recalled this memory, stamped with the mark, at once irritating and solemn, of riddles left for ever insoluble by the death of the one person who could have interpreted them. Might I not at least try to make certain that Albertine had never done anything wrong in that bathing establishment. By sending some one to Balbec, I might perhaps succeed. While she was alive, I should doubtless have been unable to learn anything. But people's tongues become strangely loosened and they are ready to report a misdeed when they need no longer fear the culprit's resentment. As the constitution of our imagination, which has remained rudimentary, simplified (not having passed through the countless transformations which improve upon the primitive models of human inventions, barely recognisable, whether it be the barometer, the balloon, the telephone, or anything else, in their ultimate perfection), allows us to see only a very few things at one time, the memory of the bathing establishment occupied the whole field of my inward vision.

Sometimes I came in collision in the dark lanes of sleep with one of those bad dreams, which are not very serious for several reasons, one of these being that the sadness which they engender lasts for barely an hour after we awake, like the weakness that is caused by an artificial soporific. For another reason also, namely that we encounter them but very rarely, no more than once in two or three years. And, moreover, it remains uncertain whether we have encountered them before, whether they have not rather that aspect of not being seen for the first time which is projected over them by an illusion, a sub-division (for duplication would not be a strong enough term).

Of course, since I entertained doubts as to the life, the death of Albertine, I ought long since to have begun to make inquiries, but the same weariness, the same cowardice which had made me give way to Albertine when she was with me prevented me from undertaking anything since I had ceased to see her. And yet from a weakness that had dragged on for years on end, a flash of energy sometimes emerged. I decided to make this investigation which, after all, was perfectly natural. One would have said that nothing else had occurred in Albertine's whole life. I asked myself whom I could best send down to make inquiries on the spot, at Balbec. Aimé seemed to me to be a suitable person. Apart from his thorough know-ledge of the place, he belonged to that category of plebeian folk who have a keen eye to their own advantage, are loyal to those whom they serve, indifferent to any thought of morality, and of whom—because, if we pay them well, in their obedience to our will, they suppress everything that might in one way or another go against it, shewing themselves as incapable of indiscretion, weakness or dis-honesty as they are devoid of scruples—we say: " They are good fellows." In such we can repose an absolute confidence. When Aimé had gone, I thought how much more to the point it would have been if, instead of sending him down to try to discover something there, I had now been able to question Albertine herself. And at once the thought of this question which I would have liked, which it seemed to me that I was about to put to her, having brought Albertine into my presence—not thanks to an effort of resurrection but as though by one of those chance encounters which, as is the case with photographs that are not posed, with snapshots, always make the person appear more alive—at the same time in which I imagined our conversation, I felt how impossible it was; I had just approached a fresh aspect of the idea that Albertine was dead, Albertine who inspired in me that affection which we have for the absent the sight of whom does not come to correct the embellished image, inspiring also sorrow that this absence must be eternal and that the poor child should be deprived for ever of the joys of life. And immediately, by an abrupt change of mood, from the torments of jealousy I passed to the despair of separation.

What filled my heart now was, in the place of odious suspicions, the affectionate memory of hours of confiding tenderness spent with the sister whom death had really made me lose, since my grief was related not to what Albertine had been to me, but to what my heart, anxious to participate in the most general emotions of love, had gradually persuaded me that she was; then I became aware that the life which had bored me so—so, at least, I thought—had been on the contrary delicious; to the briefest moments spent in talking to her of things that were quite insignificant, I felt now that there was added, amalgamated a pleasure which at the time had not—it is true—been perceived by me, but which was already responsible for making me turn so perseveringly to those moments to the exclusion of any others; the most trivial incidents which I recalled, a movement that she had made in the carriage by my side, or to sit down facing me in my room, dispersed through my spirit an eddy of sweetness and sorrow which little by little overwhelmed it altogether.

This room in which we used to dine had never seemed to me attractive, I had told Albertine merely that it was attractive in order that my mistress might be content to live in it. Now the curtains, the chairs, the books, had ceased to be unimportant. Art is not alone in imparting charm and mystery to the most insignificant things; the same power of bringing them into intimate relation with ourself is committed also to grief. At the moment I had paid no attention to the dinner which we had eaten together after our return from the Bois, before I went to the Verdurins', and towards the beauty, the solemn sweetness of which I now turned, my eyes filled with tears. An impression of love is out of proportion to the other impressions of life, but it is not when it is lost in their midst that we can take account of it. It is not from its foot, in the tumult of the street and amid the thronging houses, it is when we are far away, that from the slope of a neighbouring hill, at a distance from which the whole town has disappeared, or appears only as a confused mass upon the ground, we can, in the calm detachment of solitude and dusk, appreciate, unique, persistent and pure, the height of a cathedral. I tried to embrace the image of Albertine through my tears as I thought of all the serious and sensible things that she had said that evening.

One morning I thought that I could see the oblong shape of a hill swathed in mist, that I could taste the warmth of a cup of chocolate, while my heart was horribly wrung by the memory of that afternoon on which Albertine had come to see me and I had kissed her for the first time: the fact was that I had just heard the hiccough of the hot-water pipes, the furnace having just been started. And I flung angrily away an invitation which Françoise brought me from Mme Verdurin; how the impression that I had felt when I went to dine for the first time at la Raspelière, that death does not strike us all at the same age, overcame me with increased force now that Albertine was dead, so young, while Brichot continued to dine with Mme Verdurin who was still entertaining and would perhaps continue to entertain for many years to come. At once the name of Brichot recalled to me the end of that evening party when he had accompanied me home, when I had seen from the street the light of Albertine's lamp. I had already thought of it upon many occasions, but I had not approached this memory from the same angle. Then when I thought of the void which I should now find upon returning home, that I should never again see from the street Albertine's room, the light in which was extinguished for ever, I realised how, that evening, in parting from Brichot, I had thought that I was bored, that I regretted my inability to stroll about the streets and make love elsewhere, I realised how greatly I had been mistaken, that it was only because the treasure whose reflections came down to me in the street had seemed to be entirely in my

possession that I had failed to calculate its value, which
meant that it seemed to me of necessity inferior to pleasures,
however slight, of which however, in seeking to imagine
them, I enhanced the value. I realised how much that
light which had seemed to me to issue from a prison contained for me of fulness, of life and sweetness, all of which
was but the realisation of what had for a moment intoxi-
cated me and had then seemed for ever impossible: I began
to understand that this life which I had led in Paris in a
home which was also her home, was precisely the realisation of that profound peace of which I had dreamed on the
night when Albertine had slept under the same roof as
myself, at Balbec. The conversation which I had had
with Albertine after our return from the Bois before that
party at the Verdurins', I should not have been consoled
had it never occurred, that conversation which had to
some extent introduced Albertine into my intellectual life
and in certain respects had made us one. For no doubt, if
I returned with melting affection to her intelligence, to
her kindness to myself, it was not because they were any
greater than those of other persons whom I had known.
Had not Mme de Cambremer said to me at Balbec:
"What! You might be spending your days with Elstir,
who is a genius, and you spend them with your cousin!"
Albertine's intelligence pleased me because, by association,
it revived in me what I called its sweetness as we call the
sweetness of a fruit a certain sensation which exists only in
our palate. And in fact, when I thought of Albertine's
intelligence, my lips instinctively protruded and tasted a
memory of which I preferred that the reality should remain
external to me and should consist in the objective superi-

ority of another person. There could be no denying that I had known people whose intelligence was greater. But the infinitude of love, or its egoism, has the result that the people whom we love are those whose intellectual and moral physiognomy is least defined objectively in our eyes, we alter them incessantly to suit our desires and fears, we do not separate them from ourself, they are only a vast and vague place in which our affections take root. We have not of our own body, into which flow perpetually so many discomforts and pleasures, as clear an outline as we have of a tree or house, or of a passer-by. And where I had gone wrong was perhaps in not making more effort to know Albertine in herself. Just as, from the point of view of her charm, I had long considered only the different positions that she occupied in my memory in the procession of years, and had been surprised to see that she had been spontaneously enriched with modifications which were due merely to the difference of perspective, so I ought to have sought to understand her character as that of an ordinary person, and thus perhaps, finding an explanation of her persistence in keeping her secret from me, might have averted the continuance between us, with that strange desperation, of the conflict which had led to the death of Albertine. And I then felt, with an intense pity for her, shame at having survived her. It seemed to me indeed, in the hours when I suffered least, that I had derived a certain benefit from her death, for a woman is of greater service to our life if she is in it, instead of being an element of happiness, an instrument of sorrow, and there is not a woman in the world the possession of whom is as precious as that of the truths which she reveals to us by causing us to suffer. In these moments, thinking at once of my grandmother's death and of Albertine's, it seemed to me that my life was stained with a double murder from which only the cowardice of the world could absolve me. I had dreamed of being understood by Albertine, of not being scorned by her, thinking that it was for the great happiness of being understood, of not being scorned, when so many other people might have served me better. We wish to be understood, because we wish to be loved, and we wish to be loved because we are in love. The understanding of other people is immaterial and their love importunate. My joy at having possessed a little of Albertine's intelligence and of her heart arose not from their intrinsic worth, but from the fact that this possession was a stage farther towards the complete possession of Albertine, a possession which had been my goal and my chimera, since the day on which I first set eyes on her. When we speak of the " kindness " of a woman, we do no more perhaps than project outside ourself the pleasure that we feel in seeing her, like children when they say: " My dear little bed, my dear little pillow, my dear little haw-thorns." Which explains incidentally why men never say of a woman who is not unfaithful to them: " She is so kind," and say it so often of a woman by whom they are betrayed. Mme de Cambremer was right in thinking that Elstir's intellectual charm was greater. But we cannot judge in the same way the charm of a person who is, like everyone else, exterior to ourself, painted upon the horizon of our mind, and that of a person who, in con-sequence of an error in localisation which has been due to certain accidents but is irreparable, has lodged herself in

our own body so effectively that the act of asking ourself
in retrospect whether she did not look at a woman on a
particular day in the corridor of a little seaside railway-
train makes us feel the same anguish as would a surgeon
probing for a bullet in our heart. A simple crescent of
bread, but one which we are eating, gives us more pleasure
than all the ortolans, young rabbits and barbavelles that
were set before Louis XV and the blade of grass which,
a few inches away, quivers before our eye, while we are
lying upon the mountain-side, may conceal from us the
sheer summit of another peak, if it is several miles away.

Furthermore, our mistake is our failure to value the
intelligence, the kindness of a woman whom we love,
however slight they may be. Our mistake is our remaining indifferent to the kindness, the intelligence of others.
Falsehood begins to cause us the indignation, and kindness
the gratitude which they ought always to arouse in us,
only if they proceed from a woman with whom we are in
love, and bodily desire has the marvellous faculty of
restoring its value to intelligence and a solid base to the
moral life. Never should I find again that divine thing,
a person with whom I might talk freely of everything, in
whom I might confide. Confide? But did not other
people offer me greater confidence than Albertine? Had
I not had with others more unrestricted conversations?
The fact is that confidence, conversation, trivial things in
themselves, what does it matter whether they are more
or less imperfect, if only there enters into them love,
which alone is divine. I could see Albertine now, seated
at her pianola, rosy beneath her dark hair, I could feel,
against my lips which she was trying to part, her tongue,

her motherly, inedible, nourishing and holy tongue whose
secret flame and dew meant that even when Albertine let
it glide over the surface of my throat or stomach, those
caresses, superficial but in a sense offered by her inmost
flesh, turned outward like a cloth that is turned to shew
its lining, assumed even in the most external touches as it
were, the mysterious delight of a penetration.

All these so pleasant moments which nothing would
ever restore to me again, I cannot indeed say that what
made me feel the loss of them was despair. To feel
despair, we must still be attached to that life which could
end only in disaster. I had been in despair at Balbec
when I saw the day break and realised that none of the
days to come could ever be a happy day for me. I had
remained fairly selfish since then, but the self to which
I was now attached, the self which constituted those vital
reserves that were set in action by the instinct of self-
preservation, this self was no longer alive; when I thought
of my strength, of my vital force, of the best elements in
myself, I thought of a certain treasure which I had possessed (which I had been alone in possessing since other
people could not know exactly the sentiment, concealed
in myself, which it had inspired in me) and which no
one could ever again take from me since I possessed it no
longer.

And, to tell the truth, when I had ever possessed it, it had
been only because I had liked to think of myself as possessing it. I had not merely committed the imprudence,
when I cast my eyes upon Albertine and lodged her in
my heart, of making her live within me, nor that other
imprudence of combining a domestic affection with sensual

pleasure. I had sought also to persuade myself that our relations were love, that we were mutually practising the relations that are called love, because she obediently returned the kisses that I gave her, and, having come in time to believe this, I had lost not merely a woman whom I loved but a woman who loved me, my sister, my child, my tender mistress. And in short, I had received a blessing and a curse which Swann had not known, for, after all, during the whole of the time in which he had been in love with Odette and had been so jealous of her, he had barely seen her, having found it so difficult, on certain days when she put him off at the last moment, to gain admission to her. But afterwards he had had her to himself, as his wife, and until the day of his death. I, on the contrary, while I was so jealous of Albertine, more fortunate than Swann, had had her with me in my own house. I had realised as a fact the state of which Swann had so often dreamed and which he did not realise materially until it had ceased to interest him. But, after all, I had not managed to keep Albertine as he had kept Odette. She had fled from me, she was dead. For nothing is ever repeated exactly, and the most analogous lives which, thanks to the kinship of the persons and the similarity of the circumstances, we may select in order to represent them as symmetrical remain in many respects opposite.

By losing my life I should not have lost very much; I should have lost now only an empty form, the empty frame of a work of art. Indifferent as to what I might in the future put in it, but glad and proud to think of what it had contained, I dwelt upon the memory of those so pleasant hours, and this moral support gave me a feeling of comfort which the approach of death itself would not have disturbed.

How she used to hasten to see me at Balbec when I sent for her, lingering only to sprinkle scent on her hair to please me. These images of Balbec and Paris which I loved to see again were the pages still so recent, and so quickly turned, of her short life. All this which for me was only memory had been for her action, action as precipitate as that of a tragedy towards a sudden death. People develop in one way inside us, but in another way outside us (I had indeed felt this on those evenings when I remarked in Albertine an enrichment of qualities which was due not only to my memory), and these two ways do not fail to react upon each other. Albeit I had, in seeking to know Albertine, then to possess her altogether, obeyed merely the need to reduce by experiment to elements meanly similar to those of our own self the mystery of every other person, I had been unable to do so without exercising an influence in my turn over Albertine's life. Perhaps my wealth, the prospect of a brilliant marriage had attracted her, my jealousy had kept her, her goodness or her intelligence, or her sense of guilt, or her cunning had made her accept, and had led me on to make harsher and harsher a captivity in chains forged simply by the internal process of my mental toil, which had, nevertheless, had, upon Albertine's life, reactions, destined themselves to set, by the natural swing of the pendulum, fresh and ever more painful problems to my psychology, since from my prison she had escaped, to go and kill herself upon a horse which but for me she would not have owned, leaving me, even after she was dead, with suspicions the verification of which, if it was to come, would perhaps be more painful to me than the discovery at Balbec that Albertine had known Mlle Vinteuil, since Albertine would no longer be present to soothe me. So that the long plaint of the soul which thinks that it is living shut up within itself is a monologue in appearance only, since the echoes of reality alter its course and such a life is like an essay in subjective psychology spontaneously pursued, but furnishing from a distance its "action" to the purely realistic novel of another reality, another existence, the vicissitudes of which come in their turn to inflect the curve and change the direction of the psychological essay. How highly geared had been the mechanism, how rapid had been the evolution of our love, and, notwithstanding the sundry delays, interruptions and hesitations of the start, as in certain of Balzac's tales or Schumann's ballads, how sudden the catastrophe! It was in the course of this last year, long as a century to me, so many times had Albertine changed her appearance in my mind between Balbec and her departure from Paris, and also, independently of me and often without my knowledge, changed in herself, that I must place the whole of that happy life of affection which had lasted so short a while, which yet appeared to me with an amplitude, almost an immensity, which now was for ever impossible and yet was indispensable to me. Indispensable without perhaps having been in itself and at the outset a thing that was necessary since I should not have known Albertine had I not read in an archæological treatise a description of the church at Balbec, had not Swann, by telling me that this church was almost Persian, directed my taste to the Byzantine Norman, had not a financial syndicate, by erecting at Balbec a hygienic and comfortable hotel, made my parents decide to hear my supplication and send me to Balbec. To be sure, in that Balbec so long desired, I had not found the Persian church of my dreams, nor the eternal mists. Even the famous train at one twenty-two had not corresponded to my mental picture of it. But in compensation for what our imagination leaves us wanting and we give ourself so much unnecessary trouble in trying to find, life does give us something which we were very far from imagining. Who would have told me at Combray, when I lay waiting for my mother's good-night with so heavy a heart, that those anxieties would be healed, and would then break out again one day, not for my mother, but for a girl who would at first be no more, against the horizon of the sea, than a flower upon which my eyes would daily be invited to gaze, but a flower that could think, and in whose mind I should be so childishly anxious to occupy a prominent place, that I should be distressed by her not being aware that I knew Mme de Villeparisis? Yes, it was the good-night, the kiss of a stranger like this, that, in years to come, was to make me suffer as keenly as I had suffered as a child when my mother was not coming up to my room. Well, this Albertine so necessary, of love for whom my soul was now almost entirely composed, if Swann had not spoken to me of Balbec, I should never have known her. Her life would perhaps have been longer, mine would have been unprovided with what was now making it a martyrdom. And also it seemed to me that, by my entirely selfish affection, I had allowed Albertine to die just as I had murdered my grandmother. Even later on, even after I

had already known her at Balbec, I should have been able
not to love her as I was to love her in the sequel. When I
gave up Gilberte and knew that I would be able one day
to love another woman, I scarcely ventured to entertain a
doubt whether, considering simply the past, Gilberte was
the only woman whom I had been capable of loving. Well,
in the case of Albertine I had no longer any doubt at all,
I was sure that it need not have been herself that I loved,
that it might have been someone else. To prove this, it
would have been sufficient that Mlle de Stermaria, on the
evening when I was going to take her to dine on the island
in the Bois, should not have put me off. It was still not
too late, and it would have been upon Mlle de Stermaria
that I would have trained that activity of the imagination
which makes us extract from a woman so special a notion
of the individual that she appears to us unique in herself
and predestined and necessary for us. At the most,
adopting an almost physiological point of view, I could
say that I might have been able to feel this same exclusive
love for another woman but not for any other woman.
For Albertine, plump and dark, did not resemble Gilberte,
tall and ruddy, and yet they were fashioned of the same
healthy stuff, and over the same sensual cheeks shone a
look in the eyes of both which it was difficult to interpret.
They were women of a sort that would never attract the
attention of men who, for their part, would do the most
extravagant things for other women who made no appeal
to me. A man has almost always the same way of catching
cold, and so forth; that is to say, he requires to bring about
the event a certain combination of circumstances; it is
natural that when he falls in love he should love a certain

class of woman, a class which for that matter is very numerous. The two first glances from Albertine which had set me dreaming were not absolutely different from Gilberte's first glances. I could almost believe that the obscure personality, the sensuality, the forward, cunning nature of Gilberte had returned to tempt me, incarnate this time in Albertine's body, a body quite different and yet not without analogies. In Albertine's case, thanks to a wholly different life shared with me into which had been unable to penetrate—in a block of thoughts among which a painful preoccupation maintained a permanent cohesion —any fissure of distraction and oblivion, her living body had indeed not, like Gilberte's, ceased one day to be the body in which I found what I subsequently recognised as being to me (what they would not have been to other men) feminine charms. But she was dead. I should, in time, forget her. Who could tell whether then, the same qualities of rich blood, of uneasy brooding would return one day to spread havoc in my life, but incarnate this time in what feminine form I could not foresee. The example of Gilberte would as little have enabled me to form an idea of Albertine and guess that I should fall in love with her, as the memory of Vinteuil's sonata would have enabled me to imagine his septet. Indeed, what was more, on the first occasions of my meeting Albertine, I might have supposed that it was with other girls that I should fall in love. Besides, she might indeed quite well have appeared to me, had I met her a year earlier, as dull as a grey sky in which dawn has not yet broken. If I had changed in relation to her, she herself had changed also, and the girl who had come and sat upon my bed on the day of my letter to Mlle de Stermaria was no longer the same girl that I had known at Balbec, whether by a mere explosion of the woman which occurs at the age of puberty, or because of some incident which I have never been able to discover. In any case, if she whom I was one day to love must to a certain extent resemble this other, that is to say, if my choice of a woman was not entirely free, this meant, nevertheless that, trained in a manner that was perhaps inevitable, it was trained upon something more considerable than a person, upon a type of womankind, and this removed all inevitability from my love for Albertine. The woman whose face we have before our eyes more constantly than light itself, since, even when our eyes are shut, we never cease for an instant to adore her beautiful eyes, her beautiful nose, to arrange opportunities of seeing them again, this unique woman—we know quite well that it would have been another woman that would now be unique to us if we had been in another town than that in which we made her acquaintance, if we had explored other quarters of the town, if we had frequented the house of a different hostess. Unique, we suppose; she is innumerable. And yet she is compact, indestructible in our loving eyes, irreplaceable for a long time to come by any other. The truth is that the woman has only raised to life by a sort of magic spell a thousand elements of affection existing in us already in a fragmentary state, which she has assembled, joined together, bridging every gap between them, it is ourself who by giving her her features have supplied all the solid matter of the beloved object. Whence it comes about that even if we are only one man among a thousand to her and perhaps the last man of them all, to us she is the only woman, the woman towards whom our whole life tends. It was, indeed, true that I had been quite well aware that this love was not inevitable since it might have occurred with Mlle de Stermaria, but even without that from my knowledge of the love itself, when I found it to be too similar to what I had known with other women, and also when I felt it to be vaster than Albertine, enveloping her, unconscious of her, like a tide swirling round a tiny rock. But gradually, by dint of living with Albertine, the chains which I myself had forged I was unable to fling off, the habit of associating Albertine's person with the sentiment which she had not inspired made me, nevertheless, believe that it was peculiar to her, as habit gives to the mere association of ideas between two phenomena, according to a certain school of philosophy, an illusion of the force, the necessity of a law of causation. I had thought that my social relations, my wealth, would dispense me from suffering, and too effectively perhaps, since this seemed to dispense me from feeling, loving, imagining; I envied a poor country girl whom her absence of social relations, even by telegraph, allows to ponder for months on end upon a grief which she cannot artificially put to sleep. And now I began to realise that if, in the case of Mme de Guermantes, endowed with everything that could make the gulf infinite between her and myself, I had seen that gulf suddenly bridged by the opinion that social advantages are nothing more than inert and transmutable matter, so, in a similar albeit converse fashion, my social relations, my wealth, all the material means by which not only my own position but the civilisation of my age enabled me to profit, had done no more than postpone the conclusion of my struggle against the contrary inflexible will of Albertine upon which no pressure had had any effect. True, I had been able to exchange telegrams, telephone messages with Saint-Loup, to remain in constant communication with the office at Tours, but had not the delay in waiting for them proved useless, the result nil? And country girls, without social advantages or relations, or human beings enjoying the perfections of civilisation, do they not suffer less, because all of us desire less, because we regret less what we have always known to be inaccessible, what for that reason has continued to seem unreal. We desire more keenly the person who is about to give herself to us; hope anticipates possession; but regret also is an amplifier of desire. Mlle de Stermaria's refusal to come and dine with me on the island in the Bois was what had prevented her from becoming the object of my love. This might have sufficed also to make me fall in love with her if afterwards I had seen her again before it was too late. As soon as I had known that she was not coming, entertaining the improbable hypothesis—which had been proved correct—that perhaps she had a jealous lover who prevented her from seeing other men, that I should never see her again, I had suffered so intensely that I would have given anything in the world to see her, and it was one of the keenest anguishes that I had ever felt that Saint-Loup's arrival had soothed. After we have reached a certain age our loves, our mistresses are begotten of our anguish; our past, and the physical lesions in which it is recorded, determine our future. In Albertine's case, the fact that it would not necessarily be she that I must love was, even without the example of those previous loves, inscribed in the history of my love for her, that is to say for herself and her friends. For it was not a single love like my love for Gilberte, but was created by division among a number of girls. That it was on her account and because they appeared to me more or less similar to her that I had amused myself with her friends was quite possible. The fact remains that for a long time hesitation among them all was possible, my choice strayed from one to another, and when I thought that I preferred one, it was enough that another should keep me waiting, should refuse to see me, to make me feel the first premonitions of love for her. Often at that time when Andrée was coming to see me at Balbec, if, shortly before Andrée was expected, Albertine failed to keep an appointment, my heart throbbed without ceasing, I felt that I would never see her again and that it was she whom I loved. And when Andrée came it was in all seriousness that I said to her (as I said it to her in Paris after I had learned that Albertine had known Mlle Vinteuil) what she supposed me to be saying with a purpose, without sincerity, what I would indeed have said and in the same words had I been enjoying myself the day before with Albertine: " Alas! If you had only come sooner, now I am in love with someone else." Again, in this case of Andrée, replaced by Albertine after I learned that the latter had known Mlle Vinteuil, my love had alternated between them, so that after all there had been only one love at a time. But a case had occurred earlier in which I had more or less quarrelled with two of the girls. The one who took the first step towards a reconciliation would restore my peace of mind, it was the other that I would love, if she remained cross with me, which does not mean that it was not with the former that I would form a definite tie, for she would console me—albeit ineffectively —for the harshness of the other, whom I would end by forgetting if she did not return to me again. Now, it so happened that, while I was convinced that one or the other at least would come back to me, for some time neither of them did so. My anguish was therefore twofold, and twofold my love, while I reserved to myself the right to cease to love the one who came back, but until that happened continued to suffer on account of them both. It is the lot of a certain period in life which may come to us quite early that we are made less amorous by a person than by a desertion, in which we end by knowing one thing and one thing only about that person, her face having grown dim, her heart having ceased to exist, our preference of her being quite recent and inexplicable; namely that what we need to make our suffering cease is a message from her: " May I come and see you ? " My separation from Albertine on the day when Françoise informed me: " Mademoiselle Albertine has gone " was like an allegory of countless other separations. For very often in order that we may discover that we are in love, perhaps indeed in order that we may fall in love, the day of separation must first have come. In the case when it is an unkept appointment, a written refusal that dictates our choice, our imagination lashed by suffering sets about its work so swiftly, fashions with so frenzied a rapidity a love that had scarcely begun, and had been quite featureless, destined, for months past, to remain a rough sketch, that now and again our intelligence which has not been able to keep pace

with our heart, cries out in astonishment: " But you must
be mad, what are these strange thoughts that are making
you so miserable? That is not real life." And indeed at
that moment, had we not been roused to action by the
betrayer, a few healthy distractions that would calm our
heart physically would be sufficient to bring our love to an
end. In any case, if this life with Albertine was not in its
essence necessary, it had become indispensable to me. I
had trembled when I was in love with Mme de Guermantes because I used to say to myself that, with her too
abundant means of attraction, not only beauty but position,
wealth, she would be too much at liberty to give herself to
all and sundry, that I should have too little hold over her.
Albertine had been penniless, obscure, she must have been
anxious to marry me. And yet I had not been able to
possess her exclusively. Whatever be our social position,
however wise our precautions, when the truth is confessed
we have no hold over the life of another person. Why
had she not said to me: " I have those tastes," I would have
yielded, would have allowed her to gratify them. In a
novel that I had been reading there was a woman whom
no objurgation from the man who was in love with her
could induce to speak. When I read the book, I had
thought this situation absurd; had I been the hero, I
assured myself, I would first of all have forced the woman
to speak, then we could have come to an understanding;
what was the good of all this unnecessary misery? But
I saw now that we are not free to abstain from forging the
chains of our own misery, and that however well we may
know our own will, other people do not obey it.

And yet those painful, those ineluctable truths which

125

dominated us and to which we were blind, the truth of our
sentiments, the truth of our destiny, how often without
knowing it, without meaning it, we have expressed them
in words in which we ourself doubtless thought that we
were lying, but the prophetic value of which has been
established by subsequent events.   I could recall many
words that each of us had uttered without knowing at the
time the truth that they contained, which indeed we had
said thinking that each was deceiving the other, words the
falsehood of which was very slight, quite uninteresting,
wholly confined within our pitiable insincerity, compared with what they contained that was unknown to us.
Lies, mistakes, falling short of the reality which neither of
us perceived, truth extending beyond it, the truth of our
natures the essential laws of which escape us and require
time before they reveal themselves, the truth of our
destinies also.   I had supposed that I was lying when I
said to her at Balbec: " The more I see you, the more I
shall love you " (and yet it was that intimacy at every
moment that had, through the channel of jealousy
attached me so strongly to her), " I know that I could be
of use to you intellectually " ;   and in Paris: " Do be
careful.   Remember that if you met with an accident, it
would break my heart."   And she: " But I may meet
with an accident "; and I in Paris on the evening when I
pretended that I wished to part from her: " Let me look
at you once again since presently I shall not be seeing you
again, and it will be for ever! " and she, when, that same
evening, she looked round the room: " To think that I
shall never see this room again, those books, that pianola,
the whole house, I cannot believe it and yet it is true."

In her last letters again, when she wrote—probably saying
to herself: " This is the stuff to tell him "—" I leave with
you the best part of myself " (and was it not now indeed
to the fidelity, to the strength, which too was, alas, frail,
of my memory that were entrusted her intelligence, her
goodness, her beauty?) and " that twofold twilight (since
night was falling and we were about to part) will be
effaced from my thoughts only when the darkness is complete," that phrase written on the eve of the day when her
mind had indeed been plunged in complete darkness, and
when, it may well have been, in the last glimmer, so brief
but stretched out to infinity by the anxiety of the moment,
she had indeed perhaps seen again our last drive together
and in that instant when everything forsakes us and we
create a faith for ourself, as atheists turn Christian upon
the battle-field, she had perhaps summoned to her aid the
friend whom she had so often cursed but had so deeply
respected, who himself—for all religions are alike—was so
cruel as to hope that she had also had time to see herself as
she was, to give her last thought to him, to confess her sins
at length to him, to die in him. But to what purpose,
since even if, at that moment, she had had time to see herself as she was, we had neither of us understood where our
happiness lay, what we ought to do, until that happiness,
because that happiness was no longer possible, until and
because we could no longer realise it. So long as things
are possible we postpone them, and they cannot assume
that force of attraction, that apparent ease of realisation
save when, projected upon the ideal void of the imagination, they are removed from their burdensome, degrading
submersion in the vital medium. The thought that we

must die is more painful than the act of dying, but less painful than the thought that another person is dead, which, becoming once more a plane surface after having engulfed a person, extends without even an eddy at the point of disappearance, a reality from which that person is excluded, in which there exists no longer any will, any knowledge, and from which it is as difficult to reascend to the thought that the person has lived, as it is difficult, with the still recent memory of her life, to think that she is now comparable with the unsubstantial images, with the memories left us by the characters in a novel which we have been reading.

At any rate, I was glad that, before she died, she had written me that letter, and above all, had sent me that final message which proved to me that she would have returned had she lived. It seemed to me that it was not merely more soothing, but more beautiful also, that the event would have been incomplete without this note, would not have had so markedly the form of art and destiny. In reality it would have been just as markedly so had it been different; for every event is like a mould of a particular shape, and, whatever it be, it imposes, upon the series of incidents which it has interrupted and seems to have concluded, a pattern which we believe to be the only one possible, because we do not know the other which might have been substituted for it. I repeated to myself: " Why had she not said to me: ' I have those tastes,' I would have yielded, would have allowed her to gratify them, at this moment I should be kissing her still." What a sorrow to have to remind myself that she had lied to me thus when she swore to me, three days before she left me,

that she had never had with Mlle Vinteuil's friend those
relations which at the moment when Albertine swore it
her blush had confessed.   Poor child, she had at least had
the honesty to refuse to swear that the pleasure of seeing
Mlle Vinteuil again had no part in her desire to go that
day to the Verdurins'.   Why had she not made her admission complete, why had she then invented that inconceiv-
able tale?   Perhaps, however, it was partly my fault that
she had never, despite all my entreaties which were powerless against her denial, been willing to say to me: " I have
those tastes."   It was perhaps partly my fault because at
Balbec, on the day when, after Mme de Cambremer's
call, I had had my first explanation with Albertine, and
when I was so far from imagining that she could have had,
in any case, anything more than an unduly passionate
friendship with Andrée, I had expressed with undue
violence my disgust at that kind of moral lapse, had condemned it in too categorical a fashion.   I could not recall
whether Albertine had blushed when I had innocently
expressed my horror of that sort of thing, I could not
recall it, for it is often only long afterwards that we would
give anything to know what attitude a person adopted at a
moment when we were paying no attention to it, an
attitude which, later on, when we think again of our
conversation, would elucidate a poignant difficulty.   But
in our memory there is a blank, there is no trace of it.
And very often we have not paid sufficient attention, at the
actual moment, to the things which might even then have
seemed to us important, we have not properly heard a
sentence, have not noticed a gesture, or else we have forgotten them.   And when later on, eager to discover a

truth, we reascend from deduction to deduction, turning over our memory like a sheaf of written evidence, when we arrive at that sentence, at that gesture, which it is impossible to recall, we begin again a score of times the same process, but in vain: the road goes no farther. Had she blushed? I did not know whether she had blushed, but she could not have failed to hear, and the memory of my speech had brought her to a halt later on when perhaps she had been on the point of making her confession to me. And now she no longer existed anywhere, I might scour the earth from pole to pole without finding Albertine. The reality which had closed over her was once more unbroken, had obliterated every trace of the creature who had sunk into its depths. She was no more now than a name, like that Mme de Charlus of whom the people who had known her said with indifference: "She was charming." But I was unable to conceive for more than an instant the existence of this reality of which Albertine had no knowledge, for in myself my mistress existed too vividly, in myself in whom every sentiment, every thought bore some reference to her life. Perhaps if she had known, she would have been touched to see that her lover had not forgotten her, now that her own life was finished, and would have been moved by things which in the past had left her indifferent. But as we would choose to refrain from infidelities, however secret they might be, so fearful are we that she whom we love is not refraining from them, I was alarmed by the thought that if the dead do exist anywhere, my grandmother was as well aware of my oblivion as Albertine of my remembrance. And when all is said, even in the case of a single dead person, can we be sure that the joy which we should feel in learning that she knows certain things would compensate for our alarm at the thought that she knows *all;* and, however agonising the sacrifice, would we not sometimes abstain from keeping after their death as friends those whom we have loved, from the fear of having them also as judges?

My jealous curiosity as to what Albertine might have done was unbounded. I suborned any number of women from whom I learned nothing. If this curiosity was so keen, it was because people do not die at once for us, they remain bathed in a sort of *aura* of life in which there is no true immortality but which means that they continue to occupy our thoughts in the same way as when they were alive. It is as though they were travelling abroad. This is a thoroughly pagan survival. Conversely, when we have ceased to love her, the curiosity which the person arouses dies before she herself is dead. Thus I would no longer have taken any step to find out with whom Gilberte had been strolling on a certain evening in the Champs-Elysées. Now I felt that these curiosities were absolutely alike, had no value in themselves, were incapable of lasting, but I continued to sacrifice everything to the cruel satisfaction of this transient curiosity, albeit I knew in advance that my enforced separation from Albertine, by the fact of her death, would lead me to the same indifference as had resulted from my deliberate separation from Gilberte.

If she could have known what was about to happen, she would have stayed with me. But this meant no more than that, once she saw herself dead, she would have preferred, in my company, to remain alive. Simply in view of the contradiction that it implied, such a supposition was absurd. But it was not innocuous, for in imagining how glad Albertine would be, if she could know, if she could retrospectively understand, to come back to me, I saw her before me, I wanted to kiss her; and alas, it was impossible, she would never come back, she was dead. My imagination sought for her in the sky, through the nights on which we had gazed at it when still together; beyond that moonlight which she loved, I tried to raise up to her my affection so that it might be a consolation to her for being no longer alive, and this love for a being so remote was like a religion, my thoughts rose towards her like prayers. Desire is very powerful, it engenders belief; I had believed that Albertine would not leave me because I desired that she might not. Because I desired it, I began to believe that she was not dead; I took to reading books upon table-turning, I began to believe in the possibility of the immortality of the soul. But that did not suffice me. I required that, after my own death, I should find her again in her body, as though eternity were like life. Life, did I say! I was more exacting still. I would have wished not to be deprived for ever by death of the pleasures of which however it is not alone in robbing us. For without her death they would eventually have grown faint, they had begun already to do so by the action of long-established habit, of fresh curiosities. Besides, had she been alive, Albertine, even physically, would gradually have changed, day by day I should have adapted myself to that change. But my memory, calling up only detached moments of her life, asked to see her again as she would already have ceased to be, had she lived; what it required was a miracle which would satisfy the natural and

arbitrary limitations of memory which cannot emerge from
the past. With the simplicity of the old theologians, I
imagined her furnishing me not indeed with the explanations which she might possibly have given me, but, by a
final contradiction, with those that she had always refused
me during her life. And thus, her death being a sort of
dream, my love would seem to her an unlooked-for happiness; I saw in death only the convenience and optimism of a
solution which simplifies, which arranges everything.
Sometimes it was not so far off, it was not in another world
that I imagined our reunion. Just as in the past, when I
knew Gilberte only from playing with her in the Champs-
Elysées, at home in the evening I used to imagine that I
was going to receive a letter from her in which she would
confess her love for me, that she was coming into the room,
so a similar force of desire, no more embarrassed by the laws
of nature which ran counter to it than on the former occasion in the case of Gilberte, when after all it had not been
mistaken since it had had the last word, made me think now
that I was going to receive a message from Albertine,
informing me that she had indeed met with an accident
while riding, but that for romantic reasons (and as, after all,
has sometimes happened with people whom we have long
believed to be dead) she had not wished me to hear of her
recovery and now, repentant, asked to be allowed to come
and live with me for ever. And, making quite clear to
myself the nature of certain harmless manias in people who
otherwise appear sane, I felt co-existing in myself the certainty that she was dead and the incessant hope that I might
see her come into the room.

I had not yet received any news from Aimé, albeit he

must by now have reached Balbec. No doubt my inquiry turned upon a secondary point, and one quite arbitrarily selected. If Albertine's life had been really culpable, it must have contained many other things of far greater importance, which chance had not allowed me to touch, as it had allowed me that conversation about the wrapper thanks to Albertine's blushes. It was quite arbitrarily that I had been presented with that particular day, which many years later I was seeking to reconstruct. If Albertine had been a lover of women, there were thousands of other days in her life her employment of which I did not know and about which it might be as interesting for me to learn; I might have sent Aimé to many other places in Balbec, to many other towns than Balbec. But these other days, precisely because I did not know how she had spent them, did not represent themselves to my imagination. They had no existence. Things, people did not begin to exist for me until they assumed in my imagination an individual existence. If there were thousands of others like them, they became for me representative of all the rest. If I had long felt a desire to know, in the matter of my suspicions with regard to Albertine, what exactly had happened in the baths, it was in the same manner in which, in the matter of my desires for women, and although I knew that there were any number of girls and lady's-maids who could satisfy them and whom chance might just as easily have led me to hear mentioned, I wished to know—since it was of them that Saint-Loup had spoken to me—the girl who frequented houses of ill fame and Mme Putbus's maid. The difficulties which my health, my indecision, my " procrastination," as M. de Charlus called it, placed in the way of my carrying out any project, had made me put off from day to day, from month to month, from year to year, the elucidation of certain suspicions as also the accomplishment of certain desires. But I kept them in my memory promising myself that I would not forget to learn the truth of them, because they alone obsessed me (since the others had no form in my eyes, did not exist), and also because the very accident that had chosen them out of the surrounding reality gave me a guarantee that it was indeed in them that I should come in contact with a trace of reality, of the true and coveted life.

Besides, from a single fact, if it is certain, can we not, like a scientist making experiments, extract the truth as to all the orders of similar facts? Is not a single little fact, if it is well chosen, sufficient to enable the experimenter to deduce a general law which will make him know the truth as to thousands of analogous facts?

Albertine might indeed exist in my memory only in the state in which she had successively appeared to me in the course of her life, that is to say subdivided according to a series of fractions of time, my mind, reestablishing unity in her, made her a single person, and it was upon this person that I sought to bring a general judgment to bear, to know whether she had lied to me, whether she loved women, whether it was in order to be free to associate with them that she had left me. What the woman in the baths would have to say might perhaps put an end for ever to my doubts as to Albertine's morals.

My doubts! Alas, I had supposed that it would be immaterial to me, even pleasant, not to see Albertine again, until her departure revealed to me my error. Similarly her death had shewn me how greatly I had been mistaken when I believed that I hoped at times for her death and supposed that it would be my deliverance. So it was that, when I received Aimé's letter, I realised that, if I had not until then suffered too painfully from my doubts as to Albertine's virtue, it was because in reality they were not doubts at all. My happiness, my life required that Albertine should be virtuous, they had laid it down once and for all time that she was. Furnished with this preservative belief, I could without danger allow my mind to play sadly with suppositions to which it gave a form but added no faith. I said to myself, " She is perhaps a woman-lover," as we say " I may die to-night "; we say it, but we do not believe it, we make plans for the morrow. This explains why, believing mistakenly that I was uncertain whether Albertine did or did not love women, and believing in consequence that a proof of Albertine's guilt would not give me anything that I had not already taken into account, I was able to feel before the pictures, insignificant to anyone else, which Aimé's letter called up to me, an unexpected anguish, the most painful that I had ever yet felt, and one that formed with those pictures, with the picture, alas! of Albertine herself, a sort of precipitate, as chemists say, in which the whole was invisible and of which the text of Aimé's letter, which I isolate in a purely conventional fashion, can give no idea whatsoever, since each of the words that compose it was immediately transformed, coloured for ever by the suffering that it had aroused.

" MONSIEUR,

" Monsieur will kindly forgive me for not having written sooner to Monsieur. The person whom Monsieur instructed me to see had gone away for a few days, and, anxious to justify the confidence which Monsieur had placed in me, I did not wish to return empty-handed. I have just spoken to this person who remembers (Mlle A.) quite well." Aimé who possessed certain rudiments of culture meant to italicise *Mlle A.* between inverted commas. But when he meant to write inverted commas, he wrote brackets, and when he meant to write something in brackets he put it between inverted commas. Thus it was that Françoise would say that someone *stayed* in my street meaning that he abode there, and that one could *abide* for a few minutes, meaning *stay*, the mistakes of popular speech consisting merely, as often as not, in interchanging—as for that matter the French language has done—terms which in the course of centuries have replaced one another. " According to her the thing that Monsieur supposed is absolutely certain. For one thing, it was she who looked after (Mlle A.) whenever she came to the baths. (Mlle A.) came very often to take her bath with a tall woman older than herself, always dressed in grey, whom the bath-woman without knowing her name recognised from having often seen her going after girls. But she took no notice of any of them after she met (Mlle A.). She and (Mlle A.) always shut themselves up in the dressing-box, remained there a very long time, and the lady in grey used to give at least 10 francs as a tip to the person to whom I spoke. As this person said to me, you can imagine that if they were just stringing beads, they wouldn't have given a tip of ten francs. (Mlle A.) used to come also sometimes with a woman with a very dark skin and long handled glasses.

But (Mlle A.) came most often with girls younger than herself, especially one with a high complexion. Apart from the lady in grey, the people whom (Mlle A.) was in the habit of bringing were not from Balbec and must indeed often have come from quite a distance. They never came in together, but (Mlle A.) would come in, and ask for the door of her box to be left unlocked—as she was expecting a friend, and the person to whom I spoke knew what that meant. This person could not give me any other details, as she does not remember very well, ' which is easily understood after so long an interval.' Besides, this person did not try to find out, because she is very discreet and it was to her advantage, for (Mlle A.) brought her in a lot of money. She was quite sincerely touched to hear that she was dead. It is true that so young it is a great calamity for her and for her friends. I await Monsieur's orders to know whether I may leave Balbec where I do not think that I can learn anything more. I thank Monsieur again for the little holiday that he has procured me, and which has been very pleasant especially as the weather is as fine as could be. The season promises well for this year. We hope that Monsieur will come and put in a little appearance.

" I can think of nothing else to say that will interest Monsieur."

To understand how deeply these words penetrated my being, the reader must bear in mind that the questions which I had been asking myself with regard to Albertine were not subordinate, immaterial questions, questions of detail, the only questions as a matter of fact which we ask ourself about anyone who is not ourself, whereby we are enabled to proceed, wrapped in an impenetrable thought, through the midst of suffering, falsehood, vice or death. No, in Albertine's case, they were essential questions: " In her heart of hearts what was she? What were her thoughts? What were her loves? Did she lie to me? Had my life with her been as lamentable as Swann's life with Odette? " And so the point reached by Aimé's reply, even although it was not a general reply—and precisely for that reason—was indeed in Albertine, in myself, the uttermost depths.

At last I saw before my eyes, in that arrival of Albertine at the baths along the narrow lane with the lady in grey, a fragment of that past which seemed to me no less mysterious, no less alarming than I had feared when I imagined it as enclosed in the memory, in the facial expression of Albertine. No doubt anyone but myself might have dismissed as insignificant these details, upon which my inability, now that Albertine was dead, to secure a denial of them from herself, conferred the equivalent of a sort of likelihood. It is indeed probable that for Albertine, even if they had been true, her own misdeeds, if she had admitted them, whether her conscience thought them innocent or reprehensible, whether her sensuality had found them exquisite or distinctly dull, would not have been accompanied by that inexpressible sense of horror from which I was unable to detach them. I myself, with the help of my own love of women, albeit they could not have been the same thing to Albertine, could more or less imagine what she felt. And indeed it was already a first degree of anguish, merely to picture her to myself desiring as I had so often desired, lying to me as I had so often lied to her, preoccupied with one girl or another, putting herself out for her, as I had done for Mlle de Stermaria and ever so many others, not to mention the peasant girls whom I met on country roads. Yes, all my own desires helped me to understand, to a certain degree, what hers had been; it was by this time an intense anguish in which all my desires, the keener they had been, had changed into torments that were all the more cruel; as though in this algebra of sensibility they reappeared with the same coefficient but with a minus instead of a plus sign. To Albertine, so far as I was capable of judging her by my own standard, her misdeeds, however anxious she might have been to conceal them from me—which made me suppose that she was conscious of her guilt or was afraid of grieving me—her misdeeds because she had planned them to suit her own taste in the clear light of imagination in which desire plays, appeared to her nevertheless as things of the same nature as the rest of life, pleasures for herself which she had not had the courage to deny herself, griefs for me which she had sought to avoid causing me by concealing them, but pleasures and griefs which might be numbered among the other pleasures and griefs of life. But for me, it was from without, without my having been forewarned, without my having been able myself to elaborate them, it was from Aimé's letter that there had come to me the visions of Albertine arriving at the baths and preparing her gratuity.

No doubt it was because in that silent and deliberate arrival of Albertine with the woman in grey I read the assignation that they had made, that convention of going to make love in a dressing-box which implied an experience of corruption, the well-concealed organisation of a double life, it was because these images brought me the terrible

tidings of Albertine's guilt that they had immediately
caused me a physical grief from which they would never in
time to come be detached. But at once my grief had re-
acted upon them: an objective fact, such as an image, differs
according to the internal state in which we approach it.
And grief is as potent in altering reality as is drunkenness.
Combined with these images, suffering had at once made of
them something absolutely different from what might be
for anyone else a lady in grey, a gratuity, a bath, the street
which had witnessed the deliberate arrival of Albertine with
the lady in grey. All these images—escaping from a life of
falsehood and misconduct such as I had never conceived—
my suffering had immediately altered in their very substance, I did not behold them in the light that illuminates
earthly spectacles, they were a fragment of another world,
of an unknown and accursed planet, a glimpse of Hell.
My Hell was all that Balbec, all those neighbouring villages
from which, according to Aimé's letter, she frequently
collected girls younger than herself whom she took to the
baths. That mystery which I had long ago imagined in
the country around Balbec and which had been dispelled
after I had stayed there, which I had then hoped to grasp
again when I knew Albertine because, when I saw her pass
me on the beach, when I was mad enough to desire that
she might not be virtuous, I thought that she must be its
incarnation, how fearfully now everything that related to
Balbec was impregnated with it. The names of those
stations, Toutaineville, Epreville, Parville, grown so
familiar, so soothing, when I heard them shouted at night
as I returned from the Verdurins, now that I thought how
Albertine had been staying at the last, had gone from there

to the second, must have often ridden on her bicycle to the first, they aroused in me an anxiety more cruel than on the first occasion, when I beheld the places with such misgivings, before arriving at a Balbec which I did not yet know. It is one of the faculties of jealousy to reveal to us the extent to which the reality of external facts and the sentiments of the heart are an unknown element which lends itself to endless suppositions. We suppose that we know exactly what things are and what people think, for the simple reason that we do not care about them. But as soon as we feel the desire to know, which the jealous man feels, then it becomes a dizzy kaleidoscope in which we can no longer make out anything. Had Albertine been unfaithful to me? With whom? In what house? Upon what day? The day on which she had said this or that to me? When I remembered that I had in the course of it said this or that? I could not tell. Nor did I know what were her sentiments towards myself, whether they were inspired by financial interest, by affection. And all of a sudden I remembered some trivial incident, for instance that Albertine had wished to go to Saint-Mars le Vêtu, saying that the name interested her, and perhaps simply because she had made the acquaintance of some peasant girl who lived there. But it was nothing that Aimé should have found out all this for me from the woman at the baths, since Albertine must remain eternally unaware that he had informed me, the need to know having always been exceeded, in my love for Albertine, by the need to shew her that I knew; for this abolished between us the partition of different illusions, without having ever had the result of making her love me more, far from it. And now, after she was dead, the second of these needs had been amalgamated with the effect of the first: I tried to picture to myself the conversation in which I would have informed her of what I had learned, as vividly as the conversation in which I would have asked her to tell me what I did not know; that is to say, to see her by my side, to hear her answering me kindly, to see her cheeks become plump again, her eyes shed their malice and assume an air of melancholy ; that is to say, to love her still and to forget the fury of my jealousy in the despair of my loneliness. The painful mystery of this impossibility of ever making her know what I had learned and of establishing our relations upon the truth of what I had only just discovered (and would not have been able, perhaps, to discover, but for the fact of her death) substituted its sadness for the more painful mystery of her conduct. What? To have so keenly desired that Albertine should know that I had heard the story of the baths, Albertine who no longer existed! This again was one of the consequences of our utter inability, when we have to consider the matter of death, to picture to ourself anything but life. Albertine no longer existed. But to me she was the person who had concealed from me that she had assignations with women at Balbec, who imagined that she had succeeded in keeping me in ignorance of them. When we try to consider what happens to us after our own death, is it not still our living self which by mistake we project before us? And is it much more absurd, when all is said, to regret that a woman who no longer exists is unaware that we have learned what she was doing six years ago than to desire that of ourself, who will be dead, the public shall still speak with approval a century hence? If there is more real foundation in the latter than in the former case, the regrets of my retrospective jealousy proceeded none the less from the same optical error as in other men the desire for posthumous fame. And yet this impression of all the solemn finality that there was in my separation from Albertine, if it had been substituted for a moment for my idea of her misdeeds, only aggravated them by bestowing upon them an irremediable character.

I saw myself astray in life as upon an endless beach where I was alone and, in whatever direction I might turn, would never meet her. Fortunately, I found most appropriately in my memory—as there are always all sorts of things, some noxious, others salutary in that heap from which individual impressions come to light only one by one—I discovered, as a craftsman discovers the material that can serve for what he wishes to make, a speech of my grandmother's. She had said to me, with reference to an improbable story which the bath-woman had told Mme de Villeparisis: " She is a woman who must suffer from a disease of mendacity." This memory was a great comfort to me. What importance could the story have that the woman had told Aimé? Especially as, after all, she had seen nothing. A girl can come and take baths with her friends without having any evil intention. Perhaps for her own glorification the woman had exaggerated the amount of the gratuity. I had indeed heard Françoise maintain once that my aunt Léonie had said in her hearing that she had " a million a month to spend," which was utter nonsense; another time that she had seen my aunt Léonie give Eulalie four thousand-franc notes, whereas a fifty-franc note folded in four seemed to me scarcely probable. And so I thought—and, in course of time, managed—to rid myself of the painful certainty which I had taken such trouble to acquire, tossed to and fro as I still was between the desire to know and the fear of suffering. Then my affection might revive afresh, but, simultaneously with it, a sorrow at being parted from Albertine, during the course of which I was perhaps even more wretched than in the recent hours when it had been jealousy that tormented me. But my jealousy was suddenly revived, when I thought of Balbec, because of the vision which at once reappeared (and which until then had never made me suffer and indeed appeared one of the most innocuous in my memory) of the dining-room at Balbec in the evening, with, on the other side of the windows, all that populace crowded together in the dusk, as before the luminous glass of an aquarium, producing a contact (of which I had never thought) in their conglomeration, between the fishermen and girls of the lower orders and the young ladies jealous of that splendour new to Balbec, that splendour from which, if not their means, at any rate avarice and tradition debarred their parents, young ladies among whom there had certainly been almost every evening Albertine whom I did not then know and who doubtless used to accost some little girl whom she would meet a few minutes later in the dark, upon the sands, or else in a deserted bathing hut at the foot of the cliff. Then it was my sorrow that revived, I had just heard like a sentence of banishment the sound of the lift, which instead of stopping at my floor, went on higher. And yet the only person from whom I could have hoped for a visit would never come again, she was dead. And in spite of this, when the lift did stop at my floor, my heart throbbed, for an instant I said to myself: " If, after all, it was only a dream! It is perhaps she, she is going to ring the bell, she has come back, Françoise will come in and say with more alarm than anger —for she is even more superstitious than vindictive, and would be less afraid of the living girl than of what she will perhaps take for a ghost—' Monsieur will never guess who is here.' " I tried not to think of anything, to take up a newspaper. But I found it impossible to read the articles written by men who felt no real grief. Of a trivial song, one of them said: " It moves one to *tears*," whereas I myself would have listened to it with joy had Albertine been alive. Another, albeit a great writer, because he had been greeted with cheers when he alighted from a train, said that he had received " an *unforgettable* welcome," whereas I, if it had been I who received that welcome, would not have given it even a moment's thought. And a third assured his readers that, but for its tiresome politics life in Paris would be " altogether delightful " whereas I knew well that even without politics that life could be nothing but atrocious to me, and would have seemed to me delightful, even with its politics, could I have found Albertine again. The sporting correspondent said (we were in the month of May): " This season of the year is positively painful, let us say rather disastrous, to the true sportsman, for there is nothing, absolutely nothing in the way of game," and the art critic said of the Salon: " In the face of this method of arranging an exhibition we are overwhelmed by an immense discouragement, by an infinite regret. . . ." If the force of the regret that I was feeling made me regard as untruthful and colourless the expressions of men who had no true happiness or sorrow in their lives, on the other hand

146

the most insignificant lines which could, however remotely, attach themselves either to Normandy, or to Touraine, or to hydropathic establishments, or to Léa, or to the
Princesse de Guermantes, or to love, or to absence, or to
infidelity, at once set before my eyes, without my having
the time to turn them away from it, the image of Albertine,
and my tears started afresh. Besides, in the ordinary
course, I could never read these newspapers, for the mere
act of opening one of them reminded me at once that I used
to open them when Albertine was alive, and that she was
alive no longer; I let them drop without having the strength
to unfold their pages. Each impression called up an impression that was identical but marred, because there had
been cut out of it Albertine's existence, so that I had never
the courage to live to the end these mutilated minutes.
Indeed, when little by little, Albertine ceased to be present
in my thoughts and all-powerful over my heart, I was
stabbed at once if I had occasion, as in the time when she
was there, to go into her room, to grope for the light, to sit
down by the pianola. Divided among the number of little
household gods, she dwelt for a long time in the flame of
the candle, the door-bell, the back of a chair, and other
domains more immaterial such as a night of insomnia or the
emotion that was caused me by the first visit of a woman
who had attracted me. In spite of this the few sentences
which I read in the course of a day of which my mind recalled that I had read, often aroused in me a cruel jealousy.
To do this, they required not so much to supply me with a
valid argument in favour of the immorality of women as
to revive an old impression connected with the life of Albertine. Transported then to a forgotten moment, the

force of which my habit of thinking of it had not dulled, and in which Albertine was still alive, her misdeeds became more immediate, more painful, more agonising. Then I asked myself whether I could be certain that the bath-woman's revelations were false. A good way of finding out the truth would be to send Aimé to Touraine, to spend a few days in the neighbourhood of Mme Bontemps's villa. If Albertine enjoyed the pleasures which one woman takes with others, if it was in order not to be deprived of them any longer that she had left me, she must, as soon as she was free, have sought to indulge in them and have succeeded, in a district which she knew and to which she would not have chosen to retire had she not expected to find greater facilities there than in my house. No doubt there was nothing extraordinary in the fact that Albertine's death had so little altered my preoccupations. When our mistress is alive, a great part of the thoughts which form what we call our loves come to us during the hours when she is not by our side. Thus we acquire the habit of having as the object of our meditation an absent person, and one who, even if she remains absent for a few hours only, during those hours is no more than a memory. And so death does not make any great difference. When Aimé returned, I asked him to go down to Chatellerault, and thus not only by my thoughts, my sorrows, the emotion caused me by a name connected, however remotely, with a certain person, but even more by all my actions, by the inquiries that I undertook, by the use that I made of my money, all of which was devoted to the discovery of Albertine's actions, I may say that throughout this year my life remained filled with love, with a true bond of affection.

And she who was its object was a corpse. We say at times that something may survive of a man after his death, if the man was an artist and took a certain amount of pains with his work. It is perhaps in the same way that a sort of cutting taken from one person and grafted on the heart of another continues to carry on its existence, even when the person from whom it had been detached has perished. Aimé established himself in quarters close to Mme Bontemps's villa; he made the acquaintance of a maidservant, of a jobmaster from whom Albertine had often hired a carriage by the day. These people had noticed nothing. In a second letter, Aimé informed me that he had learned from a young laundress in the town that Albertine had a peculiar way of gripping her arm when she brought back the clean linen. "But," she said, "the young lady never did anything more." I sent Aimé the money that paid for his journey, that paid for the harm which he had done me by his letter, and at the same time I was making an effort to discount it by telling myself that this was a familiarity which gave no proof of any vicious desire when I received a telegram from Aimé: "Have learned most interesting things have abundant proofs letter follows." On the following day came a letter the envelope of which was enough to make me tremble; I had guessed that it came from Aimé, for everyone, even the humblest of us, has under his control those little familiar spirits at once living and couched in a sort of trance upon the paper, the characters of his handwriting which he alone possesses. "At first the young laundress refused to tell me anything, she assured me that Mlle Albertine had never done anything more than pinch her arm. But to get her to talk, I took her out to dinner, I made her drink. Then she told me that Mlle Albertine used often to meet her on the bank of the Loire, when she went to bathe, that Mlle Albertine who was in the habit of getting up very early to go and bathe was in the habit of meeting her by the water's edge, at a spot where the trees are so thick that nobody can see you, and besides there is nobody who can see you at that hour in the morning. Then the young laundress brought her friends and they bathed and afterwards, as it was already very hot down here and the sun scorched you even through the trees, they used to lie about on the grass getting dry and playing and caressing each other. The young laundress confessed to me that she loved to amuse herself with her young friends and that seeing Mlle Albertine was always wiggling against her in her wrapper she made her take it off and used to caress her with her tongue along the throat and arms, even on the soles of her feet which Mlle Albertine stretched out to her. The laundress undressed too, and they played at pushing each other into the water; after that she told me nothing more, but being entirely at your orders and ready to do anything in the world to please you, I took the young laundress to bed with me. She asked me if I would like her to do to me what she used to do to Mlle Albertine when she took off her bathing-dress. And she said to me: ' If you could have seen how she used to quiver, that young lady, she said to me (oh, it's just heavenly) and she got so excited that she could not keep from biting me.' I could still see the marks on the girl's arms. And I can understand Mlle Albertine's pleasure, for the girl is really a very good performer."

I had indeed suffered at Balbec when Albertine told me

of her friendship with Mlle Vinteuil. But Albertine was there to comfort me. Afterwards when, by my excessive curiosity as to her actions, I had succeeded in making Albertine leave me, when Françoise informed me that she was no longer in the house and I found myself alone, I had suffered more keenly still. But at least the Albertine whom I had loved remained in my heart. Now, in her place—to punish me for having pushed farther a curiosity to which, contrary to what I had supposed, death had not put an end—what I found was a different girl, heaping up lies and deceits one upon another, in the place where the former had so sweetly reassured me by swearing that she had never tasted those pleasures, which in the intoxication of her recaptured liberty, she had gone down to enjoy to the point of swooning, of biting that young laundress whom she used to meet at sunrise on the bank of the Loire, and to whom she used to say " Oh, it's just heavenly." A different Albertine, not only in the sense in which we understand the word different when it is used of other people. If people are different from what we have supposed, as this difference cannot affect us profoundly, as the pendulum of intuition cannot move outward with a greater oscillation than that of its inward movement, it is only in the superficial regions of the people themselves that we place these differences. Formerly, when I learned that a woman loved other women, she did not for that reason seem to me a different woman, of a peculiar essence. But when it is a question of a woman with whom we are in love, in order to rid ourself of the grief that we feel at the thought that such a thing is possible, we seek to find out not only what she has done, but what she felt while she was doing it, what idea she had in her mind of the thing that she was doing; then descending and advancing farther and farther, by the profundity of our grief we attain to the mystery, to the essence. I was pained internally, in my body, in my heart—far more than I should have been pained by the fear of losing my life—by this curiosity with which all the force of my intellect and of my subconscious self collaborated; and similarly it was into the core of Albertine's own being that I now projected everything that I learned about her. And the grief that had thus caused to penetrate to so great a depth in my own being the fact of Albertine's vice, was to render me later on a final service. Like the harm that I had done my grandmother, the harm that Albertine had done me was a last bond between her and myself which outlived memory even, for with the conservation of energy which belongs to everything that is physical, suffering has no need of the lessons of memory. Thus a man who has forgotten the charming night spent by moonlight in the woods, suffers still from the rheumatism which he then contracted. Those tastes which she had denied but which were hers, those tastes the discovery of which had come to me not by a cold process of reasoning but in the burning anguish that I had felt on reading the words: " Oh, it's just heavenly," a suffering which gave them a special quality of their own, those tastes were not merely added to the image of Albertine as is added to the hermit-crab the new shell which it drags after it, but, rather, like a salt which comes in contact with another salt, alters its colour, and what is more, its nature. When the young laundress must have said to her young friend: " Just fancy, I would never have believed it, well, the young lady is one too! " to me it was not merely a vice hitherto unsuspected by them that they added to Albertine's person, but the discovery that she was another person, a person like themselves, speaking the same language, which, by making her the compatriot of other women made her even more alien to myself, proved that what I had possessed of her, what I carried in my heart, was only quite a small part of her, and that the rest which was made so extensive by not being merely that thing so mysteriously important, an individual desire, but being shared with others, she had always concealed from me, she had kept me aloof from it, as a woman might have concealed from me that she was a native of an enemy country and a spy; and would indeed have been acting even more treacherously than a spy, for a spy deceives us only as to her nationality, whereas Albertine had deceived me as to her profoundest humanity, the fact that she did not belong to the ordinary human race, but to an alien race which moves among it; conceals itself among it and never blends with it. I had as it happened seen two paintings by Elstir shewing against a leafy background nude women.   In one of them, one of the girls is raising her foot as Albertine must have raised hers when she offered it to the laundress.   With her other foot she is pushing into the water the other girl, who gaily resists, her hip bent, her foot barely submerged in the blue water.   I remembered now that the raising of the thigh made the same swan's-neck curve with the angle of the knee that was made by the droop of Albertine's thigh when she was lying by my side on the bed, and I had often meant to tell her that she reminded me of those paintings. But I had refrained from doing so, in order not to awaken in her mind the image of nude female bodies.   Now I saw her, side by side with the laundress and her friends, recomposing the group which I had so admired when I was seated among Albertine's friends at Balbec. And if I had been an enthusiast sensitive to absolute beauty, I should have recognised that Albertine recomposed it with a thousand times more beauty, now that its elements were the nude statues of goddesses like those which consummate sculptors scattered about the groves of Versailles or plunged in the fountains to be washed and polished by the caresses of their eddies. Now I saw her by the side of the laundress girls by the water's edge, in their two-fold nudity of marble maidens in the midst of a grove of vegetation and dipping into the water like bas-reliefs of Naiads. Remembering how Albertine looked as she lay upon my bed, I thought I could see her bent hip, I saw it, it was a swan's neck, it was seeking the hips of the other girl. Then I beheld no longer a leg, but the bold neck of a swan, like that which in a frenzied sketch seeks the lips of a Leda whom we see in all the palpitation peculiar to feminine pleasures, because there is nothing else but a swan, and she seems more alone, just as we discover upon the telephone the inflexions of a voice which we do not distinguish so long as it is not dissociated from a face in which we materialise its expression. In this sketch, the pleasure, instead of going to seek the face which inspires it and which is absent, replaced by a motionless swan, is concentrated in her who feels it. At certain moments the communication was cut between my heart and my memory. What Albertine had done with the laundress was indicated to me now only by almost algebraical abbreviations which no longer meant anything to me; but a hundred times in an hour the interrupted current was

restored, and my heart was pitilessly scorched by a fire from
hell, while I saw Albertine, raised to life by my jealousy,
really alive, stiffen beneath the caresses of the young laundress, to whom she was saying: " Oh, it's just heavenly."
As she was alive at the moment when she committed her
misdeeds, that is to say at the moment at which I myself
found myself placed, it was not sufficient to know of the
misdeed, I wished her to know that I knew. And so, if
at those moments I thought with regret that I should never
see her again, this regret bore the stamp of my jealousy,
and, very different from the lacerating regret of the moments in which I loved her, was only regret at not being
able to say to her: " You thought that I should never
know what you did after you left me, well, I know everything, the laundress on the bank of the Loire, you said to
her: ' Oh, it's just heavenly,' I have seen the bite." No
doubt I said to myself: " Why torment myself? She who
took her pleasure with the laundress no longer exists, and
consequently was not a person whose actions retain any
importance. She is not telling herself that I know. But
no more is she telling herself that I do not know, since she
tells herself nothing." But this line of reasoning convinced me less than the visual image of her pleasure which
brought me back to the moment in which she had tasted it.
What we feel is the only thing that exists for us, and we
project it into the past, into the future, without letting ourself be stopped by the fictitious barriers of death. If my
regret that she was dead was subjected at such moments to
the influences of my jealousy and assumed this so peculiar
form, that influence extended over my dreams of occultism,
of immortality, which were no more than an effort to

realise what I desired. And so at those moments if I could have succeeded in evoking her by turning a table as Bergotte had at one time thought possible, or in meeting her in the other life as the abbé X thought, I would have wished to do so only in order to repeat to her: " I know about the laundress. You said to her: ' Oh, it's just heavenly,' I have seen the bite." What came to my rescue against this image of the laundress, was—certainly when it had endured for any while—the image itself, because we really know only what is novel, what suddenly introduces into our sensibility a change of tone which strikes us, the things for which habit has not yet substituted its colourless facsimiles. But it was, above all, this subdivision of Albertine in many fragments, in many Albertines, which was her sole mode of existence in me. Moments recurred in which she had merely been good, or intelligent, or serious, or even addicted to nothing but sport. And this subdivision, was it not after all proper that it should soothe me? For if it was not in itself anything real, if it depended upon the successive form of the hours in which it had appeared to me, a form which remained that of my memory as the curve of the projections of my magic lantern depended upon the curve of the coloured slides, did it not represent in its own manner a truth, a thoroughly objective truth too, to wit that each one of us is not a single person, but contains many persons who have not all the same moral value and that if a vicious Albertine had existed, it did not mean that there had not been others, she who enjoyed talking to me about Saint-Simon in her room, she who on the night when I had told her that we must part had said so sadly: " That pianola, this room, to think that I shall never see any of

these things again " and, when she saw the emotion which
my lie had finally communicated to myself, had exclaimed
with a sincere pity: "Oh, no, anything rather than make
you unhappy, I promise that I will never try to see you
again." Then I was no longer alone. I felt the wall that
separated us vanish. At the moment in which the good
Albertine had returned, I had found again the one person
from whom I could demand the antidote to the sufferings
which Albertine was causing me. True, I still wanted to
speak to her about the story of the laundress, but it was no
longer by way of a cruel triumph, and to shew her malici-
ously how much I knew. As I should have done had
Albertine been alive, I asked her tenderly whether the tale
about the laundress was true. She swore to me that it was
not, that Aimé was not truthful and that, wishing to appear
to have earned the money which I had given him, he had
not liked to return with nothing to shew, and had made the
laundress tell him what he wished to hear. No doubt Albertine had been lying to me throughout. And yet, in the
flux and reflux of her contradictions, I felt that there had
been a certain progression due to myself. That she had not
indeed made me, at the outset, admission (perhaps, it is true,
involuntary in a phrase that escaped her lips) I would not
have sworn. I no longer remembered. And besides she
had such odd ways of naming certain things, that they
might be interpreted in one sense or the other, but the feeling that she had had of my jealousy had led her afterwards
to retract with horror what at first she had complacently
admitted. Anyhow, Albertine had no need to tell me
this. To be convinced of her innocence it was enough for
me to embrace her, and I could do so now that the wall was

down which parted us, like that impalpable and resisting wall which after a quarrel rises between two lovers and against which kisses would be shattered. No, she had no need to tell me anything. Whatever she might have done, whatever she might have wished to do, the poor child, there were sentiments in which, over the barrier that divided us, we could be united. If the story was true, and if Albertine had concealed her tastes from me, it was in order not to make me unhappy. I had the pleasure of hearing this Albertine say so. Besides, had I ever known any other? The two chief causes of error in our relations with another person are, having ourself a good heart, or else being in love with the other person. We fall in love for a smile, a glance, a bare shoulder. That is enough; then, in the long hours of hope or sorrow, we fabricate a person, we compose a character. And when later on we see much of the beloved person, we can no more, whatever the cruel reality that confronts us, strip off that good character, that nature of a woman who loves us, from the person who bestows that glance, bares that shoulder, than we can when she has grown old eliminate her youthful face from a person whom we have known since her girlhood. I called to mind the noble glance, kind and compassionate, of that Albertine, her plump cheeks, the coarse grain of her throat. It was the image of a dead woman, but, as this dead woman was alive, it was easy for me to do immediately what I should inevitably have done if she had been by my side in her living body (what I should do were I ever to meet her again in another life), I forgave her.

The moments which I had spent with this Albertine were so precious to me that I would not have let any of them escape me. Now, at times, as we recover the remnants of a squandered fortune, I recaptured some of these which I had thought to be lost; as I tied a scarf behind my neck instead of in front, I remembered a drive of which I had never thought again, before which, in order that the cold air might not reach my throat, Albertine had arranged my scarf for me in this way after first kissing me. This simple drive, restored to my memory by so humble a gesture, gave me the same pleasure as the intimate objects once the property of a dead woman who was dear to us which her old servant brings to us and which are so precious to us; my grief found itself enriched by it, all the more so as I had never given another thought to the scarf in question.

And now Albertine, liberated once more, had resumed her flight; men, women followed her. She was alive in me. I became aware that this prolonged adoration of Albertine was like the ghost of the sentiment that I had felt for her, reproduced its various elements and obeyed the same laws as the sentimental reality which it reflected on the farther side of death. For I felt quite sure that if I could place some interval between my thoughts of Albertine, or if, on the other hand, I had allowed too long an interval to elapse, I should cease to love her; a clean cut would have made me unconcerned about her, as I was now about my grandmother. A period of any length spent without thinking of her would have broken in my memory the continuity which is the very principle of life, which however may be resumed after a certain interval of time. Had not this been the case with my love for Albertine when she was alive, a love which had been able to revive after a quite long interval during which I had never given her a thought? Well, my memory must have been obedient to the same laws, have been unable to endure longer intervals, for all that it did was, like an aurora borealis, to reflect after Albertine's death the sentiment that I had felt for her, it was like the phantom of my love.

At other times my grief assumed so many forms that occasionally I no longer recognised it; I longed to be loved in earnest, decided to seek for a person who would live with me; this seemed to me to be the sign that I no longer loved Albertine, whereas it meant that I loved her still; for the need to be loved in earnest was, just as much as the desire to kiss Albertine's plump cheeks, merely a part of my regret. It was when I had forgotten her that I might feel it to be wiser, happier to live without love. And so my regret for Albertine, because it was it that aroused in me the need of a sister, made that need insatiable. And in proportion as my regret for Albertine grew fainter, the need of a sister, which was only an unconscious form of that regret, would become less imperious. And yet these two residues of my love did not proceed to shrink at an equal rate. There were hours in which I had made up my mind to marry, so completely had the former been eclipsed, the latter on the contrary retaining its full strength. And then, later on, my jealous memories having died away, suddenly at times a feeling welled up into my heart of affection for Albertine, and then, thinking of my own love affairs with other women, I told myself that she would have understood, would have shared them—and her vice became almost a reason for loving her. At times my jealousy revived in moments when I no longer remembered Albertine, albeit it was of her that I was jealous. I thought that I was jealous of Andrée, of one of whose recent adventures I had just been informed. But Andrée was to me merely a substitute, a bypath, a conduit which brought me indirectly to Albertine. So it is that in our dreams we give a different face, a different name to a person as to whose underlying identity we are not mistaken. When all was said, notwithstanding the flux and reflux which upset in these particular instances the general law, the sentiments that Albertine had left with me were more difficult to extinguish than the memory of their original cause. Not only the sentiments, but the sensations. Different in this respect from Swann who, when he had begun to cease to love Odette, had not even been able to recreate in himself the sensation of his love, I felt myself still reliving a past which was no longer anything more than the history of another person; my ego in a sense cloven in twain, while its upper extremity was already hard and frigid, burned still at its base whenever a spark made the old current pass through it, even after my mind had long ceased to conceive Albertine. And as no image of her accompanied the cruel palpitations, the tears that were brought to my eyes by a cold wind blowing as at Balbec upon the apple trees that were already pink with blossom, I was led to ask myself whether the renewal of my grief was not due to entirely pathological causes and whether what I took to be the revival of a memory and the final period of a state of love was not rather the first stage of heart-disease.

There are in certain affections secondary accidents which the sufferer is too apt to confuse with the malady itself. When they cease, he is surprised to find himself nearer to recovery than he has supposed. Of this sort had been the suffering caused me—the complication brought about—by

Aimé's letters with regard to the bathing establishment and the young laundress. But a healer of broken hearts, had such a person visited me, would have found that, in other respects, my grief itself was on the way to recovery. No doubt in myself, since I was a man, one of those amphibious creatures who are plunged simultaneously in the past and in the reality of the moment, there still existed a contradiction between the living memory of Albertine and my consciousness of her death. But this contradiction was so to speak the opposite of what it had been before. The idea that Albertine was dead, this idea which at first used to contest so furiously with the idea that she was alive that I was obliged to run away from it as children run away from a breaking wave, this idea of her death, by the very force of its incessant onslaught, had ended by capturing the place in my mind that, a short while ago, was still occupied by the idea of her life. Without my being precisely aware of it, it was now this idea of Albertine's death—no longer the present memory of her life—that formed the chief subject of my unconscious musings, with the result that if I interrupted them suddenly to reflect upon myself, what surprised me was not, as in earlier days, that Albertine so living in myself could be no longer existent upon the earth, could be dead, but that Albertine, who no longer existed upon the earth, who was dead, should have remained so living in myself. Built up by the contiguity of the memories that followed one another, the black tunnel, in which my thoughts had been straying so long that they had even ceased to be aware of it, was suddenly broken by an interval of sunlight, allowing me to see in the distance a blue and smiling universe in which Albertine was no more than a memory, unimportant and full of charm. Is it this, I asked myself, that is the true Albertine, or is it indeed the person who, in the darkness through which I have so long been rolling, seemed to me the sole reality? The person that I had been so short a time ago, who lived only in the perpetual expectation of the moment when Albertine would come in to bid him good-night and to kiss him, a sort of multiplication of myself made this person appear to me as no longer anything more than a feeble part, already half-detached from myself, and like a fading flower I felt the rejuvenating refreshment of an exfoliation. However, these brief illuminations succeeded perhaps only in making me more conscious of my love for Albertine, as happens with every idea that is too constant and has need of opposition to make it affirm itself. People who were alive during the war of 1870, for instance, say that the idea of war ended by seeming to them natural, not because they were not thinking sufficiently of the war, but because they could think of nothing else. And in order to understand how strange and important a fact war is, it was necessary that, some other thing tearing them from their permanent obsession, they should forget for a moment that war was being waged, should find themselves once again as they had been in a state of peace, until all of a sudden upon the momentary blank there stood out at length distinct the monstrous reality which they had long ceased to see, since there had been nothing else visible.

If, again, this withdrawal of my different impressions of Albertine had at least been carried out not in echelon but simultaneously, equally, by a general retirement, along the whole line of my memory, my impressions of her infidelities retiring at the same time as those of her kindness, oblivion would have brought me solace. It was not so. As upon a beach where the tide recedes unevenly, I would be assailed by the rush of one of my suspicions when the image of her tender presence had already withdrawn too far from me to be able to bring me its remedy. As for the infidelities, they had made me suffer, because, however remote the year in which they had occurred, to me they were not remote; but I suffered from them less when they became remote, that is to say when I pictured them to myself less vividly, for the remoteness of a thing is in proportion rather to the visual power of the memory that is looking at it than to the real interval of the intervening days, like the memory of last night's dream which may seem to us more distant in its vagueness and obliteration than an event which is many years old. But albeit the idea of Albertine's death made headway in me, the reflux of the sensation that she was alive, if it did not arrest that progress, obstructed it nevertheless and prevented its being regular. And I realise now that during this period (doubtless because of my having forgotten the hours in which she had been cloistered in my house, hours which, by dint of relieving me from my pain at misdeeds which seemed to me almost unimportant because I knew that she was not committing them, had become almost tantamount to so many proofs of her innocence), I underwent the martyrdom of living in the constant company of an idea quite as novel as the idea that Albertine was dead (previously I had always started from the idea that she was alive), with an idea which I should have supposed it to be equally impossible to endure and which, without my noticing it, was gradually forming the basis of my consciousness, was substituting itself for the

idea that Albertine was innocent: the idea that she was
guilty. When I believed that I was doubting her, I was
on the contrary believing in her; similarly I took as the
starting point of my other ideas the certainty—often proved
false as the contrary idea had been—the certainty of her
guilt, while I continued to imagine that I still felt doubts.
I must have suffered intensely during this period, but I
realise that it was inevitable. We are healed of a suffering
only by experiencing it to the full. By protecting Albertine from any contact with the outer world, by forging the
illusion that she was innocent, just as later on when I
adopted as the basis of my reasoning the thought that she
was alive, I was merely postponing the hour of my recovery, because I was postponing the long hours that must
elapse as a preliminary to the end of the necessary sufferings.
Now with regard to these ideas of Albertine's guilt, habit,
were it to come into play, would do so according to the
same laws that I had already experienced in the course of
my life. Just as the name Guermantes had lost the significance and the charm of a road bordered with flowers in
purple and ruddy clusters and of the window of Gilbert the
Bad, Albertine's presence, that of the blue undulations of
the sea, the names of Swann, of the lift boy, of the Princesse
de Guermantes and ever so many others had lost all that
they had signified for me—that charm and that significance
leaving in me a mere word which they considered important enough to live by itself, as a man who has come to set a
subordinate to work gives him his instructions and after a
few weeks withdraws—similarly the painful knowledge of
Albertine's guilt would be expelled from me by habit.
Moreover, between now and then, as in the course of an

attack launched from both flanks at once, in this action by habit two allies would mutually lend a hand. It was because this idea of Albertine's guilt would become for me an idea more probable, more habitual, that it would become less painful. But on the other hand, because it would be less painful, the objections raised to my certainty of her guilt, which were inspired in my mind only by my desire not to suffer too acutely, would collapse one by one, and as each action precipitates the next, I should pass quickly enough from the certainty of Albertine's innocence to the certainty of her guilt. It was essential that I should live with the idea of Albertine's death, with the idea of her misdeeds, in order that these ideas might become habitual, that is to say that I might be able to forget these ideas and in the end to forget Albertine herself.

I had not yet reached this stage. At one time it was my memory made more clear by some intellectual excitement —such as reading a book—which revived my grief, at other times it was on the contrary my grief—when it was aroused, for instance, by the anguish of a spell of stormy weather—which raised higher, brought nearer to the light, some memory of our love.

Moreover these revivals of my love for Albertine might occur after an interval of indifference interspersed with other curiosities, as after the long interval that had dated from her refusal to let me kiss her at Balbec, during which I had thought far more about Mme de Guermantes, about Andrée, about Mlle de Stermaria; it had revived when I had begun again to see her frequently. But even now various preoccupations were able to bring about a separation —from a dead woman, this time—in which she left me more indifferent. And even later on when I loved her less, this remained nevertheless for me one of those desires of which we soon grow tired, but which resume their hold when we have allowed them to lie quiet for some time. I pursued one living woman, then another, then I returned to my dead. Often it was in the most obscure recesses of myself, when I could no longer form any clear idea of Albertine, that a name came by chance to stimulate painful reactions, which I supposed to be no longer possible, like those dying people whose brain is no longer capable of thought and who are made to contract their muscles by the prick of a needle. And, during long periods, these stimulations occurred to me so rarely that I was driven to seek for myself the occasions of a grief, of a crisis of jealousy, in an attempt to reattach myself to the past, to remember her better. Since regret for a woman is only a recrudescence of love and remains subject to the same laws, the keenness of my regret was enhanced by the same causes which in Albertine's lifetime had increased my love for her and in the front rank of which had always appeared jealousy and grief. But as a rule these occasions—for an illness, a war, can always last far longer than the most prophetic wisdom has calculated—took me unawares and caused me such violent shocks that I thought far more of protecting myself against suffering than of appealing to them for a memory.

Moreover a word did not even need to be connected, like " Chaumont," with some suspicion (even a syllable common to different names was sufficient for my memory—as for an electrician who is prepared to use any substance that is a good conductor—to restore the contact between Albertine and my heart) in order to reawaken that suspicion,

to be the password, the triumphant " Open, Sesame " un-
locking the door of a past which one had ceased to take into
account, because, having seen more than enough of it,
strictly speaking one no longer possessed it; one had been
shorn of it, had supposed that by this subtraction one's own
personality had changed its form, like a geometrical figure
which by the removal of an angle would lose one of its
sides; certain phrases for instance in which there occurred
the name of a street, of a road, where Albertine might have
been, were sufficient to incarnate a potential, non-existent
jealousy, in the quest of a body, a dwelling, some material
location, some particular realisation.   Often it was simply
during my sleep that these " repetitions," these " da capo "
of our dreams which turn back in an instant many pages of
our memory, many leaves of the calendar, brought me
back, made me return to a painful but remote impression
which had long since yielded its place to others but which
now became present once more.   As a rule, it was accompanied by a whole stage-setting, clumsy but appealing,
which, giving me the illusion of reality, brought before my
eyes, sounded in my ears what thenceforward dated from
that night.   Besides, in the history of a love-affair and of
its struggles against oblivion, do not our dreams occupy an
even larger place than our waking state, our dreams which
take no account of the infinitesimal divisions of time, suppress transitions, oppose sharp contrasts, undo in an instant
the web of consolation so slowly woven during the day, and
contrive for us, by night, a meeting with her whom we
would eventually have forgotten, provided always that we
did not see her again.   For whatever anyone may say, we
can perfectly well have in a dream the impression that what

is happening is real. This could be impossible only for reasons drawn from our experience which at that moment is hidden from us. With the result that this improbable life seems to us true. Sometimes, by a defect in the internal lighting which spoiled the success of the play, the appearance of my memories on the stage giving me the illusion of real life, I really believed that I had arranged to meet Albertine, that I was seeing her again, but then I found myself incapable of advancing to meet her, of uttering the words which I meant to say to her, to rekindle in order to see her the torch that had been quenched, impossibilities which were simply in my dream the immobility, the dumbness, the blindness of the sleeper—as suddenly one sees in the faulty projection of a magic lantern a huge shadow, which ought not to be visible, obliterate the figures on the slide, which is the shadow of the lantern itself, or that of the operator. At other times Albertine appeared in my dream, and proposed to leave me once again, without my being moved by her determination. This was because from my memory there had been able to filter into the darkness of my dream a warning ray of light which, lodged in Albertine, deprived her future actions, the departure of which she informed me, of any importance, this was the knowledge that she was dead. Often this memory that Albertine was dead was combined, without destroying it, with the sensation that she was alive. I conversed with her; while I was speaking, my grandmother came and went at the other end of the room. Part of her chin had crumbled away like a corroded marble, but I found nothing unusual in that. I told Albertine that I had various questions to ask her with regard to the bathing establishment at Balbec, and to a

certain laundress in Touraine, but I postponed them to
another occasion since we had plenty of time and there was
no longer any urgency. She assured me that she was not
doing anything wrong and that she had merely, the day
before, kissed Mlle Vinteuil on the lips. "What? Is
she here?" "Yes, in fact it is time for me to leave you, for
I have to go and see her presently." And since, now that
Albertine was dead, I no longer kept her a prisoner in my
house as in the last months of her life, her visit to Mlle
Vinteuil disturbed me. I sought to prevent Albertine
from seeing her. Albertine told me that she had done no
more than kiss her, but she was evidently beginning to lie
again as in the days when she used to deny everything.
Presently she would not be content, probably, with kissing
Mlle Vinteuil. No doubt from a certain point of view I
was wrong to let myself be disturbed like this, since, according to what we are told, the dead can feel, can do nothing.
People say so, but this did not explain the fact that my
grandmother, who was dead, had continued nevertheless to
live for many years, and at that moment was passing to and
fro in my room. And no doubt, once I was awake, this
idea of a dead woman who continued to live ought to have
become as impossible for me to understand as it is to explain.
But I had already formed it so many times in the course of
those transient periods of insanity which are our dreams,
that I had become in time familiar with it; our memory of
dreams may become lasting, if they repeat themselves
sufficiently often. And long after my dream had ended, I
remained tormented by that kiss which Albertine had told
me that she had bestowed in words which I thought that I
could still hear. And indeed, they must have passed very

close to my ear since it was I myself that had uttered them.

All day long, I continued to converse with Albertine, I questioned her, I forgave her, I made up for my forgetfulness of the things which I had always meant to say to her during her life. And all of a sudden I was startled by the thought that to the creature invoked by memory to whom all these remarks were addressed, no reality any longer corresponded, that death had destroyed the various parts of the face to which the continual urge of the will to live, now abolished, had alone given the unity of a person. At other times, without my having dreamed, as soon as I awoke, I felt that the wind had changed in me; it was blowing coldly and steadily from another direction, issuing from the remotest past, bringing back to me the sound of a clock striking far-off hours, of the whistle of departing trains which I did not ordinarily hear. One day I tried to interest myself in a book, a novel by Bergotte, of which I had been especially fond. Its congenial characters appealed to me strongly, and very soon, reconquered by the charm of the book, I began to hope, as for a personal pleasure, that the wicked woman might be punished; my eyes grew moist when the happiness of the young lovers was assured. "But then," I exclaimed in despair, " from my attaching so much importance to what Albertine may have done, I must conclude that her personality is something real which cannot be destroyed, that I shall find her one day in her own likeness in heaven, if I invoke with so many prayers, await with such impatience, learn with such floods of tears the success of a person who has never existed save in Bergotte's imagination, whom I have never seen, whose appearance I am at liberty to imagine as I please!" Besides, in this novel, there were seductive girls, amorous correspondences, deserted paths in which lovers meet, this reminded me that one may love clandestinely, it revived my jealousy, as though Albertine had still been able to stroll along deserted paths. And there was also the incident of a man who meets after fifty years a woman whom he loved in her youth, does not recognise her, is bored in her company. And this reminded me that love does not last for ever and crushed me as though I were destined to be parted from Albertine and to meet her again with indifference in my old age. If I caught sight of a map of France, my timorous eyes took care not to come upon Touraine so that I might not be jealous, nor, so that I might not be miserable, upon Normandy, where the map marked at least Balbec and Doncières, between which I placed all those roads that we had traversed so many times together. In the midst of other names of towns or villages of France, names which were merely visible or audible, the name of Tours for instance seemed to be differently composed, no longer of immaterial images, but of venomous substances which acted in an immediate fashion upon my heart whose beatings they quickened and made painful. And if this force extended to certain names, which it had made so different from the rest, how when I remained more shut up in myself, when I confined myself to Albertine herself, could I be astonished that, emanating from a girl who was probably just like any other girl, this force which I found irresistible, and to produce which any other woman might have served, had been the result of a confusion and of the bringing in contact of dreams, desires, habits, affections, with the requisite interference of alternate pains and pleasures? And this continued after her death, memory being sufficient to carry on the real life, which is mental. I recalled Albertine alighting from a railway-carriage and telling me that she wanted to go to Saint-Mars le Vêtu, and I saw her again also with her " polo " pulled down over her cheeks, I found once more possibilities of pleasure, towards which I sprang saying to myself: " We might have gone on together to Incarville, to Doncières." There was no watering-place in the neighbourhood of Balbec in which I did not see her, with the result that that country, like a mythological land which had been preserved, restored to me, living and cruel, the most ancient, the most charming legends, those that had been most obliterated by the sequel of my love. Oh! what anguish were I ever to have to lie down again upon that bed at Balbec around whose brass frame, as around an immovable pivot, a fixed bar, my life had moved, and evolved, bringing successively into its compass gay conversations with my grandmother, the nightmare of her death, Albertine's soothing caresses, the discovery of her vice, and now a new life in which, looking at the glazed bookcases upon which the sea was reflected, I knew that Albertine would never come into the room again! Was it not, that Balbec hotel, like the sole indoor set of a provincial theatre, in which for years past the most diverse plays have been performed, which has served for a comedy, for one tragedy, for another, for a purely poetical drama, that hotel which already receded quite far into my past? The fact that this part alone remained always the same, with its walls, its bookcases, its glass panes, through the course of fresh epochs in my life, made me more conscious that, in the total, it was the rest, it was myself that had changed, and gave me thus that impression that the mysteries of life, of love, of death, in which children imagine in their optimism that they have no share, are not set apart, but that we perceive with a dolorous pride that they have embodied themselves in the course of years in our own life.

I tried at times to take an interest in the newspapers. But I found the act of reading them repellent, and moreover it was not without danger to myself. The fact is that from each of our ideas, as from a clearing in a forest, so many roads branch in different directions that at the moment when I least expected it I found myself faced by a fresh memory. The title of Fauré's melody *le Secret* had led me to the Duc de Broglie's *Secret du Roi*, the name Broglie to that of Chaumont, or else the words " Good Friday " had made me think of Golgotha, Golgotha of the etymology of the word which is, it seems, the equivalent of *Calvus Mons*, Chaumont. But, whatever the path by which I might have arrived at Chaumont, at that moment I received so violent a shock that I could think only of how to guard myself against pain. Some moments after the shock, my intelligence, which like the sound of thunder travels less rapidly, taught me the reason. Chaumont had made me think of the Buttes-Chaumont to which Mme Bontemps had told me that Andrée used often to go with Albertine, whereas Albertine had told me that she had never seen the Buttes-Chaumont. After a certain age our memories are so intertwined with one another that the thing of which we are thinking, the book that we are reading are of scarcely any importance. We have put something of ourself everywhere, everything is fertile, everything is dangerous, and we can make discoveries no less precious than in Pascal's Pensées in an advertisement of soap.

No doubt an incident such as this of the Buttes-Chaumont which at the time had appeared to me futile was in itself far less serious, far less decisive evidence against Albertine than the story of the bath-woman or the laundress. But, for one thing, a memory which comes to us by chance finds in us an intact capacity for imagining, that is to say in this case for suffering, which we have partly exhausted when it is on the contrary ourself that have deliberately applied our mind to recreating a memory. And to these latter memories (those that concerned the bath-woman and the laundress) ever present albeit obscured in my consciousness, like the furniture placed in the semi-darkness of a gallery which, without being able to see them, we avoid as we pass, I had grown accustomed. It was on the contrary, a long time since I had given a thought to the Buttes-Chaumont, or, to take another instance, to Albertine's scrutiny of the mirror in the casino at Balbec, or to her unexplained delay on the evening when I had waited so long for her after the Guermantes party, to any of those parts of her life which remained outside my heart and which I would have liked to know in order that they might become assimilated, annexed to it, become joined with the more pleasant memories which formed in it an Albertine internal and genuinely possessed. When I raised a corner of the heavy curtain of habit (and stupefying habit which during the whole course of our life conceals from us almost the whole universe, and in the dead of night, without changing the label, substitutes for the most dangerous or intoxicating poisons of life some kind of anodyne which does not procure any delight), such a memory would come back to me as on the day of the incident itself with that fresh and piercing novelty of a recurring season, of a change in the routine of our hours, which, in the realm of pleasures also, if we get into a carriage on the first fine day in spring, or leave the house at sunrise, makes us observe our own insignificant actions with a lucid exaltation which makes that intense minute worth more than the sum-total of the preceding days. I found myself once more coming away from the party at the Princesse de Guermantes's and awaiting the coming of Albertine. Days in the past cover up little by little those that preceded them and are themselves buried beneath those that follow them. But each past day has remained deposited in us, as, in a vast library in which there are older books, a volume which, doubtless, nobody will ever ask to see. And yet should this day from the past, traversing the lucidity of the subsequent epochs, rise to the surface and spread itself over us whom it entirely covers, then for a moment the names resume their former meaning, people their former aspect, we ourself our state of mind at the time, and we feel, with a vague suffering which how-ever is endurable and will not last for long, the problems which have long ago become insoluble and which caused us such anguish at the time. Our ego is composed of the superimposition of our successive states. But this super-imposition is not unalterable like the stratification of a mountain. Incessant upheavals raise to the surface ancient deposits. I found myself as I had been after the party at the Princesse de Guermantes's, awaiting the coming of Albertine. What had she been doing that evening? Had she been unfaithful to me? With whom? Aimé's revelations, even if I accepted them, in no way diminished for me the anxious, despairing interest of this unexpected question, as though each different Albertine, each fresh memory, set a special problem of jealousy, to which the solutions of the other problems could not apply. But I would have liked to know not only with what woman she had spent that evening, but what special pleasure the action represented to her, what was occurring in that moment in herself. Sometimes, at Balbec, Françoise had gone to fetch her, had told me that she had found her leaning out of her window, with an uneasy, questing air, as though she were expecting somebody. Supposing that I learned that the girl whom she was awaiting was Andrée. What was the state of mind in which Albertine awaited her, that state of mind concealed behind the uneasy, questing gaze? That tendency, what importance did it have for Albertine? How large a place did it occupy in her thoughts? Alas, when I recalled my own agitation, whenever I had caught sight of a girl who attracted me, sometimes when I had merely heard her mentioned without having seen her, my anxiety to look my best, to enjoy every advantage, my cold sweats, I had only, in order to torture myself, to imagine the same voluptuous emotion in Albertine. And already it was sufficient to torture me, if I said to myself that, compared with this other thing, her serious conversations with me about Stendhal and Victor Hugo must have had very little weight with her, if I felt her heart attracted towards other people, detach itself from mine, incarnate itself elsewhere. But even the importance which this desire must have had for her and the reserve with which she surrounded it could not reveal to me what, qualitatively, it had been, still less how she qualified it when she spoke of it to herself. In bodily suffering, at least we do not have ourself to choose our pain. The malady decides it and imposes it on us. But in jealousy we have to some extent to make trial of sufferings of every sort and degree, before we arrive at the one which seems appropriate. And what could be more difficult, when it is a question of a suffering such as that of feeling that she whom we loved is finding pleasure with persons different from ourself who give her sensations which we are not capable of giving her, or who at least by their configuration, their aspect, their ways, represent to her anything but ourself. Ah! if only Albertine had fallen in love with Saint-Loup! How much less, it seemed to me, I should have suffered! It is true that we are unaware of the peculiar sensibility of each of our fellow-creatures, but as a rule we do not even know that we are unaware of it, for this sensibility of other people leaves us cold. So far as Albertine was concerned, my misery or happiness would have depended upon the nature of this sensibility; I knew well enough that it was unknown to me, and the fact that it was unknown to me was already a grief. The unknown desires and pleasures that Albertine felt, once I was under the illusion that I beheld them, when, some time after Albertine's death Andrée came to see me.

For the first time she seemed to me beautiful, I said to myself that her almost woolly hair, her dark, shadowed eyes, were doubtless what Albertine had so dearly loved, the materialisation before my eyes of what she used to take with her in her amorous dreams, of what she beheld with the prophetic eyes of desire on the day when she had so suddenly decided to leave Balbec.

Like a strange, dark flower that was brought to me from beyond the grave, from the innermost being of a person in whom I had been unable to discover it, I seemed to see before me, the unlooked-for exhumation of a priceless relic, the incarnate desire of Albertine which Andrée was to me, as Venus was the desire of Jove.   Andrée regretted Albertine, but I felt at once that she did not miss her.   Forcibly removed from her friend by death, she seemed to have easily taken her part in a final separation which I would not have dared to ask of her while Albertine was alive, so afraid would I have been of not succeeding in obtaining Andrée's consent.   She seemed on the contrary to accept without difficulty this renunciation, but precisely at the moment when it could no longer be of any advantage to me. Andrée abandoned Albertine to me, but dead, and when she had lost for me not only her life but retrospectively a little of her reality, since I saw that she was not indispensable, unique to Andrée who had been able to replace her with other girls.

While Albertine was alive, I would not have dared to ask Andrée to take me into her confidence as to the nature of their friendship both mutually and with Mlle Vinteuil's friend, since I was never absolutely certain that Andrée did not repeat to Albertine everything that I said to her.   But now such an inquiry, even if it must prove fruitless, would at least be unattended by danger.   I spoke to Andrée not in a questioning tone but as though I had known all the time, perhaps from Albertine, of the fondness that Andrée herself had for women and of her own relations with Mlle Vinteuil's friend.   She admitted everything without the slightest reluctance, smiling as she spoke.   From this avowal, I might derive the most painful consequences; first of all because Andrée, so affectionate and coquettish with many of the young men at Balbec, would never have been suspected by anyone of practices which she made no attempt to deny, so that by analogy, when I discovered this novel Andrée, I might think that Albertine would have confessed them with the same ease to anyone other than myself whom she felt to be jealous. But on the other hand, Andrée having been Albertine's dearest friend, and the friend for whose sake she had probably returned in haste from Balbec, now that Andrée was proved to have these tastes, the conclusion that was forced upon my mind was that Albertine and Andrée had always indulged them together. Certainly, just as in a stranger's presence, we do not always dare to examine the gift that he has brought us, the wrapper of which we shall not unfasten until the donor has gone, so long as Andrée was with me I did not retire into myself to examine the grief that she had brought me, which I could feel, was already causing my bodily servants, my nerves, my heart, a keen disturbance which, out of good breeding, I pretended not to notice, speaking on the contrary with the utmost affability to the girl who was my guest without diverting my gaze to these internal incidents. It was especially painful to me to hear Andrée say, speaking of Albertine: "Oh, yes, she always loved going to the Chevreuse valley." To the vague and non-existent universe in which Albertine's excursions with Andrée occurred, it seemed to me that the latter had, by a posterior and diabolical creation, added an accursed valley. I felt that Andrée was going to tell me everything that she was in the habit of doing with Albertine, and, while I endeavoured from politeness, from force of habit, from self-esteem, perhaps from gratitude, to appear more and more affectionate, while the space that I had still been able to concede to Albertine's innocence became smaller and smaller, I seemed to perceive that, despite my efforts, I presented the paralysed aspect of an animal round which a steadily narrowing circle is slowly traced by the hypnotising bird of prey which makes no haste because it is sure of reaching when it chooses the victim that can no longer escape. I gazed at her nevertheless, and, with such liveliness, naturalness and assurance as a person can muster who is trying to make it appear that he is not afraid of being hypnotised by the other's stare, I said casually to Andrée: " I have never mentioned the subject to you for fear of offending you, but now that we both find a pleasure in talking about her, I may as well tell you that I found out long ago all about the things of that sort that you used to do with Albertine. And I can tell you something that you will be glad to hear although you know it already: Albertine adored you." I told Andrée that it would be of great interest to me if she would allow me to see her, even if she simply confined herself to caresses which would not embarrass her unduly in my presence, performing such actions with those of Albertine's friends who shared her tastes, and I mentioned Rosemonde, Berthe, each of Albertine's friends, in the hope of finding out something. " Apart from the fact that not for anything in the world would I do the things you mention in your presence," Andrée replied, " I do not believe that any of the girls whom you have named have those tastes." Drawing closer in spite of myself to the monster that was attracting me, I answered: "What! You are not going

181

to expect me to believe that, of all your band, Albertine was the only one with whom you did that sort of thing! " " But I have never done anything of the sort with Albertine." " Come now, my dear Andrée, why deny things which I have known for at least three years, I see no harm in them, far from it. Talking of such things, that evening when she was so anxious to go with you the next day to Mme Verdurin's, you may remember perhaps. . . ." Before I had completed my sentence, I saw in Andrée's eyes, which it sharpened to a pin-point like those stones which for that reason jewellers find it difficult to use, a fleeting, worried stare, like the heads of persons privileged to go behind the scenes who draw back the edge of the curtain before the play has begun and at once retire in order not to be seen. This uneasy stare vanished, everything had become quite normal, but I felt that anything which I might see hereafter would have been specially arranged for my benefit. At that moment I caught sight of myself in the mirror; I was struck by a certain resemblance between myself and Andrée. If I had not long since ceased to shave my upper lip and had had but the faintest shadow of a moustache, this resemblance would have been almost complete. It was perhaps when she saw, at Balbec, my moustache which had scarcely begun to grow, that Albertine had suddenly felt that impatient, furious desire to return to Paris. " But I cannot, all the same, say things that are not true, for the simple reason that you see no harm in them. I swear to you that I never did anything with Albertine, and I am convinced that she detested that sort of thing. The people who told you were lying to you, probably with some ulterior motive," she said with a questioning, defiant

air. " Oh, very well then, since you won't tell me," I
replied. I preferred to appear to be unwilling to furnish a
proof which I did not possess. And yet I uttered vaguely
and at random the name of the Buttes-Chaumont. " I
may have gone to the Buttes-Chaumont with Albertine,
but is it a place that has a particularly evil reputation? " I
asked her whether she could not mention the subject to
Gisèle who had at one time been on intimate terms with
Albertine. But Andrée assured me that after the out-
rageous way in which Gisèle had behaved to her recently,
asking a favour of her was the one thing that she must
absolutely decline to do for me. " If you see her," she
went on, " do not tell her what I have said to you about
her, there is no use in making an enemy of her. She
knows what I think of her, but I have always preferred to
avoid having violent quarrels with her which only have to
be patched up afterwards. And besides, she is a dangerous
person. But you can understand that when one has read
the letter which I had in my hands a week ago, and in
which she lied with such absolute treachery, nothing, not
even the noblest actions in the world, can wipe out the
memory of such a thing." In short, if, albeit Andrée had
those tastes to such an extent that she made no pretence of
concealing them, and Albertine had felt for her that strong
affection which she had undoubtedly felt, notwithstanding
this Andrée had never had any carnal relations with Albertine and had never been aware that Albertine had those
tastes, this meant that Albertine did not have them, and
had never enjoyed with anyone those relations which,
rather than with anyone else, she would have enjoyed with
Andrée. And so when Andrée had left me, I realised that

183

so definite a statement had brought me peace of mind. But perhaps it had been dictated by a sense of the obligation, which Andrée felt that she owed to the dead girl whose memory still survived in her, not to let me believe what Albertine had doubtless, while she was alive, begged her to deny.

Novelists sometimes pretend in an introduction that while travelling in a foreign country they have met somebody who has told them the story of a person's life. They then withdraw in favour of this casual acquaintance, and the story that he tells them is nothing more or less than their novel. Thus the life of Fabrice del Dongo was related to Stendhal by a Canon of Padua. How gladly would we, when we are in love, that is to say when another person's existence seems to us mysterious, find some such well-informed narrator! And undoubtedly he exists. Do we not ourself frequently relate, without any trace of passion, the story of some woman or other, to one of our friends, or to a stranger, who has known nothing of her love-affairs and listens to us with keen interest? The person that I was when I spoke to Bloch of the Duchesse de Guermantes, of Mme Swann, that person still existed, who could have spoken to me of Albertine, that person exists always . . . but we never come across him. It seemed to me that, if I had been able to find women who had known her, I should have learned everything of which I was unaware. And yet to strangers it must have seemed that nobody could have known so much of her life as myself. Did I even know her dearest friend, Andrée? Thus it is that we suppose that the friend of a Minister must know the truth about some political affair or cannot be implicated in a scandal. Having tried and failed, the friend has found that whenever he discussed politics with the Minister the latter confined himself to generalisations and told him nothing more than what had already appeared in the newspapers, or that if he was in any trouble, his repeated attempts to secure the Minister's help have ended invariably in an: " It is not in my power " against which the friend is himself powerless. I said to myself: " If I could have known such and such witnesses! " from whom, if I had known them, I should probably have been unable to extract anything more than from Andrée, herself the custodian of a secret which she refused to surrender. Differing in this respect also from Swann who, when he was no longer jealous, ceased to feel any curiosity as to what Odette might have done with Forcheville, even after my jealousy had subsided, the thought of making the acquaintance of Albertine's laundress, of the people in her neighbourhood, of reconstructing her life in it, her intrigues, this alone had any charm for me. And as desire always springs from a preliminary sense of value, as had happened to me in the past with Gilberte, with the Duchesse de Guermantes, it was, in the districts in which Albertine had lived in the past, the women of her class that I sought to know, and whose presence alone I could have desired. Even without my being able to learn anything from them, they were the only women towards whom I felt myself attracted, as being those whom Albertine had known or whom she might have known, women of her class or of the classes with which she liked to associate, in a word those women who had in my eyes the distinction of resembling her or of being of the type that had appealed to her. As I recalled thus either Albertine herself, or the type for which she had doubtless felt a preference, these women aroused in me an agonising feeling of jealousy or regret, which afterwards when my grief had been dulled changed into a curiosity not devoid of charm. And among them especially the women of the working class, on account of that life, so different from the life that I knew, which is theirs. No doubt it is only in our mind that we possess things, and we do not possess a picture because it hangs in our dining-room if we are incapable of understanding it, or a landscape because we live in front of it without even glancing at it. But still I had had in the past the illusion of recapturing Balbec, when in Paris Albertine came to see me and I held her in my arms. Similarly I obtained a contact, restricted and furtive as it might be, with Albertine's life, the atmosphere of workrooms, a conversation across a counter, the spirit of the slums, when I kissed a seamstress. Andrée, these other women, all of them in relation to Albertine—as Albertine herself had been in relation to Balbec—were to be numbered among those substitutes for pleasures, replacing one another, in a gradual degradation, which enable us to dispense with the pleasure to which we can no longer attain, a holiday at Balbec, or the love of Albertine (as the act of going to the Louvre to look at a Titian which was originally in Venice consoles us for not being able to go there), for those pleasures which, separated one from another by indistinguishable gradations, convert our life into a series of concentric, contiguous, harmonic and graduated zones, encircling an initial desire which has set the tone, eliminated everything that does not combine with it and spread the dominant colour (as had, for instance, occurred to me also in the cases of the Duchesse de Guermantes and of Gilberte). Andrée, these women, were to the desire, for the gratification of which I knew that it was hopeless, now, to pray, to have Albertine by my side, what one evening, before I knew Albertine save by sight, had been the many-faceted and refreshing lustre of a bunch of grapes.

Associated now with the memory of my love, Albertine's physical and social attributes, in spite of which I had loved her, attracted my desire on the contrary towards what at one time it would least readily have chosen: dark girls of the lower middle class. Indeed what was beginning to a certain extent to revive in me was that immense desire which my love for Albertine had not been able to assuage, that immense desire to know life which I used to feel on the roads round Balbec, in the streets of Paris, that desire which had caused me so much suffering when, supposing it to exist in Albertine's heart also, I had sought to deprive her of the means of satisfying it with anyone but myself. Now that I was able to endure the thought of her desire, as that thought was at once aroused by my own desire, these two immense appetites coincided, I would have liked us to be able to indulge them together, I said to myself: "That girl would have appealed to her," and led by this sudden digression to think of her and of her death, I felt too unhappy to be able to pursue my own desire any farther. As, long ago, the Méséglise and Guermantes ways had established the conditions of my liking for the country and had prevented me from finding any real charm in a village where there was no old church, nor cornflowers, nor buttercups, so it was by attaching them in myself to a past full of charm that my love for Albertine made me seek out exclusively a certain type of woman; I began again, as before I was in love with her, to feel the need of things in harmony with her which would be interchangeable with a memory that had become gradually less exclusive. I could not have found any pleasure now in the company of a golden-haired and haughty duchess, because she would not have aroused in me any of the emotions that sprang from Albertine, from my desire for her, from the jealousy that I had felt of her love-affairs, from my sufferings, from her death. For our sensations in order to be strong, need to release in us something different from themselves, a sentiment, which will not find any satisfaction in pleasure, but which adds itself to desire, enlarges it makes it cling desperately to pleasure. In proportion as the love that Albertine had felt for certain women ceased to cause me pain, it attached those women to my past, gave them something that was more real, as to buttercups, to hawthorn-blossom the memory of Combray gave a greater reality than to unfamiliar flowers. Even of Andrée, I no longer said to myself with rage: " Albertine loved her," but on the contrary, so as to explain my desire to myself, in a tone of affection: " Albertine loved her dearly." I could now understand the widowers whom we suppose to have found consolation and who prove on the contrary that they are inconsolable because they marry their deceased wife's sister. Thus the decline of my love seemed to make fresh loves possible for me, and Albertine like those women long loved for themselves who, later, feeling their lover's desire grow

feeble, maintain their power by confining themselves to
the office of panders, provided me, as the Pompadour
provided Louis XV, with fresh damsels. Even in the
past, my time had been divided into periods in which I
desired this woman or that. When the violent pleasures
afforded by one had grown dull, I longed for the other who
would give me an almost pure affection until the need of
more sophisticated caresses brought back my desire for the
first. Now these alternations had come to an end, or at
least one of the periods was being indefinitely prolonged.
What I would have liked was that the newcomer should
take up her abode in my house, and should give me at
night, before leaving me, a friendly, sisterly kiss. In
order that I might have believed—had I not had experience of the intolerable presence of another person—that I
regretted a kiss more than a certain pair of lips, a pleasure
more than a love, a habit more than a person. I would
have liked also that the newcomers should be able to play
Vinteuil's music to me like Albertine, to talk to me as
she had talked about Elstir. All this was impossible.
Their love would not be equivalent to hers, I thought,
whether because a love to which were annexed all those
episodes, visits to picture galleries, evenings spent at
concerts, the whole of a complicated existence which
allows correspondences, conversations, a flirtation preliminary to the more intimate relations, a serious friendship afterwards, possesses more resources than love for a
woman who can only offer herself, as an orchestra possesses more resources than a piano, or because, more
profoundly, my need of the same sort of affection that
Albertine used to give me, the affection of a girl of a

certain culture who would at the same time be a sister to
me, was—like my need of women of the same class as
Albertine—merely a recrudescence of my memory of
Albertine, of my memory of my love for her. And once
again, I discovered, first of all that memory has no power
of invention, that it is powerless to desire anything else,
even anything better than what we have already possessed,
secondly that it is spiritual in the sense that reality cannot
furnish it with the state which it seeks, lastly that, when
applied to a person who is dead, the resurrection that it
incarnates is not so much that of the need to love in which
it makes us believe as that of the need of the absent person.
So that the resemblance to Albertine of the woman whom
I had chosen, the resemblance of her affection even, if I
succeeded in winning it, to Albertine's, made me all the
more conscious of the absence of what I had been unconsciously seeking, of what was indispensable to the revival
of my happiness, that is to say, Albertine herself, the time
during which we had lived together, the past in quest of
which I had unconsciously gone. Certainly, upon fine
days, Paris seemed to me innumerably aflower with all
these girls, whom I did not desire, but who thrust down
their roots into the obscurity of the desire and the mysterious nocturnal life of Albertine. They were like the
girls of whom she had said to me at the outset, when she
had not begun to distrust me: "That girl is charming,
what nice hair she has." All the curiosity that I had felt
about her life in the past when I knew her only by sight,
and on the other hand all my desires in life were blended
in this sole curiosity, to see Albertine in company with
other women, perhaps because thus, when they had left

her, I should have remained alone with her, the last and the master. And when I observed her hesitations, her uncertainty when she asked herself whether it would be worth her while to spend the evening with this or that girl, her satiety when the other had gone, perhaps her disappointment, I should have brought to the light of day, I should have restored to its true proportions the jealousy that Albertine inspired in me, because seeing her thus experience them I should have taken the measure and discovered the limit of her pleasures. Of how many pleasures, of what an easy life she has deprived us, I said to myself, by that stubborn obstinacy in denying her instincts! And as once again I sought to discover what could have been the reason for her obstinacy, all of a sudden, the memory came to me of a remark that I had made to her at Balbec on the day when she gave me a pencil. As I rebuked her for not having allowed me to kiss her, I had told her that I thought a kiss just as natural as I thought it degrading that a woman should have relations with another woman. Alas, perhaps Albertine had never forgotten that imprudent speech.

I took home with me the girls who had appealed to me least, I stroked their virginal tresses, I admired a well-modelled little nose, a Spanish pallor. Certainly, in the past, even with a woman of whom I had merely caught sight on a road near Balbec, in a street in Paris, I had felt the individuality of my desire and that it would be adulterating it to seek to assuage it with another person. But life, by disclosing to me, little by little, the permanence of our needs, had taught me that, failing one person, we must content ourself with another—and I felt that what I had demanded of Albertine another woman, Mlle de Stermaria, could have given me. But it had been Albertine; and what with the satisfaction of my need of affection and the details of her body, an interwoven tangle of memories had become so inextricable that I could no longer detach from a desire for affection all that embroidery of my memories of Albertine's body. She alone could give me that happiness. The idea of her uniqueness was no longer a metaphysical *a priori* based upon what was individual in Albertine, as in the case of the women I passed in the street long ago, but an *a posteriori* created by the contingent and indissoluble overlapping of my memories. I could no longer desire any affection without feeling a need of her, without grief at her absence. Also the mere resemblance of the woman I had selected, of the affection that I asked of her to the happiness that I had known made me all the more conscious of all that was lacking before that happiness could revive. The same vacuum that I had found in my room after Albertine had left, and had supposed that I could fill by taking women in my arms, I found in them. They had never spoken to me, these women, of Vinteuil's music, of Saint-Simon's memoirs, they had not sprayed themselves with too strong a scent before coming to visit me, they had not played at interlacing their eyelashes with mine, all of which things were important because, apparently, they allow us to weave dreams round the sexual act itself and to give ourself the illusion of love, but in reality because they formed part of my memory of Albertine and it was she whom I would fain have seen again. What these women had in common with Albertine made me feel all the more clearly what was lacking of her in them, which was everything, and would never be anything again since Albertine was dead. And so my love for Albertine which had drawn me towards these women made me indifferent to them, and perhaps my regret for Albertine and the persistence of my jealousy, which had already outlasted the period fixed for them in my most pessimistic calculations, would never have altered appreciably, had their existence, isolated from the rest of my life, been subjected merely to the play of my memories, to the actions and reactions of a psychology applicable to immobile states, and had it not been drawn into a vaster system in which souls move in time as bodies move in space. As there is a geometry in space, so there is a psychology in time, in which the calculations of a plane psychology would no longer be accurate because we should not be taking into account time and one of the forms that it assumes, oblivion; oblivion, the force of which I was beginning to feel and which is so powerful an instrument of adaptation to reality because it gradually destroys in us the surviving past which is a perpetual contradiction of it. And I ought really to have discovered sooner that one day I should no longer be in love with Albertine. When I had realised, from the difference that existed between what the importance of her person and of her actions was to me and what it was to other people, that my love was not so much a love for her as a love in myself, I might have deduced various consequences from this subjective nature of my love and that, being a mental state, it might easily long survive the person, but also that having no genuine connection with that person, it must, like every mental state, even the most permanent, find itself one day obsolete, be " replaced," and that when that day came everything that seemed to attach me so pleasantly, indissolubly, to the memory of Albertine would no longer exist for me. It is the tragedy of other people that they are to us merely showcases for the very perishable collections of our own mind. For this very reason we base upon them projects which have all the ardour of our mind; but our mind grows tired, our memory crumbles, the day would arrive when I would readily admit the first comer to Albertine's room, as I had without the slightest regret given Albertine the agate marble or other gifts that I had received from Gilberte.[1]

[1] In the French text of *Albertine Disparue*, Volume I ends with this chapter.

CHAPTER II

MADEMOISELLE DE FORCHEVILLE

IT was not that I was not still in love with Albertine, but no longer in the same fashion as in the final phase. No, it was in the fashion of the earliest times, when everything that had any connection with her, places or people, made me feel a curiosity in which there was more charm than suffering. And indeed I was quite well aware now that before I forgot her altogether, before I reached the initial stage of indifference, I should have, like a traveller who returns by the same route to his starting-point, to traverse in the return direction all the sentiments through which I had passed before arriving at my great love. But these fragments, these moments of the past are not immobile, they have retained the terrible force, the happy ignorance of the hope that was then yearning towards a time which has now become the past, but which a hallucination makes us for a moment mistake retrospectively for the future. I read a letter from Albertine, in which she had said that she was coming to see me that evening, and I felt for an instant the joy of expectation. In these return journeys along the same line from a place to which we shall never return, when we recall the names, the appearance of all the places which we have passed on the outward journey, it happens that, while our train is halting at one of the stations, we feel for an instant the illusion that we are setting off again, but in the direction of the place from which we have come, as on the former journey. Soon the illusion vanishes, but for an instant we felt ourself carried away once again: such is the cruelty of memory.

At times the reading of a novel that was at all sad carried me sharply back, for certain novels are like great but temporary bereavements, they abolish our habits, bring us in contact once more with the reality of life, but for a few hours only, like a nightmare, since the force of habit, the oblivion that it creates, the gaiety that it restores to us because our brain is powerless to fight against it and to recreate the truth, prevails to an infinite extent over the almost hypnotic suggestion of a good book which, like all suggestions, has but a transient effect.

And yet, if we cannot, before returning to the state of indifference from which we started, dispense ourself from covering in the reverse direction the distances which we had traversed in order to arrive at love, the trajectory, the line that we follow, are not of necessity the same. They have this in common, that they are not direct, because oblivion is no more capable than love of progressing along a straight line. But they do not of necessity take the same paths. And on the path which I was taking on my return journey, there were in the course of a confused passage three halting-points which I remember, because of the light that shone round about me when I was already nearing my goal, stages which I recall especially, doubtless because I perceived in them things which had no place in my love for Albertine, or at most were attached to it only to the extent to which what existed already in our heart before a great passion associates itself with it, whether

196

by feeding it, or by fighting it, or by offering to our
analytical mind, a contrast with it.

The first of these halting-points began with the coming
of winter, on a fine Sunday, which was also All Saints'
Day, when I had ventured out of doors. As I came
towards the Bois, I recalled with sorrow how Albertine
had come back to join me from the Trocadéro, for it was
the same day, only without Albertine. With sorrow
and yet not without pleasure all the same, for the repetition in a minor key, in a despairing tone, of the same
motif that had filled my day in the past, the absence even
of Françoise's telephone message, of that arrival of Albertine which was not something negative, but the suppression in reality of what I had recalled, of what had given
the day a sorrowful aspect, made of it something more
beautiful than a simple, unbroken day, because what was
no longer there, what had been torn from it, remained
stamped upon it as on a mould.

In the Bois, I hummed phrases from Vinteuil's sonata.
I was no longer hurt by the thought that Albertine had
fooled me, for almost all my memories of her had entered
into that secondary chemical state in which they no longer
cause any anxious oppression of the heart, but rather
comfort. Now and then, at the passages which she used
to play most often, when she was in the habit of uttering
some reflection which I had thought charming at the time,
of suggesting some reminiscence, I said to myself: " Poor
little girl," but without melancholy, merely adding to the
musical phrase an additional value, a value that was so to
speak, historic and curious like that which the portrait of
Charles I by Van Dyck, so beautiful already in itself,

acquires from the fact that it found its way into the national collection because of Mme du Barry's desire to impress the King. When the little phrase, before disappearing altogether, dissolved into its various elements in which it floated still for a moment in scattered fragments, it was not for me as it had been for Swann a messenger from Albertine who was vanishing. It was not altogether the same association of ideas that the little phrase had aroused in me as in Swann. I had been impressed, most of all, by the elaboration, the attempts, the repetitions, the " outcome " of a phrase which persisted throughout the sonata as that love had persisted throughout my life. And now, when I realised how, day by day, one element after another of my love departed, the jealous side of it, then some other, drifted gradually back in a vague remembrance to the feeble bait of the first outset, it was my love that I seemed, in the scattered notes of the little phrase, to see dissolving before my eyes.

As I followed the paths separated by undergrowth, carpeted with a grass that diminished daily, the memory of a drive during which Albertine had been by my side in the carriage, from which she had returned home with me, during which I felt that she was enveloping my life, floated now round about me, in the vague mist of the darkening branches in the midst of which the setting sun caused to gleam, as though suspended in the empty air, a horizontal web embroidered with golden leaves. Moreover my heart kept fluttering at every moment, as happens to anyone in whose eyes a rooted idea gives to every woman who has halted at the end of a path, the appearance, the possible identity of the woman of whom he is thinking.

" It is perhaps she! " We turn round, the carriage continues on its way and we do not return to the spot. These leaves, I did not merely behold them with the eyes of my memory, they interested me, touched me, like those purely descriptive pages into which an artist, to make them more complete, introduces a fiction, a whole romance; and this work of nature thus assumed the sole charm of melancholy which was capable of reaching my heart. The reason for this charm seemed to me to be that I was still as much in love with Albertine as ever, whereas the true reason was on the contrary that oblivion was continuing to make such headway in me that the memory of Albertine was no longer painful to me, that is to say, it had changed; but however clearly we may discern our impressions, as I then thought that I could discern the reason for my melancholy, we are unable to trace them back to their more remote meaning. Like those maladies the history of which the doctor hears his patient relate to him, by the help of which he works back to a more profound cause, of which the patient is unaware, similarly our impressions, our ideas, have only a symptomatic value. My jealousy being held aloof by the impression of charm and agreeable sadness which I was feeling, my senses reawakened. Once again, as when I had ceased to see Gilberte, the love of woman arose in me rid of any exclusive association with any particular woman already loved, and floated like those spirits that have been liberated by previous destructions and stray suspended in the springtime air, asking only to be allowed to embody themselves in a new creature. Nowhere do there bud so many flowers, forget-me-not though they be styled, as in a cemetery. I looked at the girls with whom this fine day so countlessly blossomed, as I would have looked at them long ago from Mme de Villeparisis's carriage or from the carriage in which, upon a similar Sunday, I had come there with Albertine. At once, the glance which I had just cast at one or other of them was matched immediately by the curious, stealthy, enterprising glance, reflecting unimaginable thoughts, which Albertine had furtively cast at them and which, duplicating my own with a mysterious, swift steel-blue wing, wafted along these paths which had hitherto been so natural the tremor of an unknown element with which my own desire would not have sufficed to animate them had it remained alone, for it, to me, contained nothing that was unknown.

Moreover at Balbec, when I had first longed to know Albertine, was it not because she had seemed to me typical of those girls the sight of whom had so often brought me to a standstill in the streets, upon country roads, and because she might furnish me with a specimen of their life? And was it not natural that now the cooling star of my love in which they were condensed should explode afresh in this scattered dust of nebulæ? They all of them seemed to me Albertines—the image that I carried inside me making me find copies of her everywhere—and indeed, at the turning of an avenue, the girl who was getting into a motor-car recalled her so strongly, was so exactly of the same figure, that I asked myself for an instant whether it were not she that I had just seen, whether people had not been deceiving me when they sent me the report of her death. I saw her again thus at the corner of an avenue, as perhaps she had been at Balbec, getting into a car in the same way, when she was so full of confidence in life. And this other girl's action in climbing into the car, I did not merely record with my eyes, as one of those superficial forms which occur so often in the course of a walk: become a sort of permanent action, it seemed to me to extend also into the past in the direction of the memory which had been superimposed upon it and which pressed so deliciously, so sadly against my heart. But by this time the girl had vanished.

A little farther on I saw a group of three girls slightly older, young women perhaps, whose fashionable, energetic style corresponded so closely with what had attracted me on the day when I first saw Albertine and her friends, that I hastened in pursuit of these three new girls and, when they stopped a carriage, looked frantically in every direction for another. I found one, but it was too late. I did not overtake them. A few days later, however, as I was coming home, I saw, emerging from the portico of our house, the three girls whom I had followed in the Bois. They were absolutely, the two dark ones especially, save that they were slightly older, the type of those young ladies who so often, seen from my window or encountered in the street, had made me form a thousand plans, fall in love with life, and whom I had never been able to know. The fair one had a rather more delicate, almost an invalid air, which appealed to me less. It was she, nevertheless, that was responsible for my not contenting myself with glancing at them for a moment, but, becoming rooted to the ground, staring at them with a scrutiny of the sort which, by their fixity which nothing can distract, their application as though to a problem, seem to be conscious that the true object is hidden far beyond what they behold. I should doubtless have allowed them to disappear as I had allowed so many others, had not (at the moment when they passed by me) the fair one—was it because I was scrutinising them so closely?—darted a stealthy glance at myself, then, having passed me and turning her head, a second glance which fired my blood. However, as she ceased to pay attention to myself and resumed her conversation with her friends, my ardour would doubtless have subsided, had it not been increased a hundredfold by the following incident. When I asked the porter who they were: " They asked for Mme la Duchesse," he informed me. " I think that only one of them knows her and that the others were simply seeing her to the door. Here's the name, I don't know whether I've taken it down properly." And I read: " Mlle Déporcheville," which it was easy to correct to " d'Eporcheville," that is to say the name, more or less, so far as I could remember, of the girl of excellent family, vaguely connected with the Guermantes, whom Robert had told me that he had met in a disorderly house, and with whom he had had relations. I now understood the meaning of her glance, why she had turned round, without letting her companions see. How often I had thought about her, imagining her in the light of the name that Robert had given me. And, lo and behold, I had seen her, in no way different from her friends, save for that concealed glance which established between me and herself a secret entry into the parts of her life which, evidently, were concealed from her friends, and which made her appear more accessible—almost half my own—more gentle than girls of noble birth generally are. In the mind of this girl, between me and herself, there was in advance the common ground of the hours that we might have spent together, had she been free to make an appointment with me. Was it not this that her glance had sought to express to me with an eloquence that was intelligible to myself alone. My heart throbbed until it almost burst, I could not have given an exact description of Mlle d'Eporcheville's appearance, I could picture vaguely a fair complexion viewed from the side, but I was madly in love with her. All of a sudden I became aware that I was reasoning as though, of the three girls, Mlle d'Eporcheville could be only the fair one who had turned round and had looked at me twice. But the porter had not told me this. I returned to his lodge, questioned him again, he told me that he could not enlighten me, but that he would ask his wife who had seen them once before. She was busy at the moment scrubbing the service stair. Which of us has not experienced in the course of his life these uncertainties more or less similar to mine, and all alike delicious? A charitable friend to whom we describe a girl that we have seen at a ball, concludes from our description that she must be one of his friends and invites us to meet her. But among so many girls, and with no guidance but a mere verbal portrait, may there not have been some mistake? The girl whom we are about to meet, will she not be a different girl from her whom we desire? Or on the contrary are we not going to see holding out her hand to us with a smile precisely the girl whom we hoped that she would be? This latter case which is frequent enough, without being justified always by arguments as conclusive as this with respect to Mlle d'Eporcheville, arises from a sort of intuition and also from that wind of fortune which favours us at times. Then, when we catch sight of her, we say to ourself: " That is indeed the girl." I recall that, among the little band of girls who used to parade along the beach, I had guessed correctly which was named Albertine Simonet. This memory caused me a keen but transient pang, and while the porter went in search of his wife, my chief anxiety—as I thought of Mlle d'Eporcheville, and since in those minutes spent in waiting in which a name, a detail of information which we have, we know not why, fitted to a face, finds itself free for an instant, ready if it shall adhere to a new face to render, retrospectively, the original face as to which it had enlightened us strange, innocent, imperceptible—was that the porter's wife was perhaps going to inform me that Mlle d'Eporcheville was, on the contrary, one of the two dark girls. In that event, there would vanish the being in whose existence I believed, whom I already loved, whom I now thought only of possessing, that fair and sly Mlle d'Eporcheville whom the fatal answer must then separate into two distinct elements, which I had arbitrarily united after the fashion of a novelist who blends together diverse elements borrowed from reality in order to create an imaginary character, elements which, taken separately —the name failing to corroborate the supposed intention of the glance—lost all their meaning. In that case my arguments would be stultified, but how greatly they found themselves, on the contrary, strengthened when the porter returned to tell me that Mlle d'Eporcheville was indeed the fair girl.

From that moment I could no longer believe in a

similarity of names. The coincidence was too remarkable
that of these three girls one should be named Mlle
d'Eporcheville, that she should be precisely (and this was
the first convincing proof of my supposition) the one who
had gazed at me in that way, almost smiling at me, and
that it should not be she who frequented the disorderly
houses.

Then began a day of wild excitement. Even before
starting to buy all the bedizenments that I thought necessary in order to create a favourable impression when I
went to call upon Mme de Guermantes two days later,
when (the porter had informed me) the young lady would
be coming again to see the Duchess, in whose house I
should thus find a willing girl and make an appointment
(or I should easily be able to take her into a corner for a
moment), I began, so as to be on the safe side, by telegraphing to Robert to ask him for the girl's exact name
and for a description of her, hoping to have his reply
within forty-eight hours (I did not think for an instant of
anything else, not even of Albertine), determined, whatever might happen to me in the interval, even if I had to
be carried down in a chair were I too ill to walk, to pay a
long call upon the Duchess. If I telegraphed to Saint-
Loup it was not that I had any lingering doubt as to the
identity of the person, or that the girl whom I had seen
and the girl of whom he had spoken were still distinct
personalities in my mind. I had no doubt whatever that
they were the same person. But in my impatience at the
enforced interval of forty-eight hours, it was a pleasure,
it gave me already a sort of secret power over her to
receive a telegram concerning her, filled with detailed

information. At the telegraph office, as I drafted my
message with the animation of a man who is fired by hope,
I remarked how much less disconcerted I was now than
in my boyhood and in facing Mlle d'Eporcheville than I
had been in facing Gilberte. From the moment in which
I had merely taken the trouble to write out my telegram,
the clerk had only to take it from me, the swiftest channels
of electric communication to transmit it across the extent
of France and the Mediterranean, and all Robert's sensual
past would be set to work to identify the person whom I
had seen in the street, would be placed at the service of the
romance which I had sketched in outline, and to which I
need no longer give a thought, for his answer would undertake to bring about a happy ending before twenty-four
hours had passed. Whereas in the old days, brought home
by Françoise from the Champs-Elysées, brooding alone
in the house over my impotent desires, unable to employ
the practical devices of civilisation, I loved like a savage,
or indeed, for I was not even free to move about, like a
flower. From this moment I was in a continual fever; a
request from my father that I would go away with him for
a couple of days, which would have obliged me to forgo
my visit to the Duchess, filled me with such rage and
desperation that my mother interposed and persuaded my
father to allow me to remain in Paris. But for many
hours my anger was unable to subside, while my desire
for Mlle d'Eporcheville was increased a hundredfold by
the obstacle that had been placed between us, by the fear
which I had felt for a moment that those hours, at which
I smiled in constant anticipation, of my call upon Mme
de Guermantes, as at an assured blessing of which nothing

could deprive me, might not occur. Certain philosophers assert that the outer world does not exist, and that it is in ourself that we develop our life. However that may be, love, even in its humblest beginnings, is a striking example of how little reality means to us. Had I been obliged to draw from memory a portrait of Mlle d'Eporcheville, to furnish a description, an indication of her, or even to recognise her in the street, I should have found it impossible. I had seen her in profile, on the move, she had struck me as being simple, pretty, tall and fair, I could not have said anything more. But all the reactions of desire, of anxiety of the mortal blow struck by the fear of not seeing her if my father took me away, all these things, associated with an image which, after all, I did not remember and as to which it was enough that I knew it to be pleasant, already constituted a state of love. Finally, on the following morning, after a night of happy sleeplessness I received Saint-Loup's telegram: "de l'Orgeville, *de* preposition, *orge* the grain barley, *ville* town, small, dark, plump, is at present in Switzerland." It was not she!

A moment before Françoise brought me the telegram, my mother had come into my room with my letters, had laid them carelessly on my bed, as though she were thinking of something else. And withdrawing at once to leave me by myself, she had smiled as she left the room. And I, who was familiar with my dear mother's little subterfuges and knew that one could always read the truth in her face, without any fear of being mistaken, if one took as a key to the cipher her desire to give pleasure to other people, I smiled and thought: "There must be something interesting for me in the post, and Mamma has assumed that indifferent air so that my surprise may be complete and so as not to be like the people who take away half your pleasure by telling you of it beforehand. And she has not stayed with me because she is afraid that in my pride I may conceal the pleasure that I shall feel and so feel it less keenly." Meanwhile, as she reached the door she met Françoise who was coming into the room, the telegram in her hand. As soon as she had handed it to me, my mother had forced Françoise to turn back, and had taken her out of the room, startled, offended and surprised. For Françoise considered that her office conferred the privilege of entering my room at any hour of the day and of remaining there if she chose. But already, upon her features, astonishment and anger had vanished beneath the dark and sticky smile of a transcendant pity and a philosophical irony, a viscous liquid that was secreted, in order to heal her wound, by her outraged self-esteem. So that she might not feel herself despised, she despised us. Also she considered that we were masters, that is to say, capricious creatures, who do not shine by their intelligence and take pleasure in imposing by fear upon clever people, upon servants, so as to shew that they are the masters, absurd tasks such as that of boiling water when there is illness in the house, of mopping the floor of my room with a damp cloth, and of leaving it at the very moment when they intended to remain in it. Mamma had left the post by my side, so that I might not overlook it. But I could see that there was nothing but newspapers. No doubt there was some article by a writer whom I admired, which, as he wrote seldom, would be a surprise to me. I went to the window, and drew back the curtains. Above the pale and misty daylight, the sky was all r(d, as at the same hour are the newly lighted fires in kitchens, and the sight of it filled me with hope and with a longing to pass the night in a train and awake at the little country station where I had seen the milk-girl with the rosy cheeks.

Meanwhile, I could hear Françoise who, indignant at having been banished from my room, into which she considered that she had the right of entry, was grumbling: " If that isn't a tragedy, a boy one saw brought into the world. I didn't see him when his mother bore him, to be sure. But when I first knew him, to say the most, it wasn't five years since he was birthed! "

I opened the *Figaro*. What a bore! The very first article had the same title as the article which I had sent to the paper and which had not appeared, but not merely the same title . . . why, there were several words absolutely identical. This was really too bad. I must write and complain. But it was not merely a few words, there was the whole thing, there was my signature at the foot. It was my article that had appeared at last! But my brain which, even at this period, had begun to shew signs of age and to be easily tired, continued for a moment longer to reason as though it had not understood that this was my article, just as we see an old man obliged to complete a movement that he has begun even if it is no longer necessary, even if an unforeseen obstacle, in the face of which he ought at once to draw back, makes it dangerous. Then I considered the spiritual bread of life that a newspaper is, still hot and damp from the press in the murky air of the morning in which it is distributed, at break of day, to the housemaids who bring it to their masters with their morning coffee, a miraculous, self-multiplying bread which is at the same time one and ten thousand, which remains the same for each person while penetrating innumerably into every house at once.

What I am holding in my hand is not a particular copy of the newspaper, it is any one out of the ten thousand, it is not merely what has been written for me, it is what has been written for me and for everyone. To appreciate exactly the phenomenon which is occurring at this moment in the other houses, it is essential that I read this article not as its author but as one of the ordinary readers of the paper. For what I held in my hand was not merely what I had written, it was the symbol of its incarnation in countless minds. And so, in order to read it, it was essential that I should cease for a moment to be its author, that I should be simply one of the readers of the *Figaro*. But then came an initial anxiety. Would the reader who had not been forewarned catch sight of this article. I open the paper carelessly as would this not forewarned reader, even assuming an air of not knowing what there is this morning in my paper, of being in a hurry to look at the social paragraphs and the political news. But my article is so long that my eye which avoids it (to remain within the bounds of truth and not to put chance on my side, as a person who is waiting counts very slowly on purpose) catches a fragment of it in its survey. But many of those readers who notice the first article and even read it do not notice the signature; I myself would be quite incapable of saying who had written the first article of the day before. And I now promise myself that I will always read them, including the author's name, but, like a jealous lover who refrains from betraying his mistress in order to believe in her fidelity, I reflect sadly that my own future attention will not compel the reciprocal attention of other people. And besides there are those who are going out shooting, those who have left the house in a hurry. And yet, after all, some of them will read it. I do as they do, I begin. I may know full well that many people who read this article will find it detestable, at the moment of reading it, the meaning that each word conveys to me seems to me to be printed on the paper, I cannot believe that each other reader as he opens his eyes will not see directly the images that I see, believing the author's idea to be directly perceived by the reader, whereas it is a different idea that takes shape in his mind, with the simplicity of people who believe that it is the actual word which they have uttered that proceeds along the wires of the telephone; at the very moment in which I mean to be a reader, my mind adjusts, as its author, the attitude of those who will read my article. If M. de Guermantes did not understand some sentences which would appeal to Bloch, he might, on the other hand, be amused by some reflection which Bloch would scorn. Thus for each part which the previous reader seemed to overlook, a fresh admirer presenting himself, the article as a whole was raised to the clouds by a swarm of readers and so prevailed over my own mistrust of myself which had no longer any need to analyse it. The truth of the matter is that the value of an article, however remarkable it may be, is like that of those passages in parliamentary reports in which the words: "Wait and see!" uttered by the Minister, derive all their importance only from their appearing in the setting: The President of the Council, Minister of the Interior and of Religious Bodies: "Wait and see!" (Outcry on the extreme Left. "Hear, hear!" from the Left and Centre)—the main part of their beauty dwells in the minds of the readers. And it is the original sin of this style of literature, of which the famous Lundis are not guiltless, that their merit resides in the impression that they make on their readers. It is a synthetic Venus, of which we have but one truncated limb if we confine ourself to the thought of the author, for it is realised in its completeness only in the minds of his readers. In them it finds its fulfilment. And as a crowd, even a select crowd, is not an artist, this final seal of approval which it sets upon the article must always retain a certain element of vulgarity. Thus Sainte-Beuve, on a Monday, could imagine Mme de Boigne in her bed with its eight columns reading his article in the *Constitutionnel*, appreciating some charming phrase in which he had long delighted and which might never, perhaps, have flowed from his pen had he not thought it expedient to load his article with it in order to give it a longer range. Doubtless the Chancellor, reading it for himself, would refer to it during the call which he would pay upon his old friend a little later. And as he took her out that evening in his carriage, the Duc de Noailles in his grey pantaloons would tell her what had been thought of it in society, unless a word let fall by Mme d'Herbouville had already informed her.

I saw thus at that same hour, for so many people, my idea or even failing my idea, for those who were incapable of understanding it, the repetition of my name and as it were, a glorified suggestion of my personality, shine upon them, in a daybreak which filled me with more strength and triumphant joy than the innumerable daybreak which at that moment was blushing at every window.

I saw Bloch, M. de Guermantes, Legrandin, extracting each in turn from every sentence the images that it enclosed; at the very moment in which I endeavour to be an ordinary reader, I read as an author, but not as an author only. In order that the impossible creature that I am endeavouring to be may combine all the contrary elements which may be most favourable to me, if I read as an author, I judge myself as a reader, without any of the scruples that may be felt about a written text by him who confronts in it the ideal which he has sought to express in it. Those phrases in my article, when I wrote them, were so colourless in comparison with my thought, so complicated and opaque in comparison with my harmonious and transparent vision, so full of gaps which I had not managed to fill, that the reading of them was a torture to me, they had only accentuated in me the sense of my own impotence and of my incurable want of talent. But now, in forcing myself to be a reader, if I transferred to others the painful duty of criticising me, I succeeded at least in making a clean sweep of what I had attempted to do in first reading what I had written. I read the article, forcing myself to imagine that it was written by someone else. Then all my images, all my reflections, all my epithets taken by themselves and without the memory of the check which they had given to my intentions, charmed me by their brilliance, their amplitude, their depth. And when I felt a weakness that was too marked, taking refuge in the spirit of the ordinary and astonished reader, I said to myself: " Bah! How can a reader notice that there is something missing there, it is quite possible. But, be damned to them, if they are not satisfied! There are plenty of pretty passages, more than they are accustomed to find." And resting upon this ten thousandfold approval which supported me, I derived as much sense of my own strength and hope in my own talent from the article which I was reading at that moment as I had derived distrust when what I had written addressed itself only to myself.

No sooner had I finished this comforting perusal than I who had not had the courage to reread my manuscript, longed to begin reading it again immediately, for there is nothing like an old article by oneself of which one can say more aptly that " when one has read it one can read it again." I decided that I would send Françoise out to buy fresh copies, in order to give them to my friends, I should tell her, in reality so as to touch with my finger the miracle of the multiplication of my thought and to read, as though I were another person who had just opened the *Figaro*, in another copy the same sentences. It was, as it happened, ever so long since I had seen the Guermantes, I must pay them, next day, the call which I had planned with such agitation in the hope of meeting Mlle d'Eporcheville, when I telegraphed to Saint-Loup. I should find out from them what people thought of my article. I imagined some female reader into whose room I would have been so glad to penetrate and to whom the newspaper would convey if not my thought, which she would be incapable of understanding, at least my name, like a tribute to myself. But these tributes paid to one whom we do not love do not enchant our heart any more than the thoughts of a mind which we are unable to penetrate reach our mind. With regard to other friends, I told myself that if the state of my health continued to grow worse and if I could not see them again, it would be pleasant to continue to write to them so as still to have, in that way, access to them, to speak to them between the lines, to make them share my thoughts, to please them, to be received into their hearts. I told myself this because, social relations having previously had a place in my daily life, a future in which they would no longer figure alarmed me, and because this expedient which would enable me to keep the attention of my friends fixed upon myself, perhaps to arouse their admiration, until the day when I should be well enough to begin to see them again, consoled me. I told myself this, but I was well aware that it was not true, that if I chose to imagine their attention as the object of my pleasure, that pleasure was an internal, spiritual, ultimate pleasure which they themselves could not give me, and which I might find not in conversing with them, but in writing remote from them, and that if I began to write in the hope of seeing them indirectly, so that they might have a better idea of myself, so as to prepare for myself a better position in society, perhaps the act of writing would destroy in me any wish to see them, and that the position which literature would perhaps give me in society I should no longer feel any wish to enjoy, for my pleasure would be no longer in society, but in literature.

After luncheon when I went down to Mme de Guermantes, it was less for the sake of Mlle d'Eporcheville who had been stripped, by Saint-Loup's telegram, of the better part of her personality, than in the hope of finding in the Duchess herself one of those readers of my article who would enable me to form an idea of the impression that it had made upon the public—subscribers and purchasers—of the *Figaro*. It was not, however, without pleasure that I went to see Mme de Guermantes. It was all very well my telling myself that what made her house different to me from all the rest was the fact that it had for so long haunted my imagination, by knowing the reason for this difference I did not abolish it. Moreover, the name Guermantes existed for me in many forms. If the form which my memory had merely noted, as in an address-book, was not accompanied by any poetry, older forms, those which dated from the time when I did not know Mme de Guermantes, were liable to renew themselves in me, especially when I had not seen her for some time and when the glaring light of the person with human features did not quench the mysterious radiance of the name. Then once again I began to think of the home of Mme de Guermantes as of something that was beyond the bounds of reality, in the same way as I began to think again of the misty Balbec of my early dreams, and as though I had not since then made that journey, of the one twenty-two train as though I had never taken it. I forgot for an instant my own knowledge that such things did not exist, as we think at times of a beloved friend forgetting for an instant that he is dead. Then the idea of reality returned as I set foot in the Duchess's hall. But I consoled myself with the reflection that in spite of every-

thing it was for me the actual point of contact between
reality and dreams.

When I entered the drawing-room, I saw the fair girl
whom I had supposed for twenty-four hours to be the girl
of whom Saint-Loup had spoken to me. It was she who
asked the Duchess to "reintroduce" me to her. And
indeed, the moment I came into the room I had the
impression that I knew her quite well, which the Duchess
however dispelled by saying: "Oh! You have met Mlle
de Forcheville before." I myself, on the contrary, was
certain that I had never been introduced to any girl of
that name, which would certainly have impressed me, so
familiar was it in my memory ever since I had been given
a retrospective account of Odette's love affairs and Swann's
jealousy. In itself my twofold error as to the name, in
having remembered " de l'Orgeville " as " d'Eporcheville "
and in having reconstructed as " d'Eporcheville " what
was in reality " Forcheville," was in no way extraordinary.
Our mistake lies in our supposing that things present
themselves ordinarily as they are in reality, names as they
are written, people as photography and psychology give
an unalterable idea of them. As a matter of fact this is
not at all what we ordinarily perceive. We see, we hear,
we conceive the world quite topsy-turvy. We repeat a
name as we have heard it spoken until experience has corrected our mistake, which does not always happen. Everyone at Combray had spoken to Françoise for five-and-
twenty years of Mme Sazerat and Françoise continued to
say " Mme Sazerin," not from that deliberate and proud
perseverance in her mistakes which was habitual with her,
was strengthened by our contradiction and was all that she

had added of herself to the France of Saint-André-des-Champs (of the equalitarian principles of 1789 she claimed only one civic right, that of not pronouncing words as we did and of maintaining that " hotel," " été " and " air " were of the feminine gender), but because she really did continue to hear " Sazerin."[1] This perpetual error which is precisely " life," does not bestow its thousand forms merely upon the visible and the audible universe, but upon the social universe, the sentimental universe, the historical universe, and so forth. The Princesse de Luxembourg is no better than a prostitute in the eyes of the Chief Magistrate's wife, which as it happens is of little importance; what is slightly more important, Odette is a difficult woman to Swann, whereupon he builds up a whole romance which becomes all the more painful when he discovers his error; what is more important still, the French are thinking only of revenge in the eyes of the Germans. We have of the universe only formless, fragmentary visions, which we complete by the association of arbitrary ideas, creative of dangerous suggestions. I should, therefore, have had no reason to be surprised when I heard the name Forcheville (and I was already asking myself whether she was related to the Forcheville of whom I had so often heard) had not the fair girl said to me at once, anxious no doubt to forestall, tactfully, questions which would have been unpleasant to her: " You don't remember that you knew me quite well long ago . . . you used to come to our house . . . your friend Gilberte. I could see that you didn't recognise me. I recognised

---

[1] See *Swann's Way*, I. 92, where, however, this error is attributed to Eulalie. C. K. S. M.

you immediately." (She said this as if she had recognised me immediately in the drawing-room, but the truth is that she had recognised me in the street and had greeted me, and later Mme de Guermantes informed me that she had told her, as something very odd and extraordinary, that I had followed her and brushed against her, mistaking her for a prostitute). I did not learn until she had left the room why she was called Mlle de Forcheville. After Swann's death, Odette, who astonished everyone by her profound, prolonged and sincere grief, found herself an extremely rich widow. Forcheville married her, after making a long tour of various country houses and ascertaining that his family would acknowledge his wife. (The family raised certain objections, but yielded to the material advantage of not having to provide for the expenses of a needy relative who was about to pass from comparative penury to opulence.) Shortly after this, one of Swann's uncles, upon whose head the successive demise of many relatives had accumulated an enormous fortune, died, leaving the whole of his fortune to Gilberte who thus became one of the wealthiest heiresses in France. But this was the moment when from the effects of the Dreyfus case there had arisen an anti-semitic movement parallel to a more abundant movement towards the penetration of society by Israelites. The politicians had not been wrong in thinking that the discovery of the judicial error would deal a fatal blow to anti-semitism. But provisionally, at least, a social anti-semitism was on the contrary, enhanced and exacerbated by it. Forcheville who, like every petty nobleman, had derived from conversations in the family circle the certainty that his name was more ancient than that of La

Rochefoucauld, considered that, in marrying the widow of a Jew, he had performed the same act of charity as a millionaire who picks up a prostitute in the street and rescues her from poverty and mire; he was prepared to extend his bounty to Gilberte, whose prospects of marriage were assisted by all her millions but were hindered by that absurd name "Swann." He declared that he would adopt her. We know that Mme de Guermantes, to the astonishment—which, however, she liked and was accustomed to provoke—of her friends, had, after Swann's marriage, refused to meet his daughter as well as his wife. This refusal had been apparently all the more cruel, inasmuch as what had long made marriage with Odette seem possible to Swann was the prospect of introducing his daughter to Mme de Guermantes. And doubtless he ought to have known, he who had already had so long an experience of life, that these pictures which we form in our mind are never realised for a diversity of reasons. Among these there is one which meant that he seldom regretted his inability to effect that introduction. This reason is that, whatever the image may be, from the trout to be eaten at sunset which makes a sedentary man decide to take the train, to the desire to be able to astonish, one evening, the proud lady at a cash desk by stopping outside her door in a magnificent carriage which makes an unscrupulous man decide to commit murder, or to long for the death of rich relatives, according to whether he is bold or lazy, whether he goes ahead in the sequence of his ideas or remains fondling the first link in the chain, the act which is destined to enable us to attain to the image, whether that act be travel, marriage, crime . . . that act modifies us so profoundly that we cease to attach any importance to the reason which made us perform it. It may even happen that there never once recurs to his mind the image which the man formed who was not then a traveller, or a husband, or a criminal, or a recluse (who has bound himself to work with the idea of fame and has at the same moment rid himself of all desire for fame.) Besides even if we include an obstinate refusal to seem to have desired to act in vain, it is probable that the effect of the sunlight would not be repeated, that feeling cold at the moment we would long for a bowl of soup by the chimney-corner and not for a trout in the open air, that our carriage would leave the cashier unmoved who perhaps for wholly different reasons had a great regard for us and in whom this sudden opulence would arouse suspicion. In short we have seen Swann, when married, attach most importance to the relations of his wife and daughter with Mme Bontemps.

To all the reasons, derived from the Guermantes way of regarding social life, which had made the Duchess decide never to allow Mme and Mlle Swann to be introduced to her, we may add also that blissful assurance with which people who are not in love hold themselves aloof from what they condemn in lovers and what is explained by their love. " Oh! I don't mix myself up in that, if it amuses poor Swann to do stupid things and ruin his life, it is his affair, but one never knows with that sort of thing, it may end in great trouble, I leave them to clear it up for themselves." It is the *Suave mari magno* which Swann himself recommended to me with regard to the Verdurins, when he had long ceased to be in love with Odette and no

longer formed a part of the little clan. It is everything
that makes so wise the judgments of third persons with
regard to the passions which they do not feel and the
complications of behaviour which those passions involve.

Mme de Guermantes had indeed applied to the os-
tracism of Mme and Mlle Swann a perseverance that
caused general surprise. When Mme Molé, Mme de
Marsantes had begun to make friends with Mme Swann
and to bring a quantity of society ladies to see her, Mme de
Guermantes had not only remained intractable but had made
arrangements to blow up the bridges and to see that her
cousin the Princesse de Guermantes followed her example.
On one of the gravest days of the crisis when, during
Rouvier's Ministry, it was thought that there was going
to be war with Germany, upon going to dine with M. de
Bréauté at Mme de Guermantes's, I found the Duchess
looking worried. I supposed that, since she was always
dabbling in politics, she intended to shew that she was
afraid of war, as one day when she had appeared at the
dinner-table so pensive, barely replying in monosyllables,
upon somebody's inquiring timidly what was the cause of
her anxiety, she had answered with a grave air: " I am
anxious about China." But a moment later Mme de
Guermantes, herself volunteering an explanation of that
anxious air which I had put down to fear of a declaration
of war, said to M. de Bréauté: " I am told that Mme
Aynard means to establish the Swanns. I simply must
go and see Marie-Gilberte to-morrow and make her help
me to prevent it. Otherwise, there will be no society
left. The Dreyfus case is all very well. But then the
grocer's wife round the corner has only to call herself a

222

Nationalist and expect us to invite her to our houses in return." And I felt at this speech, so frivolous in comparison with the speech that I expected to hear, the astonishment of the reader who, turning to the usual column of the *Figaro* for the latest news of the Russo-Japanese war, finds instead the list of people who have given wedding-presents to Mlle de Mortemart, the importance of an aristocratic marriage having displaced to the end of the paper battles upon land and sea. The Duchess had come in time, moreover, to derive from this perseverance, pursued beyond all normal limits, a satisfaction to her pride which she lost no opportunity of expressing. "Babal" she said "maintains that we are the two smartest people in Paris because he and I are the only two people who do not allow Mme and Mlle Swann to bow to us. For he assures me that smartness consists in not knowing Mme Swann." And the Duchess ended in a peal of laughter.

However, when Swann was dead, it came to pass that her determination not to know his daughter had ceased to furnish Mme de Guermantes with all the satisfaction of pride, independence, self-government, persecution which she was capable of deriving from it, which had come to an end with the passing of the man who had given her the exquisite sensation that she was resisting him, that he was unable to make her revoke her decrees.

Then the Duchess had proceeded to the promulgation of other decrees which, being applied to people who were still alive, could make her feel that she was free to act as she might choose. She did not speak to the Swann girl, but, when anyone mentioned the girl to her, the Duchess felt a curiosity, as about some place that she had never visited, which could no longer be suppressed by her desire to stand out against Swann's pretensions. Besides, so many different sentiments may contribute to the formation of a single sentiment that it would be impossible to say whether there was not a lingering trace of affection for Swann in this interest. No doubt—for in every grade of society a worldly and frivolous life paralyses our sensibility and robs us of the power to resuscitate the dead—the Duchess was one of those people who require a personal presence—that presence which, like a true Guermantes, she excelled in protracting—in order to love truly, but also, and this is less common, in order to hate a little. So that often her friendly feeling for people, suspended during their lifetime by the irritation that some action or other on their part caused her, revived after their death. She then felt almost a longing to make reparation, because she pictured them now—though very vaguely—with only their good qualities, and stripped of the petty satisfactions, of the petty pretensions which had irritated her in them when they were alive. This imparted at times, notwithstanding the frivolity of Mme de Guermantes, something that was distinctly noble—blended with much that was base—to her conduct. Whereas three-fourths of the human race flatter the living and pay no attention to the dead, she would often do, after their death, what the people would have longed for her to do whom she had maltreated while they were alive.

As for Gilberte, all the people who were fond of her and had a certain respect for her dignity, could not rejoice at the change in the Duchess's attitude towards her except by thinking that Gilberte, scornfully rejecting advances that came after twenty-five years of insults, would be avenging these at length. Unfortunately, moral reflexes are not always identical with what commonsense imagines. A man who, by an untimely insult, thinks that he had forfeited for all time all hope of winning the friendship of a person to whom he is attached finds that on the contrary, he has established his position. Gilberte, who remained quite indifferent to the people who were kind to her, never ceased to think with admiration of the insolent Mme de Guermantes, to ask herself the reasons for such insolence; once indeed (and this would have made all the people who shewed some affection for her die with shame on her account) she had decided to write to the Duchess to ask her what she had against a girl who had never done her any injury. The Guermantes had assumed in her eyes proportions which their birth would have been powerless to give them. She placed them not only above all the nobility, but even above all the royal houses.

Certain women who were old friends of Swann took a great interest in Gilberte. When the aristocracy learned of her latest inheritance, they began to remark how well bred she was and what a charming wife she would make. People said that a cousin of Mme de Guermantes, the Princesse de Nièvre, was thinking of Gilberte for her son. Mme de Guermantes hated Mme de Nièvre. She announced that such a marriage would be a scandal. Mme de Nièvre took fright and swore that she had never thought of it. One day, after luncheon, as the sun was shining, and M. de Guermantes was going to take his wife out, Mme de Guermantes was arranging her hat in front of the mirror, her blue eyes gazing into their own reflection, and at her still golden hair, her maid holding in her hand various sunshades among which her mistress might choose. The sun came flooding in through the window and they had decided to take advantage of the fine weather to pay a call at Saint-Cloud, and M. de Guermantes, ready to set off, wearing pearl-grey gloves and a tall hat on his head said to himself: "Oriane is really astounding still. I find her delicious," and went on, aloud, seeing that his wife seemed to be in a good humour: " By the way, I have a message for you from Mme de Virelef. She wanted to ask you to come on Monday to the Opera, but as she's having the Swann girl, she did not dare and asked me to explore the ground. I don't express any opinion, I simply convey the message. But really, it seems to me that we might. . . ." he added evasively, for their attitude towards anyone else being a collective attitude and taking an identical form in each of them, he knew from his own feelings that his wife's hostility to Mlle Swann had subsided and that she was anxious to meet her. Mme de Guermantes settled her veil to her liking and chose a sunshade. " But just as you like, what difference do you suppose it can make to me, I see no reason against our meeting the girl. I simply did not wish that we should appear to be countenancing the dubious establishments of our friends. That is all." " And you were perfectly right," replied the Duke. " You are wisdom incarnate, Madame, and you are more ravishing than ever in that hat." " You are very kind," said Mme de Guermantes with a smile at her husband as she made her way to the door. But, before entering the carriage, she felt it her duty to give him a further explanation: " There are plenty of people now who call upon the mother, besides she has the sense to be ill for nine months of the year. . . . It seems that the child is quite charming. Everybody knows that we were greatly attached to Swann. People will think it quite natural," and they set off together for Saint-Cloud.

A month later, the Swann girl, who had not yet taken the name of Forcheville, came to luncheon with the Guermantes. Every conceivable subject was discussed; at the end of the meal, Gilberte said timidly: " I believe you knew my father quite well." " Why of course we did," said Mme de Guermantes in a melancholy tone which proved that she understood the daughter's grief and with a deliberate excess of intensity which gave her the air of concealing the fact that she was not sure whether she did remember the father. " We knew him quite well, I remember him *quite well*." (As indeed she might, seeing that he had come to see her almost every day for twenty-five years.) " I know quite well who he was, let me tell you," she went on, as though she were seeking to explain to the daughter whom she had had for a father and to give the girl information about him, " he was a great friend of my mother-in-law and besides he was very intimate with my brother-in-law Palamède." " He used to come here too, indeed he used to come to luncheon here," added M. de Guermantes with an ostentatious modesty and a scrupulous exactitude. " You remember, Oriane. What a fine man your father was. One felt that he must come of a respectable family; for that matter I saw once, long ago, his own father and mother. They and he, what worthy people! "

One felt that if they had, parents and son, been still alive, the Duc de Guermantes would not have had a moment's hesitation in recommending them for a post as gardeners! And this is how the Faubourg Saint-Germain speaks to any bourgeois of the other bourgeois, whether in order to flatter him with the exception made—during the course of the conversation—in favour of the listener, or rather and at the same time in order to humiliate him. Thus it is that an anti-semite in addressing a Jew, at the very moment when he is smothering him in affability, speaks evil of Jews, in a general fashion which enables him to be wounding without being rude.

But while she could shower compliments upon a person, when she met him, and could then never bring herself to let him take his leave, Mme de Guermantes was also a slave to this need of personal contact. Swann might have managed, now and then, in the excitement of conversation, to give the Duchess the illusion that she regarded him with a friendly feeling, he could do so no longer. " He was charming," said the Duchess with a wistful smile and fastening upon Gilberte a kindly gaze which would at least, supposing the girl to have delicate feelings, shew her that she was understood, and that Mme de Guermantes, had the two been alone together and had circumstances allowed it, would have loved to reveal to her all the depth of her own feelings. But M. de Guermantes, whether because he was indeed of the opinion that the circumstances forbade such effusions, or because he considered that any exaggeration of sentiment was a matter for women and that men had no more part in it than in the other feminine departments, save the kitchen and the wine-cellar which he had reserved to himself, knowing more about them than the Duchess, felt it incumbent upon him not to encourage, by taking part in it, this conversation to which he listened with a visible impatience.

Moreover Mme de Guermantes, when this outburst of sentiment had subsided, added with a worldly frivolity, addressing Gilberte: " Why, he was not only a great friend of my brother-in-law Charlus, he was also a great favourite at Voisenon " (the country house of the Prince de Guermantes), as though Swann's acquaintance with M. de Charlus and the Prince had been a mere accident, as though the Duchess's brother-in-law and cousin were two men with whom Swann had happened to be intimate for some special reason, whereas Swann had been intimate with all the people in that set, and as though Mme de Guermantes were seeking to make Gilberte understand who, more or less, her father had been, to " place " him by one of those character sketches by which, when we seek to explain how it is that we happen to know somebody whom we would not naturally know, or to give an additional point to our story, we name the sponsors by whom a certain person was introduced.

As for Gilberte, she was all the more glad to find that the subject was dropped, in that she herself was anxious only to change it, having inherited from Swann his exquisite tact combined with an intellectual charm that was appreciated by the Duke and Duchess who begged her to come again soon. Moreover, with the minute observation of people whose lives have no purpose, they would discern, one after another, in the people with whom they associated, the most obvious merits, exclaiming their

wonder at them with the artless astonishment of a towns-
man who on going into the country discovers a blade of
grass, or on the contrary magnifying them as with a
microscope, making endless comments, taking offence at
the slightest faults, and often applying both processes
alternately to the same person. In Gilberte's case it was
first of all upon these minor attractions that the idle
perspicacity of M. and Mme de Guermantes was brought
to bear: " Did you notice the way in which she pro-
nounced some of her words? " the Duchess said to her
husband after the girl had left them; " it was just like
Swann, I seemed to hear him speaking." " I was just
about to say the very same, Oriane." " She is witty, she
is just like her father." " I consider that she is even far
superior to him. Think how well she told that story
about the sea-bathing, she has a vivacity that Swann never
had." " Oh! but he was, after all, quite witty." " I
am not saying that he was not witty, I say that he lacked
vivacity," said M. de Guermantes in a complaining tone,
for his gout made him irritable, and when he had no one
else upon whom to vent his irritation, it was to the Duchess that he displayed it. But being incapable of any clear
understanding of its causes, he preferred to adopt an air of
being misunderstood.

This friendly attitude on the part of the Duke and
Duchess meant that, for the future, they might at the most
let fall an occasional " your poor father " to Gilberte,
which, for that matter, was quite unnecessary, since it was
just about this time that Forcheville adopted the girl.
She addressed him as " Father ", charmed all the dowagers
by her politeness and air of breeding, and it was admitted

that, if Forcheville had behaved with the utmost generosity towards her, the girl had a good heart and knew how to reward him for his pains. Doubtless because she was able, now and then, and desired to shew herself quite at her ease, she had reintroduced herself to me and in conversation with me had spoken of her true father. But this was an exception and no one now dared utter the name Swann in her presence.

I had just caught sight, in the drawing-room, of two sketches by Elstir which formerly had been banished to a little room upstairs in which it was only by chance that I had seen them. Elstir was now in fashion. Mme de Guermantes could not forgive herself for having given so many of his pictures to her cousin, not because they were in fashion, but because she now appreciated them. Fashion is, indeed, composed of the appreciations of a number of people of whom the Guermantes are typical. But she could not dream of buying others of his pictures, for they had long ago begun to fetch absurdly high prices. She was determined to have something, at least, by Elstir in her drawing-room and had brought down these two drawings which, she declared, she " preferred to his paintings."

Gilberte recognised the drawings. " One would say Elstir," she suggested. " Why, yes," replied the Duchess without thinking, " it was, as a matter of fact, your fa . . . some friends of ours who made us buy them. They are admirable. To my mind, they are superior to his paintings." I who had not heard this conversation went closer to the drawings to examine them. " Why, this is the Elstir that. . . ." I saw Mme de Guermantes's signals of despair. " Ah, yes! The Elstir that

I admired upstairs. It shews far better here than in that passage. Talking of Elstir, I mentioned him yesterday in an article in the *Figaro*. Did you happen to read it? " " You have written an article in the *Figaro?* " exclaimed M. de Guermantes with the same violence as if he had exclaimed: " Why, she is my cousin." " Yes, yesterday." " In the *Figaro*, you are certain? That is a great surprise. For we each of us get our *Figaro*, and if one of us had missed it, the other would certainly have noticed it. That is so, ain't it, Oriane, there was nothing in the paper." The Duke sent for the *Figaro* and accepted the facts, as though, previously, the probability had been that I had made a mistake as to the newspaper for which I had written. " What's that, I don't understand, do you mean to say, you have written an article in the *Figaro?* " said the Duchess, making an effort in order to speak of a matter which did not interest her. " Come, Basin, you can read it afterwards." " No, the Duke looks so nice like that with his big beard sweeping over the paper," said Gilberte. " I shall read it as soon as I am at home." " Yes, he wears a beard now that everybody is clean-shaven," said the Duchess, " he never does anything like other people. When we were first married, he shaved not only his beard but his moustaches as well. The peasants who didn't know him by sight thought that he couldn't be French. He was called at that time the Prince des Laumes." " Is there still a Prince des Laumes? " asked Gilberte, who was interested in everything that concerned the people who had refused to bow to her during all those years. " Why, no ! " the Duchess replied with a melancholy, caressing gaze. " Such a charming title!

One of the finest titles in France!" said Gilberte, a certain sort of banality emerging inevitably, as a clock strikes the hour, from the lips of certain quite intelligent persons. "Yes, indeed, I regret it too. Basin would have liked his sister's son to take it, but it is not the same thing; after all it is possible, since it is not necessarily the eldest son, the title may pass to a younger brother. I was telling you that in those days Basin was clean-shaven; one day, at a pilgrimage—you remember, my dear," she turned to her husband, "that pilgrimage at Paray-le-Monial—my brother-in-law Charlus who always enjoys talking to peasants, was saying to one after another: 'where do you come from?' and as he is extremely generous, he would give them something, take them off to have a drink. For nobody was ever at the same time simpler and more haughty than Mémé. You'll see him refuse to bow to a Duchess whom he doesn't think duchessy enough, and shower compliments upon a kennelman. And so, I said to Basin: 'Come, Basin, say something to them too.' My husband, who is not always very inventive—" "Thank you, Oriane," said the Duke, without interrupting his reading of my article in which he was immersed— "approached one of the peasants and repeated his brother's question in so many words: 'Where do you come from?' 'I am from Les Laumes.' 'You are from Les Laumes. Why, I am your Prince.' Then the peasant looked at Basin's smooth face and replied: ''s not true. You're an English.'"[1] One saw thus in these anecdotes told by the Duchess those great and eminent titles, such as that

---

[1] Mme de Guermantes forgets that she had already told this story at the expense of the Prince de Léon. See *The Captive, p.* 39.

of the Prince des Laumes, rise to their true position, in their original state and their local colour, as in certain Books of Hours one sees, amid the mob of the period, the soaring steeple of Bourges.

Some cards were brought to her which a footman had just left at the door. " I can't think what has come over her, I don't know her. It is to you that I am indebted for this, Basin. Not that they have done you any good, all these people, my poor dear," and, turning to Gilberte: " I really don't know how to explain to you who she is, you certainly have never heard of her, she calls herself Lady Rufus Israel."

Gilberte flushed crimson: " I do not know her," she said (which was all the more untrue in that Lady Israel and Swann had been reconciled two years before the latter's death and she addressed Gilberte by her Christian name), " but I know quite well, from hearing about her, who it is that you mean." The truth is that Gilberte had become a great snob. For instance, another girl having one day, whether in malice or from a natural want of tact, asked her what was the name of her real—not her adoptive—father, in her confusion, and as though to mitigate the crudity of what she had to say, instead of pronouncing the name as " Souann " she said " Svann," a change, as she soon realised, for the worse, since it made this name of English origin a German patronymic. And she had even gone on to say, abasing herself so as to rise higher: " All sorts of stories have been told about my birth, but of course, I know nothing about that."

Ashamed as Gilberte must have felt at certain moments when she thought of her parents (for even Mme Swann

234

represented to her and was a good mother) of such an attitude towards life, we must, alas, bear in mind that its elements were borrowed doubtless from her parents, for we do not create the whole of our own personality. But with a certain quantity of egoism which exists in the mother, a different egoism, inherent in the father's family, is combined, which does not invariably mean that it is added, nor even precisely that it serves as a multiple, but rather that it creates a fresh egoism infinitely stronger and more redoubtable. And, in the period that has elapsed since the world began, during which families in which some defect exists in one form have been intermarrying with families in which the same defect exists in another, thereby creating a peculiarly complex and detestable variety of that defect in the offspring, the accumulated egoisms (to confine ourselves, for the moment, to this defect) would have acquired such force that the whole human race would have been destroyed, did not the malady itself bring forth, with the power to reduce it to its true dimensions, natural restrictions analogous to those which prevent the infinite proliferation of the infusoria from destroying our planet, the unisexual fertilisation of plants from bringing about the extinction of the vegetable kingdom, and so forth. From time to time a virtue combines with this egoism to produce a new and disinterested force.

The combinations by which, in the course of generations, moral chemistry thus stabilises and renders inoffensive the elements that were becoming too formidable, are infinite and would give an exciting variety to family history. Moreover, with these accumulated egoisms such as must have been embodied in Gilberte there co-exists some charming virtue of the parents; it appears for a moment to perform an interlude by itself, to play its touching part with an entire sincerity.

No doubt Gilberte did not always go so far as when she insinuated that she was perhaps the natural daughter of some great personage, but as a rule she concealed her origin. Perhaps it was simply too painful for her to confess it and she preferred that people should learn of it from others. Perhaps she really believed that she was hiding it, with that uncertain belief which at the same time is not doubt, which reserves a possibility for what we would like to think true, of which Musset furnishes an example when he speaks of Hope in God. " I do not know her personally," Gilberte went on. Had she, after all, when she called herself Mlle de Forcheville, a hope that people would not know that she was Swann's daughter? Some people, perhaps, who, she hoped, would in time become everybody. She could not be under any illusion as to their number at the moment, and knew doubtless that many people must be murmuring: " Isn't that Swann's daughter? " But she knew it only with that information which tells us of people taking their lives in desperation while we are going to a ball, that is to say, a remote and vague information for which we are at no pains to substitute a more precise knowledge, founded upon a direct impression. Gilberte belonged, during these years at least, to the most widespread variety of the human ostrich, the kind which buries its head in the hope not of not being seen, which it considers hardly probable, but of not seeing that other people see it, which seems to it something to the good and enables it to leave the rest to chance. As distance makes things smaller, more uncertain, less dangerous, Gilberte preferred not to be near other people at the moment when they made the discovery that she was by birth a Swann.

And as we are near the people whom we picture to ourself, as we can picture people reading their newspaper, Gilberte preferred the papers to style her Mlle de Forcheville. It is true that with the writings for which she herself was responsible, her letters, she prolonged the transition for some time by signing herself " G. S. Forcheville." The real hypocrisy in this signature was made manifest by the suppression not so much of the other letters of the word " Swann " as of those of the word " Gilberte." In fact, by reducing the innocent Christian name to a simple " G," Mlle de Forcheville seemed to insinuate to her friends that the similar amputation applied to the name " Swann " was due merely to the necessity of abbreviation. Indeed she gave a special importance to the " S," and gave it a sort of long tail which ran across the " G," but which one felt to be transitory and destined to disappear like the tail which, still long in the monkey, has ceased to exist in man.

Notwithstanding this, in her snobbishness, there remained the intelligent curiosity of Swann. I remember that, during this same afternoon, she asked Mme de Guermantes whether she could meet M. du Lau, and that when the Duchess replied that he was an invalid and never went out, Gilberte asked what sort of man he was, for, she added with a faint blush, she had heard a great deal about him. (The Marquis du Lau had indeed been one of Swann's most intimate friends before the latter's marriage, and Gilberte may perhaps herself have seen him, but at a time when she was not interested in such people.) " Would M. de Bréauté or the Prince d'Agrigente be at all like him? " she asked. " Oh! not in the least," exclaimed Mme de Guermantes, who had a keen sense of these provincial differences and drew portraits that were sober, but coloured by her harsh, golden voice, beneath the gentle blossoming of her violet eyes. " No, not in the least. Du Lau was the gentleman from the Périgord, charming, with all the good manners and the absence of ceremony of his province. At Guermantes, when we had the King of England, with whom du Lau was on the friendliest terms, we used to have a little meal after the men came in from shooting. . . . It was the hour when du Lau was in the habit of going to his room to take off his boots and put on big woollen slippers. Very well, the presence of King Edward and all the Grand Dukes did not disturb him in the least, he came down to the great hall at Guermantes in his woollen slippers, he felt that he was the Marquis du Lau d'Ollemans who had no reason to put himself out for the King of England. He and that charming Quasimodo de Breteuil, they were the two that I liked best. They were, for that matter, great friends of. . . ." (she was about to say " your father " and stopped short). " No, there is no resemblance at all, either to Gri-gri, or to Bréauté. He was the genuine nobleman from the Périgord. For that matter, Mémé quotes a page from Saint-Simon about a Marquis d'Ollemans, it is just like him." I repeated the opening words of the portrait: " M. d'Ollemans who was a man of great distinction among the nobility of the Périgord, from his own birth and from his merit, and was regarded by every soul alive there as a general arbiter to whom each had recourse because of his probity, his capacity and the suavity of his manners, as it were, the cock of his province." "Yes, he's like that," said Mme de Guermantes, "all the more so as du Lau was always as red as a cock." "Yes, I remember hearing that description quoted," said Gilberte, without adding that it had been quoted by her father, who was, as we know, a great admirer of Saint-Simon.

She liked also to speak of the Prince d'Agrigente and of M. de Bréauté, for another reason. The Prince d'Agrigente was prince by inheritance from the House of Aragon, but his lordship was Poitevin. As for his country house, the house, that is to say, in which he lived, it was not the property of his own family, but had come to him from his mother's former husband, and was situated almost halfway between Martinville and Guermantes. And so Gilberte spoke of him and of M. de Bréauté as of neighbours in the country who reminded her of her old home. Strictly speaking there was an element of falsehood in this attitude, since it was only in Paris, through the Comtesse Molé, that she had come to know M. de Bréauté, albeit he had been an old friend of her father. As for her pleasure in speaking of the country round Tansonville, it may have been sincere. Snobbishness is, with certain people, analogous to those pleasant beverages with which they mix nutritious substances. Gilberte took an interest in some lady of fashion because she possessed priceless books and portraits by Nattier which my former friend would probably not have taken the trouble to inspect in the

National Library or at the Louvre, and I imagine that not-withstanding the even greater proximity, the magnetic influence of Tansonville would have had less effect in drawing Gilberte towards Mme Sazerat or Mme Goupil than towards M. d'Agrigente.

"Oh! poor Babal and poor Gri-gri," said Mme de Guermantes, "they are in a far worse state than du Lau, I'm afraid they haven't long to live, either of them."

When M. de Guermantes had finished reading my article, he paid me compliments which however he took care to qualify. He regretted the slightly hackneyed form of a style in which there were "emphasis, metaphors as in the antiquated prose of Chateaubriand "; on the other hand he congratulated me without reserve upon my " occupying myself ": " I like a man to do something with his ten fingers. I do not like the useless creatures who are always self-important or agitators. A fatuous breed! "

Gilberte, who was acquiring with extreme rapidity the ways of the world of fashion, announced how proud she would be to say that she was the friend of an author. "You can imagine that I shall tell people that I have the pleasure, the honour of your acquaintance."

"You wouldn't care to come with us, to-morrow, to the Opéra-Comique? " the Duchess asked me; and I thought that it would be doubtless in that same box in which I had first beheld her, and which had seemed to me then as inaccessible as the submarine realm of the Nereids. But I replied in a melancholy tone: " No, I am not going to the theatre just now; I have lost a friend to whom I was greatly attached." The tears almost came to my eyes as I said this, and yet, for the first time, I felt a sort of pleasure in speaking of my bereavement. It was from this moment that I began to write to all my friends that I had just experienced a great sorrow, and to cease to feel it.

When Gilberte had gone, Mme de Guermantes said to me: "You did not understand my signals, I was trying to hint to you not to mention Swann." And, as I apologised: "But I quite understand. I was on the point of mentioning him myself, but I stopped short just in time, it was terrible, fortunately I bridled my tongue. You know, it is a great bore," she said to her husband, seeking to mitigate my own error by appearing to believe that I had yielded to a propensity common to everyone, and difficult to resist. "What do you expect me to do," replied the Duke. "You have only to tell them to take those drawings upstairs again, since they make you think about Swann. If you don't think about Swann, you won't speak about him."

On the following day I received two congratulatory letters which surprised me greatly, one from Mme Goupil whom I had not seen for many years and to whom, even at Combray, I had not spoken more than twice. A public library had given her the chance of seeing the *Figaro*. Thus, when anything occurs in our life which makes some stir, messages come to us from people situated so far outside the zone of our acquaintance, our memory of whom is already so remote that these people seem to be placed at a great distance, especially in the dimension of depth. A forgotten friendship of our school days, which has had a score of opportunities of recalling itself to our mind, gives us a sign of life, not that there are not negative results also. For example, Bloch, from whom I would have been so glad to learn what he thought of my article, did not write to me.

It is true that he had read the article and was to admit it later, but by a counterstroke. In fact, he himself contributed, some years later, an article to the *Figaro* and was anxious to inform me immediately of the event. As he ceased to be jealous of what he regarded as a privilege, as soon as it had fallen to him as well, the envy that had made him pretend to ignore my article ceased, as though by the raising of a lever; he mentioned it to me but not at all in the way in which he hoped to hear me mention his article: " I know that you too," he told me, " have written an article. But I do not think that I ought to mention it to you, for fear of hurting your feelings, for we ought not to speak to our friends of the humiliations that occur to them. And it is obviously a humiliation to supply the organ of sabres and aspergills with ' five-o'clocks,' not forgetting the holy-water-stoup." His character remained unaltered, but his style had become less precious, as happens to certain people who shed their mannerisms, when, ceasing to compose symbolist poetry, they take to writing newspaper serials.

To console myself for his silence, I read Mme Goupil's letter again; but it was lacking in warmth, for if the aristocracy employ certain formulas which slip into watertight compartments, between the initial " *Monsieur* " and the " *sentiments distingués* " of the close, cries of joy, of admiration may spring up like flowers, and their clusters waft over the barriers their entrancing fragrance. But middle-class conventionality enwraps even the content of letters in a net of " your well-deserved success," at best " your great success." Sisters-in-law, faithful to their upbringing and tight-laced in their respectable stays, think that they have overflowed into the most distressing enthusiasm if they have written: " my kindest regards." " Mother joins me " is a superlative of which they are seldom wearied.

I received another letter as well as Mme Goupil's, but the name of the writer was unknown to me. It was an illiterate hand, a charming style. I was desolate at my inability to discover who had written to me.

While I was asking myself whether Bergotte would have liked this article, Mme de Forcheville had replied that he would have admired it enormously and could not have read it without envy. But she had told me this while I slept: it was a dream.

Almost all our dreams respond thus to the questions which we put to ourself with complicated statements, presentations of several characters on the stage, which however lead to nothing.

As for Mlle de Forcheville, I could not help feeling appalled when I thought of her. What? The daughter of Swann who would so have loved to see her at the Guermantes', for whom they had refused their great friend the favour of an invitation, they had now sought out of their own accord, time having elapsed which refashions everything for us, instils a fresh personality, based upon what we have been told about them, into people whom we have not seen during a long interval, in which we ourself have grown a new skin and acquired fresh tastes. I recalled how, to this girl, Swann used to say at times as he hugged her and kissed her: " It is a comfort, my darling, to have a child like you; one day when I am no longer here, if people still mention your poor papa, it will be only to you and because of you." Swann in anticipating thus after his own death a timorous and anxious hope of his survival in his daughter was as greatly mistaken as the old banker who having made a will in favour of a little dancer whom he is keeping and who behaves admirably, tells himself that he is nothing more to her than a great friend, but that she will remain faithful to his memory. She did behave admirably, while her feet under the table sought the feet of those of the old banker's friends who appealed to her, but all this was concealed, beneath an excellent exterior. She will wear mourning for the worthy man, will feel that she is well rid of him, will enjoy not only the ready money, but the real estate, the motor-cars that he has bequeathed to her, taking care to remove the monogram of the former owner, which makes her feel slightly ashamed, and with her enjoyment of the gift will never associate any regret for the giver. The illusions of paternal affection are perhaps no less deceiving than those of the other kind; many girls regard their fathers only as the old men who are going to leave them a fortune. Gilberte's presence in a drawing-room, instead of being an opportunity for speaking occasionally still of her father, was an obstacle in the way of people's seizing those opportunities, increasingly more rare, that they might still have had of referring to him. Even in connection with the things that he had said, the presents that he had made, people acquired the habit of not mentioning him, and she who ought to have refreshed, not to say perpetuated his memory, found herself hastening and completing the process of death and oblivion.

And it was not merely with regard to Swann that Gilberte was gradually completing the process of oblivion, she had accelerated in me that process of oblivion with regard to Albertine.

Under the action of desire, and consequently of the desire for happiness which Gilberte had aroused in me during those hours in which I had supposed her to be someone else, a certain number of miseries, of painful preoccupations which only a little while earlier had obsessed my mind, had been released, carrying with them a whole block of memories, probably long since crumbled and become precarious, with regard to Albertine. For if many memories, which were connected with her, had at the outset helped to keep alive in me my regret for her death, in return that regret had itself fixed those memories. So that the modification of my sentimental state, prepared no doubt obscurely day by day by the constant disintegration of oblivion, but realised abruptly as a whole, gave me the impression which I remember that I felt that day for the first time, of a void, of the suppression in myself of a whole portion of my associations of ideas, which a man feels in whose brain an artery, long exhausted, has burst, so that a whole section of his memory is abolished or paralysed.

The vanishing of my suffering and of all that it carried away with it, left me diminished as does often the healing of a malady which occupied a large place in our life. No doubt it is because memories are not always genuine that love is not eternal, and because life is made up of a perpetual renewal of our cells. But this renewal, in the case of memories, is nevertheless retarded by the attention which arrests and fixes a moment that is bound to change. And since it is the case with grief as with the desire for women that we increase it by thinking about it, the fact of having plenty of other things to do should, like chastity, make oblivion easy.

By another reaction (albeit it was the distraction—the desire for Mlle d'Eporcheville—that had made my oblivion suddenly apparent and perceptible), if the fact remains that it is time that gradually brings oblivion, oblivion does not fail to alter profoundly our notion of time. There are optical errors in time as there are in space. The persistence in myself of an old tendency to work, to make up for lost time, to change my way of life, or rather to begin to live gave me the illusion that I was still as young as in the past; and yet the memory of all the events that had followed one another in my life (and also of those that had followed one another in my heart, for when we have greatly changed, we are led to suppose that our life has been longer) in the course of those last months of Albertine's existence, had made them seem to me much longer than a year, and now this oblivion of so many things, separating me by gulfs of empty space from quite recent events which they made me think remote, because I had had what is called "the time" to forget them, by its fragmentary, irregular interpolation in my memory—like a thick fog at sea which obliterates all the landmarks—confused, destroyed my sense of distances in time, contracted in one place, extended in another, and made me suppose myself now farther away from things, now far closer to them than I really was. And as in the fresh spaces, as yet unexplored, which extended before me, there would be no more trace of my love for Albertine than there had been, in the time past which I had just traversed, of my love for my grandmother, my life appeared to me—offering a succession of periods in which, after a certain interval, nothing of what had sustained the previous period survived in that which followed

—as something so devoid of the support of an individual, identical and permanent self, something so useless in the future and so protracted in the past, that death might just as well put an end to its course here or there, without in the least concluding it, as with those courses of French history which, in the Rhetoric class, stop short indifferently, according to the whim of the curriculum or the professor, at the Revolution of 1830, or at that of 1848, or at the end of the Second Empire.

Perhaps then the fatigue and distress which I was feeling were due not so much to my having loved in vain what I was already beginning to forget, as to my coming to take pleasure in the company of fresh living people, purely social figures, mere friends of the Guermantes, offering no interest in themselves. It was easier perhaps to reconcile myself to the discovery that she whom I had loved was nothing more, after a certain interval of time, than a pale memory, than to the rediscovery in myself of that futile activity which makes us waste time in decorating our life with a human vegetation that is alive but is parasitic, which likewise will become nothing when it is dead, which already is alien to all that we have ever known, which, nevertheless, our garrulous, melancholy, conceited senility seeks to attract. The newcomer who would find it easy to endure the prospect of life without Albertine had made his appearance in me, since I had been able to speak of her at Mme de Guermantes's in the language of grief without any real suffering. These strange selves which were to bear each a different name, the possibility of their coming had, by reason of their indifference to the object of my love, always alarmed me, long ago in connection with Gilberte when her father told me that if I went to live in Oceania I would never wish to return, quite recently when I had read with such a pang in my heart the passage in Bergotte's novel where he treats of the character who, separated by the events of life from a woman whom he had adored when he was young, as an old man meets her without pleasure, without any desire to see her again.   Now, on the contrary, he was bringing me with oblivion an almost complete elimination of suffering, a possibility of comfort, this person so dreaded, so beneficent who was none other than one of those spare selves whom destiny holds in reserve for us, and, without paying any more heed to our entreaties than a clear-sighted and so all the more authoritative physician, substitutes without our aid, by an opportune intervention, for the self that has been too seriously injured.   This renewal, as it happens, nature performs from time to time, as by the decay and refashioning of our tissues, but we notice this only if the former self contained a great grief, a painful foreign body, which we are surprised to find no longer there, in our amazement at having become another self to whom the sufferings of his precursor are nothing more than the sufferings of a stranger, of which we can speak with compassion because we do not feel them.   Indeed we are unaffected by our having undergone all those sufferings, since we have only a vague remembrance of having suffered them.   It is possible that similarly our dreams, during the night, may be terrible.   But when we awake we are another person to whom it is of no importance that the person whose place he takes has had to fly during our sleep from a band of cut-throats.

No doubt this self had maintained some contact with the

old self, as a friend, unconcerned by a bereavement, speaks of it nevertheless, to those who come to the house, in a suitable tone of sorrow, and returns from time to time to the room in which the widower who has asked him to receive the company for him may still be heard weeping. I made this contact even closer when I became once again for a moment the former friend of Albertine. But it was into a new personality that I was tending to pass altogether. It is not because other people are dead that our affection for them grows faint, it is because we ourself are dying. Albertine had no cause to rebuke her friend. The man who was usurping his name had merely inherited it. We may be faithful to what we remember, we remember only what we have known. My new self, while it grew up in the shadow of the old, had often heard the other speak of Albertine; through that other self, through the information that it gathered from it, it thought that it knew her, it found her attractive, it was in love with her, but this was merely an affection at second hand.

Another person in whom the process of oblivion, so far as concerned Albertine, was probably more rapid at this time, and enabled me in return to realise a little later a fresh advance which that process had made in myself (and this is my memory of a second stage before the final oblivion), was Andrée. I can scarcely, indeed, refrain from citing this oblivion of Albertine as, if not the sole cause, if not even the principal cause, at any rate a conditioning and necessary cause of a conversation between Andrée and myself about six months after the conversation which I have already reported, when her words were so different from those that she had used on the former occasion. I remem-

ber that it was in my room because at that moment I found
a pleasure in having semi-carnal relations with her, because
of the collective form originally assumed and now being
resumed by my love for the girls of the little band, a love
that had long been undivided among them, and for a while
associated exclusively with Albertine's person during the
months that had preceded and followed her death.

We were in my room for another reason as well which
enables me to date this conversation quite accurately.
This was that I had been banished from the rest of the
apartment because it was Mamma's day. Notwithstanding its being her day, and after some hesitation, Mamma
had gone to luncheon with Mme Sazerat thinking that as
Mme Sazerat always contrived to invite one to meet boring
people, she would be able without sacrificing any pleasure
to return home in good time. And she had indeed returned in time and without regret, Mme Sazerat having
had nobody but the most deadly people who were frozen
from the start by the special voice that she adopted when
she had company, what Mamma called her Wednesday
voice. My mother was, nevertheless, extremely fond of
her, was sorry for her poverty—the result of the extrava-
gance of her father who had been ruined by the Duchesse
de X. . . .—a poverty which compelled her to live all the
year round at Combray, with a few weeks at her cousin's
house in Paris and a great " pleasure-trip " every ten years.

I remember that the day before this, at my request repeated for months past, and because the Princess was always
begging her to come, Mamma had gone to call upon the
Princesse de Parme, who, herself, paid no calls, and at
whose house people as a rule contented themselves with

writing their names, but who had insisted upon my mother's coming to see her, since the rules and regulations prevented Her from coming to us. My mother had come home thoroughly cross: "You have sent me on a fool's errand," she told me, "the Princesse de Parme barely greeted me, she turned back to the ladies to whom she was talking without paying me any attention, and after ten minutes, as she hadn't uttered a word to me, I came away without her even offering me her hand. I was extremely annoyed; however, on the doorstep, as I was leaving, I met the Duchesse de Guermantes who was very kind and spoke to me a great deal about you. What a strange idea that was to tell her about Albertine. She told me that you had said to her that her death had been such a grief to you. I shall never go near the Princesse de Parme again. You have made me make a fool of myself."

Well, the next day, which was my mother's at-home day, as I have said, Andrée came to see me. She had not much time, for she had to go and call for Gisèle with whom she was very anxious to dine. "I know her faults, but she is after all my best friend and the person for whom I feel most affection," she told me. And she even appeared to feel some alarm at the thought that I might ask her to let me dine with them. She was hungry for people, and a third person who knew her too well, such as myself, would, by preventing her from letting herself go, at once prevent her from enjoying complete satisfaction in their company.

The memory of Albertine had become so fragmentary in me that it no longer caused me any sorrow and was no more now than a transition to fresh desires, like a chord which announced a change of key. And indeed the idea of a momentary sensual caprice being ruled out, in so far as I was still faithful to Albertine's memory, I was happier at having Andrée in my company than I would have been at having an Albertine miraculously restored to life. For Andrée could tell me more things about Albertine than Albertine herself had ever told me. Now the problems concerning Albertine still remained in my mind when my affection for her, both physical and moral, had already vanished. And my desire to know about her life, because it had diminished less, was now relatively greater than my need of her presence. On the other hand, the thought that a woman had perhaps had relations with Albertine no longer provoked in me anything save the desire to have relations myself also with that woman. I told Andrée this, caressing her as I spoke. Then, without making the slightest effort to harmonise her speech with what she had said a few months earlier, Andrée said to me with a lurking smile: " Ah! yes, but you are a man. And so we can't do quite the same things as I used to do with Albertine." And whether it was that she considered that this increased my desire (in the hope of extracting confidences, I had told her that I would like to have relations with a woman who had had them with Albertine) or my grief, or perhaps destroyed a sense of superiority to herself which she might suppose me to feel at being the only person who had had relations with Albertine: " Ah! we spent many happy hours together, she was so caressing, so passionate. Besides, it was not only with me that she liked to enjoy herself. She had met a nice boy at Mme Verdurin's, Morel. They understood each other at once. He undertook (with her permission to enjoy himself with them too, for he liked

virgins), to procure little girls for her.   As soon as he had
set their feet on the path, he left them.   And so he made
himself responsible for attracting young fisher-girls in some
quiet watering-place, young laundresses, who would fall in
love with a boy, but would not have listened to a girl's
advances.   As soon as the girl was well under his control,
he would bring her to a safe place, where he handed her
over to Albertine.   For fear of losing Morel, who took
part in it all too, the girl always obeyed, and yet she lost
him all the same, for, as he was afraid of what might happen and also as once or twice was enough for him, he would
slip away leaving a false address.   Once he had the nerve to
bring one of these girls, with Albertine, to a brothel, at
Corliville, where four or five of the women had her at once,
or in turn.   That was his passion, and Albertine's also.
But Albertine suffered terrible remorse afterwards.   I
believe that when she was with you she had conquered her
passion and put off indulging it from day to day.   Then her
affection for yourself was so strong that she felt scruples.
But it was quite certain that, if she ever left you, she would
begin again.   She hoped that you would rescue her, that
you would marry her.   She felt in her heart that it was a
sort of criminal lunacy, and I have often asked myself
whether it was not after an incident of that sort, which
had led to a suicide in a family, that she killed herself on
purpose.   I must confess that in the early days of her life
with you she had not entirely given up her games with me.
There were days when she seemed to need it, so much so
that once, when it would have been so easy elsewhere, she
could not say good-bye without taking me to bed with her,
in your house.   We had no luck, we were very nearly

caught. She had taken her opportunity when Françoise had gone out on some errand, and you had not come home. Then she had turned out all the lights so that when you let yourself in with your key it would take you some time to find the switch, and she had not shut the door of her room. We heard you come upstairs, I had just time to make myself tidy and begin to come down. Which was quite unnecessary, for by an incredible accident you had left your key at home and had to ring the bell. But we lost our heads all the same, so that to conceal our awkwardness we both of us, without any opportunity of discussing it, had the same idea: to pretend to be afraid of the scent of syringa which as a matter of fact we adored. You were bringing a long branch of it home with you, which enabled me to turn my head away and hide my confusion. This did not prevent me from telling you in the most idiotic way that perhaps Françoise had come back and would let you in, when a moment earlier I had told you the lie that we had only just come in from our drive and that when we arrived Françoise had not left the house and was just going on an errand. But our mistake was—supposing you to have your key—turning out the light, for we were afraid that as you came upstairs you would see it turned on again, or at least we hesitated too long. And for three nights on end Albertine could not close an eye, for she was always afraid that you might be suspicious and ask Françoise why she had not turned on the light before leaving the house. For Albertine was terribly afraid of you, and at times she would assure me that you were wicked, mean, that you hated her really. After three days she gathered from your calm that you had said nothing to Françoise, and she was able to sleep again. But she never did anything with me after that, perhaps from fear, perhaps from remorse, for she made out that she did really love you, or perhaps she was in love with some other man. In any case, nobody could ever mention syringa again in her hearing without her turning crimson and putting her hand over her face in the hope of hiding her blushes."

As there are strokes of good fortune, so there are misfortunes that come too late, they do not assume all the importance that they would have had in our eyes a little earlier. Among these was the calamity that Andrée's terrible revelation was to me. No doubt, even when bad tidings ought to make us unhappy, it so happens that in the diversion, the balanced give and take of conversation, they pass by us without stopping, and that we ourself, preoccupied with a thousand things which we have to say in response, transformed by the desire to please our present company into someone else protected for a few moments in this new environment against the affections, the sufferings that he has discarded upon entering it and will find again when the brief spell is broken, have not the time to take them in. And yet if these affections, these sufferings are too predominant, we enter only distractedly into the zone of a new and momentary world, in which, too faithful to our sufferings, we are incapable of becoming another person, and then the words that we hear said enter at once into relation with our heart, which has not remained out of action. But for some time past words that concerned Albertine, had, like a poison that has evaporated, lost their toxic power. She was already too remote from me.

As a wayfarer seeing in the afternoon a misty crescent in

the sky, says to himself: " That is it, the vast moon," so I said to myself: " What, so that truth which I have sought so earnestly, which I have so dreaded, is nothing more than these few words uttered in the course of conversation, words to which we cannot even give our whole attention since we are not alone! " Besides, it took me at a serious disadvantage, I had exhausted myself with Andrée. With a truth of such magnitude, I would have liked to have more strength to devote to it; it remained outside me, but this was because I had not yet found a place for it in my heart. We would like the truth to be revealed to us by novel signs, not by a phrase similar to those which we have constantly repeated to ourself. The habit of thinking prevents us at times from feeling reality, makes us immune to it, makes it seem no more than another thought.

There is no idea that does not carry in itself a possible refutation, no word that does not imply its opposite. In any case, if all this was true, how futile a verification of the life of a mistress who exists no longer, rising up from the depths and coming to the surface just when we are no longer able to make any use of it. Then, thinking doubt-less of some other woman whom we now love and with regard to whom the same change may occur (for to her whom we have forgotten we no longer give a thought), we lose heart. We say to ourself: " If she were alive! " We say to ourself: " If she who is alive could understand all this and that when she is dead I shall know everything that she is hiding from me." But this is a vicious circle. If I could have brought Albertine back to life, the immedi-ate consequence would have been that Andrée would have revealed nothing. It is the same thing as the everlasting:

" You'll see what it's like when I no longer love you "
which is so true and so absurd, since as a matter of fact we
should elicit much if we were no longer in love, but then
we should no longer think of enquiring. It is precisely
the same. For the woman whom we see again when we
are no longer in love with her, if she tells us everything, the
fact is that she is no longer herself, or that we are no longer
ourself: the person who was in love has ceased to exist.
There also death has passed by, and has made everything
easy and unnecessary. I pursued these reflections, adopting the hypothesis that Andrée had been telling the truth—
which was possible—and had been prompted to sincerity
with me, precisely because she had now had relations with
me, by that Saint-André-des-Champs side of her nature
which Albertine, too, had shewn me at the start. She was
encouraged in this case by the fact that she was no longer
afraid of Albertine, for other people's reality survives their
death for only a short time in our minds, and after a few
years they are like those gods of obsolete religions whom we
insult without fear, because people have ceased to believe in
their existence. But the fact that Andrée no longer
believed in the reality of Albertine might mean that she no
longer feared (any more than to betray a secret which she
had promised not to reveal) to invent a falsehood which
slandered retrospectively her alleged accomplice. Had
this absence of fear permitted her to reveal at length, in
speaking as she did, the truth, or rather to invent a falsehood, if, for some reason, she supposed me to be full of
happiness and pride, and wished to pain me? Perhaps the
sight of me caused her a certain irritation (held in suspense
so long as she saw that I was miserable, unconsoled) be-

cause I had had relations with Albertine and she envied me, perhaps—supposing that I considered myself on that account more highly favoured than her—an advantage which she herself had never, perhaps, obtained, nor even sought. Thus it was that I had often heard her say how ill they were looking to people whose air of radiant health, and what was more their consciousness of their own air of radiant health, exasperated her, and say in the hope of annoying them that she herself was very well, a fact that she did not cease to proclaim when she was seriously ill until the day when, in the detachment of death, it no longer mattered to her that other fortunate people should be well and should know that she was dying. But this day was still remote. Perhaps she had turned against me, for what reason I knew not, in one of those rages in which she used, long ago, to turn against the young man so learned in sporting matters, so ignorant of everything else, whom we had met at Balbec, who since then had been living with Rachel, and at the mention of whom Andrée overflowed in defamatory speeches, hoping to be sued for libel in order to be able to launch against his father disgraceful accusations the falsehood of which he would not be able to prove. Quite possibly this rage against myself had simply revived, having doubtless ceased when she saw how miserable I was. Indeed, the very same people whom she, her eyes flashing with rage, had longed to disgrace, to kill, to send to prison, by false testimony if need be, she had only to know that they were unhappy, crushed, to cease to wish them any harm, and to be ready to overwhelm them with kindness. For she was not fundamentally wicked, and if her non-apparent, somewhat buried nature was not the kindness which one divined at first from her delicate attentions, but rather envy and pride, her third nature, buried more deeply still, the true but not entirely realised nature, tended towards goodness and the love of her neighbour.   Only, like all those people who, being in a certain state of life, desire a better state, but knowing it only by desire, do not realise that the first condition is to break away from the former state—like the neurasthenics or morphinomaniacs who are anxious to be cured, but at the same time do not wish to be deprived of their manias or their morphine, like the religious hearts or artistic spirits attached to the world who long for solitude but seek nevertheless to imagine it as not implying an absolute renunciation of their former existence —Andrée was prepared to love all her fellow-creatures, but on the condition that she should first of all have succeeded in not imagining them as triumphant, and to that end should have humiliated them in advance.   She did not understand that we ought to love even the proud, and to conquer their pride by love and not by a more overweening pride.   But the fact is that she was like those invalids who wish to be cured by the very means that prolong their malady, which they like and would cease at once to like if they renounced them.   But people wish to learn to swim and at the same time to keep one foot on the ground.   As for the young sportsman, the Verdurins' nephew, whom I had met during my two visits to Balbec, I am bound to add, as an accessory statement and in anticipation, that some time after Andrée's visit, a visit my account of which will be resumed in a moment, certain events occurred which caused a great sensation.   First of all, this young man (perhaps remembering Albertine with whom I did not then know that he had been in love) became engaged to Andrée and married her, notwithstanding the despair of Rachel to which he paid not the slightest attention. Andrée no longer said then (that is to say some months after the visit of which I have been speaking) that he was a wretch, and I realised later on that she had said so only because she was madly in love with him and thought that he did not want to have anything to do with her. But another fact impressed me even more. This young man produced certain sketches for the theatre, with settings and costumes designed by himself, which have effected in the art of to-day a revolution at least equal to that brought about by the Russian ballet. In fact, the best qualified critics regarded his work as something of capital importance, almost as works of genius and for that matter I agree with them, confirming thus, to my own astonishment, the opinion long held by Rachel. The people who had known him at Balbec, anxious only to be certain whether the cut of the clothes of the men with whom he associated was or was not smart, who had seen him spend all his time at baccarat, at the races, on the golf-course or on the polo-ground, who knew that at school he had always been a dunce, and had even been expelled from the lycée (to annoy his parents, he had spent two months in the smart brothel in which M. de Charlus had hoped to surprise Morel), thought that perhaps his work was done by Andrée, who, in her love for him, chose to leave him the renown, or that more probably he was paying, out of his huge private fortune at which his excesses had barely nibbled, some inspired but needy professional to create it. People in this kind of wealthy society, not purified by mingling with the aristocracy, and having no idea of what constitutes an artist—a word which to them is represented only by an actor whom they engage to recite monologues at the party given for their daughter's betrothal, at once handing him his fee discreetly in another room, or by a painter to whom they make her sit after she is married, before the children come and when she is still at her best—are apt to believe that all the people in society who write, compose or paint, have their work done for them and pay to obtain a reputation as an author as other men pay to make sure of a seat in Parliament. But all this was false, and the young man was indeed the author of those admirable works. When I learned this, I was obliged to hesitate between contrary suppositions. Either he had indeed been for years on end the " coarse brute " that he appeared to be, and some physiological cataclysm had awakened in him the dormant genius, like a Sleeping Beauty, or else at the period of his tempestuous schooldays, of his failures to matriculate in the final examination, of his heavy gambling losses at Balbec, of his reluctance to shew himself in the tram with his aunt Verdurin's faithful, because of their unconventional attire, he was already a man of genius, distracted perhaps from his genius, having left its key beneath the door mat in the effervescence of juvenile passions; or again, already a conscious man of genius, and at the bottom of his classes, because, while the master was uttering platitudes about Cicero, he himself was reading Rimbaud or Goethe. Certainly, there was no ground for any such hypothesis when I met him at Balbec, where his interests seemed to me to be centred solely in turning out a smart carriage and pair and in mixing cocktails. But even this is not an insuperable objection. He might be extremely vain, and this may be allied to genius, and might seek to shine in the manner which he knew to be dazzling in the world in which he lived, which did not mean furnishing a profound knowledge of elective affinities, but far rather a knowledge of how to drive four-in-hand. Moreover, I am not at all sure that later on, when he had become the author of those fine and so original works, he would have cared greatly, outside the theatres in which he was known, to greet anyone who was not in evening dress, like the " faithful " in their earlier manner, which would be a proof in him not of stupidity, but of vanity, and indeed of a certain practical sense, a certain clairvoyance in adapting his vanity to the mentality of the imbeciles upon whose esteem he depended and in whose eyes a dinner-jacket might perhaps shine with a more brilliant radiance than the eyes of a thinker. Who can say whether, seen from without, some man of talent, or even a man devoid of talent, but a lover of the things of the mind, myself for instance, would not have appeared, to anyone who met him at Rivebelle, at the hotel at Balbec, or on the beach there, the most perfect and pretentious imbecile. Not to mention that for Octave matters of art must have been a thing so intimate, a thing that lived so in the most secret places of his heart that doubtless it would never have occurred to him to speak of them, as Saint-Loup, for instance, would have spoken, for whom the fine arts had the importance that horses and carriages had for Octave. Besides, he may have had a passion for gambling, and it is said that he has retained it. All the same, even if the piety which brought to light the unknown work of Vinteuil arose from amid the troubled life of Montjouvain, I was no less impressed by the thought that the masterpieces which are perhaps the most extraordinary of our day have emerged not from the university certificate, from a model, academic education, upon Broglie lines, but from the frequentations of "paddocks" and fashionable bars. In any case, in those days at Balbec, the reasons which made me anxious to know him, which made Albertine and her friends anxious that I should not know him, were equally detached from his merit, and could only have brought into prominence the eternal misunderstanding between an "intellectual" (represented in this instance by myself) and people in society (represented by the little band) with regard to a person in society (the young golfer). I had no inkling of his talent, and his prestige in my eyes, like that, in the past, of Mme Blatin, had been that of his being—whatever they might say—the friend of my girl friends, and more one of their band than myself. On the other hand, Albertine and Andrée, symbolising in this respect the incapacity of people in society to bring a sound judgment to bear upon the things of the mind and their propensity to attach themselves in that connection to false appearances, not only thought me almost idiotic because I took an interest in such an imbecile, but were astonished beyond measure that, taking one golfer with another, my choice should have fallen upon the poorest player of them all. If, for instance, I had chosen to associate with young Gilbert de Bellœuvre; apart from golf, he was a boy who had the gift of conversation, who had secured a *proxime* in the examinations and wrote quite good poetry (as a matter of fact he was the stupidest of them all). Or again, if my object had been to "make a study for a book," Guy Saumoy who was completely insane, who had abducted two girls, was at least a singular type who might "interest" me. These two might have been allowed me, but the other, what attraction could I find in him, he was the type of the "great brute," of the "coarse brute." To return to Andrée's visit, after the disclosure that she had just made to me of her relations with Albertine, she added that the chief reason for which Albertine had left me was the thought of what her friends of the little band might think, and other people as well, when they saw her living like that with a young man to whom she was not married. "Of course I know, it was in your mother's house. But that makes no difference. You can't imagine what all those girls are like, what they conceal from one another, how they dread one another's opinion. I have seen them being terribly severe with young men simply because the men knew their friends and they were afraid that certain things might be repeated, and those very girls, I have happened to see them in a totally different light, much to their disgust." A few months earlier, this knowledge which Andrée appeared to possess of the motives that swayed the girls of the little band would have seemed to me the most priceless thing in the world. What she said was perhaps sufficient to explain why Albertine, who had given herself to me afterwards in Paris, had refused to yield to me at Balbec where I was constantly meeting her friends which I had absurdly supposed to be so great an advantage in winning her affection. Perhaps indeed it was because she had seen me display some sign of intimacy with Andrée or because I had rashly told the latter that Albertine was coming to spend the night at the Grand Hotel, that Albertine who perhaps, an hour earlier, was ready to let me take certain favours, as though that were the simplest thing in the world, had abruptly changed her mind and threatened to ring the bell. But then, she must have been accommodating to lots of others. This thought rekindled my jealousy and I told Andrée that there was something that I wished to ask her. "You did those things in your grandmother's empty apartment?" "Oh, no, never, we should have been disturbed." "Why, I thought . . . it seemed to me. . . ." "Besides, Albertine loved doing it in the country." "And where, pray?" "Originally, when she hadn't time to go very far, we used to go to the Buttes-Chaumont. She knew a house there. Or else we would lie under the trees, there is never anyone about; in the grotto of the Petit Trianon, too." "There, you see; how am I to believe you? You swore to me, not a year ago, that you had never done anything at the Buttes-Chaumont." "I was afraid of distressing you." As I have said, I thought (although not until much later) that on the contrary it was on this second occasion, the day of her confessions, that Andrée had sought to distress me. And this thought would have occurred to me at once, because I should have felt the need of it, if I had still been as much in love with Albertine. But Andrée's words did not hurt me sufficiently to make it indispensable to me to dismiss them immediately as untrue. In short if what Andrée said was true, and I did not doubt it at the time, the real Albertine whom I discovered, after having known so many diverse forms of Albertine, differed very little from the young Bacchanal who had risen up and whom I had detected, on the first day, on the front at Balbec, and who had offered me so many different aspects in succession, as a town gradually alters the position of its buildings so as to overtop, to obliterate the principal monument which alone we beheld from a distance, as we approach it, whereas when we know it well and can judge it exactly, its true proportions prove to be those which the perspective of the first glance had indicated, the rest, through which we passed, being no more than that continuous series of lines of defence which everything in creation raises against our vision, and which we must cross one after another, at the cost of how much suffering, before we arrive at the heart. If, however, I had no need to believe absolutely in Albertine's innocence because my suffering had diminished, I can say that reciprocally if I did not suffer unduly at this revelation, it was because, some time since, for the belief that I feigned in Albertine's innocence, there had been substituted gradually and without my taking it into account the belief, ever present in my mind, in her guilt. Now if I no longer believed in Albertine's innocence, it was because I had already ceased to feel the need, the passionate desire to believe in it. It is desire that engenders belief and if we fail as a rule to take this into account, it is because most of the desires that create beliefs end—unlike the desire which had persuaded me that Albertine was innocent—only with our own life. To all the evidence that corroborated my original version I had stupidly preferred simple statements by Albertine. Why had I believed them? Falsehood is essential to humanity. It plays as large a part perhaps as the quest of pleasure and is moreover commanded by that quest. We lie in order to protect our pleasure or our honour if the disclosure of our pleasure runs counter to our honour. We lie all our life long, especially indeed, perhaps only, to those people who love us. Such people in fact alone make us fear for our pleasure and desire their esteem. I had at first thought Albertine guilty, and it was only my desire devoting to a process of doubt the strength of my intelligence that had set me upon the wrong track. Perhaps we live surrounded by electric, seismic signs, which we must interpret in good faith in order to know the truth about the characters of other people. If the truth must be told, saddened as I was in spite of everything by Andrée's words, I felt it to be better that the truth should at last agree with what my instinct had originally foreboded, rather than with the miserable optimism to which I had since made a cowardly surrender. I would have preferred that life should remain at the high level of my intuitions. Those moreover which I had felt, that first day upon the beach, when I had supposed that those girls embodied the frenzy of pleasure, were vice incarnate, and again on the evening when I had seen Albertine's governess leading that passionate girl home to the little villa, as one thrust into its cage a wild animal which nothing in the future, despite appearances, will ever succeed in taming, did they not agree with what Bloch had told me when he had made the world seem so fair to me by shewing me, making me palpitate on all my walks, at every encounter, the universality of desire. Perhaps, when all was said, it was better that I should not have found those first intuitions verified afresh until now. While the whole of my love for Albertine endured, they would have made me suffer too keenly and it was better that there should have subsisted of them only a trace, my perpetual suspicion of things which I did not see and which nevertheless happened continually so close to me, and perhaps another trace as well, earlier, more vast, which was *my love itself*. Was it not indeed, despite all the denials of my reason, tantamount to knowing Albertine in all her hideousness, merely to choose her, to love her; and even in the moments when suspicion is lulled, is not love the persistence and a transformation of that suspicion, is it not a proof of clairvoyance (a proof unintelligible to the lover himself), since desire going always in the direction of what is most opposite to ourself forces us to love what will make us suffer? Certainly there enter into a person's charm, into the attraction of her eyes, her lips, her figure, the elements unknown to us which are capable of making us suffer most intensely, so much so that to feel ourself attracted by the person, to begin to love her, is, however innocent we may pretend it to be, to read already, in a different version, all her betrayals and her faults. And those charms which, to attract me, materialised thus the noxious, dangerous, fatal parts of a person, did they perhaps stand in a more direct relation of cause to effect to those secret poisons than do the seductive luxuriance and the toxic juice of certain venomous flowers? It was perhaps, I told myself, Albertine's vice itself, the cause of my future sufferings, that had produced in her that honest, frank manner, creating the illusion that one could enjoy with her the same loyal and unrestricted comradeship as with a man, just as a parallel vice had produced in M. de Charlus a feminine refinement of sensibility and mind. Through a period of the most utter blindness, perspicacity persists beneath the very form of predilection and affection. Which means that we are wrong in speaking of a bad choice in love, since whenever there is a choice it can only be bad. " Did those excursions to the Buttes-Chaumont take place when you used to call for her here? " I asked Andrée. " Oh! no, from the day when Albertine came back from Balbec with you, except the time I told you about, she never did anything again with me. She would not even allow me to mention such things to her." " But, my dear Andrée, why go on lying to me? By the merest chance, for I never try to find out anything, I have learned in the minutest details things of that sort which Albertine did, I can tell you exactly, on the bank of the river with a laundress, only a few days before her death." " Ah! perhaps after she had left you, that I can't say. She felt that she had failed, that she would never again be able to regain your confidence." These last words appalled me. Then I thought again of the evening of the branch of syringa, I remembered that about a fortnight later, as my jealousy kept seeking a fresh object, I had asked Albertine whether she had ever had relations with Andrée, and she had replied: " Oh! never! Of course, I adore Andrée; I have a profound affection for her, but as though we were sisters, and even if I had the tastes which you seem to suppose, she is the last person that would have entered my head. I can swear to you by anything you like, by my aunt, by my poor mother's grave." I had believed her. And yet even if I had not been made suspicious by the contradiction between her former partial admissions with regard to certain matters and the firmness with which she had afterwards denied them as soon as she saw that I was not unaffected, I ought to have remembered Swann, convinced of the platonic nature of M. de Charlus's friendships and assuring me of it on the evening of the very day on which I had seen the tailor and the Baron in the courtyard. I ought to have reflected that if there are, one covering the other, two worlds, one consisting of the things that the best, the sincerest people say, and behind it the world composed of those same people's successive actions; so that when a married woman says to you of a young man: "Oh! It is perfectly true that I have an immense affection for him, but it is something quite innocent, quite pure, I could swear it upon the memory of my parents," we ought ourself, instead of feeling any hesitation, to swear that she has probably just come from her bath room to which, after every assignation that she has with the young man in question, she dashes, to prevent any risk of his giving her a child. The spray of syringa made me profoundly sad, as did also the discovery that Albertine could have thought or called me cruel and hostile; most of all perhaps, certain lies so unexpected that I had difficulty in grasping them. One day Albertine had told me that she had been to an aerodrome, that the airman was in love with her (this doubtless in order to divert my suspicion from women, thinking that I was less jealous of other men); that it had been amusing to watch Andrée's raptures at the said airman, at all the compliments that he paid Albertine, until finally Andrée had longed to go in the air with him. Now this was an entire fabrication; Andrée had never visited the aerodrome in question.

When Andrée left me, it was dinner-time. "You will never guess who has been to see me and stayed at least three hours," said my mother. "I call it three hours, it was perhaps longer, she arrived almost on the heels of my first visitor, who was Mme Cottard, sat still and watched everybody come and go—and I had more than thirty callers—

and left me only a quarter of an hour ago. If you hadn't had your friend Andrée with you, I should have sent for you." "Why, who was it?" "A person who never pays calls." "The Princesse de Parme?" "Why, I have a cleverer son than I thought I had. There is no fun in making you guess a name, for you hit on it at once." "Did she come to apologise for her rudeness yesterday?" "No, that would have been stupid, the fact of her calling was an apology. Your poor grandmother would have thought it admirable. It seems that about two o'clock she had sent a footman to ask whether I had an at-home day. She was told that this was the day and so up she came." My first thought, which I did not dare mention to Mamma, was that the Princesse de Parme, surrounded, the day before, by people of rank and fashion with whom she was on intimate terms and enjoyed conversing, had when she saw my mother come into the room felt an annoyance which she had made no attempt to conceal. And it was quite in the style of the great ladies of Germany, which for that matter the Guermantes had largely adopted, this stiffness, for which they thought to atone by a scrupulous affability. But my mother believed, and I came in time to share her opinion, that all that had happened was that the Princesse de Parme, having failed to recognise her, had not felt herself bound to pay her any attention, that she had learned after my mother's departure who she was, either from the Duchesse de Guermantes whom my mother had met as she was leaving the house, or from the list of her visitors, whose names, before they entered her presence, the servants recorded in a book. She had thought it impolite to send word or to say to my mother: "I did not recognise you," but—and this was no less in harmony with the good manners of the German courts and with the Guermantes' code of behaviour than my original theory—had thought that a call, an exceptional action on the part of a royal personage, and what was more a call of several hours' duration, would convey the explanation to my mother in an indirect but no less convincing form, which is just what did happen. But I did not waste any time in asking my mother to tell me about the Princess's call, for I had just recalled a number of incidents with regard to Albertine as to which I had meant but had forgotten to question Andrée. How little, for that matter, did I know, should I ever know, of this story of Albertine, the only story that could be of particular interest to me, or did at least begin to interest me afresh at certain moments. For man is that creature without any fixed age, who has the faculty of becoming, in a few seconds, many years younger, and who, surrounded by the walls of the time through which he has lived, floats within them but as though in a basin the surface-level of which is constantly changing, so as to bring him into the range now of one epoch, now of another. I wrote to Andrée asking her to come again. She was unable to do so until a week had passed. Almost as soon as she entered the room, I said to her: "Very well, then, since you maintain that Albertine never did that sort of thing while she was staying here, according to you, it was to be able to do it more freely that she left me, but for which of her friends?" "Certainly not, it was not that at all." "Then because I was too unkind to her?" "No, I don't think so. I believe that she was forced to leave you by her aunt who had designs for her future upon that guttersnipe, you know, the young man

whom you used to call ' I am in the soup,' the young man
who was in love with Albertine and had proposed for her.
Seeing that you did not marry her, they were afraid that the
shocking length of her stay in your house might prevent
the young man from proposing.   Mme Bontemps, after
the young man had brought continual pressure to bear upon
her, summoned Albertine home.   Albertine after all
needed her uncle and aunt, and when she found that they
expected her to make up her mind she left you."   I had
never in my jealousy thought of this explanation, but only
of Albertine's desire for other women and of my own vigilance, I had forgotten that there was also Mme Bontemps
who might presently regard as strange what had shocked my
mother from the first.   At least Mme Bontemps was
afraid that it might shock this possible husband whom she
was keeping in reserve for Albertine, in case I failed to
marry her.   Was this marriage really the cause of Albertine's departure, and out of self-respect, so as not to appear to
be dependent on her aunt, or to force me to marry her, had
she preferred not to mention it?   I was beginning to realise
that the system of multiple causes for a single action, of
which Albertine shewed her mastery in her relations with
her girl friends when she allowed each of them to suppose
that it was for her sake that she had come, was only a sort of
artificial, deliberate symbol of the different aspects that an
action assumes according to the point of view that we adopt.
The astonishment, I might almost say the shame that I felt
at never having even once told myself that Albertine, in my
house, was in a false position, which might give offence to
her aunt, it was not the first, nor was it the last time that I
felt it.   How often has it been my lot, after I have sought

to understand the relations between two people and the crises that they bring about, to hear, all of a sudden, a third person speak to me of them from his own point of view, for he has even closer relations with one of the two, a point of view which has perhaps been the case of the crisis. And if people's actions remain so indefinite, how should not the people themselves be equally indefinite? If I listened to the people who maintained that Albertine was a schemer who had tried to get one man after another to marry her, it was not difficult to imagine how they would have defined her life with me. And yet to my mind she had been a victim, a victim who perhaps was not altogether pure, but in that case guilty for other reasons, on account of vices to which people did not refer. But we must above all say to ourself this: on the one hand, lying is often a trait of character; on the other hand, in women who would not otherwise be liars, it is a natural defence, improvised at first, then more and more organised, against that sudden danger which would be capable of destroying all life: love. On the other hand again, it is not the effect of chance if men who are intelligent and sensitive invariably give themselves to insensitive and inferior women, and are at the same time so attached to them that the proof that they are not loved does not in the least cure them of the instinct to sacrifice everything else in the attempt to keep such a woman with them. If I say that such men need to suffer, I am saying something that is accurate while suppressing the preliminary truths which make that need—involuntary in a sense—to suffer a perfectly comprehensible consequence of those truths. Without taking into account that, complete nature being rare, a man who is highly sensitive and highly intelligent

will generally have little will-power, will be the plaything
of habit and of that fear of suffering in the immediate
present which condemns us to perpetual suffering—and
that in those conditions he will never be prepared to repudi-
ate the woman who does not love him. We may be surprised that he should be content with so little love, but we
ought rather to picture to ourself the grief that may be
caused him by the love which he himself feels. A grief
which we ought not to pity unduly, for those terrible com-
motions which are caused by an unrequited love, by the
departure, the death of a mistress, are like those attacks of
paralysis which at first leave us helpless, but after which our
muscles begin by degrees to recover their vital elasticity and
energy. What is more, this grief does not lack compensation. These sensitive and intelligent men are as a rule
little inclined to falsehood. This takes them all the more
by surprise inasmuch as, intelligent as they may be, they
live in the world of possibilities, react little, live in the grief
which a woman has just inflicted on them, rather than in
the clear perception of what she had in mind, what she was
doing, of the man with whom she was in love, a perception
granted chiefly to deliberate natures which require it in
order to prepare against the future instead of lamenting the
past. And so these men feel that they are betrayed without
quite knowing how. Wherefore the mediocre woman
with whom we are surprised to see them fall in love en-
riches the universe for them far more than an intelligent
woman would have done. Behind each of her words, they
feel that a lie is lurking, behind each house to which she
says that she has gone, another house, behind each action,
each person, another action, another person. Doubtless

they do not know what or whom, have not the energy, would not perhaps find it possible to discover. A lying woman, by an extremely simple trick, can beguile, without taking the trouble to change her method, any number of people, and, what is more, the very person who ought to have discovered the trick. All this creates, in front of the sensitive and intelligent man a universe all depth, which his jealousy would fain plumb and which is not without interest to his intelligence.

Albeit I was not exactly a man of that category, I was going perhaps, now that Albertine was dead, to learn the secret of her life. Here again, do not these indiscretions which occur only after a person's life on earth is ended, prove that nobody believes, really, in a future state. If these indiscretions are true, we ought to fear the resentment of her whose actions we are revealing fully as much on the day when we shall meet her in heaven, as we feared it so long as she was alive, when we felt ourself bound to keep her secret. And if these indiscretions are false, invented because she is no longer present to contradict them, we ought to be even more afraid of the dead woman's wrath if we believed in heaven. But no one does believe in it. So that it was possible that a long debate had gone on in Albertine's heart between staying with me and leaving me, but that her decision to leave me had been made on account of her aunt, or of that young man, and not on account of women to whom perhaps she had never given a thought. The most serious thing to my mind was that Andrée, albeit she had nothing now to conceal from me as to Albertine's morals, swore to me that nothing of the sort had ever occurred between Albertine on the one hand and Mlle

Vinteuil or her friend on the other. (Albertine herself was unconscious of her own instincts when she first met the girls, and they, from that fear of making a mistake in the object of our desire, which breeds as many errors as desire itself, regarded her as extremely hostile to that sort of thing. Perhaps later on they had learned that her tastes were similar to their own, but by that time they knew Albertine too well and Albertine knew them too well for there to be any thought of their doing things together.) In short I did not understand any better than before why Albertine had left me. If the face of a woman is perceived with difficulty by our eyes which cannot take in the whole of its moving surface, by our lips, still more by our memory, if it is shrouded in obscurity according to her social position, according to the level at which we are situated, how much thicker is the veil drawn between the actions of her whom we see and her motives. Her motives are situated in a more distant plane, which we do not perceive, and engender moreover actions other than those which we know and often in absolute contradiction to them. When has there not been some man in public life, regarded as a saint by his friends, who is discovered to have forged documents, robbed the State, betrayed his country? How often is a great nobleman robbed by a steward whom he has brought up from childhood, ready to swear that he was an honest man, as possibly he was. Now this curtain that screens another person's motives, how much more impenetrable does it become if we are in love with that person, for it clouds our judgment and also obscures the actions of her who, feeling that she is loved, ceases at once to attach any value to what otherwise would doubtless have seemed to her important, such as wealth for example. Perhaps moreover she is impelled to pretend, to a certain extent, this scorn of wealth in the hope of obtaining more money by making us suffer. The bargaining instinct also may be involved. And so with the actual incidents in her life, an intrigue which she has confided to no one for fear of its being revealed to us, which many people might, for all that, have discovered, had they felt the same passionate desire to know it as ourself, while preserving freer minds, arousing fewer suspicions in the guilty party, an intrigue of which certain people have not been unaware—but people whom we do not know and should not know how to find. And among all these reasons for her adopting an inexplicable attitude towards us, we must include those idiosyncrasies of character which impel a person, whether from indifference to his own interests, or from hatred, or from love of freedom, or from sudden bursts of anger, or from fear of what certain people will think, to do the opposite of what we expected. And then there are the differences of environment, of upbringing, in which we refuse to believe because, when we are talking together, they are effaced by our speech, but which return, when we are apart, to direct the actions of each of us from so opposite a point of view that there is no possibility of their meeting. " But, my dear Andrée, you are lying again. Remember—you admitted it to me yourself,—I telephoned to you the evening before; you remember Albertine had been so anxious, and kept it from me as though it had been something that I must not know about, to go to the afternoon party at the Verdurins' at which Mlle Vinteuil was expected." " Yes, but Albertine had not the slightest idea that Mlle Vinteuil was to be there." "What? You yourself told me that she had met Mme Verdurin a few days earlier. Besides, Andrée, there is no point in our trying to deceive one another. I found a letter one morning in Albertine's room, a note from Mme Verdurin begging her to come that afternoon." And I shewed her the note which, as a matter of fact, Françoise had taken care to bring to my notice by placing it on the surface of Albertine's possessions a few days before her departure, and, I am afraid, leaving it there to make Albertine suppose that I had been rummaging among her things, to let her know in any case that I had seen it. And I had often asked myself whether Françoise's ruse had not been largely responsible for the departure of Albertine, who saw that she could no longer conceal anything from me, and felt disheartened, vanquished. I shewed Andrée the letter: " I feel no compunction, everything is excused by this strong family feeling. . . ." " You know very well, Andrée, that Albertine used always to say that Mlle Vinteuil's friend was indeed a mother, an elder sister to her." " But you have misinterpreted this note. The person that Mme Verdurin wished Albertine to meet that afternoon was not at all Mlle Vinteuil's friend, it was the young man you call ' I am in the soup,' and the strong family feeling is what Mme Verdurin felt for the brute who is after all her nephew. At the same time I think that Albertine did hear afterwards that Mlle Vinteuil was to be there, Mme Verdurin may have let her know separately. Of course the thought of seeing her friend again gave her pleasure, reminded her of happy times in the past, but just as you would be glad, if you were going to some place, to know that Elstir would be there, but no more than that, not even as much. No, if Albertine was unwilling to say why she wanted to go to Mme Verdurin's, it is because it was a rehearsal to which Mme Verdurin had invited a very small party, including that nephew of hers whom you had met at Balbec, to whom Mme Bontemps was hoping to marry Albertine and to whom Albertine wanted to talk. A fine lot of people!" And so Albertine, in spite of what Andrée's mother used to think, had had after all the prospect of a wealthy marriage. And when she had wanted to visit Mme Verdurin, when she spoke to her in secret, when she had been so annoyed that I should have gone there that evening without warning her, the plot that had been woven by her and Mme Verdurin had had as its object her meeting not Mlle Vinteuil but the nephew with whom Albertine was in love and for whom Mme Verdurin was acting as go-between, with the satisfaction in working for the achievement of one of those marriages which surprise us in certain families into whose state of mind we do not enter completely, supposing them to be intent upon a rich bride. Now I had never given another thought to this nephew who had perhaps been the initiator thanks to whom I had received her first kiss. And for the whole plane of Albertine's motives which I had constructed, I must now substitute another, or rather superimpose it, for perhaps it did not exclude the other, a preference for women did not prevent her from marrying. "And anyhow there is no need to seek out all these explanations," Andrée went on. "Heaven only knows how I loved Albertine and what a good creature she was, but really, after she had typhoid (a year before you first met us all) she was an absolute madcap. All of a sudden she would be disgusted with what she was doing, all her plans would have to be changed at once, and she herself probably could not tell you why. You remember the year when you first came to Balbec, the year when you met us all? One fine day she made someone send her a telegram calling her back to Paris, she had barely time to pack her trunks. But there was absolutely no reason for her to go. All the excuses that she made were false. Paris was impossible for her at the moment. We were all of us still at Balbec. The golf club wasn't closed, indeed the heats for the cup which she was so keen on winning weren't finished. She was certain to win it. It only meant staying on for another week. Well, off she went. I have often spoken to her about it since. She said herself that she didn't know why she had left, that she felt home-sick (the home being Paris, you can imagine how likely that was), that she didn't feel happy at Balbec, that she thought that there were people there who were laughing at her." And I told myself that there was this amount of truth in what Andrée said that, if differences between minds account for the different impressions produced upon one person and another by the same work, for differences of feeling, for the impossibility of captivating a person to whom we do not appeal, there are also the differences between characters, the peculiarities of a single character, which are also motives for action. Then I ceased to think about this explanation and said to myself how difficult it is to know the truth in this world. I had indeed observed Albertine's anxiety to go to Mme Verdurin's and her concealment of it and I had not been mistaken. But then even if we do manage to grasp one fact like this, there are others which we perceive only in their outward appearance, for the reverse of the tapestry, the real side of the action, of the intrigue,—as well as that of the intellect, of the heart—is hidden from us and we see pass before us only flat silhouettes of which we say to ourself: it is this, it is that; it is on her account, or on someone's else. The revelation of the fact that Mlle Vinteuil was expected had seemed to me an explanation all the more logical seeing that Albertine had anticipated it by mentioning her to me. And subsequently had she not refused to swear to me that Mlle Vinteuil's presence gave her no pleasure? And here, with regard to this young man, I remembered a point which I had forgotten; a little time earlier, while Albertine was staying with me, I had met him, and he had been—in contradiction of his attitude at Balbec—extremely friendly, even affectionate with me, had begged me to allow him to call upon me, which I had declined to do for a number of reasons. And now I realised that it was simply because, knowing that Albertine was staying in the house, he had wished to be on good terms with me so as to have every facility for seeing her and for carrying her off from me, and I concluded that he was a scoundrel. Some time later, when I attended the first performances of this young man's works, no doubt I continued to think that if he had been so anxious to call upon me, it was for Albertine's sake, but, while I felt this to be reprehensible, I remembered that in the past if I had gone down to Doncières, to see Saint-Loup, it was really because I was in love with Mme de Guermantes. It is true that the situation was not identical, since Saint-Loup had not been in love with Mme de Guermantes, with the result that there was in my affection for him a trace of duplicity perhaps, but no treason. But I reflected afterwards that this affection which we feel for the person who controls the object of our desire, we feel equally if the person controls that object while loving it himself. No doubt, we have then to struggle against a friendship which will lead us straight to treason. And I think that this is what I have always done. But in the case of those who have not the strength to struggle, we cannot say that in them the friendship that they affect for the controller is a mere ruse; they feel it sincerely and for that reason display it with an ardour which, once the betrayal is complete, means that the betrayed husband or lover is able to say with a stupefied indignation: " If you had heard the protestations of affection that the wretch showered on me! That a person should come to rob a man of his treasure, that I can understand. But that he should feel the diabolical need to assure him first of all of his friendship, is a degree of ignominy and perversity which it is impossible to imagine." Now, there is no such perversity in the action, nor even an absolutely clear falsehood. The affection of this sort which Albertine's pseudo-fiancé had manifested for me that day had yet another excuse, being more complex than a simple consequence of his love for Albertine. It had been for a short time only that he had known himself, confessed himself, been anxious to be proclaimed an intellectual. For the first time values other than sporting or amatory, existed for him. The fact that I had been regarded with esteem by Elstir, by Bergotte, that Albertine had perhaps told him of the way in which I criticised writers which led her to imagine that I might myself be able to write, had the result that all of a sudden I had become to him (to the new man whom he at least realised himself to be) an interesting person with whom he would like to be associated, to whom he would like to confide his plans, whom he would ask perhaps for an introduction to Elstir. With the result that he was sincere when he asked if he might call upon me, expressing a regard for me to which intellectual reasons as well as the thought of Albertine imparted sincerity. No doubt it was not *for that* that he was so anxious to come and see me and would have sacrificed everything else with that object. But of this last reason which did little more than raise to a sort of impassioned paroxysm the two other reasons, he was perhaps unaware himself, and the other two existed really, as might have existed really in Albertine when she been anxious to go, on the afternoon of the rehearsal, to Mme Verdurin's, the perfectly respectable pleasure that she would feel in meeting again friends of her childhood, who in her eyes were no more vicious than she was in theirs, in talking to them, in shewing them, by the mere fact of her presence at the Verdurins', that the poor little girl whom they had known was now invited to a distinguished house, the pleasure also that she might perhaps have felt in listening to Vinteuil's music. If all this was true, the blush that had risen to Albertine's cheeks when I mentioned Mlle Vinteuil was due to what I had done with regard to that afternoon party which she had tried to keep secret from me, because of that proposal of marriage of which I was not to know. Albertine's refusal to swear to me that she would not have felt any pleasure in meeting Mlle Vinteuil again at that party had at the moment intensified my torment, strengthened my suspicions, but proved to me in retrospect that she had been determined to be sincere, and even over an innocent matter, perhaps simply because it was an innocent matter. There remained what Andrée had told me about her relations with Albertine. Perhaps, however, even without going so far as to believe that Andrée had invented the story solely in order that I might not feel happy and might not feel myself superior to her, I might still suppose that she had slightly exaggerated her account of what she used to do with Albertine, and that Albertine, by a mental restriction, diminished slightly also what she had done with Andrée, making use systematically of certain definitions which I had stupidly formulated upon the subject, finding that her relations with Andrée did not enter into the field of what she was obliged to confess to me and that she could deny them without lying. But why should I believe that it was she rather than Andrée who was lying? Truth and life are very arduous, and there remained to me from them, without my really knowing them, an impression in which sorrow was perhaps actually dominated by exhaustion.

As for the third occasion on which I remember that I was conscious of approaching an absolute indifference with regard to Albertine (and on this third occasion I felt that I had entirely arrived at it), it was one day, at Venice, a long time after Andrée's last visit.

CHAPTER III

VENICE

MY mother had brought me for a few weeks to Venice and—as there may be beauty in the most precious as well as in the humblest things—I was receiving there impressions analogous to those which I had felt so often in the past at Combray, but transposed into a wholly different and far richer key. When at ten o'clock in the morning my shutters were thrown open, I saw ablaze in the sunlight, instead of the black marble into which the slates of Saint-Hilaire used to turn, the Golden Angel on the Campanile of San Marco. In its dazzling glitter, which made it almost impossible to fix it in space, it promised me with its outstretched arms, for the moment, half an hour later, when I was to appear on the Piazzetta, a joy more certain than any that it could ever in the past have been bidden to announce to men of good will. I could see nothing but itself, so long as I remained in bed, but as the whole world is merely a vast sun-dial, a single lighted segment of which enables us to tell what o'clock it is, on the very first morning I was reminded of the shops in the Place de l'Eglise at Combray, which, on Sunday mornings, were always on the point of shutting when I arrived for mass, while the straw in the market place smelt strongly in the already hot sunlight. But on the second morning, what I saw, when I awoke, what made me get out of bed (because they had taken the place in my consciousness and in my desire of my

287

memories of Combray), were the impressions of my first morning stroll in Venice, Venice whose daily life was no less real than that of Combray, where as at Combray on Sunday mornings one had the delight of emerging upon a festive street, but where that street was paved with water of a sapphire blue, refreshed by little ripples of cooler air, and of so solid a colour that my tired eyes might, in quest of relaxation and without fear of its giving way, rest their gaze upon it. Like, at Combray, the worthy folk of the Rue de l'Oiseau, so in this strange town also, the inhabitants did indeed emerge from houses drawn up in line, side by side, along the principal street, but the part played there by houses that cast a patch of shade before them was in Venice entrusted to palaces of porphyry and jasper, over the arched door of which the head of a bearded god (projecting from its alignment, like the knocker on a door at Combray) had the effect of darkening with its shadow, not the brownness of the soil but the splendid blue of the water. On the piazza, the shadow that would have been cast at Combray by the linen-draper's awning and the barber's pole, turned into the tiny blue flowers scattered at its feet upon the desert of sun-scorched tiles by the silhouette of a Renaissance façade, which is not to say that, when the sun was hot, we were not obliged, in Venice as at Combray, to pull down the blinds between ourselves and the Canal, but they hung behind the quatrefoils and foliage of gothic windows. Of this sort was the window in our hotel behind the pillars of which my mother sat waiting for me, gazing at the Canal with a patience which she would not have displayed in the old days at Combray, at that time when, reposing in myself hopes which had never been realised, she was unwilling to let me see how much she loved me. Nowadays she was well aware that an apparent coldness on her part would alter nothing, and the affection that she lavished upon me was like those forbidden foods which are no longer withheld from invalids, when it is certain that they are past recovery. To be sure, the humble details which gave an individuality to the window of my aunt Léonie's bedroom, seen from the Rue de l'Oiseau, the asymmetry of its position not mid-way between the windows on either side of it, the exceptional height of its wooden ledge, the slanting bar which kept the shutters closed, the two curtains of glossy blue satin, divided and kept apart by their rod, the equivalent of all these things existed in this hotel in Venice where I could hear also those words, so distinctive, so eloquent, which enable us to recognise at a distance the house to which we are going home to luncheon, and afterwards remain in our memory as testimony that, during a certain period of time, that house was ours; but the task of uttering them had, in Venice, devolved not, as at Combray, and indeed, to a certain extent, everywhere, upon the simplest, that is to say the least beautiful things, but upon the almost oriental arch of a façade which is reproduced among the casts in every museum as one of the supreme achievements of the domestic architecture of the middle ages; from a long way away and when I had barely passed San Giorgio Maggiore, I caught sight of this arched window which had already seen me, and the spring of its broken curves added to its smile of welcome the distinction of a loftier, scarcely comprehensible gaze. And since, behind those pillars of differently coloured marble, Mamma was sitting reading while she waited for me to return, her face shrouded in a tulle veil as agonising in its whiteness as her hair to myself who felt that my mother, wiping away her tears, had pinned it to her straw hat, partly with the idea of appearing " dressed " in the eyes of the hotel staff, but principally so as to appear to me less " in mourning," less sad, almost consoled for the death of my grandmother; since, not having recognised me at first, as soon as I called to her from the gondola, she sent out to me, from the bottom of her heart, a love which stopped only where there was no longer any material substance to support it on the surface of her impassioned gaze which she brought as close to me as possible, which she tried to thrust forward to the advanced post of her lips, in a smile which seemed to be kissing me, in the framework and beneath the canopy of the more discreet smile of the arched window illuminated by the midday sun; for these reasons, that window has assumed in my memory the precious quality of things that have had, simultaneously, side by side with ourself, their part in a certain hour that struck, the same for us and for them; and however full of admirable tracery its mullions may be, that illustrious window retains in my sight the intimate aspect of a man of genius with whom we have spent a month in some holiday resort, where he has acquired a friendly regard for us; and if, ever since then, whenever I see a cast of that window in a museum, I feel the tears starting to my eyes, it is simply because the window says to me the thing that touches me more than anything else in the world: " I remember your mother so well."

And as I went indoors to join my mother who had left the window, I did indeed recapture, coming from the warm air outside, that feeling of coolness that I had known long ago at Combray when I went upstairs to my room, but at Venice it was a breeze from the sea that kept the air cool, and no longer upon a little wooden staircase with narrow steps, but upon the noble surfaces of blocks of marble, splashed at every moment by a shaft of greenish sunlight, which to the valuable instruction in the art of Chardin, acquired long ago, added a lesson in that of Veronese. And since at Venice it is to works of art, to things of priceless beauty, that the task is entrusted of giving us our impressions of everyday life, we may sketch the character of this city, using the pretext that the Venice of certain painters is coldly æsthetic in its most celebrated parts, by representing only (let us make an exception of the superb studies of Maxime Dethomas) its poverty-stricken aspects, in the quarters where everything that creates its splendour is concealed, and to make Venice more intimate and more genuine give it a resemblance to Aubervilliers. It has been the mistake of some very great artists, that, by a quite natural reaction from the artificial Venice of bad painters, they have attached themselves exclusively to the Venice which they have found more realistic, to some humble *campo*, some tiny deserted *rio*. It was this Venice that I used often to explore in the afternoon, when I did not go out with my mother. The fact was that it was easier to find there women of the industrial class, match-makers, pearl-stringers, workers in glass or lace, working women in black shawls with long fringes. My gondola followed the course of the small canals; like the mysterious hand of a Genie leading me through the maze of this oriental city, they seemed, as I advanced, to be carving a road for me through the heart of a crowded quarter which they clove asunder, barely dividing with a slender fissure, arbitrarily carved, the tall houses with their tiny Moorish windows; and, as though the magic guide had been holding a candle in his hand and were lighting the way for me, they kept casting ahead of them a ray of sunlight for which they cleared a path.

One felt that between the mean dwellings which the canal had just parted and which otherwise would have formed a compact whole, no open space had been reserved. With the result that the belfry of the church, or the garden-trellis rose sheer above the *rio* as in a flooded city. But with churches as with gardens, thanks to the same transposition as in the Grand Canal, the sea formed so effective a way of communication, a substitute for street or alley, that on either side of the *canaletto* the churches rose from the water in this ancient, plebeian quarter, degraded into humble, much frequented mission chapels, bearing upon their surface the stamp of their necessity, of their use by crowds of simple folk, that the gardens crossed by the line of the canal allowed their astonished leaves or fruit to trail in the water and that on the doorstep of the house whose roughly hewn stone was still wrinkled as though it had only just been sawn, little boys surprised by the gondola and keeping their balance allowed their legs to dangle vertically, like sailors seated upon a swing-bridge the two halves of which have been swung apart, allowing the sea to pass between them.

Now and again there appeared a handsomer building that happened to be there, like a surprise in a box which we have just opened, a little ivory temple with its Corinthian columns and its allegorical statue on the pediment, somewhat out of place among the ordinary buildings in the midst of which it had survived, and the peristyle with which the canal provided it resembled a landing-stage for market gardeners.

The sun had barely begun to set when I went to fetch my mother from the Piazzetta. We returned up the Grand Canal in our gondola, we watched the double line of palaces between which we passed reflect the light and angle of the sun upon their rosy surfaces, and alter with them, seeming not so much private habitations and historic buildings as a chain of marble cliffs at the foot of which people go out in the evening in a boat to watch the sunset. In this way, the mansions arranged along either bank of the canal made one think of objects of nature, but of a nature which seemed to have created its works with a human imagination. But at the same time (because of the character of the impressions, always urban, which Venice gives us almost in the open sea, upon those waves whose flow and ebb make themselves felt twice daily, and which alternately cover at high tide and uncover at low tide the splendid outside stairs of the palaces), as we should have done in Paris upon the boulevards, in the Champs-Elysées, in the Bois, in any wide thoroughfare that was a fashionable resort, in the powdery evening light, we passed the most beautifully dressed women, almost all foreigners, who, propped luxuriously upon the cushions of their floating vehicle, took their place in the procession, stopped before a palace in which there was a friend whom they wished to see, sent to inquire whether she was at home; and while, as they waited for the answer, they prepared to leave a card, as they would have done at the door of the Hôtel de Guermantes, they turned to their guide-book to find out the period, the style of the palace, not without being shaken, as though upon the crest of a blue wave, by the thrust of the flashing, prancing water, which took alarm on finding itself pent between the dancing gondola and the slapping marble. And thus any excursion, even when it was only to pay calls or to go shopping, was threefold and unique in this Venice where the simplest social coming and going assumed at the same time the form and the charm of a visit to a museum and a trip on the sea.

Several of the palaces on the Grand Canal had been converted into hotels, and, feeling the need of a change, or wishing to be hospitable to Mme Sazerat whom we had encountered—the unexpected and inopportune acquaintance whom we invariably meet when we travel abroad—and whom Mamma had invited to dine with us, we decided one evening to try an hotel which was not our own, and in which we had been told that the food was better. While my mother was paying the gondolier and taking Mme Sazerat to the room which she had engaged, I slipped away to inspect the great hall of the restaurant with its fine marble pillars and walls and ceiling that were once entirely covered with frescoes, recently and badly restored. Two waiters were conversing in an Italian which I translate:

"Are the old people going to dine in their room? They never let us know. It's the devil, I never know whether I am to reserve their table (*non so se bisogna conservargli la loro tavola*). And then, suppose they come down and find their table taken! I don't understand how they can

294

take in *forestieri* like that in such a smart hotel. They're not our style."

Notwithstanding his contempt, the waiter was anxious to know what action he was to take with regard to the table, and was going to get the lift-boy sent upstairs to inquire, when, before he had had time to do so, he received his answer: he had just caught sight of the old lady who was entering the room. I had no difficulty, despite the air of melancholy and weariness that comes with the burden of years, and despite a sort of eczema, a red leprosy that covered her face, in recognising beneath her bonnet, in her black jacket, made by W——, but to the untutored eye exactly like that of an old charwoman, the Marquise de Villeparisis. As luck would have it, the spot upon which I was standing, engaged in studying the remains of a fresco, between two of the beautiful marble panels, was directly behind the table at which Mme de Villeparisis had just sat down.

"Then M. de Villeparisis won't be long. They've been here a month now, and it's only once that they didn't have a meal together," said the waiter.

I was asking myself who the relative could be with whom she was travelling, and who was named M. de Villeparisis, when I saw, a few moments later, advance towards the table and sit down by her side, her old lover, M. de Norpois.

His great age had weakened the resonance of his voice, but had in compensation given to his language, formerly so reserved, a positive intemperance. The cause of this was to be sought, perhaps, in certain ambitions for the realisation of which little time, he felt, remained to him and which filled him all the more with vehemence and ardour; perhaps in the fact that, having been discarded from a world of politics to which he longed to return, he imagined, in the simplicity of his desire, that he could turn out of office, by the pungent criticisms which he launched at them, the men whose places he was anxious to fill. Thus we see politicians convinced that the Cabinet of which they are not members cannot hold out for three days. It would, however, be an exaggeration to suppose that M. de Norpois had entirely lost the traditions of diplomatic speech. Whenever "important matters" were involved, he at once became, as we shall see, the man whom we remember in the past, but at all other times he would inveigh against this man and that with the senile violence of certain octogenarians which hurls them into the arms of women to whom they are no longer capable of doing any serious damage.

Mme de Villeparisis preserved, for some minutes, the silence of an old woman who in the exhaustion of age finds it difficult to rise from memories of the past to consideration of the present. Then, turning to one of those eminently practical questions that indicate the survival of a mutual affection:

" Did you call at Salviati's? "

" Yes."

" Will they send it to-morrow? "

" I brought the bowl back myself. You shall see it after dinner. Let us look what there is to eat."

" Did you send instructions about my Suez shares? "

" No; at the present moment the market is entirely taken up with oil shares. But there is no hurry, they are still fetching an excellent price. Here is the bill of fare. First of all, there are red mullets. Shall we try them? "

"For me, yes, but you are not allowed them. Ask for a risotto instead. But they don't know how to cook it."

"That doesn't matter. Waiter, some mullets for Madame and a risotto for me."

A fresh and prolonged silence.

"Why, I brought you the papers, the *Corriere della Sera*, the *Gazzetta del Popolo*, and all the rest of them. Do you know, there is a great deal of talk about a diplomatic change, the first scapegoat in which is to be Paléologue, who is notoriously inadequate in Serbia. He will perhaps be succeeded by Lozé, and there will be a vacancy at Constantinople. But," M. de Norpois hastened to add in a bitter tone, "for an Embassy of such scope, in a capital where it is obvious that Great Britain must always, whatever may happen, occupy the chief place at the council-table, it would be prudent to turn to men of experience better armed to resist the ambushes of the enemies of our British ally than are diplomats of the modern school who would walk blindfold into the trap." The angry volubility with which M. de Norpois uttered the last words was due principally to the fact that the newspapers, instead of suggesting his name, as he had requested them to do, named as a " hot favourite " a young official of the Foreign Ministry. "Heaven knows that the men of years and experience may well hesitate, as a result of all manner of tortuous manœuvres, to put themselves forward in the place of more or less incapable recruits. I have known many of these self-styled diplomats of the empirical method who centred all their hopes in a soap bubble which it did not take me long to burst. There can be no question about it, if the Government is so lacking in wisdom as to entrust the reins of state to turbulent hands, at the call of duty an old conscript will always answer ' Present! ' But who knows " (and here M. de Norpois appeared to know perfectly well to whom he was referring) " whether it would not be the same on the day when they came in search of some veteran full of wisdom and skill. To my mind, for everyone has a right to his own opinion, the post at Constantinople should not be accepted until we have settled our existing difficulties with Germany. We owe no man anything, and it is intolerable that every six months they should come and demand from us, by fraudulent machinations, and extort, by force and fear, the payment of some debt or other, always hastily offered by a venal press. This must cease, and naturally a man of high distinction who has proved his merit, a man who would have, if I may say so, the Emperor's ear, would wield greater authority than any ordinary person in bringing the conflict to an end."

A gentleman who was finishing his dinner bowed to M. de Norpois.

" Why, there is Prince Foggi," said the Marquis.

" Ah, I'm not sure that I know whom you mean," muttered Mme de Villeparisis.

" Why, of course you do. It is Prince Odone. The brother-in-law of your cousin Doudeauville. You cannot have forgotten that I went shooting with him at Bonnétable? "

" Ah! Odone, that is the one who went in for paint-ing? "

" Not at all, he's the one who married the Grand Duke N—'s sister."

M. de Norpois uttered these remarks in the cross tone of a schoolmaster who is dissatisfied with his pupil, and stared fixedly at Mme de Villeparisis out of his blue eyes.

When the Prince had drunk his coffee and was leaving his table, M. de Norpois rose, hastened towards him and with a majestic wave of his arm, himself retiring into the background, presented him to Mme de Villeparisis. And during the next few minutes while the Prince was standing beside their table, M. de Norpois never ceased for an instant to keep his azure pupils trained on Mme de Villeparisis, from the weakness or severity of an old lover, principally from fear of her making one of those mistakes in Italian which he had relished but which he dreaded. Whenever she said anything to the Prince that was not quite accurate he corrected her mistake and stared into the eyes of the abashed and docile Marquise with the steady intensity of a hypnotist.

A waiter came to tell me that my mother was waiting for me, I went to her and made my apologies to Mme Sazerat, saying that I had been interested to see Mme de Villeparisis. At the sound of this name, Mme Sazerat turned pale and seemed about to faint. Controlling herself with an effort: " Mme de Villeparisis, who was Mlle de Bouillon? " she inquired.

" Yes."

" Couldn't I just get a glimpse of her for a moment? It has been the desire of my life."

" Then there is no time to lose, Madame, for she will soon have finished her dinner. But how do you come to take such an interest in her? "

" Because Mme de Villeparisis was, before her second marriage, the Duchesse d'Havré, beautiful as an angel, wicked as a demon, who drove my father out of his senses, ruined him and then forsook him immediately. Well, she may have behaved to him like any girl out of the gutter, she may have been the cause of our having to live, my family and myself, in a humble position at Combray; now that my father is dead, my consolation is to think that he was in love with the most beautiful woman of his generation, and as I have never set eyes on her, it will, after all, be a pleasure. . . ."

I escorted Mme Sazerat, trembling with emotion, to the restaurant and pointed out Mme de Villeparisis.

But, like a blind person who turns his face in the wrong direction, so Mme Sazerat did not bring her gaze to rest upon the table at which Mme de Villeparisis was dining, but, looking towards another part of the room, said:

" But she must have gone, I don't see her in the place you're pointing to."

And she continued to gaze round the room, in quest of the loathed, adored vision that had haunted her imagination for so long.

" Yes, there she is, at the second table."

" Then we can't be counting from the same point. At what I call the second table there are only two people, an old gentleman and a little hunchbacked, red-faced woman, quite hideous."

" That is she! "

In the meantime, Mme de Villeparisis having asked M. de Norpois to make Prince Foggi sit down, a friendly conversation followed among the three of them; they discussed politics, the Prince declared that he was not interested in the fate of the Cabinet and would spend another week at least at Venice. He hoped that in the interval all risk of a ministerial crisis would have been obviated. Prince Foggi supposed for a moment that these political topics did not interest M. de Norpois, for the latter who until then had been expressing himself with such vehemence had become suddenly absorbed in an almost angelic silence which he seemed capable of breaking, should his voice return, only by singing some innocent melody by Mendelssohn or César Franck. The Prince supposed also that this silence was due to the reserve of a Frenchman who naturally would not wish to discuss Italian affairs in the presence of an Italian. Now in this, the Prince was completely mistaken. Silence, an air of indifference were, in M. de Norpois, not a sign of reserve but the regular prelude to an intervention in important affairs. The Marquis had his eye upon nothing less (as we have seen) than Constantinople, with a preliminary settlement of the German question, with a view to which he hoped to force the hand of the Rome Cabinet. He considered, in fact, that an action on his part of international range might be the worthy crown of his career, perhaps even an avenue to fresh honours, to difficult tasks to which he had not relinquished his pretensions. For old age makes us incapable of performing our duties but not, at first, of desiring them. It is only in a third period that those who live to a very great age have relinquished desire, as they have had already to forgo action. They no longer present themselves as candidates at futile elections which they tried so often to win, the Presidential election, for instance. They content themselves with taking the air, eating, reading the newspapers, they have outlived themselves.

The Prince, to put the Marquis at his ease and to shew him that he regarded him as a compatriot, began to speak of the possible successors to the Prime Minister then in office. A successor who would have a difficult task before him. When Prince Foggi had mentioned more than twenty names of politicians who seemed to him suitable for office, names to which the ex-ambassador listened with his eyelids drooping over his blue eyes and without moving a muscle, M. de Norpois broke his silence at length to utter those words which were for a score of years to supply the Chanceries with food for conversation, and afterwards, when they had been forgotten, would be exhumed by some personage signing himself "One Who Knows" or "Testis" or "Machiavelli" in a newspaper in which the very oblivion into which they had fallen entitled them to create a fresh sensation. As I say, Prince Foggi had mentioned more than twenty names to the diplomat who remained as motionless and mute as though he were stone deaf when M. de Norpois raised his head slightly, and, in the form that had been assumed by those of his diplomatic interventions which had had the most far-reaching consequences, albeit this time with greater audacity and less brevity, asked shrewdly: "And has no one mentioned the name of Signor Giolitti?" At these words the scales fell from Prince Foggi's eyes; he could hear a celestial murmur. Then at once M. de Norpois began to speak about one thing and another, no longer afraid to make a sound, as, when the last note of a sublime aria by Bach has been played, the audience are no longer afraid to talk aloud, to call for their hats and coats in the cloakroom. He made the difference even more marked by begging the Prince to pay his most humble respects to Their Majesties the King and Queen when next he should see them, a phrase of dismissal which corresponds to the shout for a coachman at the end of a concert: "Auguste, from the Rue de Belloy." We cannot say what exactly were Prince Foggi's impressions. He must certainly have been delighted to have heard the gem: "And Signor Giolitti, has no one mentioned his name?" For M. de Norpois, in whom age had destroyed or deranged his most outstanding qualities, had on the other hand, as he grew older, perfected his bravura, as certain aged musicians, who in all other respects have declined, acquire and retain until the end, in the matter of chamber-music, a perfect virtuosity which they did not formerly possess.

However that may be, Prince Foggi, who had intended to spend a fortnight in Venice, returned to Rome that very night and was received a few days later in audience by the King in connection with the property which, as we may perhaps have mentioned already, the Prince owned in Sicily. The Cabinet hung on for longer than could have been expected. When it fell, the King consulted various statesmen as to the most suitable head of the new Cabinet. Then he sent for Signor Giolitti who accepted. Three months later a newspaper reported Prince Foggi's meeting with M. de Norpois. The conversation was reported as we have given it here, with the difference that, instead of: " M. de Norpois asked shrewdly," one read: " M. de Norpois said with that shrewd and charming smile which is so characteristic of him." M. de Norpois considered that "shrewdly" had in itself sufficient explosive force for a diplomat and that this addition was, to say the least, untimely. He had even asked the Quai d'Orsay to issue an official contradiction, but the Quai d'Orsay did not know which way to turn. As a matter of fact, ever since the conversation had been made public, M. Barrère had been telegraphing several times hourly to Paris, pointing out that there was already an accredited Ambassador at the Quirinal and describing the indignation with which the incident had been received throughout the whole of Europe. This indignation was non-existent, but the other Ambassadors were too polite to contradict M. Barrère when he assured them that there could be no question about everybody's being furious. M. Barrère, listening only to his own thoughts, mistook this courteous silence for assent. Immediately he telegraphed to Paris: " I have just had an hour's conversation with the Marchese Visconti-Venosta," and so forth. His secretaries were worn to skin and bone.

M. de Norpois, however, could count upon the devotion of a French newspaper of very long standing, which indeed in 1870, when he was French Minister in a German capital, had rendered him an important service. This paper (especially its leading article, which was unsigned) was admirably written. But the paper became a thousand times more interesting when this leading article (styled " premier-Paris " in those far off days and now, no one knows why, " editorial ") was on the contrary badly expressed, with endless repetitions of words. Everyone felt then, with emotion, that the article had been " inspired." Perhaps by M. de Norpois, perhaps by some other leading man of the hour. To give an anticipatory idea of the Italian incident, let us shew how M. de Norpois made use of this paper in 1870, to no purpose, it may be thought, since war broke out nevertheless—most efficaciously, according to M. de Norpois, whose axiom was that we ought first and foremost to prepare public opinion. His articles, every word in which was weighed, resembled those optimistic bulletins which are at once followed by the death of the patient. For instance, on the eve of the declaration of war, in 1870, when mobilisation was almost complete, M. de Norpois (remaining, of course, in the background) had felt it to be his duty to send to this famous newspaper the following " editorial " :

" The opinion seems to prevail in authoritative circles that since the afternoon hours of yesterday, the situation, without of course being of an alarming nature, might well be envisaged as serious and even, from certain angles, as susceptible of being regarded as critical. M. le Marquis de Norpois would appear to have held several conversations with the Prussian Minister, in order to examine in a firm and conciliatory spirit, and in a wholly concrete fashion, the different causes of friction that, if we may say so, exist. Unfortunately, we have not yet heard, at the hour of going to press, that Their Excellencies have been able to agree upon a formula that may serve as base for a diplomatic instrument."

Latest intelligence: " We have learned with satisfaction in well-informed circles that a slight slackening of tension appears to have occurred in Franco-Prussian relations. We may attach a specially distinct importance to the fact that M. de Norpois is reported to have met the British Minister ' unter den Linden ' and to have conversed with him for fully twenty minutes. This report is regarded as highly satisfactory." (There was added, in brackets, after the word " satisfactory " its German equivalent " *befriedigend* "). And on the following day one read in the editorial: " It would appear that, notwithstanding all the dexterity of M. de Norpois, to whom everyone must hasten to render homage for the skill and energy with which he has managed to defend the inalienable rights of France, a rupture is now, so to speak, virtually inevitable."

The newspaper could not refrain from following an editorial couched in this vein with a selection of comments, furnished of course by M. de Norpois. The reader may perhaps have observed in these last pages that the " conditional mood " was one of the Ambassador's favourite grammatical forms, in the literature of diplomacy. (" One would attach a special importance " for " it appears that people attach a special importance.") But the " present indicative " employed not in its regular sense but in that of the old " optative " was no less dear to M. de Norpois. The comments that followed the editorial were as follows:

" Never have the public shewn themselves so admirably calm " (M. de Norpois would have liked to believe that this was true but feared that it was precisely the opposite of the truth.) " They are weary of fruitless agitation and have learned with satisfaction that His Majesty's Government would assume their responsibilities according to the eventualities that might occur. The public ask " (optative) " nothing more. To their splendid coolness, which is in itself a token of victory, we shall add a piece of intelligence amply qualified to reassure public opinion, were there any need of that. We are, indeed, assured that M. de Norpois who, for reasons of health, was ordered long ago to return to Paris for medical treatment, would appear to have left Berlin where he considered that his presence no longer served any purpose."

Latest intelligence: " His Majesty the Emperor left Compiègne this morning for Paris in order to confer with the Marquis de Norpois, the Minister for War and Marshal Bazaine upon whom public opinion relies with absolute confidence. H. M. the Emperor has cancelled the banquet which he was about to give for his sister-in-law the Duchess of Alba. This action created everywhere, as soon as it became known, a particularly favourable impression. The Emperor has held a review of his troops whose enthusiasm is indescribable. Several Corps, by virtue of a mobilisation order issued immediately upon the Sovereign's arrival in Paris, are, in any contingency, ready to move in the direction of the Rhine."

* * *

Sometimes at dusk as I returned to the hotel I felt that the Albertine of long ago invisible to my eyes was nevertheless enclosed within me as in the dungeons of an internal Venice, the solid walls of which some incident occasionally slid apart so as to give me a glimpse of that past.

Thus for instance one evening a letter from my stockbroker reopened for me for an instant the gates of the prison in which Albertine abode within me alive, but so remote, so profoundly buried that she remained inaccessible to me. Since her death I had ceased to take any interest in the speculations that I had made in order to have more money for her. But time had passed; the wisest judgments of the previous generation had been proved unwise by this generation, as had occurred in the past to M. Thiers who had said that railways could never prove successful. The stocks of which M. de Norpois had said to us: " even if your income from them is nothing very great, you may be certain of never losing any of your capital," were, more often than not, those which had declined most in value. Calls had been made upon me for considerable sums and in a rash moment I decided to sell out everything and found that I now possessed barely a fifth of the fortune that I had had when Albertine was alive. This became known at Combray among the survivors of our family circle and their friends, and, as they knew that I went about with the Marquis de Saint-Loup and the Guermantes family, they said to themselves: " Pride goes before a fall! " They would have been greatly astonished to learn that it was for a girl of Albertine's humble position that I had made these speculations.

Besides, in that Combray world in which everyone is classified for ever according to the income that he is known to enjoy, as in an Indian caste, it would have been impossible for anyone to form any idea of the great freedom that prevailed in the world of the Guermantes where people attached no importance to wealth, and where poverty was regarded as being as disagreeable, but no more degrading, as having no more effect on a person's social position than would a stomach-ache. Doubtless they imagined, on the contrary, at Combray that Saint-Loup and M. de Guermantes must be ruined aristocrats, whose estates were mortgaged, to whom I had been lending money, whereas if I had been ruined they would have been the first to offer in all sincerity to come to my assistance. As for my comparative penury, it was all the more awkward at the moment, inasmuch as my Venetian interests had been concentrated for some little time past on a rosy-cheeked young glass-vendor who offered to the delighted eye a whole range of orange tones and filled me with such a longing to see her again daily that, feeling that my mother and I would soon be leaving Venice, I had made up my mind that I would try to create some sort of position for her in Paris which would save me the distress of parting from her. The beauty of her seventeen summers was so noble, so radiant, that it was like acquiring a genuine Titian before leaving the place. And would the scant remains of my fortune be sufficient temptation to her to make her leave her native land and come to live in Paris for my sole convenience? But as I came to the end of the stockbroker's letter, a passage in which he said: " I shall look after your credits " reminded me of a scarcely less hypocritically professional expression which the bath-attendant at Balbec had used in speaking to Aimé of Albertine. " It was I that looked after her," she had said, and these words which had never again entered my mind acted like an " Open, sesame! " upon the hinges of the prison door. But a moment later the door closed once more upon the immured victim—whom I was not to blame for not wishing to join, since I was no longer able to see her, to call her to mind, and since other people exist for us only to the extent of the idea that we retain of them —who had for an instant seemed to me so touching because of my desertion of her, albeit she was unaware of it, that I had for the duration of a lightning-flash thought with longing of the time, already remote, when I used to suffer night and day from the companionship of her memory. Another time at San Giorgio degli Schiavoni, an eagle accompanying one of the Apostles and conventionalised in the same manner revived the memory and almost the suffering caused by the two rings the similarity of which Françoise had revealed to me, and as to which I had never learned who had given them to Albertine. Finally, one evening, an incident occurred of such a nature that it seemed as though my love must revive. No sooner had our gondola stopped at the hotel steps than the porter handed me a telegram which the messenger had already brought three times to the hotel, for owing to the inac-curate rendering of the recipient's name (which I recog-nised nevertheless, through the corruptions introduced by Italian clerks, as my own) the post-office required a signed receipt certifying that the telegram was addressed to myself. I opened it as soon as I was in my own room, and, as I cast my eye over the sheet covered with inaccurately transmitted words, managed, nevertheless, to make out: " My dear, you think me dead, forgive me, I am quite alive, should like to see you, talk about marriage, when do you return? Love. Albertine." Then there occurred in me in inverse order a process parallel to that which had occurred in the case of my grandmother: when I had learned the fact of my grandmother's death, I had not at first felt any grief. And I had been really grieved by her death only when spontaneous memories had made her seem to me to be once again alive. Now that Albertine was no longer alive for me in my mind, the news that she was alive did not cause me the joy that I might have expected. Albertine had been nothing more to me than a bundle of thoughts, she had survived her bodily death so long as those thoughts were alive in me; on the other hand, now that those thoughts were dead, Albertine did not in any way revive for me, in her bodily form. And when I realised that I felt no joy at the thought of her being alive, that I no longer loved her, I ought to have been more astounded than a person who, looking at his reflection in the glass, after months of travel, or of sickness, discovers that he has white hair and a different face, that of a middle-aged or an old man. This appals us because its message is: " the man that I was, the fair young man no longer exists, I am another person." And yet, was not the impression that I now felt the proof of as profound a change, as total a death of my former self and of the no less complete substitution of a new self for that former self, as is proved by the sight of a wrinkled face capped with a snowy poll instead of the face of long ago? But we are no more disturbed by the fact of our having become another person, after a lapse of years and in the natural order of events, than we are disturbed at any given moment by the fact of our being, one after another, the incompatible persons, crafty, sensitive, refined, coarse, disinterested, ambitious which we are, in turn, every day of our life. And the reason why this does not disturb us is the same, namely that the self which has been eclipsed—momentarily in this latter case and when it is a question of character, permanently in the former case and when it is a matter of passions—is not present to deplore the other, the other which is for the moment, or for all time, our whole self; the coarse self laughs at his own coarseness, for he is a coarse person, and the forgetful man does not worry about his loss of memory, simply because he has forgotten.

I should have been incapable of resuscitating Albertine because I was incapable of resuscitating myself, of resuscitating the self of those days. Life, according to its habit which is, by incessant, infinitesimal labours, to change the face of the world, had not said to me on the morrow of Albertine's death: " Become another person," but, by changes too imperceptible for me to be conscious even that I was changing, had altered almost every element in me, with the result that my mind was already accustomed to its new master—my new self—when it became aware that it had changed; it was upon this new master that it depended. My affection for Albertine, my jealousy depended, as we have seen, upon the irradiation by the association of ideas of certain pleasant or painful impressions, upon the memory of Mlle Vinteuil at Montjouvain, upon the precious good-night kisses that Albertine used to bestow on my throat. But in proportion as these impressions had grown fainter, the vast field of impressions which they coloured with a hue that was agonising or soothing began to resume its neutral tint. As soon as oblivion had taken hold of certain dominant points of suffering and pleasure, the resistance offered by my love was overcome, I was no longer in love with Albertine. I tried to recall her image to my mind. I had been right in my presentiment when, a couple of days after Albertine's flight, I was appalled by the discovery that I had been able to live for forty-eight hours without her. It had been the same thing when I wrote to Gilberte long ago saying to myself: " If this goes on for a year or two, I shall no longer be in love with her." And if, when Swann asked me to come and see Gilberte again, this had seemed to me as embarrassing as greeting a dead woman, in Albertine's case death—or what I had supposed to be death—had achieved the same result as a prolonged rupture in Gilberte's. Death acts only in the same way as absence. The monster at whose apparition my love had trembled, oblivion, had indeed, as I had feared, ended by devouring that love. Not only did the news that she was alive fail to revive my love, not only did it allow me to realise how far I had already proceeded on the way towards indifference, it at once and so abruptly accelerated that process that I asked myself whether in the past the converse report that of Albertine's death, had not in like manner, by completing the effect of her departure, exalted my love and delayed its decline. And now that the knowledge that she was alive and the possibility of our reunion made her all of a sudden so worthless in my sight, I asked myself whether Françoise's insinuations, our rupture itself, and even her death (imaginary, but supposed to be true) had not prolonged my love, so true is it that the efforts of third persons and even those of fate, in separating us from a woman, succeed only in attaching us to her. Now it was the contrary process that had occurred. Anyhow, I tried to recall her image and perhaps because I had only to raise my finger to have her once more to myself, the memory that came to me was that of a very stout, masculine girl from whose colourless face protruded already, like a sprouting seed, the profile of Mme Bontemps. What she might or might not have done with Andrée or with other girls no longer interested me. I no longer suffered from the malady which I had so long thought to be incurable and really I might have foreseen this. Certainly, regret for a lost mistress, jealousy that survives her death are physical maladies fully as much as tuberculosis or leucaemia. And yet among physical maladies it is possible to distinguish those which are caused by a purely physical agency, and those which act upon the body only through the channel of the mind. If the part of the mind which serves as carrier is the memory—that is to say if the cause is obliterated or remote—however agonising the pain, however profound the disturbance to the organism may appear to be, it is very seldom (the mind having a capacity for renewal or rather an incapacity for conservation which the tissues lack) that the prognosis is not favourable. At the end of a given period after which a man who has been attacked by cancer will be dead, it is very seldom that the grief of an inconsolable widower or father is not healed. Mine was healed. Was it for this girl whom I saw in my mind's eye so fleshy and who had certainly grown older as the girls whom she had loved had grown older, was it for her that I must renounce the dazzling girl who was my memory of yesterday, my hope for to-morrow (to whom I could give nothing, any more than to any other, if I married Albertine), renounce that new Albertine not "such as hell had beheld her" but faithful, and "indeed a trifle shy"? It was she who was now what Albertine had been in the past: my love for Albertine had been but a transitory form of my devotion to girlhood. We think that we are in love with a girl, whereas we love in her, alas! only that dawn the glow of which is momentarily reflected on her face. The night passed. In the morning I gave the telegram back to the hotel porter explaining that it had been brought to me by mistake and that it was not addressed to me. He told me that now that it had been opened he might get into trouble, that it would be better if I kept it; I put it back in my pocket, but determined that I would act as though I had never received it. I had definitely ceased to love Albertine. So that this love after departing so widely from the course that I had anticipated, when I remembered my love for Gilberte, after obliging me to make so long and painful a detour, itself too ended, after furnishing an exception, by merging itself, just like my love for Gilberte, in the general rule of oblivion.

But then I reflected: I used to value Albertine more than myself; I no longer value her now because for a certain time past I have ceased to see her. But my desire not to be parted from myself by death, to rise again after my death, this desire was not like the desire never to be parted from Albertine, it still persisted. Was this due to the fact that I valued myself more highly than her, that when I was in love with her I loved myself even more? No, it was because, having ceased to see her, I had ceased to love her, whereas I had not ceased to love myself because my everyday attachments to myself had not been severed like my attachments to Albertine. But if the attachments to my body, to my self were severed also. . . ? Obviously, it would be the same. Our love of life is only an old connection of which we do not know how to rid ourself. Its strength lies in its permanence. But death which severs it will cure us of the desire for immortality.

After luncheon, when I was not going to roam about Venice by myself, I went up to my room to get ready to go out with my mother. In the abrupt angles of the walls I could read the restrictions imposed by the sea, the parsimony of the soil. And when I went downstairs to join Mamma who was waiting for me, at that hour when, at Combray, it was so pleasant to feel the sun quite close at hand, in the darkness guarded by closed shutters, here, from top to bottom of the marble staircase as to which one knew no better than in a Renaissance picture, whether it was built in a palace or upon a galley, the same coolness and the same feeling of the splendour of the scene outside were imparted, thanks to the awning which stirred outside the ever-open windows through which, upon an incessant stream of air, the cool shade and the greenish sunlight moved as though over a liquid surface and suggested the weltering proximity, the glitter, the mirroring instability of the sea.

After dinner, I went out by myself, into the heart of the enchanted city where I found myself wandering in strange regions like a character in the Arabian Nights. It was very seldom that I did not, in the course of my wanderings, hit upon some strange and spacious piazza of which no guide-book, no tourist had ever told me.

I had plunged into a network of little alleys, *calli* dissecting in all directions by their ramifications the quarter of Venice isolated between a canal and the lagoon, as if it had crystallised along these innumerable, slender, capillary lines. All of a sudden, at the end of one of those little streets, it seemed as though a bubble had occurred in the crystallised matter. A vast and splendid *campo* of which I could certainly never, in this network of little streets, have guessed the importance, or even found room for it, spread out before me flanked with charming palaces silvery in the moonlight. It was one of those architectural wholes towards which, in any other town, the streets converge, lead you and point the way. Here it seemed to be deliberately concealed in a labyrinth of alleys, like those palaces in oriental tales to which mysterious agents convey by night a person who, taken home again before daybreak, can never again find his way back to the magic dwelling which he ends by supposing that he visited only in a dream.

On the following day I set out in quest of my beautiful nocturnal piazza, I followed *calli* which were exactly like one another and refused to give me any information, except such as would lead me farther astray. Sometimes a vague landmark which I seemed to recognise led me to suppose that I was about to see appear, in its seclusion, solitude and silence, the beautiful exiled piazza. At that moment,

317

some evil genie which had assumed the form of a fresh *calle* made me turn unconsciously from my course, and I found myself suddenly brought back to the Grand Canal. And as there is no great difference between the memory of a dream and the memory of a reality, I ended by asking myself whether it was not during my sleep that there had occurred in a dark patch of Venetian crystallisation that strange interruption which offered a vast piazza flanked by romantic palaces, to the meditative eye of the moon.

On the day before our departure, we decided to go so far afield as Padua where were to be found those Vices and Virtues of which Swann had given me reproductions; after walking in the glare of the sun across the garden of the Arena, I entered the Giotto chapel the entire ceiling of which and the background of the frescoes are so blue that it seems as though the radiant day has crossed the threshold with the human visitor, and has come in for a moment to stow away in the shade and coolness its pure sky, of a slightly deeper blue now that it is rid of the sun's gilding, as in those brief spells of respite that interrupt the finest days, when, without our having noticed any cloud, the sun having turned his gaze elsewhere for a moment, the azure, more exquisite still, grows deeper. In this sky, upon the blue-washed stone, angels were flying with so intense a celestial or at least an infantile ardour, that they seemed to be birds of a peculiar species that had really existed, that must have figured in the natural history of biblical and Apostolic times, birds that never fail to fly before the saints when they walk abroad; there are always some to be seen fluttering above them, and as they are real creatures with a genuine power of flight, we see them soar upwards, describe curves,

" loop the loop " without the slightest difficulty, plunge towards the earth head downwards with the aid of wings which enable them to support themselves in positions that defy the law of gravitation, and they remind us far more of a variety of bird or of young pupils of Garros practising the *vol-plané*, than of the angels of the art of Renaissance and later periods whose wings have become nothing more than emblems and whose attitude is generally the same as that of heavenly beings who are not winged.

    ●   ●   ●

When I heard, on the very day upon which we were due to start for Paris, that Mme Putbus, and consequently her maid, had just arrived in Venice, I asked my mother to put off our departure for a few days; her air of not taking my request into consideration, of not even listening to it seriously, reawakened in my nerves, excited by the Venetian springtime, that old desire to rebel against an imaginary plot woven against me by my parents (who imagined that I would be forced to obey them), that fighting spirit, that desire which drove me in the past to enforce my wishes upon the people whom I loved best in the world, prepared to conform to their wishes after I had succeeded in making them yield. I told my mother that I would not leave Venice, but she, thinking it more to her purpose not to appear to believe that I was saying this seriously, did not even answer. I went on to say that she would soon see whether I was serious or not. And when the hour came at which accompanied by all my luggage, she set off for the station, I ordered a cool drink to be brought out to me on the terrace overlooking the canal, and installed myself there, watching the sunset, while from a boat that had stopped in front of the hotel a musician sang "sole mio."

The sun continued to sink. My mother must be nearing the station. Presently, she would be gone, I should be left alone in Venice, alone with the misery of knowing that I had distressed her, and without her presence to comfort me. The hour of the train approached. My irrevocable solitude was so near at hand that it seemed to me to have begun already and to be complete. For I felt myself to be alone. Things had become alien to me. I was no longer calm enough to draw from my throbbing heart and introduce into them a measure of stability. The town that I saw before me had ceased to be Venice. Its personality, its name, seemed to me to be lying fictions which I no longer had the courage to impress upon its stones. I saw the palaces reduced to their constituent parts, lifeless heaps of marble with nothing to choose between them, and the water as a combination of hydrogen and oxygen, eternal, blind, anterior and exterior to Venice, unconscious of Doges or of Turner. And yet this unremarkable place was as strange as a place at which we have just arrived, which does not yet know us—as a place which we have left and which has forgotten us already. I could not tell it anything more about myself, I could leave nothing of myself imprinted upon it, it left me diminished, I was nothing

more than a heart that throbbed, and an attention strained
to follow the development of " sole mio." In vain might
I fix my mind despairingly upon the beautiful and characteristic arch of the Rialto, it seemed to me, with the mediocrity of the obvious, a bridge not merely inferior to but as
different from the idea that I possessed of it as an actor with
regard to whom, notwithstanding his fair wig and black
garments, we know quite well that in his essential quality
he is not Hamlet. So the palaces, the canal, the Rialto
became divested of the idea that created their individuality
and disintegrated into their common material elements.
But at the same time this mediocre place seemed to me
remote. In the basin of the arsenal, because of an element
which itself also was scientific, namely latitude, there was
that singularity in things which, even when similar in appearance to those of our own land, reveal that they are
aliens, in exile beneath a foreign sky; I felt that that horizon
so close at hand, which I could have reached in an hour, was
a curve of the earth quite different from those made by the
seas of France, a remote curve which, by the accident of
travel, happened to be moored close to where I was; so that
this arsenal basin, at once insignificant and remote, filled
me with that blend of disgust and alarm which I had felt as
a child when I first accompanied my mother to the Deligny
baths; indeed in that fantastic place consisting of a dark
water reflecting neither sky nor sun, which nevertheless
amid its fringe of cabins one felt to be in communication
with invisible depths crowded with human bodies in bathing dresses, I had asked myself whether those depths, concealed from mortal eyes by a row of cabins which prevented
anyone in the street from suspecting that they existed,

were not the entry to arctic seas which began at that point, whether the Poles were not comprised in them and whether that narrow space was not indeed the open water that surrounds the Pole. This Venice without attraction for myself in which I was going to be left alone, seemed to me no less isolated, no less unreal, and it was my distress which the sound of " sole mio," rising like a dirge for the Venice that I had known, seemed to be calling to witness. No doubt I ought to have ceased to listen to it if I wished to be able to overtake my mother and to join her on the train, I ought to have made up my mind without wasting another instant that I was going, but this is just what I was powerless to do; I remained motionless, incapable not merely of rising, but even of deciding that I would rise from my chair.

My mind, doubtless in order not to have to consider the question of making a resolution, was entirely occupied in following the course of the successive lines of " sole mio," singing them mentally with the singer, in anticipating for each of them the burst of melody that would carry it aloft, in letting myself soar with it, and fall to earth again with it afterwards.

No doubt this trivial song which I had heard a hundred times did not interest me in the least degree. I could afford no pleasure to anyone else, or to myself, by listening to it religiously like this to the end. In fact, none of the elements, familiar beforehand, of this popular ditty was capable of furnishing me with the resolution of which I stood in need; what was more, each of these phrases when it came and passed in its turn, became an obstacle in the way of my making that resolution effective, or rather it forced me to adopt the contrary resolution not to leave Venice, for it made me too late for the train. Wherefore this occupation, devoid of any pleasure in itself, of listening to " sole mio," was charged with a profound, almost despairing melancholy. I knew very well that in reality it was the resolution not to go that I had adopted by the mere act of remaining where I was; but to say to myself: " I am not going," a speech which in that direct form was impossible, became possible in this indirect form: " I am going to listen to one more line of ' sole mio ' "; but the practical significance of this figurative language did not escape me and, while I said to myself: " After all, I am only listening to another line," I knew that the words meant: " I shall remain by myself at Venice." And it was perhaps this melancholy, like a sort of numbing cold, that constituted the desperate but fascinating charm of the song. Each note that the singer's voice uttered with a force and ostentation that were almost muscular came and pierced my heart; when he had uttered his last flourish and the song seemed to be at an end, the singer had not had enough and repeated it an octave higher as though he needed to proclaim once again my solitude and despair.

My mother must by now have reached the station. In a little while she would be gone. My heart was wrung by the anguish that was caused me by—with a view of the Canal that had become quite tiny now that the soul of Venice had escaped from it, of that commonplace Rialto which was no longer the Rialto,—the wail of despair that " sole mio " had become, which, declaimed thus before the unsubstantial palaces, reduced them to dust and ashes and completed the ruin of Venice; I looked on at the slow realisation of my misery built up artistically, without haste, note by note, by the singer as he stood beneath the astonished gaze of the sun arrested in its course beyond San Giorgio Maggiore,[1] with the result that the fading light was to combine for ever in my memory with the throb of my emotion and the bronze voice of the singer in a dubious, unalterable and poignant alloy.

Thus I remained motionless with a disintegrated will-power, with no apparent decision; doubtless at such moments our decision has already been made: our friends can often predict it themselves. But we, we are unable to do so, otherwise how much suffering would we be spared!

But at length, from caverns darker than that from which flashes the comet which we can predict,—thanks to the unimaginable defensive force of inveterate habit, thanks to the hidden reserves which by a sudden impulse habit hurls at the last moment into the fray—my activity was roused at length; I set out in hot haste and arrived, when the carriage doors were already shut, but in time to find my mother flushed with emotion, overcome by the effort to restrain her tears, for she thought that I was not coming. Then the train started and we saw Padua and Verona come to meet us, to speed us on our way, almost on to the platforms of their stations, and, when we had drawn away from them, return—they who were not travelling and were about to resume their normal life—one to its plain the other to its hill.

The hours went by. My mother was in no hurry to read two letters which she had in her hand and had merely

---

[1] The geography of this chapter is confusing, but it is evident that Proust has transferred the name of San Giorgio Maggiore to one of the churches on the Grand Canal. Compare also page 289 C. K. S. M.

opened, and tried to prevent me from pulling out my pocket-book at once so as to take from it the letter which the hotel porter had given me. My mother was always afraid of my finding journeys too long, too tiring, and put off as long as possible, so as to keep me occupied during the final hours, the moment at which she would seek fresh distractions for me, bring out the hard-boiled eggs, hand me newspapers, untie the parcel of books which she had bought without telling me. We had long passed Milan when she decided to read the first of her two letters. I began by watching my mother who sat reading it with an air of astonishment, then raised her head, and her eyes seemed to come to rest upon a succession of distinct, incompatible memories, which she could not succeed in bringing together. Meanwhile I had recognised Gilberte's hand on the envelope which I had just taken from my pocket-book. I opened it. Gilberte wrote to inform me that she was marrying Robert de Saint-Loup. She told me that she had sent me a telegram about it to Venice but had had no reply. I remembered that I had been told that the telegraphic service there was inefficient, I had never received her telegram. Perhaps, she would refuse to believe this. All of a sudden, I felt in my brain a fact which had installed itself there in the guise of a memory, leave its place which it surrendered to another fact. The telegram that I had received a few days earlier, and had supposed to be from Albertine, was from Gilberte. As the somewhat laboured originality of Gilberte's handwriting consisted chiefly, when she wrote one line, in introducing into the line above the strokes of her *t*'s which appeared to be underlining the words, or the dots over her *i*'s which appeared to be punctuating the sentence above them, and on the other hand in interspersing the line below with the tails and flourishes of the words immediately above it, it was quite natural that the clerk who dispatched the telegram should have read the tail of an *s* or *z* in the line above as an " -ine " attached to the word " Gilberte." The dot over the *i* of Gilberte had risen above the word to mark the end of the message. As for her capital *G*, it resembled a gothic *A*. Add that, apart from this, two or three words had been misread, dove-tailed into one another (some of them as it happened had seemed to me incomprehensible), and this was quite enough to explain the details of my error and was not even necessary. How many letters are actually read into a word by a careless person who knows what to expect, who sets out with the idea that the message is from a certain person, how many words into the sentence? We guess as we read, we create; everything starts from an initial mistake, the mistakes that follow (and not only in the reading of letters and telegrams, not only in reading as a whole), extraordinary as they may appear to a person who has not begun at the same starting-point, are all quite natural. A large part of what we believe to be true (and this applies even to our final conclusions) with a persistence equalled only by our sincerity, springs from an original misconception of our premises.

CHAPTER IV

A FRESH LIGHT UPON ROBERT DE SAINT-LOUP

"OH, it is unheard of," said my mother. "Listen, at my age, one has ceased to be astonished at anything, but I assure you that there could be nothing more unexpected than what I find in this letter." "Listen, first to me," I replied, "I don't know what it is, but however astonishing it may be, it cannot be quite so astonishing as what I have found in my letter. It is a marriage. It is Robert de Saint-Loup who is marrying Gilberte Swann." "Ah!" said my mother, "then that is no doubt what is in the other letter, which I have not yet opened, for I recognised your friend's hand." And my mother smiled at me with that faint trace of emotion which, ever since she had lost her own mother, she felt at every event however insignificant, that concerned human creatures who were capable of grief, of memory, and who themselves also mourned their dead. And so my mother smiled at me and spoke to me in a gentle voice, as though she had been afraid, were she to treat this marriage lightly, of belittling the melancholy feelings that it might arouse in Swann's widow and daughter, in Robert's mother who had resigned herself to parting from her son, all of whom my mother, in her kindness of heart, in her gratitude for their kindness to me, endowed with her own faculty of filial, conjugal and maternal emotion. "Was I right in telling you that you would find nothing more astonishing?" I asked her. "On the contrary! " she replied in a gentle tone, " it is I who can impart the most extraordinary news, I shall not say the greatest, the smallest, for that quotation from Sévigné which everyone makes who knows nothing else that she ever wrote used to distress your grandmother as much as ' what a charming thing it is to smoke.' We scorn to pick up such stereotyped Sévigné. This letter is to announce the marriage of the Cambremer boy." " Oh! " I remarked with indifference, " to whom? But in any case the personality of the bridegroom robs this marriage of any sensational element." " Unless the bride's personality supplies it." " And who is the bride in question? " " Ah, if I tell you straight away, that will spoil everything; see if you can guess," said my mother who, seeing that we had not yet reached Turin, wished to keep something in reserve for me as meat and drink for the rest of the journey. " But how do you expect me to know? Is it anyone brilliant? If Legrandin and his sister are satisfied, we may be sure that it is a brilliant marriage." " As for Legrandin, I cannot say, but the person who informs me of the marriage says that Mme de Cambremer is delighted. I don't know whether you will call it a brilliant marriage. To my mind, it suggests the days when kings used to marry shepherdesses, though in this case the shepherdess is even humbler than a shepherdess, charming as she is. It would have stupefied your grandmother, but would not have shocked her." " But who in the world is this bride? " " It is Mlle d'Oloron." " That sounds to me tremendous and not in the least shepherdessy, but I don't quite gather who she can be. It is a title that used to be in the Guermantes family." " Precisely, and M. de Charlus conferred it, when he

328

adopted her, upon Jupien's niece." "Jupien's niece! It isn't possible!" "It is the reward of virtue. It is a marriage from the last chapter of one of Mme Sand's novels," said my mother. "It is the reward of vice, it is a marriage from the end of a Balzac novel," thought I. "After all," I said to my mother, " when you come to think of it, it is quite natural. Here are the Cambremers established in that Guermantes clan among which they never hoped to pitch their tent; what is more, the girl, adopted by M. de Charlus, will have plenty of money, which was indispensable now that the Cambremers have lost theirs; and after all she is the adopted daughter, and, in the Cambremer's eyes, probably the real daughter—the natural daughter—of a person whom they regard as a Prince of the Blood Royal. A bastard of a semi-royal house has always been regarded as a flattering alliance by the nobility of France and other countries. Indeed, without going so far back, only the other day, not more than six months ago, don't you remember, the marriage of Robert's friend and that girl, the only possible justification of which was that she was supposed, rightly or wrongly, to be the natural daughter of a sovereign prince." My mother, without abandoning the caste system of Combray which meant that my grandmother would have been scandalised by such a marriage, being principally anxious to echo her mother's judgment, added: " Anyhow, the girl is worth her weight in gold, and your dear grandmother would not have had to draw upon her immense goodness, her unbounded indulgence, to keep her from condemning young Cambremer's choice. Do you remember how distinguished she thought the girl, years ago, one day when she went into the shop to have a stitch put in her skirt? She was only a child then. And now, even if she has rather run to seed, and become an old maid, she is a different woman, a thousand times more perfect. But your grandmother saw all that at a glance. She found the little niece of a jobbing tailor more ' noble ' than the Duc de Guermantes." But even more necessary than to extol my grandmother was it for my mother to decide that it was " better " for her that she had not lived to see the day. This was the supreme triumph of her filial devotion, as though she were sparing my grandmother a final grief. " And yet, can you imagine for a moment," my mother said to me, " what old father Swann—not that you ever knew him, of course—would have felt if he could have known that he would one day have a great-grandchild in whose veins the blood of mother Moser who used to say: ' Ponchour Mezieurs ' would mingle with the blood of the Duc de Guise! " " But, listen, Mamma, it is a great deal more surprising than that. For the Swanns were very respectable people, and, given the position that their son occupied, his daughter, if he himself had made a decent marriage, might have married very well indeed. But all her chances were ruined by his marrying a courtesan." " Oh, a courtesan, you know, people were perhaps rather hard on her, I never quite believed." " Yes, a courtesan, indeed I can let you have some startling revelations one of these days." Lost in meditation, my mother said: " The daughter of a woman to whom your father would never allow me to bow marrying the nephew of Mme de Ville-parisis, upon whom your father wouldn't allow me to call at first because he thought her too grand for me! " Then: " The son of Mme de Cambremer to whom Legrandin

330

was so afraid of having to give us a letter of introduction because he didn't think us smart enough, marrying the niece of a man who would never dare to come to our flat except by the service stairs! . . . All the same your poor grandmother was right—you remember—when she said that the great nobility could do things that would shock the middle classes and that Queen Marie-Amélie was spoiled for her by the overtures that she made to the Prince de Condé's mistress to persuade him to leave his fortune to the Duc d'Aumale. You remember too, it shocked her that for centuries past daughters of the house of Gramont who have been perfect saints have borne the name Corisande, in memory of Henri IV's connection with one of their ancestresses. These are things that may happen also, perhaps, among the middle classes, but we conceal them better. Can't you imagine how it would have amused her, your poor grandmother? " said Mamma sadly, for the joys of which it grieved us to think that my grandmother was deprived were the simplest joys of life, a tale, a play, something more trifling still, a piece of mimicry, which would have amused her, " can't you imagine her astonishment? I am sure, however, that your grandmother would have been shocked by these marriages, that they would have grieved her, I feel that it is better that she never knew about them," my mother went on, for, when confronted with any event, she liked to think that my grandmother would have received a unique impression of it which would have been caused by the marvellous singularity of her nature and had an extraordinary importance. Did anything painful occur, which could not have been foreseen in the past, the disgrace or ruin of one of our old friends, some public calamity, an epidemic, a war, a revolution, my mother would say to herself that perhaps it was better that Grandmamma had known nothing about it, that it would have distressed her too keenly, that perhaps she would not have been able to endure it. And when it was a question of something startling like this, my mother, by an impulse directly opposite to that of the malicious people who like to imagine that others whom they do not like have suffered more than is generally supposed, would not, in her affection for my grandmother, allow that anything sad, or depressing, could ever have happened to her. She always imagined my grandmother as raised above the assaults even of any malady which ought not to have developed, and told herself that my grandmother's death had perhaps been a good thing on the whole, inasmuch as it had shut off the too ugly spectacle of the present day from that noble character which could never have become resigned to it. For optimism is the philosophy of the past. The events that have occurred being, among all those that were possible, the only ones which we have known, the harm that they have caused seems to us inevitable, and, for the slight amount of good that they could not help bringing with them, it is to them that we give the credit, imagining that without them it would not have occurred. But she sought at the same time to form a more accurate idea of what my grandmother would have felt when she learned these tidings, and to believe that it was impossible for our minds, less exalted than hers, to form any such idea. " Can't you imagine," my mother said to me first of all, " how astonished your poor grandmother would have been! " And I felt that my mother was pained by her inability to tell her the news, regretted that my grandmother could not learn it, and felt it to be somehow unjust that the course of life should bring to light facts which my grandmother would never have believed, rendering thus retrospectively the knowledge which my grandmother had taken with her of people and society false, and incomplete, the marriage of the Jupien girl and Legrandin's nephew being calculated to modify my grandmother's general ideas of life, no less than the news—had my mother been able to convey it to her—that people had succeeded in solving the problems, which my grandmother had regarded as insoluble, of aerial navigation and wireless telegraphy.

The train reached Paris before my mother and I had finished discussing these two pieces of news which, so that the journey might not seem to me too long, she had deliberately reserved for the latter part of it, not mentioning them until we had passed Milan. And my mother continued the discussion after we had reached home: " Just imagine, that poor Swann who was so anxious that his Gilberte should be received by the Guermantes, how happy he would be if he could see his daughter become a Guermantes! " " Under another name, led to the altar as Mlle de Forcheville, do you think he would be so happy after all? " " Ah, that is true. I had not thought of it. That is what makes it impossible for me to congratulate the little chit, the thought that she has had the heart to give up her father's name, when he was so good to her.—Yes, you are right, when all is said and done, it is perhaps just as well that he knows nothing about it." With the dead as with the living, we cannot tell whether a thing would cause them joy or sorrow. " It appears that the Saint-Loups are

333

going to live at Tansonville. Old father Swann, who was so anxious to shew your poor grandmother his pond, could he ever have dreamed that the Duc de Guermantes would see it constantly, especially if he had known of his son's marriage? And you yourself who have talked so often to Saint-Loup about the pink hawthorns and lilacs and irises at Tansonville, he will understand you better. They will be his property." Thus there developed in our dining-room, in the lamplight that is so congenial to them, one of those talks in which the wisdom not of nations but of families, taking hold of some event, a death, a betrothal, an inheritance, a bankruptcy, and slipping it under the magnifying glass of memory, brings it into high relief, detaches, thrusts back one surface of it, and places in perspective at different points in space and time what, to those who have not lived through the period in question, seems to be amalgamated upon a single surface, the names of dead people, successive addresses, the origins and changes of fortunes, transmissions of property. Is not this wisdom inspired by the Muse whom it is best to ignore for as long as possible, if we wish to retain any freshness of impressions, any creative power, but whom even those people who have ignored her meet in the evening of their life in the nave of the old country church, at the hour when all of a sudden they feel that they are less moved by eternal beauty as expressed in the carvings of the altar than by the thought of the vicissitudes of fortune which those carvings have undergone, passing into a famous private collection, to a chapel, from there to a museum, then returning at length to the church, or by the feeling as they tread upon a marble slab that is almost endowed with thought, that it covers the last remains of

Arnault or Pascal, or simply by deciphering (forming perhaps a mental picture of a fair young worshipper) on the brass plate of the wooden prayer-desk, the names of the daughters of country squire or leading citizen? The Muse who has gathered up everything that the more exalted Muses of philosophy and art have rejected, everything that is not founded upon truth, everything that is merely contingent, but that reveals other laws as well, is History.

What I was to learn later on—for I had been unable to keep in touch with all this affair from Venice—was that Mlle de Forcheville's hand had been sought first of all by the Prince de Silistrie, while Saint-Loup was seeking to marry Mlle d'Entragues, the Duc de Luxembourg's daughter. This is what had occurred. Mlle de Forcheville possessing a hundred million francs, Mme de Marsantes had decided that she would be an excellent match for her son. She made the mistake of saying that the girl was charming, that she herself had not the slightest idea whether she was rich or poor, that she did not wish to know, but that even without a penny it would be a piece of good luck for the most exacting of young men to find such a wife. This was going rather too far for a woman who was tempted only by the hundred millions, which blinded her eyes to everything else. At once it was understood that she was thinking of the girl for her own son. The Princesse de Silistrie went about uttering loud cries, expatiated upon the social importance of Saint-Loup, and proclaimed that if he should marry Odette's daughter by a Jew then there was no longer a Faubourg Saint-Germain. Mme de Marsantes, sure of herself as she was, dared not advance farther and retreated before the cries of the Princesse de

Silistrie, who immediately made a proposal in the name of her own son. She had protested only in order to keep Gilberte for herself. Meanwhile Mme de Marsantes, refusing to own herself defeated, had turned at once to Mlle d'Entragues, the Duc de Luxembourg's daughter. Having no more than twenty millions, she suited her purpose less, but Mme de Marsantes told everyone that a Saint-Loup could not marry a Mlle Swann (there was no longer any mention of Forcheville). Some time later, somebody having carelessly observed that the Duc de Châtellerault was thinking of marrying Mlle d'Entragues, Mme de Marsantes, who was the most captious woman in the world mounted her high horse, changed her tactics, returned to Gilberte, made a formal offer of marriage on Saint-Loup's behalf, and the engagement was immediately announced. This engagement provoked keen comment in the most different spheres. Some old friends of my mother, who belonged more or less to Combray, came to see her to discuss Gilberte's marriage, which did not dazzle them in the least. "You know who Mlle de Forcheville is, she is simply Mlle Swann. And her witness at the marriage, the 'Baron' de Charlus, as he calls himself, is the old man who used to keep her mother at one time, under Swann's very nose, and no doubt to his advantage." "But what do you mean?" my mother protested, "In the first place, Swann was extremely rich." "We must assume that he was not as rich as all that if he needed other people's money. But what is there in the woman, that she keeps her old lovers like that? She has managed to persuade the third to marry her and she drags out the second when he has one foot in the grave to make him act at the marriage of the daughter she had by the first or by someone else, for how is one to tell who the father was? She can't be certain herself! I said the third, it is the three hundredth I should have said. But then, don't you know, if she's no more a Forcheville than you or I, that puts her on the same level as the bridegroom who of course isn't noble at all. Only an adventurer would marry a girl like that. It appears he's just a plain Monsieur Dupont or Durand or something. If it weren't that we have a Radical mayor now at Combray, who doesn't even lift his hat to the priest, I should know all about it. Because, you understand, when they published the banns, they were obliged to give the real name. It is all very nice for the newspapers or for the stationer who sends out the intimations, to describe yourself as the Marquis de Saint-Loup. That does no harm to anyone, and if it can give any pleasure to those worthy people, I should be the last person in the world to object! What harm can it do me? As I shall never dream of going to call upon the daughter of a woman who has let herself be talked about, she can have a string of titles as long as my arm before her servants. But in an official document it's not the same thing. Ah, if my cousin Sazerat were still deputy-mayor, I should have written to him, and he would certainly have let *me* know what name the man was registered under."

Other friends of my mother who had met Saint-Loup in our house came to her " day," and inquired whether the bridegroom was indeed the same person as my friend. Certain people went so far as to maintain, with regard to the other marriage, that it had nothing to do with the Legrandin Cambremers. They had this on good authority, for the Marquise, *née* Legrandin, had contradicted the rumour on the very eve of the day on which the engagement was announced. I, for my part, asked myself why M. de Charlus on the one hand, Saint-Loup on the other, each of whom had had occasion to write to me quite recently, had made various friendly plans and proposed expeditions which must have clashed with the wedding ceremonies, and had said nothing whatever to me about these. I came to the conclusion, forgetting the secrecy which people always preserve until the last moment in affairs of this sort, that I was less their friend than I had supposed, a conclusion which, so far as Saint-Loup was concerned, distressed me. Though why, when I had already remarked that the affability, the " one-man-to-another " attitude of the aristocracy was all a sham, should I be surprised to find myself its victim? In the establishment for women— where men were now to be procured in increasing numbers —in which M. de Charlus had surprised Morel, and in which the " assistant matron," a great reader of the *Gaulois*, used to discuss the social gossip with her clients, this lady, while conversing with a stout gentleman who used to come to her incessantly to drink champagne with young men, because, being already very stout, he wished to become obese enough to be certain of not being " called up," should there ever be a war, declared: " It seems, young Saint-Loup is ' one of those ' and young Cambremer too. Poor wives!—In any case, if you know the bridegrooms, you must send them to us, they will find everything they want here, and there's plenty of money to be made out of them." Whereupon the stout gentleman, albeit he was himself " one of those," protested, replied, being something of a snob, that he often met Cambremer and Saint-Loup at his cousins' the Ardouvillers, and that they were great womanisers, and quite the opposite of " all that." " Ah! " the assistant matron concluded in a sceptical tone, but without any proof of the assertion, and convinced that in our generation the perversity of morals was rivalled only by the absurd exaggeration of slanderous rumours. Certain people whom I no longer saw wrote to me and asked me " what I thought " of these two marriages, precisely as though they had been inviting a public discussion of the height of women's hats in the theatre or the psychological novel. I had not the heart to answer these letters. Of these two marriages, I thought nothing at all, but I did feel an immense melancholy, as when two parts of our past existence, which have been anchored near to us, and upon which we have perhaps been basing idly from day to day an unacknowledged hope, remove themselves finally, with a joyous crackling of flames, for unknown destinations, like two vessels on the high seas. As for the prospective bride-grooms themselves, they regarded their own marriages from a point of view that was quite natural, since it was a question not of other people but of themselves. They had never tired of mocking at such " grand marriages " founded upon some secret shame. And indeed the Cambremer family, so ancient in its lineage and so modest in its pretensions, would have been the first to forget Jupien and to remember only the unimaginable grandeur of the House of Oloron, had not an exception occurred in the person who ought to have been most gratified by this marriage, the Marquise de Cambremer-Legrandin. For, being of a malicious nature, she reckoned the pleasure of humiliating

339

her family above that of glorifying herself. And so, as she had no affection for her son, and was not long in taking a dislike to her daughter-in-law, she declared that it was a calamity for a Cambremer to marry a person who had sprung from heaven knew where, and had such bad teeth. As for young Cambremer, who had already shewn a certain tendency to frequent the society of literary people, we may well imagine that so brilliant an alliance had not the effect of making him more of a snob than before, but that feeling himself to have become the successor of the Ducs d'Oloron —"sovereign princes" as the newspapers said—he was sufficiently persuaded of his own importance to be able to mix with the very humblest people. And he deserted the minor nobility for the intelligent bourgeoisie on the days when he did not confine himself to royalty. The notices in the papers, especially when they referred to Saint-Loup, invested my friend, whose royal ancestors were enumerated in a fresh importance, which however could only depress me—as though he had become someone else, the descendant of Robert the Strong, rather than the friend who, only a little while since, had taken the back seat in the carriage in order that I might be more comfortable in the other; the fact that I had had no previous suspicion of his marriage with Gilberte, the prospect of which had been revealed to me suddenly in a letter, so different from anything that I could have expected of either him or her the day before, and the fact that he had not let me know pained me, whereas I ought to have reflected that he had had a great many other things to do, and that moreover in the fashionable world marriages are often arranged like this all of a sudden, generally as a substitute for a different combination which has come to grief—unexpectedly—like a chemical precipitation. And the feeling of sadness, as depressing as a household removal, as bitter as jealousy, that these marriages caused me by the accident of their sudden impact was so profound, that later on people used to remind me of it, paying absurd compliments to my perspicacity, as having been just the opposite of what it was at the time, a two-fold, nay a three-fold and four-fold presentiment.

The people in society who had taken no notice of Gilberte said to me with an air of serious interest: " Ah! It is she who is marrying the Marquis de Saint-Loup " and studied her with the attentive gaze of people who not merely relish all the social gossip of Paris but are anxious to learn, and believe in the profundity of their own introspection. Those who on the other hand had known Gilberte alone gazed at Saint-Loup with the closest attention, asked me (these were often people who barely knew me) to introduce them and returned from their presentation to the bridegroom radiant with the bliss of fatuity, saying to me: " He is very nice-looking." Gilberte was convinced that the name " Marquis de Saint-Loup " was a thousand times more important than " Duc d'Orléans."

" It appears that it is the Princesse de Parme who arranged young Cambremer's marriage," Mamma told me. And this was true. The Princess had known for a long time, on the one hand, by his works, Legrandin whom she regarded as a distinguished man, on the other hand Mme de Cambremer who changed the conversation whenever the Princess asked her whether she was not Legrandin's sister. The Princess knew how keenly Mme de Cambremer felt her position on the doorstep of the great aristo-

cratic world, in which she was invited nowhere. When
the Princesse de Parme, who had undertaken to find a
husband for Mlle d'Oloron, asked M. de Charlus
whether he had ever heard of a pleasant, educated man who
called himself Legrandin de Méséglise (thus it was that M.
Legrandin now styled himself), the Baron first of all replied in the negative, then suddenly a memory occurred to
him of a man whose acquaintance he had made in the train,
one night, and who had given him his card. He smiled a
vague smile. " It is perhaps the same person," he said to
himself. When he discovered that the prospective bridegroom was the son of Legrandin's sister, he said: " Why,
that would be really extraordinary! If he takes after his
uncle, after all, that would not alarm me, I have always
said that they make the best husbands." " Who are
they? " inquired the Princess. " Oh, Ma'am, I could explain it all to you if we met more often. With you one
can talk freely. Your Highness is so intelligent," said
Charlus, seized by a desire to confide in someone which,
however, went no farther. The name Cambremer appealed to him, although he did not like the boy's parents,
but he knew that it was one of the four Baronies of Brittany
and the best that he could possibly hope for his adopted
daughter; it was an old and respected name, with solid connections in its native province. A Prince would have been
out of the question and, moreover, not altogether desirable.
This was the very thing. The Princess then invited Legrandin to call. In appearance he had considerably
altered, and, of late, distinctly to his advantage. Like
those women who deliberately sacrifice their faces to the
slimness of their figures and never stir from Marienbad,

Legrandin had acquired the free and easy air of a cavalry officer. In proportion as M. de Charlus had grown coarse and slow, Legrandin had become slimmer and moved more rapidly, the contrary effect of an identical cause. This velocity of movement had its psychological reasons as well. He was in the habit of frequenting certain low haunts where he did not wish to be seen going in or coming out: he would hurl himself into them. Legrandin had taken up tennis at the age of fifty-five. When the Princesse de Parme spoke to him of the Guermantes, of Saint-Loup, he declared that he had known them all his life, making a sort of composition of the fact of his having always known by name the proprietors of Guermantes and that of his having met, at my aunt's house, Swann, the father of the future Mme de Saint-Loup, Swann upon whose wife and daughter Legrandin, at Combray, had always refused to call. " Indeed, I travelled quite recently with the brother of the Duc de Guermantes, M. de Charlus. He began the conversation spontaneously, which is always a good sign, for it proves that a man is neither a tongue-tied lout nor stuck-up. Oh, I know all the things that people say about him. But I never pay any attention to gossip of that sort. Besides, the private life of other people does not concern me. He gave me the impression of a sensitive nature, and a cultivated mind." Then the Princesse de Parme spoke of Mlle d'Oloron. In the Guermantes circle people were moved by the nobility of heart of M. de Charlus who, generous as he had always been, was securing the future happiness of a penniless but charming girl. And the Duc de Guermantes, who suffered from his brother's reputation, let it be understood that, fine as this conduct was, it was wholly natural. " I don't know if I make myself clear, everything in the affair is natural," he said, speaking ineptly by force of habit. But his object was to indicate that the girl was a daughter of his brother whom the latter was acknowledging. This accounted at the same time for Jupien. The Princesse de Parme hinted at this version of the story to shew Legrandin that after all young Cambremer would be marrying something in the nature of Mlle de Nantes, one of those bastards of Louis XIV who were not scorned either by the Duc d'Orléans or by the Prince de Conti.

These two marriages which I had already begun to discuss with my mother in the train that brought us back to Paris had quite remarkable effects upon several of the characters who have figured in the course of this narrative. First of all upon Legrandin; needless to say that he swept like a hurricane into M. de Charlus's town house for all the world as though he were entering a house of ill-fame where he must on no account be seen, and also, at the same time, to display his activity and to conceal his age—for our habits accompany us even into places where they are no longer of any use to us—and scarcely anybody observed that when M. de Charlus greeted him he did so with a smile which it was hard to intercept, harder still to interpret; this smile was similar in appearance, and in its essentials was diametrically opposite to the smile which two men, who are in the habit of meeting in good society, exchange if they happen to meet in what they regard as disreputable surroundings (such as the Elysée where General de Froberville, whenever, in days past, he met Swann there, would assume, on catching sight of him, an expression of ironical and mysterious complicity appropriate between two frequenters of the drawing-room of the Princesse des Laumes who were compromising themselves by visiting M. Grevy). Legrandin had been cultivating obscurely for a long time past—ever since the days when I used to go as a child to spend my holidays at Combray—relations with the aristocracy, productive at the most of an isolated invitation to a sterile house party. All of a sudden, his nephew's marriage having intervened to join up these scattered fragments, Legrandin stepped into a social position which derived retroactively from his former relations with people who had known him only as a private person but had known him well a sort of solidity. Ladies to whom people offered to introduce him informed them that for the last twenty years he had stayed with them in the country for a fortnight annually, and that it was he who had given them the beautiful old barometer in the small drawing-room. It so happened that he had been photographed in " groups " which included Dukes who were related to them. But as soon as he had acquired this social position, he ceased to make any use of it. This was not merely because, now that people knew him to be received everywhere, he no longer derived any pleasure from being invited, it was because, of the two vices that had long struggled for the mastery of him, the less natural, snobbishness, yielded its place to another that was less artificial, since it did at least shew a sort of return, albeit circuitous, towards nature. No doubt the two are not incompatible, and a nocturnal tour of exploration of a slum may be made immediately upon leaving a Duchess's party. But the chilling effect of age made Legrandin reluctant to accumulate such an abundance of pleasures, to stir out of doors except with a definite purpose, and had also the effect that the pleasures of nature became more or less platonic, consisting chiefly in friendships, in conversations which took up time, and made him spend almost all his own among the lower orders, so that he had little left for a social existence. Mme de Cambremer herself became almost indifferent to the friendly overtures of the Duchesse de Guermantes. The latter, obliged to call upon the Marquise, had noticed, as happens whenever we come to see more of our fellow creatures, that is to say combinations of good qualities, which we end by discovering, with defects to which we end by growing accustomed, that Mme de Cambremer was a woman endowed with an innate intelligence and an acquired culture of which for my part I thought but little, but which appeared remarkable to the Duchess. And so she often came, late in the afternoon, to see Mme de Cambremer and paid her long visits. But the marvellous charm which her hostess imagined as existing in the Duchesse de Guermantes vanished as soon as she saw that the other sought her company, and she received her rather out of politeness than for her own pleasure. A more striking change was manifest in Gilberte, a change at once symmetrical with and different from that which had occurred in Swann after his marriage. It is true that during the first few months Gilberte had been glad to open her doors to the most select company. It was doubtless only with a view to an eventual inheritance that she invited the intimate friends to whom her mother was attached, but on certain days only when there was no one but themselves, secluded apart from the fashionable people, as though the contact of Mme Bontemps or Mme Cottard with the Princesse de

Guermantes or the Princesse de Parme might, like that of two unstable powders, have produced irreparable catastrophes. Nevertheless the Bontemps, the Cottards and such, although disappointed by the smallness of the party were proud of being able to say: " We were dining with the Marquise de Saint-Loup," all the more so as she ventured at times so far as to invite, with them, Mme de Marsantes, who was emphatically the " great lady " with a fan of tortoiseshell and ostrich feathers, this again being a piece of legacy-hunting. She only took care to pay from time to time a tribute to the discreet people whom one never sees except when they are invited, a warning with which she bestowed upon her audience of the Cottard-Bontemps class her most gracious and distant greeting. Perhaps I should have preferred to be included in these parties. But Gilberte, in whose eyes I was now principally a friend of her husband and of the Guermantes, (and who—perhaps even in the Combray days, when my parents did not call upon her mother—had, at the age when we do not merely add this or that to the value of things but classify them according to their species, endowed me with that prestige which we never afterwards lose) regarded these evenings as unworthy of me, and when I took my leave of her would say: " It has been delightful to see you, but come again the day after to-morrow, you will find my aunt Guermantes, and Mme de Poix; to-day I just had a few of Mamma's friends, to please Mamma." But this state of things lasted for a few months only, and very soon everything was altered. Was this because Gilberte's social life was fated to exhibit the same contrasts as Swann's? However that may be, Gilberte had been only for a short time Marquise de Saint-

Loup (in the process of becoming, as we shall see, Duchesse de Guermantes)[1] when, having attained to the most brilliant and most difficult position, she decided that the name Saint-Loup was now embodied in herself like a glowing enamel and that, whoever her associates might be, from now onwards she would remain for all the world Marquise de Saint-Loup, wherein she was mistaken, for the value of a title of nobility, like that of shares in a company, rises with the demand and falls when it is offered in the market. Everything that seems to us imperishable tends to destruction; a position in society, like anything else, is not created once and for all time, but, just as much as the power of an Empire, reconstructs itself at every moment by a sort of perpetual process of creation, which explains the apparent anomalies in social or political history in the course of half a century. The creation of the world did not occur at the beginning of time, it occurs every day. The Marquise de Saint-Loup said to herself, " I am the Marquise de Saint-Loup," she knew that, the day before, she had refused three invitations to dine with Duchesses. But if, to a certain extent, her name exalted the class of people, as little aristocratic as possible, whom she entertained, by an inverse process, the class of people whom the Marquise entertained depreciated the name that she bore. Nothing can hold out against such processes, the greatest names succumb to them in the end. Had not Swann known a Duchess of the House of France whose drawing-room, because any Tom, Dick or Harry was welcomed there, had fallen to the lowest rank? One day when the Princesse des Laumes had gone

[1] This is quite inexplicable, Gilberte reappears as Saint-Loup's widow while the Duc de Guermantes and his wife are still alive. C. K. S. M.

from a sense of duty to call for a moment upon this Highness, in whose drawing-room she had found only the most
ordinary people, arriving immediately afterwards at Mme
Leroi's, she had said to Swann and the Marquise de Mod-
ène: "At last I find myself upon friendly soil. I have
just come from Mme la Duchesse de X—, there weren't
three faces I knew in the room." Sharing, in short, the
opinion of the character in the operetta who declares:
"My name, I think, dispenses me from saying more,"
Gilberte set to work to flaunt her contempt for what she
had so ardently desired, to proclaim that all the people in the
Faubourg Saint-Germain were idiots, people to whose
houses one could not go, and, suiting the action to the word,
ceased to go to them. People who did not make her acquaintance until after this epoch, and who, in the first
stages of that acquaintance, heard her, by that time Duchesse de Guermantes, make the most absurd fun of the world
in which she could so easily have moved, seeing that she
never invited a single person out of that world, and that if
any of them, even the most brilliant, ventured into her
drawing-room, she would yawn openly in their faces, blush
now in retrospect at the thought that they themselves could
ever have seen any claim to distinction in the fashionable
world, and would never dare to confess this humiliating
secret of their past weaknesses to a woman whom they suppose to have been, owing to an essential loftiness of her
nature, incapable from her earliest moments of understanding such things. They hear her poke such delicious fun at
Dukes, and see her (which is more significant) make her
behaviour accord so entirely with her mockery! No
doubt they do not think of inquiring into the causes of the

accident which turned Mlle Swann into Mlle de Forcheville, Mlle de Forcheville into the Marquise de Saint-
Loup, and finally into the Duchesse de Guermantes.
Possibly it does not occur to them either that the effects of
this accident would serve no less than its causes to explain
Gilberte's subsequent attitude, the habit of mixing with up-
starts not being regarded quite in the same light in which
Mlle Swann would have regarded it by a lady whom
everybody addresses as " Madame la Duchesse " and the
other Duchesses who bore her as " cousin." We are always ready to despise a goal which we have not succeeded in
reaching, or have permanently reached. And this contempt seems to us to form part of the character of people
whom we do not yet know. Perhaps if we were able to
retrace the course of past years, we should find them de-
voured, more savagely than anyone, by those same weaknesses which they have succeeded so completely in concealing or conquering that we reckon them incapable not only
of having ever been attacked by them themselves but even
of ever excusing them in other people, let alone being capable of imagining them. Anyhow, very soon the drawing-
room of the new Marquise de Saint-Loup assumed its permanent aspect, from the social point of view at least, for
we shall see what troubles were brewing in it in another
connection; well, this aspect was surprising for the following reason: people still remembered that the most formal,
the most exclusive parties in Paris, as brilliant as those
given by the Marquise de Guermantes, were those of Mme
de Marsantes, Saint-Loup's mother. On the other hand,
in recent years, Odette's drawing-room, infinitely lower in
the social scale, had been no less dazzling in its elegance and

splendour. Saint-Loup, however, delighted to have, thanks to his wife's vast fortune, everything that he could desire in the way of comfort, wished only to rest quietly in his armchair after a good dinner with a musical entertainment by good performers. And this young man who had seemed at one time so proud, so ambitious, invited to share his luxury old friends whom his mother would not have admitted to her house. Gilberte, on her side, put into effect Swann's saying: "Quality doesn't matter, what I dread is quantity." And Saint-Loup, always on his knees before his wife, and because he loved her, and because it was to her that he owed these extremes of comfort, took care not to interfere with tastes that were so similar to his own. With the result that the great receptions given by Mme de Marsantes and Mme de Forcheville, given year after year with an eye chiefly to the establishment, upon a brilliant footing, of their children, gave rise to no reception by M. and Mme de Saint-Loup. They had the best of saddle-horses on which to go out riding together, the finest of yachts in which to cruise—but they never took more than a couple of guests with them. In Paris, every evening, they would invite three or four friends to dine, never more; with the result, that by an unforeseen but at the same time quite natural retrogression, the two vast maternal aviaries had been replaced by a silent nest.

The person who profited least by these two marriages was the young Mademoiselle d'Oloron who, already suffering from typhoid fever on the day of the religious ceremony, was barely able to crawl to the church and died a few weeks later. The letter of intimation that was sent out some time after her death blended with names such as Jupien's those of almost all the greatest families in Europe, such as the Vicomte and Vicomtesse de Montmorency, H.R.H. the Comtesse de Bourbon-Soissons, the Prince of Modena-Este, the Vicomtesse d'Edumea, Lady Essex, and so forth. No doubt even to a person who knew that the deceased was Jupien's niece, this plethora of grand connections would not cause any surprise. The great thing, after all, is to have grand connections. Then, the *casus foederis* coming into play, the death of a simple little shop-girl plunges all the princely families of Europe in mourning. But many young men of a later generation, who were not familiar with the facts, might, apart from the possibility of their mistaking Marie-Antoinette d'Oloron, Marquise de Cambremer, for a lady of the noblest birth, have been guilty of many other errors when they read this communication. Thus, supposing their excursions through France to have given them some slight familiarity with the country round Combray, when they saw that the Comte de Méséglise figured among the first of the signatories, close to the Duc de Guermantes, they might not have felt any surprise. " The Méséglise way," they might have said, " converges with the Guermantes way, old and noble families of the same region may have been allied for generations. Who knows? It is perhaps a branch of the Guermantes family which bears the title of Comte de Méséglise." As it happened, the Comte de Méséglise had no connection with the Guermantes and was not even enrolled on the Guermantes side, but on the Cambremer side, since the Comte de Méséglise, who by a rapid advancement, had been for two years, only Legrandin de Méséglise, was our old friend Legrandin. No doubt, taking one false title with another, there were few that could have been so disagreeable to the Guermantes as this. They had been connected in the past with the authentic Comtes de Méséglise, of whom there survived only one female descendant, the daughter of obscure and unassuming parents, married herself to one of my aunt's tenant farmers named Ménager, who had become rich and bought Mirougrain from her and now styled himself " Ménager de Mirougrain," with the result that when you said that his wife was born " de Méséglise " people thought that she must simply have been born at Méséglise and that she was " of Méséglise " as her husband was " of Mirougrain."

Any other sham title would have caused less annoyance to the Guermantes family. But the aristocracy knows how to tolerate these irritations and many others as well, the moment that a marriage which is deemed advantageous, from whatever point of view, is in question. Shielded by the Duc de Guermantes, Legrandin was, to part of that generation, and will be to the whole of the generation that follows it, the true Comte de Méséglise.

Yet another mistake which any young reader not acquainted with the facts might have been led to make was that of supposing that the Baron and Baronne de Forcheville figured on the list in the capacity as parents-in-law of the Marquis de Saint-Loup, that is to say on the Guermantes side. But on this side, they had no right to appear since it was Robert who was related to the Guermantes and not Gilberte. No, the Baron and Baronne de Forcheville, despite this misleading suggestion, did figure on the wife's side, it is true, and not on the **Cambremer side, because not of the Guermantes, but of**

Jupien, who, the reader must now be told, was a cousin of Odette.

All M. de Charlus's favours had been lavished since the marriage of his adopted niece upon the young Marquis de Cambremer; the young man's tastes which were similar to those of the Baron, since they had not prevented the Baron from selecting him as a husband for Mlle d'Oloron, made him, as was only natural, appreciate him all the more when he was left a widower. This is not to say that the Marquis had not other qualities which made him a charming companion for M. de Charlus. But even in the case of a man of real merit, it is an advantage that is not disdained by the person who admits him into his private life and one that makes him particularly useful that he can also play whist. The intelligence of the young Marquis was remarkable and as they had already begun to say at Féterne when he was barely out of his cradle, he "took" entirely after his grandmother, had the same enthusiasms, the same love of music. He reproduced also some of her peculiarities, but these more by imitation, like all the rest of the family, than from atavism. Thus it was that, some time after the death of his wife, having received a letter signed "Léonor," a name which I did not remember as being his, I realised who it was that had written to me only when I had read the closing formula: "*Croyez à ma sympathie vraie*," the word "*vraie*," coming in that order, added to the Christian name Léonor the surname Cambremer.

About this time I used to see a good deal of Gilberte with whom I had renewed my old intimacy: for our life, in the long run, is not calculated according to the duration of our friendships. Let a certain period of time elapse and you will see reappear (just as former Ministers reappear in politics, as old plays are revived on the stage) friendly relations that have been revived between the same persons as before, after long years of interruption, and revived with pleasure. After ten years, the reasons which made one party love too passionately, the other unable to endure a too exacting despotism, no longer exist. Convention alone survives, and everything that Gilberte would have refused me in the past, that had seemed to her intolerable, impossible, she granted me quite readily—doubtless because I no longer desired it. Although neither of us avowed to himself the reason for this change, if she was always ready to come to me, never in a hurry to leave me, it was because the obstacle had vanished: my love.

I went, moreover, a little later to spend a few days at Tansonville. The move I found rather a nuisance, for I was keeping a girl in Paris who slept in the bachelor flat which I had rented. As other people need the aroma of forests or the ripple of a lake, so I needed her sleep near at hand during the night and by day to have her always by my side in the carriage. For even if one love passed into oblivion, it may determine the form of the love that is to follow it. Already, in the heart even of the previous love, daily habits existed, the origin of which we did not ourself recall. It was an anguish of a former day that had made us think with longing, then adopt in a permanent fashion, like customs the meaning of which has been forgotten, those homeward drives to the beloved's door, or her residence in our home, our presence or the presence of someone in whom we have confidence upon all her outings, all these habits, like great uniform highroads along which our love

355

passes daily and which were forged long ago in the volcanic fire of an ardent emotion. But these habits survive the woman, survive even the memory of the woman. They become the pattern, if not of all our loves, at least of certain of our loves which alternate with the others. And thus my home had demanded, in memory of a forgotten Albertine, the presence of my mistress of the moment whom I concealed from visitors and who filled my life as Albertine had filled it in the past. And now before I could go to Tansonville I had to make her promise that she place herself in the hands of one of my friends who did not care for women, for a few days.

I had heard that Gilberte was unhappy, betrayed by Robert, but not in the fashion which everyone supposed, which perhaps she herself still supposed, which in any case she alleged. An opinion that was justified by self-esteem, the desire to hoodwink other people, to hoodwink herself, not to mention the imperfect knowledge of his infidelities which is all that betrayed spouses ever acquire, all the more so as Robert, a true nephew of M. de Charlus, went about openly with women whom he compromised, whom the world believed and whom Gilberte supposed more or less to be his mistresses. It was even thought in society that he was too barefaced, never stirring, at a party, from the side of some woman whom he afterwards accompanied home, leaving Mme de Saint-Loup to return as best she might. Anyone who had said that the other woman whom he compromised thus was not really his mistress would have been regarded as a fool, incapable of seeing what was staring him in the face, but I had been pointed, alas. in the direction of the truth, a truth which caused me infinite distress, by a few words let fall by Jupien. What had been my amazement, when, having gone, a few months before my visit to Tansonville to enquire for M. de Charlus, in whom certain cardiac symptoms had been causing his friends great anxiety and having mentioned to Jupien, whom I found by himself, some love-letters addressed to Robert and signed Bobette which Mme de Saint-Loup had discovered, I learned from the Baron's former factotum that the person who used the signature Bobette was none other than the violinist who had played so important a part in the life of M. de Charlus. Jupien could not speak of him without indignation: "The boy was free to do what he chose. But if there was one direction in which he ought never to have looked, that was the Baron's nephew. All the more so as the Baron loved his nephew like his own son. He has tried to separate the young couple, it is scandalous. And he must have gone about it with the most devilish cunning, for no one was ever more opposed to that sort of thing than the Marquis de Saint-Loup. To think of all the mad things he has done for his mistress! No, that wretched musician may have deserted the Baron, as he did, by a mean trick, I don't mind saying; still, that was his business. But to take up with the nephew, there are certain things that are not done." Jupien was sincere in his indignation; among people who are styled immoral, moral indignation is quite as violent as among other people, only its object is slightly different. What is more, people whose own hearts are not directly engaged, always regard unfortunate entanglements, disastrous marriages as though we were free to choose the inspiration of our love, and do not take into account the exquisite mirage which love projects and which envelops so entirely and so uniquely the person with whom we are in love that the " folly " with which a man is charged who marries his cook or the mistress of his best friend is as a rule the only poetical action that he performs in the course of his existence.

I gathered that Robert and his wife had been on the brink of a separation (albeit Gilberte had not yet discovered the precise nature of the trouble) and that it was Mme de Marsantes, a loving, ambitious and philosophical mother who had arranged and enforced their reconciliation. She moved in those circles in which the inbreeding of incessantly crossed strains and a gradual impoverishment bring to the surface at every moment in the realm of the passions as in that of pecuniary interest, inherited vices and compromises. With the same energy with which she had in the past protected Mme Swann, she had assisted the marriage of Jupien's niece and brought about that of her own son to Gilberte, employing thus on her own account, with a pained resignation, the same primeval wisdom which she dispensed throughout the Faubourg. And perhaps what had made her at a certain moment expedite Robert's marriage to Gilberte—which had certainly caused her less trouble and cost fewer tears than making him break with Rachel—had been the fear of his forming with another courtesan—or perhaps with the same one, for Robert took a long time to forget Rachel—a fresh attachment which might have been his salvation. Now I understood what Robert had meant when he said to me at the Princesse de Guermantes's: " It is a pity that your young friend at Balbec has not the fortune that my mother insists upon. I believe she and I would have got on very well together."

He had meant that she belonged to Gomorrah as he belonged to Sodom, or perhaps, if he was not yet enrolled there, that he had ceased to enjoy women whom he could not love in a certain fashion and in the company of other women. Gilberte, too, might be able to enlighten me as to Albertine. If then, apart from rare moments of retrospect, I had not lost all my curiosity as to the life of my dead mistress, I should have been able to question not merely Gilberte but her husband. And it was, after all, the same thing that had made both Robert and myself anxious to marry Albertine (to wit, the knowledge that she was a lover of women). But the causes of our desire, like its objects for that matter, were opposite. In my case, it was the desperation in which I had been plunged by the discovery, in Robert's the satisfaction; in my case to prevent her, by perpetual vigilance, from indulging her predilection; in Robert's to cultivate it, and by granting her her freedom to make her bring her girl friends to him. If Jupien traced back to a quite recent origin the fresh orientation, so divergent from their original course, that Robert's carnal desires had assumed, a conversation which I had with Aimé and which made me very miserable shewed me that the headwaiter at Balbec traced this divergence, this inversion to a far earlier date. The occasion of this conversation had been my going for a few days to Balbec, where Saint-Loup himself had also come with his wife, whom during this first phase he never allowed out of his sight. I had marvelled to see how Rachel's influence over Robert still made itself felt. Only a young husband who has long been keeping a mistress knows how to take off his wife's cloak as they enter a restaurant, how to treat her with befitting courtesy.

He has, during his illicit relations, learned all that a good husband should know. Not far from him at a table adjoining my own, Bloch among a party of pretentious young university men, was assuming a false air of being at his ease and shouted at the top of his voice to one of his friends, as he ostentatiously passed him the bill of fare with a gesture which upset two water-bottles: " No, no, my dear man, order! Never in my life have I been able to make head or tail of these documents. I have never known how to order dinner! " he repeated with a pride that was hardly sincere and, blending literature with gluttony, decided at once upon a bottle of champagne which he liked to see " in a purely symbolic fashion " adorning a conversation. Saint-Loup, on the other hand, did know how to order dinner. He was seated by the side of Gilberte—already pregnant (he was, in the years that followed, to keep her continually supplied with offspring[1])—as he would presently lie down by her side in their double bed in the hotel. He spoke to no one but his wife, the rest of the hotel appeared not to exist for him, but at the moment when a waiter came to take his order, and stood close beside him, he swiftly raised his blue eyes and darted a glance at him which did not last for more than two seconds, but in its limpid penetration seemed to indicate a kind of curiosity and investigation entirely different from that which might have animated any ordinary diner studying, even at greater length, a page or messenger, with a view to making humorous or other observations which he would communicate to his friends. This little quick glance, apparently quite disinterested, revealed to

[1] *Dis aliter visum.* We shall see, in the sequel, that the widowed Gilberte appears to be the mother of an only daughter. C. K. S. M.

those who had intercepted it that this excellent husband, this once so passionate lover of Rachel, possessed another plane in his life, and one that seemed to him infinitely more interesting than that upon which he moved from sense of duty. But it was to be discerned only in that glance. Already his eyes had returned to Gilberte who had seen nothing, he introduced a passing friend and left the room to stroll with her outside. Now, Aimé was speaking to me at that moment of a far earlier time, time when I had made Saint-Loup's acquaintance, through Mme de Villeparisis, at this same Balbec. "Why, surely, sir," he said to me, "it is common knowledge, I have known it for ever so long. The year when Monsieur came first to Balbec, M. le Marquis shut himself up with my lift-boy, on the excuse of developing some photographs of Monsieur's grandmother. The boy made a complaint, we had the greatest difficulty in hushing the matter up. And besides, Monsieur, Monsieur remembers the day, no doubt, when he came to luncheon at the restaurant with M. le Marquis de Saint-Loup and his mistress, whom M. le Marquis was using as a screen. Monsieur doubtless remembers that M. le Marquis left the room, pretending that he had lost his temper. Of course I don't suggest for a moment that Madame was in the right. She was leading him a regular dance. But as to that day, no one will ever make me believe that M. le Marquis's anger wasn't put on, and that he hadn't a good reason to get away from Monsieur and Madame." So far as this day was concerned, I am convinced that, if Aimé was not lying consciously, he was entirely mistaken. I remembered quite well the state Robert was in, the blow he struck the journalist. And, for that matter, it was the same with the

Balbec incident; either the lift-boy had lied, or it was Aimé who was lying. At least, I supposed so; certainly I could not feel, for we never see more than one aspect of things. Had it not been that the thought distressed me, I should have found a refreshing irony in the fact that, whereas to me sending the lift-boy to Saint-Loup had been the most convenient way of conveying a letter to him and receiving his answer, to him it had meant making the acquaintance of a person who had taken his fancy. Everything, indeed, is at least twofold. Upon the most insignificant action that we perform, another man will graft a series of entirely different actions; it is certain that Saint-Loup's adventure with the lift-boy, if it occurred, no more seemed to me to be involved in the commonplace dispatch of my letter than a man who knew nothing of Wagner save the duet in *Lohengrin* would be able to foresee the prelude to *Tristan*. Certainly to men, things offer only a limited number of their innumerable attributes, because of the paucity of our senses. They are coloured because we have eyes, how many other epithets would they not merit if we had hundreds of senses? But this different aspect which they might present is made more comprehensible to us by the occurrence in life of even the most trivial event of which we know a part which we suppose to be the whole, and at which another person looks as though through a window opening upon another side of the house and offering a different view. Supposing that Aimé had not been mistaken, Saint-Loup's blush when Bloch spoke to him of the lift-boy had not, perhaps, been due after all to my friend's pronouncing the word as "lighft." But I was convinced that Saint-Loup's physiological evolution had not begun at that period and that he

then had been still exclusively a lover of women. More
than by any other sign, I could tell this retrospectively by
the friendship that Saint-Loup had shewn for myself at Balbec.   It was only while he was in love with women that he
was really capable of friendship.   Afterwards, for some
time at least, to the men who did not attract him physically
he displayed an indifference which was to some extent, I
believe, sincere—for he had become very curt—and which
he exaggerated as well in order to make people think that he
was interested only in women.   But I remember all the
same that one day at Doncières, as I was on my way to dine
with the Verdurins, and after he had been gazing rather
markedly at Morel, he had said to me: " Curious, that
fellow, he reminds me in some ways of Rachel.   Don't you
notice the likeness?   To my mind, they are identical in
certain respects.   Not that it can make any difference to
me."   And nevertheless his eyes remained for a long time
gazing abstractedly at the horizon, as when we think, before returning to the card-table or going out to dinner, of
one of those long voyages which we shall never make, but
for which we feel a momentary longing.   But if Robert
found certain traces of Rachel in Charlie, Gilberte, for her
part, sought to present some similarity to Rachel, so as to
attract her husband, wore like her bows of scarlet or pink or
yellow ribbon in her hair, which she dressed in a similar
style, for she believed that her husband was still in love with
Rachel, and so was jealous of her.   That Robert's love
may have hovered at times over the boundary which divides
the love of a man for a woman from the love of a man for a
man was quite possible.   In any case, the part played by his
memory of Rachel was now purely æsthetic.   It is indeed

improbable that it could have played any other part. One day Robert had gone to her to ask her to dress up as a man, to leave a long tress of hair hanging down, and nevertheless had contented himself with gazing at her without satisfying his desire. He remained no less attached to her than before and paid her scrupulously but without any pleasure the enormous allowance that he had promised her, not that this prevented her from treating him in the most abominable fashion later on. This generosity towards Rachel would not have distressed Gilberte if she had known that it was merely the resigned fulfilment of a promise which no longer bore any trace of love. But love was, on the contrary, precisely what he pretended to feel for Rachel. Homosexuals would be the best husbands in the world if they did not make a show of being in love with other women. Not that Gilberte made any complaint. It was the thought that Robert had been loved, for years on end, by Rachel that had made her desire him, had made her refuse more eligible suitors; it seemed that he was making a sort of concession to her when he married her. And indeed, at first, any comparison between the two women (incomparable as they were nevertheless in charm and beauty) did not favour the delicious Gilberte. But the latter became enhanced later on in her husband's esteem whereas Rachel grew visibly less important. There was another person who contradicted herself, namely, Mme Swann. If, in Gilberte's eyes, Robert before their marriage was already crowned with the two-fold halo which was created for him on the one hand by his life with Rachel, perpetually proclaimed in Mme de Marsantes's lamentations, on the other hand by the prestige which the Guermantes family had always had in her father's eyes and which she had inherited from him, Mme de Forcheville would have preferred a more brilliant, perhaps a princely marriage (there were royal families that were impoverished and would have accepted the dowry—which, for that matter, proved to be considerably less than the promised millions—purged as it was by the name Forcheville) and a son-in-law less depreciated in social value by a life spent in comparative seclusion. She had not been able to prevail over Gilberte's determination, had complained bitterly to all and sundry, denouncing her son-in-law. One fine day she had changed her tune, her son-in-law had become an angel, nothing was ever said against him except in private. The fact was that age had left unimpaired in Mme Swann (become Mme de Forcheville) the need that she had always felt of financial support, but, by the desertion of her admirers, had deprived her of the means. She longed every day for another necklace, a new dress studded with brilliants, a more sumptuous motor-car, but she had only a small income, Forcheville having made away with most of it, and—what Israelite strain controlled Gilberte in this?— she had an adorable, but a fearfully avaricious daughter, who counted every penny that she gave her husband, not to mention her mother. Well, all of a sudden she had discerned, and then found her natural protector in Robert. That she was no longer in her first youth mattered little to a son-in-law who was not a lover of women. All that he asked of his mother-in-law was to smooth down some little difficulty that had arisen between Gilberte and himself, to obtain his wife's consent to his going for a holiday with Morel. Odette had lent her services, and was at once rewarded with a magnificent ruby. To pay for this, it was necessary that Gilberte should treat her husband more generously. Odette preached this doctrine to her with all the more fervour in that it was she herself who would benefit by her daughter's generosity. Thus, thanks to Robert, she was enabled, on the threshold of her fifties (some people said, of her sixties) to dazzle every table at which she dined, every party at which she appeared, with an unparalleled splendour without needing to have, as in the past, a " friend " who now would no longer have stood for it, in other words have paid the piper. And so she had entered finally, it appeared, into the period of ultimate chastity, and yet she had never been so smart.

It was not merely the malice, the rancour of the once poor boy against the master who has enriched him and has moreover (this was in keeping with the character and still more with the vocabulary of M. de Charlus) made him feel the difference of their positions, that had made Charlie turn to Saint-Loup in order to add to the Baron's sorrows. He may also have had an eye to his own profit. I formed the impression that Robert must be giving him a great deal of money. After an evening party at which I had met Robert before I went down to Combray, and where the manner in which he displayed himself by the side of a lady of fashion who was reputed to be his mistress, in which he attached himself to her, never leaving her for a moment, enveloped publicly in the folds of her skirt, made me think, but with an additional nervous trepidation, of a sort of involuntary rehearsal of an ancestral gesture which I had had an op-

portunity of observing in M. de Charlus, when he appeared
to be robed in the finery of Mme Molé or some other
woman, the banner of a gynaecophil cause which was not
his own but which he loved, albeit, without having the
right to flaunt it thus, whether because he found it useful
as a protection or æsthetically charming, I had been struck,
as we came away, by the discovery that this young man,
so generous when he was far less rich, had become so
stingy. That a man clings only to what he possesses,
and that he who used to scatter money when he so rarely
had any now hoards that with which he is amply supplied,
is no doubt a common enough phenomenon, and yet in
this instance it seemed to me to have assumed a more
individual form. Saint-Loup refused to take a cab, and I
saw that he had kept a tramway transfer-ticket. No
doubt in so doing Saint-Loup was exercising with a
different object, talents which he had acquired in the
course of his intimacy with Rachel. A young man who
has lived for years with a woman is not as inexperienced
as the novice for whom the girl that he marries is the first.
Similarly, having had to enter into the minutest details of
Rachel's domestic economy, partly because she herself
was useless as a housekeeper, and afterwards because his
jealousy made him determined to keep a firm control over
her private life, he was able, in the administration of his
wife's property and the management of their household,
to continue playing the part with a skill and experience
which Gilberte would perhaps have lacked, who gladly
relinquished the duties to him. But no doubt he was
doing this principally in order to be able to support Charlie
with every penny saved by his cheeseparing, maintaining

him in affluence without Gilberte's either noticing or suffering by his peculations. Tears came to my eyes when I reflected that I had felt in the past for a different Saint-Loup an affection which had been so great and which I could see quite well, from the cold and evasive manner which he now adopted, that he no longer felt for me, since men, now that they were capable of arousing his desires, could no longer inspire his friendship. How could these tastes have come to birth in a young man who had been so passionate a lover of woman that I had seen him brought to a state of almost suicidal frenzy because "Rachel, when from the Lord" had threatened to leave him? Had the resemblance between Charlie and Rachel —invisible to me—been the plank which had enabled Robert to pass from his father's tastes to those of his uncle, in order to complete the physiological evolution which even in that uncle had occurred quite late in life? At times, however, Aimé's words came back to my mind to make me uneasy; I remembered Robert that year at Balbec; he had had a trick, when he spoke to the lift-boy, of not paying any attention to him which strongly resembled M. de Charlus's manner when he addressed certain men. But Robert might easily have derived this from M. de Charlus, from a certain stiffness and a certain bodily attitude proper to the Guermantes family, without for a moment sharing the peculiar tastes of the Baron. For instance, the Duc de Guermantes, who was free from any taint of the sort, had the same nervous trick as M. de Charlus of turning his wrist, as though he were straightening a lace cuff round it, and also in his voice certain shrill and affected intonations, mannerisms to all of which, in

M. de Charlus, one might have been tempted to ascribe another meaning, to which he would have given another meaning himself, the individual expressing his peculiarities by means of impersonal and atavistic traits which are perhaps nothing more than ingrained peculiarities fixed in his gestures and voice. By this latter hypothesis, which borders upon natural history, it would not be M. de Charlus that we ought to style a Guermantes marked with a blemish and expressing it to a certain extent by means of traits peculiar to the Guermantes race, but the Duc de Guermantes who would be in a perverted family the exceptional example, whom the hereditary malady has so effectively spared that the outward signs which it has left upon him lose all their meaning. I remembered that on the day when I had seen Saint-Loup for the first time at Balbec, so fair complexioned, fashioned of so rare and precious a substance, gliding between the tables, his monocle fluttering in front of him, I had found in him an effeminate air which was certainly not suggested by what I was now learning about him, but sprang rather from the grace peculiar to the Guermantes, from the fineness of that Dresden china in which the Duchess too was moulded. I recalled his affections for myself, his tender, sentimental way of expressing it, and told myself that this also, which might have deceived anyone else, meant at the time something quite different, indeed the direct opposite of what I had just learned about him. But from when did the change date? If it had occurred before my return to Balbec, how was it that he had never once come to see the lift-boy, had never once mentioned him to me? And as for the first year, how could he have paid any attention to the boy, passionately enamoured as he then was of Rachel? That first year, I had found Saint-Loup peculiar, as was every true Guermantes. Now he was even more individual than I had supposed. But things of which we have not had a direct intuition, which we have learned only through other people, we have no longer any opportunity, the time has passed in which we could inform our heart of them; its communications with reality are suspended; and so we cannot profit by the discovery, it is too late. Besides, upon any consideration, this discovery pained me too intensely for me to be able to derive spiritual advantage from it. No doubt, after what M. de Charlus had told me in Mme Verdurin's house in Paris, I no longer doubted that Robert's case was that of any number of respectable people, to be found even among the best and most intelligent of men. To learn this of anyone else would not have affected me, of anyone in the world save Robert. The doubt that Aimé's words had left in my mind tarnished all our friendship at Balbec and Doncières, and albeit I did not believe in friendship, nor did I believe that I had ever felt any real friendship for Robert, when I thought about those stories of the lift-boy and of the restaurant in which I had had luncheon with Saint-Loup and Rachel, I was obliged to make an effort to restrain my tears.

I should, as it happens, have no need to pause to consider this visit which I paid to the Combray district, which was perhaps the time in my life when I gave least thought to Combray, had it not furnished what was at least a provisional verification of certain ideas which I had formed long ago of the "Guermantes way," and also a verification of certain other ideas which I had formed of the " Méséglise way." I repeated every evening, in the opposite direction, the walks which we used to take at Combray, in the afternoon, when we went the " Méséglise way." We dined now at Tansonville at an hour at which in the past I had long been asleep at Combray. And this on account of the heat of the sun. And also because, as Gilberte spent the afternoon painting in the chapel attached to the house, we did not take our walks until about two hours before dinner. For the pleasure of those earlier walks which was that of seeing as we returned home the purple sky frame the Calvary or mirror itself in the Vivonne, there was substituted the pleasure of setting forth when dusk had already gathered, when we encountered nothing in the village save the blue-grey, irregular and shifting triangle of a flock of sheep being driven home. Over half the fields night had already fallen; above the evening star the moon had already lighted her lamp which presently would bathe their whole extent. It would happen that Gilberte let me go without her, and I would move forward, trailing my shadow behind me, like a boat that glides across enchanted waters. But as a rule Gilberte came with me. The walks that we took thus together were very often those that I used to take as a child: how, then, could I help feeling far more keenly now than in the past on the " Guermantes way " the conviction that I would never be able to write anything, combined with the conviction that my imagination and my sensibility had grown more feeble, when I found how little interest I took in Combray? And it distressed me to find how little I relived my early years. I found the

Vivonne a meagre, ugly rivulet beneath its towpath. Not that I noticed any material discrepancies of any magnitude from what I remembered. But, separated from the places which I happened to be revisiting by the whole expanse of a different life, there was not, between them and myself, that contiguity from which is born, before even we can perceive it, the immediate, delicious and total deflagration of memory. Having no very clear conception, probably, of its nature, I was saddened by the thought that my faculty of feeling and imagining things must have diminished since I no longer took any pleasure in these walks. Gilberte herself, who understood me even less than I understood myself, increased my melancholy by sharing my astonishment. " What," she would say, " you feel no excitement when you turn into this little footpath which you used to climb? " And she herself had so entirely altered that I no longer thought her beautiful, which indeed she had ceased to be. As we walked, I saw the landscape change, we had to climb hillocks then came to a downward slope. We conversed, very pleasantly for me—not without difficulty however. In so many people there are different strata which are not alike (there were in her father's character, and her mother's); we traverse first one, then the other. But, next day, their order is reversed. And finally we do not know who is going to allot the parts, to whom we are to appeal for a hearing. Gilberte was like one of those countries with which we dare not form an alliance because of their too frequent changes of government. But in reality this is a mistake. The memory of the most constant personality establishes a sort of identity in the person, with the result that he would not fail to abide by promise, which he remembers even if he has not endorsed them. As for intelligence, it was in Gilberte, with certain absurdities that she had inherited from her mother, very keen. I remember that, in the course of our conversations while we took these walks, she said things which often surprised me greatly. The first was: " If you were not too hungry and if it was not so late, by taking the road to the left and then turning to the right, in less than a quarter of an hour we should be at Guermantes." It was as though she had said: " Turn to the left, then the first turning on the right and you will touch the intangible, you will reach the inaccessibly remote tracts of which we never upon earth know anything but the direction, but " (what I thought long ago to be all that I could ever know of Guermantes, and perhaps in a sense I had not been mistaken) " the ' way.' " One of my other surprises was that of seeing the " source of the Vivonne " which I imagined as something as extra-terrestrial as the Gates of Hell, and which was merely a sort of rectangular basin in which bubbles rose to the surface. And the third occasion was when Gilberte said to me: " If you like, we might go out one afternoon and then we can go to Guermantes, taking the road by Méséglise, it is the nicest walk," a sentence which upset all my childish ideas by informing me that the two " ways " were not as irreconcilable as I had supposed. But what struck me most forcibly was how little, during this visit, I lived over again my childish years, how little I desired to see Combray, how meagre and ugly I thought the Vivonne. But where Gilberte made some of the things come true that I had imagined about the Méséglise way was during one of those walks which, after all, were nocturnal even if we took them before dinner—for she dined so late. Before descending into the mystery of a perfect and profound valley carpeted with moonlight, we stopped for a moment, like two insects about to plunge into the blue calyx of a flower. Gilberte then uttered, perhaps simply out of the politeness of a hostess who is sorry that you are going away so soon and would have liked to shew you more of a country which you seem to appreciate, a speech of the sort in which her practice as a woman of the world skilled in putting to the best advantage silence, simplicity, sobriety in the expression of her feelings, makes you believe that you occupy a place in her life which no one else could fill. Showering abruptly over her the sentiment with which I was filled by the delicious air, the breeze that was wafted to my nostrils, I said to her: " You were speaking the other day of the little footpath, how I loved you then! " She replied: " Why didn't you tell me? I had no idea of it. I was in love with you. Indeed, I flung myself twice at your head." " When? " " The first time at Tanson-ville, you were taking a walk with your family, I was on my way home, I had never seen such a dear little boy. I was in the habit," she went on with a vague air of modesty, " of going out to play with little boys I knew in the ruins of the keep of Roussainville. And you will tell me that I was a very naughty girl, for there were girls and boys there of all sorts who took advantage of the darkness. The altar-boy from Combray church, Théodore, who, I am bound to confess, was very nice indeed (Heavens, how charming he was!) and who has become quite ugly (he is the chemist now at Méséglise), used to amuse himself with all the peasant girls of the district. As they let me go out by myself, whenever I was able to get away, I used to fly there. I can't tell you how I longed for you to come there too; I remember quite well that, as I had only a moment in which to make you understand what I wanted, at the risk of being seen by your people and mine, I signalled to you so vulgarly that I am ashamed of it to this day. But you stared at me so crossly that I saw that you didn't want it." And, all of a sudden, I said to myself that the true Gilberte—the true Albertine—were perhaps those who had at the first moment yielded themselves in their facial expression, one behind the hedge of pink hawthorn, the other upon the beach. And it was I who, having been incapable of understanding this, having failed to recapture the impression until much later in my memory after an interval in which, as a result of our conversations, a dividing hedge of sentiment had made them afraid to be as frank as in the first moments—had ruined everything by my clumsiness. I had lost them more completely—albeit, to tell the truth, the comparative failure with them was less absurd—for the same reasons that had made Saint-Loup lose Rachel.

" And the second time," Gilberte went on, " was years later when I passed you in the doorway of your house, a couple of days before I met you again at my aunt Oriane's, I didn't recognise you at first, or rather I did unconsciously recognise you because I felt the same longing that I had felt at Tansonville." " But between these two occasions there were, after all, the Champs-Elysées." " Yes, but there you were too fond of me, I felt that you were spying upon me all the time." I did not ask her at the moment who the young man was with whom she had been walking along the Avenue des Champs-Elysées, on the day on which I had started out to call upon her, on which I would have been reconciled with her while there was still time, that day which would perhaps have changed the whole course of my life, if I had not caught sight of those two shadowy forms advancing towards me side by side in the dusk. If I had asked her, I told myself, she would perhaps have confessed the truth, as would Albertine had she been restored to life. And indeed when we are no longer in love with women whom we meet after many years, is there not the abyss of death between them and ourself, just as much as if they were no longer of this world, since the fact that we are no longer in love makes the people that they were or the person that we were then as good as dead? It occurred to me that perhaps she might not have remembered, or that she might have lied to me. In any case, it no longer interested me in the least to know, since my heart had changed even more than Gilberte's face. This last gave me scarcely any pleasure, but what was most striking was that I was no longer wretched, I should have been incapable of conceiving, had I thought about it again, that I could have been made so wretched by the sight of Gilberte tripping along by the side of a young man, and thereupon saying to myself: "It is all over, I shall never attempt to see her again." Of the state of mind which, in that far off year, had been simply an unending torture to me, nothing survived. For there is in this world in which everything wears out, everything perishes, one thing that crumbles into dust, that destroys itself still more completely, leaving behind still fewer traces of itself than Beauty: namely Grief.

And so I am not surprised that I did not ask her then with whom she had been walking in the Champs-Elysées, for I have already seen too many examples of this incuriosity that is brought about by time, but I am a little surprised that I did not tell Gilberte that, before I saw her that evening, I had sold a bowl of old Chinese porcelain in order to buy her flowers. It had indeed been, during the dreary time that followed, my sole consolation to think that one day I should be able without danger to tell her of so delicate an intention. More than a year later, if I saw another carriage bearing down upon mine, my sole reason for wishing not to die was that I might be able to tell this to Gilberte. I consoled myself with the thought: " There is no hurry, I have a whole lifetime in which to tell her." And for this reason I was anxious not to lose my life. Now it would have seemed to me a difficult thing to express in words, almost ridiculous, and a thing that would " involve consequences." " However," Gilberte went on, " even on the day when I passed you in the doorway, you were still just the same as at Combray; if you only knew how little you have altered ! " I pictured Gilberte again in my memory. I could have drawn the rectangle of light which the sun cast beneath the hawthorns, the trowel which the little girl was holding in her hand, the slow gaze that she fastened on myself. Only I had supposed, because of the coarse gesture that accompanied it, that it was a contemptuous gaze because what I longed for it to mean seemed to me to be a thing that little girls did not know about and did only in my imagination, during my hours of solitary desire. Still less could I have supposed that so easily, so rapidly, almost under the eyes of my grandfather, one of them would have had the audacity to suggest it.

Long after the time of this conversation, I asked Gilberte with whom she had been walking along the Avenue des Champs-Elysées on the evening on which I had sold the bowl: it was Léa in male attire. Gilberte knew that she was acquainted with Albertine, but could not tell me any more. Thus it is that certain persons always reappear in our life to herald our pleasures or our griefs.

What reality there had been beneath the appearance on that occasion had become quite immaterial to me. And yet for how many days and nights had I not tormented myself with wondering who the man was, had I not been obliged, when I thought of him, to control the beating of my heart even more perhaps than in the effort not to go downstairs to bid Mamma good-night in that same Combray. It is said, and this is what accounts for the gradual disappearance of certain nervous affections, that our nervous system grows old. This is true not merely of our permanent self which continues throughout the whole duration of our life, but of all our successive selves which, after all, to a certain extent compose the permanent self.

And so I was obliged, after an interval of so many years, to add fresh touches to an image which I recalled so well, an operation which made me quite happy by shewing me that the impassable gulf which I had then supposed to exist between myself and a certain type of little girl with golden hair was as imaginary as Pascal's gulf, and which I felt to be poetic because of the long series of years at the end of which I was called upon to perform it. I felt a stab of desire and regret when I thought of the dungeons of Roussainville. And yet I was glad to be able to say to myself that the pleasure towards which I used to strain every nerve in those days, and which nothing could restore to me now had indeed existed elsewhere than in my mind, in reality, and so close at hand, in that Roussainville of which I spoke so often, which I could see from the window of the orris-scented closet. And I had known nothing! In short Gilberte embodied everything that I had desired upon my walks, even my inability to make up my mind to return home, when I thought I could see the tree-trunks part asunder, take human form. The things for which at that time I so feverishly longed, she had been ready, if only I had had the sense to understand and to meet her again, to let me taste in my boyhood. More completely even than I had supposed, Gilberte had been in those days truly part of the " Méséglise way."

And indeed on the day when I had passed her in a doorway, albeit she was not Mlle de l'Orgeville, the girl whom Robert had met in houses of assignation (and what an absurd coincidence that it should have been to her future husband that I had applied for information about her), I had not been altogether mistaken as to the meaning of her glance, nor as to the sort of woman that she was and confessed to me now that she had been. " All that is a long time ago," she said to me, " I have

379

never given a thought to anyone but Robert since the day of our engagement. And, let me tell you, that childish caprice is not the thing for which I blame myself most."